"Scotland Yard! Step... Sherlock Holmes?"

"He is not here," I shouted from the top of the stairs. "What is it you want?" I realized instantly, of course, that these men had come to arrest Holmes.

"You must be Dr. Watson," said the police official.

"He is not here," I said. "I have nothing else to say to you." I turned and walked into the parlor.

The policeman followed me and stood in the doorway. "Very well, then," he said. "Have it your way." He shouted to our landlady. "Mrs. Hudson, my men must search this house. I trust you will not impede them."

"He's not here," I repeated, more forcefully this time.

"You won't tell me where he is, Doctor?"

"I have no idea where he is," I said.

"Come now. You don't really expect me to be-lieve that."

My back was against the fireplace hearth. He took two steps toward me, any closer and he'd have been in my vest pocket. He was taller by a good ten inches, so he was able to look down at me. It was all I could do to resist the urge to jam the heel of my boot into the top of his instep. But I was quite certain that would only land me in jail. . . .

The Jewel
of
Covent Garden

———◦«O»◦———

Wayne Worcester

A SIGNET BOOK

SIGNET
Published by New American Library, a division of
Penguin Putnam Inc., 375 Hudson Street,
New York, New York 10014, U.S.A.
Penguin Books Ltd, 27 Wrights Lane,
London W8 5TZ, England
Penguin Books Australia Ltd, Ringwood,
Victoria, Australia
Penguin Books Canada Ltd, 10 Alcorn Avenue,
Toronto, Ontario, Canada M4V 3B2
Penguin Books (N.Z.) Ltd, 182–190 Wairau Road,
Auckland 10, New Zealand

Penguin Books Ltd, Registered Offices:
Harmondsworth, Middlesex, England

First published by Signet, an imprint of New American Library,
a division of Penguin Putnam Inc.

First Printing, December 2000
10 9 8 7 6 5 4 3 2 1

 REGISTERED TRADEMARK—MARCA REGISTRADA

Printed in the United States of America

PUBLISHER'S NOTE
This is a work of fiction. Names, characters, places, and incidents either are
the product of the author's imagination or are used fictitiously, and any
resemblance to actual persons, living or dead, business establishments, events
or locales is entirely coincidental.

For Maureen

ACKNOWLEDGMENTS

My special and most sincere thanks to my wife, Maureen Croteau; without her thoughtful ideas, timely suggestions and skilled editing this novel might not have been written. Many thanks, too, to John J. Breen, Garret Condon and Laura Osterweis for their reading of the manuscript and for their candid contributions; also my agent, Philip G. Spitzer, for his attentiveness and professionalism, and to my editor, Laura Anne Gilman, her assistant, Jennifer Heddle, and the staff at New American Library for their inestimable help in bringing this project to fruition.

Introduction

February 25, 2000

Antiquities experts at Oxford University reported yesterday that the battered tin box found last year during the renovation of offices in Hastings on the outskirts of Eastbourne, may well have been the property of Dr. John H. Watson, the well-known chronicler and compatriot of the famous detective Sherlock Holmes of 221B Baker Street, London.

"We are vastly more interested in the authenticity of the letters and manuscripts found inside the box, of course," said Dr. Reginald F. St. John-Smythe, curator, "but this is a start. This is a critically important first step in the long and painstaking process of dating the material."

St. John-Smythe said his team of experts was led to its conclusion by a nearly obliterated serial number on the bottom of the container.

"We found it quite by accident," he said. "One doesn't try to clean such items for fear of compromising their authenticity. But we did dust the box under a magnifying glass, and some of our tracing powder adhered to the partial outline of two numbers.

"Using the most modern scientific methods," said St. John-Smythe, "we were able to raise additional numbers without substantially altering the box. This is not a simple process, because tin is so soft and malleable, you see."

Under St. John-Smythe's direction, the team traced the serial number to an army inventory list.

"We are quite certain the box was one of several apportioned to the Royal Berkshire Regiment, specifically the

Fifth Northumberland Fusiliers, in late spring, 1880," said St. John-Smythe.

"We all know that by late July of that year, Dr. Watson had been attached to that very regiment as an assistant surgeon, and that he was, in fact, with the Fusiliers when he was wounded at the Battle of Maiwand in the Second Afghan War.

"So the probability of authenticity appears great," St. John-Smythe said.

He cautioned, however, "We must be careful not to make the leap from that fact to a proclamation regarding the several manuscripts themselves—even though the box did contain a rather convincing letter, purportedly from the good doctor himself."

The letter reads:

To Whom It May Concern:

The cases I have set down here are among the most perilous and sensitive that my good friend and compatriot, Sherlock Holmes of 221B Baker Street, London, encountered during his long and illustrious career as the world's first consulting detective.

Untimely disclosure of the facts brought to light by my stories about these cases would have had dire consequences throughout the empire, which doubtless any modern reader with even a modest familiarity with history will appreciate. What's more, Holmes' reading public—and mine, of course—most assuredly would have been scandalized by the unavoidable luridness of some episodes contained in the stories.

It took some arguing on my part, but my agent, Mr. Conan Doyle, reluctantly agreed to mask Holmes' involvement in these heretofore undisclosed cases by filling the appropriate time period with other stories of which the reading public by now, I am sure, is familiar. Such is the nature of poetic license. Given the gravity of the issues at hand, however, I have no qualms about having undertaken such a minor deceit, and neither did Mr. Conan Doyle, once he clearly understood the implications.

I rest easy now, knowing that, albeit in secrecy, once

more I have done right by Holmes, my Queen and my country.

John H. Watson, M.D.
June 6, 1889

"The fact that events in several of the manuscripts occurred after that date suggests that Dr. Watson used the tin box as a repository for quite some time," St. John-Smythe said.

Authorities have postulated that the manuscripts may be among those reported missing from Watson's estate in 1941. When Nazi Germany laid siege to London in World War II, many venerable buildings in some of the city's most stolid commercial areas were demolished, among them a repository jointly maintained by banks and insurers in the Borough of St. Marylebone in the city's West End, where Watson and Holmes lived.

Police were not surprised that such a potentially important and valuable discovery might be made in the Hastings area, a once renowned South Coast resort that has become a haven for those on society's fringes.

"That sort come out here because they can live cheaper than in the city," said Inspector William Barrows of New Scotland Yard, "and there are so many of them out here now they don't have s'much as a mite of trouble blending in.

"Doctor Watson's journals," Barrow said, "wouldn't be the first good swag we've turned up in these parts."

The disused offices were among several flats being renovated in Dabney Shopping Center, which is set in a large council estate that features a Tesco superstore.

The tin box toppled out of the rubble when Thomas Langley, crew foreman for J. Anthony Johnstone, Restorationists, and two of his assistants, caved in a deep partition between two offices.

"There was an old safe in that wall, but she was rotted out and wide open, so I thought she was empty or I'd not have brought her down like I did," Langley said. "I'm thankful the writings were sealed up tight, is all.

"As best I can figure," Langley said, "the tin box must have slipped down inside the walls when the floor of the safe rotted through."

Chapter 1

It has occurred to me often that of the countless evenings I spent in the company of my old friend Sherlock Holmes, many were passed, not in complete silence, but in what I can only describe as the comfortable and welcomed absence of obligatory noise. It was not necessary that Holmes and I talk incessantly in order to enjoy good fellowship. It helped, I suppose, that neither of us was especially garrulous by nature; in fact, when we were not involved in a case, which as it happened was not often, we tended toward the studious and even the sedentary, though generally speaking Holmes possessed an insistent vitality and natural athleticism that I did not. As a youth I had played many a good rugby game for Blackheath, but owing to the wounds I suffered in the Second Afghan War and, I must confess, to some innate lethargy, I tended toward a deliberateness that befitted my early middle age.

I wish I could report that I always finished the day completely engrossed in the latest issue of *The Lancet* or the *British Medical Journal*. That, however, would be a lie. While I no doubt should have been spending time with readings suited to my medical practice, as I once had, the truth was that by 1889 the world usually was still very much with me by day's end. That being the case, it was considerably more likely that I could be found whiling away my leisurely hours with a beaker of whiskey or a pipe or cigar in one hand and a collection of Clark Russell's fine sea stories in the other.

On the particular late December evening on which our adventure began, a visitor to our lodgings at 221B Baker Street would have found the great detective seated across from me in his easy chair by the fireplace. After an early supper, I had turned to my sea stories and Holmes had immersed himself in that evening's work. There was never any telling what that might comprise.

On this night, he had turned his attention to an obscure treatise on some aspect of musicological research. Holmes was an avid student of medieval European cultures and their music. He was especially intrigued by the works of the fifteenth-century composer Orlando Lassos, and already had taken copious notes for a monograph on the Italian maestro's polyphonic motets.

Holmes added to those notes while I was still at sea with my reading, so to speak, and then had turned to his library chores, which entailed scouring accumulated issues of London's many daily and weekly newspapers and magazines. Nothing seemed to escape his notice. He sat erect and intent before his work like a tall, gangly and wide-eyed bird of prey. His beak was the long, sharply pointed paper shears he held in his right hand. Every few minutes he would spy an item of interest and descend upon it. The target might be a few suggestive or revealing lines from the agony columns or an article of police or shipping news, or something of particular note from the society pages. As Holmes worked, both hands fully occupied, he kept his straight-stemmed briar pipe clenched between his teeth. Smoke rose from it lazily and sporadically in thin white curls and diaphanous plumes. Apart from the rub of steel on steel as Holmes worked his shears, the only noise in the house was the low sibilant hiss of the gas lamps that lighted the room.

Holmes' dissected periodicals fell to one side of him as he worked. The cuttings mounted up on the opposite side in a small and tidy pile. These, I knew from experience, he would dutifully paste into one of his many commonplace books, which he then would scrupulously catalog and index. The need for any trained investigator to have just such a catalog of crime was not only self-evident but crucial. But I am certain there was no similar chronicle anywhere in London's numerous public and private libraries or in the stacks and archives of any of England's hallowed colleges and universities or, for that matter, even in the files locked away in the offices of Scotland Yard.

It remained for Sherlock Holmes to fill the void, and this he did enthusiastically. His unique compendium already had proven invaluable, for it served to mirror the ebb and flow of the two powerful tides in which our burgeoning city always was awash. One was roiling, dark and treacherous, and it emanated from the violent and unpredictable world of the downtrodden and the dispossessed. The other was clear, strong and brutally cold, and it flowed from the privileged upper orders. Together they formed an immense steaming caldron of humanity, and from it Holmes drew the cases that formed his unique practice as the world's first consulting detective.

Increasingly, whenever the Yard's staff of so-called investigators faced a seemingly insoluble crime, they turned to Holmes for help. They did so reluctantly and often rather quietly, so as to not arouse suspicions about their own competence. In return, Holmes was granted remarkable entree wherever the police were involved.

Though Holmes often was willing to suppress mention of his involvement as being in the best interests of the Crown, I know that just as often he regretted having to do so. His ego sometimes seemed to rival his massive intellect; I do him no disservice to note this trait. The man relished flattering notice, and I am certain that were I to press him on this point, he would acknowledge as much. It is true that he chided me rather often for paying more attention in my stories to plot than to science, but I am inclined to think that despite himself, Holmes always rather liked the stories for the public notice they brought. I am quite certain that even had he chosen to forgo my literary help, he still would have solved his cases with a flourish, for drama was as much a natural part of the man as an appreciation of line, light and color was to a consummate artist.

To those of us who were most familiar with Holmes' work—especially me, for as Holmes' companion and the chronicler of his exploits I have shared many of his experiences—these professional cases were complex and frustrating Gordian knots. To Holmes' way of thinking, however, each was a delight, a stimulation and a supreme and intensely personal test, the absence of which too quickly rendered his very existence intolerable. And therein lay considerable danger. Without intellectual, and often physical, activity and constant challenge, Holmes in those years quite readily fell victim to a self-destructive kind of lassitude and ennui.

The condition manifested itself as a need for opiates, most commonly an injection of a seven percent solution of cocaine. It took no great investigative power to read as much in the ugly pattern of small scars that pocketed the insides of both of his long and sinewy forearms. I found myself constantly warning him away from the needle. Sometimes he seemed to agree, albeit begrudgingly, that no good ever could come of his habit. At other times he simply nodded in assent and acknowledgment of my complaints and admonitions, and then did as he pleased. I was determined that with my help Holmes some day would rid himself of this vile habit, but I knew, too, that I had to be reasonable. I reminded myself that although Holmes' retreats into the void had commenced over a long period, they now were relatively infrequent. I also forced myself to recall having seen enough of the world to know full well that it did not abide absolute perfection in any form.

Addiction or no, in the eleven years since Holmes had officially begun his work, he had built an extraordinary reputation for solving the insoluble. He insisted that no mystery could for very long withstand the effects of keen observation, logical analysis, cool deductive reasoning, dogged persistence and, often enough, a bit of well-calculated daring. And most often he was right. Little wonder that with every success his list of clients had grown longer and longer. It was only logical that as the demand for his services increased, it had become necessary and appropriate for the great detective to become all the more selective.

From the beginning, Holmes' cases were rather more likely to come to him from members of the city's higher echelons than from the lower. The poor were accustomed to having to shoulder alone, and usually in silence, whatever misfortune or unfair burden life imposed. By now Holmes had been of service to the royalty of Scandinavia, Holland, Bohemia and, of course, our own great nation. He had little cause for financial concern, though even in earlier years the wealth and station of a prospective client had

mattered to Holmes precious little or not at all. He had
always exhibited an abiding and heartfelt need to see justice
meted out and order restored. But, in truth, what he longed
for most earnestly in all of his cases was "some interesting
feature," some peculiar and arresting aspect or problem
which might demand that a measure of ingenuity, if not
genius, be employed in its solution. And as 1889 drew
toward a close, this somewhat self-indulgent notion was
ceasing to be a preference; it was becoming a requirement
and a perquisite of success for which Sherlock Holmes apologized to no one.

However, never had a case begun in such a curious fashion as on the evening of December 20, when a dirty-faced
and ragged-looking little boy named Tommy Rogers scooted
past our vigilant and redoubtable landlady, Mrs. Hudson,
ran up the stairs to our rooms and shattered the evening's
comfortable silence by fairly launching himself against our
door.

Chapter 2

On this moonlit evening, one that bore in its clean sharp chill a hint of the winter to come, Mrs. Hudson had opened the door to an insistent knock and, quite naturally, peered directly out across the pavement and into the gaslight of Baker Street, rather than sharply downward to the space inhabited by our short intruder. He was accustomed to taking advantage of his diminutive size, and he did so quickly. By the time Mrs. Hudson inclined her head, the boy had jostled her aside. She was not amused.

"Whaa—" Mrs. Hudson shouted with the upset. "Here, you! Where do you think you're going? Come back here."

The boy paused before running up the flight of stairs to our rooms, and that was his mistake. By the time he neared the top, Mrs. Hudson was on him. As he reached the landing, she managed to get one cuff of his dirty trousers in her fist. He lurched forward, pulling her with him. The boy's head smacked into our door with a crack that was so sharp I upset my drink.

"Good Lord!" I exclaimed. "What was that?"

"I believe," Holmes said coolly, "that we have an unexpected visitor, Watson, a rather small one, as I can approximate the spot at which he smacked into the door. You had better get your medical bag. I think our visitor may need some tending to."

I opened the door to find the boy unconscious at my feet. I turned him over and saw that a bump was already rising on the top of his forehead, just below the hairline. I knelt over him and gently manipulated his neck to be sure there were no broken bones. Mrs. Hudson was just getting to her feet on the landing.

"Oh, dear," she said. "Oh, good Lord. I didn't mean to

hurt the boy, Dr. Watson. You know I wouldn't do such a thing. But he—"

"Shush," I told her. "I think he's all right, but he does have a nasty bump. Here, help me get him inside, will you?"

We laid him on the divan. Without my asking, Mrs. Hudson procured a washcloth, towel and a ceramic basin filled with hot water. She wiped the boy's face, taking special care with his reddening bump, and when she rinsed the towel, the basin water turned dark gray.

"It would seem there's a small boy beneath all of that grime," Holmes said. He had been quietly standing behind us, smoking his pipe and watching. He was now leaning forward, peering intently at the boy and examining him visually from head to toe.

"Hmmm," Holmes said, more or less to himself. "That would seem right. Most interesting."

The boy stirred and moaned and opened his eyes. Mrs. Hudson dabbed his face gently some more, and with every touch of the damp cloth the boy turned his head away from her.

"Cor! Wouldja stop 'at? Stop 'at!" He was semiconscious. As his eyes gained focus, he found himself looking directly at Mrs. Hudson. His defenses dissolved when he saw that the kindly woman meant no harm.

"I'm all right, ma'am. Really, and I'm . . . I'm sorry for bustin' in like I did."

He cleared his throat several times, and it was clear from the grimace on his face that the effort caused him some pain.

"I thought if I didn't give you the slip, I'd never get to see Mr. 'Omes, and I needs to see 'im, I do. I got bidness. Important bidness."

"You are employed by a costerman, are you not?" Holmes asked the boy. "He works in Covent Garden, and I would say that the two of you also sell your goods off Oxford Square or thereabouts. These days, perhaps most importantly, you also serve as his crier."

The boy turned his attention away from Mrs. Hudson for the first time. "How'd you know 'at?" he asked. "I ain't met you gentlemens before."

"No matter," Holmes said dismissively. "What—"

"You must be 'im!" the boy said. "You must be Mr. Sherlock 'Olmes!"

"You have the better of me, young man," the tall detective said.

The boy looked puzzled.

"He is Sherlock Holmes," I said, "And I am Dr. John H. Watson. This is Mrs. Hudson, our landlady. Can you see us all right?" I asked. "Can you see the way you normally do?"

"Um, yes. I think so," he said. "But my head hurts sump'n awful." He reached a hand to his forehead for the first time and winced. "Oww!"

"That will be sore for a while," I told him. "I'll give you something for the pain. You took a nasty fall. Open your mouth, please. Open. Open. Say, 'Aaah.' Again: 'Aaah.' Well, you most certainly have a sore throat."

"Aye," the boy said. "It's from the shoutin' all day."

"I feel so bad about this," Mrs. Hudson said, "but, young man, you had no business—"

Holmes interrupted, "Mrs. Hudson, the fault was not yours. Surely, our visitor knows that. Perhaps it's time that he told us about this business of his that's so important as to merit getting knocked unconscious. But first, young man, your name?"

"Tommy Rog— It's Thomas Payton Rogers, Mr. 'Olmes . . . sir."

"Well now, Mr. Thomas Payton Rogers," Holmes said, "what is this all about? Why do you think you require the services of this agency?"

I liked the boy, this Tommy Rogers. He had bright blue eyes, blond hair turned dirty from the streets and unabashed pluck that could only arise from a fundamental honesty. I had no idea how Holmes knew the boy was a crier for a costerman out of Covent Garden, but I knew better than to question his deductions; I would ask later.

"Mrs. Hudson," I said, "perhaps in the kitchen you have some biscuits or scones or the like and maybe some nice hot tea to wash it down. With honey. That would be good for the boy's throat."

"I just might, Doctor," she said with a smile and left the room.

Holmes, however, was growing impatient. "If you don't mind, Watson, before you try to adopt the boy, there are some questions I would like answered. Now. Thomas . . . may I call you Thomas, young man?"

Holmes smiled uncertainly at the boy, as if it were a calculated action, not one that came naturally; I can't say that I was surprised. The detective was greatly compassionate where children were concerned, but he never seemed especially comfortable with them. I suspect his awkwardness arose from the fact that he was not certain which standards of conduct should be applied to children. Absent clear rules, or at least rules with which he was intimately familiar, he chose to treat children as though they were uneducated, malnourished and foreshortened adults. I rather enjoyed watching Holmes deal with his dilemma. He was a remarkable paragon in nearly every other field of endeavor, but in this area he was awkward and ill-equipped, and I found that refreshingly human.

Thomas Payton Rogers, for his part, did not seem quite certain why a man as wise as the great Sherlock Holmes would wonder what to call him.

"I wouldn't know who you'd be talkin' to, if you'll be calling me Thomas," the boy said. "Be all right, you were to call me Tommy. Everybody does, see."

"Very well . . . Tommy," Holmes said. "What is that—"

"What should I call you?" the boy asked. "Um, beggin' your pardon, sir."

"You may call me Mr. Holmes."

"Mr. 'Olmes," the boy repeated. "I guess Sherlock is kind of a odd name, ain't it?"

The detective's eyes popped open wide. I coughed into my fist to stifle a laugh. He gave me a stern look.

"Indeed," Holmes said, "it is a singular name, but it was not of my choosing. You, on the other hand, are fortunate enough to have quite a nice name . . . common, but nice."

Holmes pursed his lips quickly as if to smile. The boy, bless him, rose to the challenge.

"It suits me, it does," our visitor said. "I'm a commoner. That's what I am. Plain an' poor. I ain't no toff. Lotsa boys got my name, an' I don't mind 'at. Tommy's a good enough name, an' it suits me . . . just like your name suits you, you get my meaning."

Holmes scowled.

"How old are you, young man?" he asked.

"Eight . . . I think. 'Ow old are you, Mr. 'Olmes?"

The detective blinked his gray eyes, but before he could speak, Mrs. Hudson came into the parlor carrying a broad tray with steaming tea, a basket filled with scones and a plate stacked with three different kinds of biscuits.

The boy's eyes went wide. "Is that all for us," he asked incredulously.

Holmes sighed. "Help yourself," he said. "You may as well take your time . . . unless you have some other engagement this evening."

The boy kept his eyes fixed on the food and shrugged off his filthy jacket. Mrs. Hudson caught it gingerly and walked out of the room, holding it at arm's length, presumably so that she could properly beat the dust out of it with a whisk. Thus unfettered, Tommy reached for the food with both hands.

"Th—thank you," he said. "I'm very hungry."

"You are entirely welcome," I said. "I think you will enjoy Mrs. Hudson's handiwork. After you've finished, perhaps the three of us can talk, hmmm?"

The boy nodded rapidly and then attacked the food. In a moment both of his cheeks were bulging. He reminded me of a chipmunk. The same thought apparently had occurred to Holmes, who was watching the boy with a rather dour expression.

"Let us hope he doesn't burrow into something and stay for the winter," he said.

Chapter 3

We left Tommy to his own gustatory devices for the moment. I drew my briar pipe from the right pocket of my jacket and felt the left pocket for my pouch of Arcadia mixture. Holmes walked over to the fireplace mantel, from which hung the Persian slipper where he always stored a supply of the noisome shag that he smoked. We filled and fired up our pipes, and a small thick cloud of smoke arose.

"You are wondering how I knew the boy is employed as a crier for a costermonger," Holmes said.

"I was mildly curious," I said, trying not to smile. Actually, I was desperate to know, but I preferred not to seem too impressed by Holmes' deductions, tired of Holmes' frequent complaint that I see but fail to observe.

"Well," Holmes said, "the dirt that seems to cover our young friend is fresh, at least at its outermost layer. It has an aroma that is unmistakable and not altogether unpleasant. It also is rich and black, quite unlike the sandy dirt of our streets, which often comes in varying colors, each of which is indigenous to a particular part of the city, depending on the weather and the nature and the extent of any major excavations that may be under way. It's even possible sometimes, you know, to deduce the exact neighborhood from which the—"

"Please, Holmes," I said, quietly and politely. "You know that I have read your monograph on the subject."

"Oh," he said. The detective seemed somewhat deflated at losing the opportunity to expound on one of his favorite topics.

"Yes. Well, the point is, dirt that black and rich is good farm dirt. I can think of nowhere in London and its outskirts where such soil would be present, in such abundance and especially at this time of year, except on volumes of produce at a greengrocery.

"It would have to be a big establishment, with considerable trade, to be handling vegetables that fresh in late December. Under the circumstances, one of the large establishments in Covent Garden seemed most likely. I believe Master Thomas Payton Rogers spent most of the day pawing over greens—turnip, chard, maybe spinach—and helping his master push and haul their cart all along Oxford Square. The boy's hands, though quite small even for a youngster his size, are substantially callused and . . . "

My mouth must have been agape, for Holmes paused.

"Oh," he said. "Yes. Well, there is a bit of turnip green stuck on the inside edge of his right shoe. I spied a bit of spinach, too, but it could be chard; I couldn't tell without my glass because it was somewhat mashed. It was caught in the pant cuff that Mrs. Hudson tore. The turned-out bottom of that same cuff also contained some of the grayish white clay that has been running in the gutters near Oxford Square of late. After a heavy rain it washes down from the construction there, you know."

"Aah," I said with a nod and a facetious smile, "I don't see how I missed it."

"Well, it *is* elementary, Watson. Really. Just the careful observation of trifles and details."

"What is elementary to you, Holmes, most often is startling to the rest of us. Surely you must know that."

He angled his head to about forty-five degrees and nodded with a grateful smile. I was not a sycophant where Sherlock Holmes was concerned. In truth, he never did cease to amaze me.

"There is something else, Watson. From those details we may infer something of Tommy's circumstances, which have worsened rather recently. The boy works for someone, presumably a man to whom he is related, who is on in years and infirm. This is someone with a penchant for rough tobacco and heavy drink or, just as likely, someone who is consumptive, but not a person who ever uses the boy badly."

"How on earth . . . ?"

"Think about it, man," Holmes said. "Tommy Rogers is a mere slip of a boy. He can't be of much service where heavy work is concerned. The best he could be expected to do is carry and load and unload small amounts of produce and help push and pull the cart. Judging from his calluses, he has been doing this for some time. That tells us he is in the hire of someone who cannot do heavy work by himself; hence advanced age or considerable infirmity, or both. The man's breathing must be severely labored, else why would he need someone to serve as a crier, to help him hawk his wares? We know that he does, because despite the boy's obvious good health, his throat is raw, as you yourself observed."

"Ingenious," I said.

He held up a forefinger; he had not finished.

"We may infer something from the cut of the boy's clothes, too," Holmes said. "In better times, someone outfitted him in the best manner possible. His clothes may be ragged now, but they are, nevertheless, of stout worsted that once fit properly; he has outgrown them, but only recently. His brogans exhibit the same attributes. They are of good thick leather, but scuffed and worn, and the fit looks as though it has grown tight. I wouldn't be surprised if the boy has callused-over blisters on the backs of both feet, where the shoes used to rub. They do not do so now because, as you will notice, both counters have been cut open just deeply enough to relieve some pressure. In short, like the rest of the boy's attire, the shoes have served him very well, but for too long."

Tommy interrupted our discussion.

"Can I interest you gentlemen in a cupa?" He had taken it upon himself to serve as our host at tea. In fact, he had properly set three places at our table and stood, teapot in hand, towel draped over his forearm, poised to pour. Mrs. Hudson could not have done it better herself.

I looked at Holmes. He looked at me. We raised our eyebrows in unison but said nothing. Instead we sat, instructed our server and enjoyed a proper tea.

"Thank you," Holmes said. "Now, please . . ."

"Did I serve the tea right?" the boy asked.

Holmes nodded.

"You did splendidly," I assured him. "Where did you learn such manners?"

In the corner of my eye, I saw Holmes' head swivel sharply in my direction. I didn't need to look at the detective to know that I had better let him get on with his questioning of the boy.

"Oh," Tommy said. "I watched through the windows at plenty o' fancy restaurants and such, and I seen how they done it."

"I see," I said. Because I am quite naturally an obstinate person who dislikes being hurried or bullied by any man, Holmes included, I added gratuitously, "Well, you've a good eye, then, my boy. You're a fine and quick study, I would say."

"Thank you, sir." he said with a smile.

Holmes cleared his throat, quite pointedly, I thought.

"Ahem! Excuse me, the two of you," Holmes said. "The evening grows late and you, young man, will have to leave soon. So now, please, do state your business and leave nothing out."

Holmes' lips pursed into that characteristically tight, nearly unnoticeable smile that I saw quite often; I suspect that it passed unseen by most people because they were not attuned to looking for it. To them Holmes always must have seemed a dour fellow, but he was not bereft of color. Sometimes, in fact, he even displayed a droll sense of humor, though when it came to his profession, he was cool and businesslike in nearly every respect.

"Aye," Tommy said, his eyes bright and wide now. "Like I said, Mr. 'Olmes, I needs your help sorely . . . wid 'dis." So saying, he reached inside his shirt and withdrew a fine hand-laid envelope of the palest white linen. He had carefully wrapped it in a clean cloth, which he let fall to the floor. He held the envelope lightly across the palms of both hands as though it would shatter into myriad fine pieces if he did not. I could see that it was addressed in a fine hand to "Master Thomas Payton Rogers," and stuck to its flap was a flattened bit of burgundy sealing wax.

" 'At's my name there," the boy said. "It is, isn't it, Mr. 'Olmes? I don't read good, but I think I knows my name when I sees it."

"Indeed," Holmes said. "May I examine the envelope, please?"

Holmes had it in his eager hand no sooner than he had finished asking the question. He withdrew from his pocket the magnifying lens that he is never without and moved it back and forth across the writing only a scant distance from the surface of the paper. As he did so, he uttered small noises and exclamations that we could barely hear and only he could understand.

"Yessss," he said. "Curious, but . . . " He passed the edge of the envelope beneath his aquiline nose several times, sniffing audibly at each pass.

Then he turned the envelope over and stared intently at the magnified impression that had been stamped into the sealing wax.

"Oh, of course! It has to be. Very well. Here. Thank you. Now pray, how did this come to you? Tell us everything. Come. Come."

Holmes noisily settled his teacup onto its saucer, leaned forward and put his elbows on the table. He tented the tips of his long fingers together and positioned them over his mouth. His nose poked directly over the top of the impromptu fortification, which seemed perfectly designed to support his piercing eyes. Suddenly, they appeared larger and more penetrating than usual. They stared directly at the boy. They took in everything and gave out nothing, not so much as a blink or a twinkle. The detective waited.

In a moment little Thomas Payton Rogers cleared his throat. He winced at the effort, though less than before, and began his story.

Chapter 4

"I got this yesterday," the boy said. "A fancy messenger came up to me with it just as we was leaving Braddock's in the morning."

"Braddock's would be one of the greengrocers in Covent Garden?" I asked.

He nodded.

"Livery?" Holmes asked, his voice somewhat muffled by the position of his hands.

The boy didn't understand.

"Was the messenger wearing a uniform or anything fancy? I think that's what Mr. Holmes wants to know," I explained.

"Oh, aye. 'E was a fine one. Right smart 'e was. His suit was all dark green, like fresh spinach leaves, and 'e 'ad a matching cap wi' gold pipin' on it."

"From Crawford & Jones, no doubt," Holmes said.

"Well, me Uncle John," Tommy said, "that's Mr. John Godey—he's the one what I work for, y'see—he stepped right up, even bein' as sick as 'e's been, an' e' puts one o' his big mitts on the messenger's shoulder straightaway, an' he says, 'What do ya think you're doin' 'ere wid 'at boy? What's yer bidness wid 'im? You got bidness wid 'im, you got bidness wid me. You unnerstan?'

"Uncle John, he looks out for me," the boy said. "It's not that I can't do for myself, mind, but I'm pretty small yet, and well, sometimes people try to pick on me, and when me Uncle John gets wind a' sump'n like that, 'e steps up quick, 'e does. But the messenger, 'e said, 'No, sir. I want no trouble here. I was hired to deliver this to Master Thomas, that's all. There is no harm intended here. No harm. No, sir. None whatsoever.'

"Uncle John, 'e wouldn't let it go, though. 'Who was it 'at hired ya?' he shouts. An' 'e brings back his big fist like this, like 'e's gonna thump him right in the gob, an' the messenger says, all proper but shaky like, 'I do not know, sir. Please. I work for the Crawford and Jones Agency. I am merely a messenger. I never know who the client is.'

"Uncle just sorta grunts, and the messenger leaves straightaway. Uncle, he opens the envelope real careful like and then reads it, and he looks all puzzled and upset. He don't say nothin' for a while, and when I ask him what's wrong, that's when 'e says I got to find you."

I was intrigued by the story, and I knew Holmes was, too, for his face now wore a scowl, but I was equally fascinated by the boy. I could not help but note that as he spoke, his voice changed with each character in his narrative. Each of them was distinctive and projected in a manner that made each seem true and alive and entirely believable. The boy was quite animated, too, and I thought to myself that with discipline and proper training he might someday become a gifted actor. Of course, he might already be a precocious liar; London's streets produced those in far greater number.

"You do not go to school, Tommy?" I asked. Holmes glared at me, and I knew at once that I should have kept quiet; my question took the boy off track.

"If'n I did," Tommy replied, "who'd be helpin' Uncle John then? 'E can't do for himself these days. 'E's 'ad a stretch of bad luck, what with his cough and all, an' 'e's losin' 'is weight, too, 'e is. I'm worried about 'im. He should be at a sawbones right now. So who'd look out for 'im if not me?"

Holmes sighed in exasperation, but now I was concerned about the boy's uncle, for Tommy's well-being obviously was inextricably wound up with his; so I continued. "Well," I said, "if you'd like, I can stop by your cart tomorrow and take a quick look at your uncle John. It wouldn't be an official doctor's visit, mind you. Just a look. You know. Perhaps I can prescribe something quickly."

"Cor', it'd be great if you could do 'at, Doc," Tommy said. " 'Bout one o'clock'd be great, it would. I'd be sure 'e's there, I would. 'At'd be—"

Holmes interrupted.

"Why did your uncle John tell you to bring the envelope here?" he asked.

" 'E wouldn't say exactly, an' I asked. 'E wouldn't even tell me what this is all about. 'E just says, 'Do's I tell ya, boy.' 'At's not like Uncle, t' be short wi' me, but 'e was mighty upset, 'e was. 'E says only bad weather an' worse ever drops from the sky. 'E said 'e din't know what to make of this fancy envelope, an 'invite,' he called it, but 'e said 'e was sure you would. 'E said 'at in all o' England, 'ere's no one 'e'd put his faith in more 'n you. 'At's exactly what he told me. 'E said we could trust you, Mr. 'Olmes. We could trust you no matter what."

"And how could he be so certain of that, do you suppose?" Holmes asked.

The slight boy shrugged. "Uncle just knows things, I guess. From all the other costermen, prob'ly."

"Well, I am flattered by your uncle John's faith in me," Holmes said, looking not at the boy but at the envelope. "You may have brought us something of considerable interest. This fine handwriting is a woman's, as is the imprint on the sealing wax, and the envelope's delicate scent is of damask rose."

Holmes closed his eyes and passed the envelope quickly back and forth beneath his nostrils.

"Aah! Unmistakable. Yes. Lady Armstrong. I am sure of it."

"The noted rosarian and industrialist from Newcastle?" I asked.

"And Berkeley Square, of course. Yes," Holmes said, "there could only be one. May I examine the contents?" he asked the boy.

Holmes opened the envelope and removed a handwritten card. A return envelope was enclosed, this one already addressed to Lady Armstrong at Berkeley Square, which was one of the very best addresses in a city that suffers from no shortage of them.

The detective read the card aloud:

"The honor of your presence is requested at a concert by the prominent violinist Signore Giacomo Famiglietti of Cremona, Italy, December 31st at Planetree, 24 Berkeley

Square, the London home of Lady Mirabelle Llewellyn Armstrong. A holiday dinner at 8 p.m. will precede the concert. Signore Famiglietti, who recently completed a most successful concert tour in America, appears under the auspices and sponsorship of the Working Man's Christian Improvement and Grace Abounding Benevolent Society of Newcastle Upon Tyne, Lady Armstrong's favorite charity.

"If the bearer of this invitation kindly presents himself to the manager of H. M. Stringfellow & Sons, 117 Savile Row, he will be provided with evening wear suitable to the occasion and at no cost to himself."

Tommy Rogers' face was screwed into a deep frown. "I don't understand," he said.

"Well," said Holmes, "it appears you have been invited to what most likely will be one of London society's most exclusive and fashionable evenings this season or, for that matter, any season."

"There!" I exclaimed. "What do you say to that?"

"Well, I . . . I don't know." And then, as if exactly the right words had come to the boy, he blurted, "Well, bugger me!"

"Young man!" I exclaimed sharply, "that will not do, not at all."

"We have our work cut out for us," Holmes muttered.

"What do you . . . ? Oh . . . " I said. His meaning had suddenly become clear. I spoke as insistently as possible. "Holmes, it is the twentieth of December. Surely you don't intend that we somehow render this boy presentable to the Berkeley Square crowd in less than two weeks? Really!"

"As lamentable as it may seem, Watson, that is precisely what we must do . . . and I am counting on your help."

"But, Holmes," I protested, "surely the boy does not have to attend this affair if he or his uncle John thinks it unwise. In all seriousness, man, why must we undertake this. And in the middle of the holidays, no less?"

"I would not want to be considered a—a . . . What was the name of that crotchety fellow in old Dickens' Christmas tale, Watson? I seem to have forgotten it."

"Scrooge," I said softly. I knew full well that Holmes never forgot a thing, and I was a bit put off by the rather pedantic manner in which he chose to drive home his point about the season. To me, of all people. How absurd! I was always of good cheer at the holidays, at least far more demonstrably than I ever had known Holmes to be. "Ebeneezer Scrooge," I answered more forcefully.

"Aah, that's right," Holmes replied. "Ebeneezer Scrooge, yes. But now, Watson, while it is true that I do not gush over the holidays, you must know I am no Scrooge. And, in fact, especially in this season, I do wish people well."

"I suppose I know that, Holmes, but I—"

"Watson, join me at the sideboard a moment, please. Excuse us, young man."

Under my breath I said to Holmes: "He is a most likable little boy, but this entire bother could simply be disregarded if—"

"Watson, you disappoint me," Holmes said. "Surely, you have a better sense of adventure than that. This boy is a puzzle piece, old fellow. A timely one, too. Just as I was beginning to lament that even the criminal element turns docile and unimaginative around the holidays, a most intriguing puzzle has been dropped in our laps. Something is very much amiss here, and I fear that this young fellow stands to be hurt by it. I'm sure you don't want to see that happen."

"Of course not, Holmes, but—"

"Take, for instance, his uncle, this John Godey. Unless I am quite mistaken, he is the very same John Godey that I helped clap in irons quite some time ago, easily before that boy was born. Godey and a couple of his pals—Jack Clough, I think it was, and . . . Oh, let me see. Let me see."

Holmes closed his eyes, tilted his head back and pinched the bridge of his nose several times, as though he could somehow squeeze the information from his memory.

"Blast," he said. "I almost had it. Perhaps it will come to me. Anyway, Watson, Clough and this other person must have had more than a dozen burglaries to their credit. They were quite a pair, certainly several cuts above your average London thieves. They devoted their talents exclusively to undoing wealthy households in the West End, especially those they knew to house precious jewelry.

"And they did their homework, these fellows. For quite a while before a burglary, they would study the house and the comings and goings of its regular occupants. They would wait patiently for the right time, and then cut a pane of glass from a window or a door and remove it. Within minutes they'd execute the robbery and be back on the street. Often, the entire household was still sound asleep and none the wiser. Their boldness was extraordinary, just extraordinary!"

Holmes was so enthused with the recounting of the thieves' exploits that I wondered out loud if he actually didn't admire them.

"Oh, yes," he replied. "I truly did. I abhorred what they were doing, of course, but admired their style, their panache, if you will. Criminals with some verve and intelligence make my job ever so much more interesting. Of course, Watson, their daring was so laced with arrogance that it was only a question of time before they were brought down.

"Eventually, Clough and his partner—why can't I think of his name!—oh, anyway, they took aim at bigger targets, and pretty quickly they found themselves having to deal with some very good safes. So they went looking for a third man and came up with John Godey. He was a locksmith by trade, and an exceptionally good one by all accounts, but he was a drinker and a bare-knuckled brawler, too. Well, that's not fair of me. In fact, Godey was a good club fighter, very good, but as it happened, he was down on his luck, and these two boyhood friends of his . . . Charles Roberts! He was the one I couldn't think of, Watson. Charles Roberts and Jack Clough recruited Godey for a few of their biggest jobs.

"As it happened, Godey took to the work quickly. He was so good that I would call him, well, gifted, really. And this despite his having, not the long nimble fingers that one normally associates with such skills, but huge boxer's hands. What distinguished him was his innate intelligence and patience. There's no question that at least for a while he was one of the best cracksmen in the city.

"But then, disaster. A safe takes some little time to work, as you know, and as luck would have it, the butler to one of the households in, I think it was Mayfair, surprised the three robbers and shot Roberts dead. Godey and Clough managed to escape, but the butler got a good look at them and gave proper descriptions to Inspector Lestrade and his fellows."

I glanced over at Tommy, who was now busying himself by carefully stacking the empty cups and saucers on Mrs. Hudson's serving tray. I tried to imagine him in the company of convicted thieves. I was having little success.

"Watson," Holmes said sharply, "are you listening?"

"Uhm, yes, Holmes. The Yarders had good descriptions of the two men."

"Yes. Clough disappeared for a time, but then his body, or rather what was left it, was found floating in the Thames weeks later. Not John Godey. For months he gave the police fits. They'd close in on him repeatedly, and he'd give them the slip. If one of the men actually got his hands on him, invariably Godey would batter him senseless.

"Lestrade asked me to help out, and it so happened that I was with two of his better detectives when we caught up with Godey behind a fetid hole of a pub at the Seven Dials."

"Seven Dials," I repeated aloud. I always took notice when anyone spoke of goings-on in what was arguably one of the city's blackest, most notorious neighborhoods. "I presume the two detectives were incognito. In uniform, they wouldn't have stood a chance anywhere in that neighborhood."

"Of course," Holmes said impatiently. "Of course.

"Well, both of the detectives were good-sized, burly men and no stranger to the job, but Godey laid them out as cold and straight as a matching pair of mackerel. Then he and I tangled. It was quite a fight, I have to say, but I won't bore you with that.

"Godey was tried, convicted and sent to prison for ten years. He served out his complete sentence without incident. The police said he left prison a changed man. I'm inclined to think that's a superficial assessment, at best, but who knows? He was out of jail only two years when he apparently stepped in as Tommy's guardian. Regardless, Watson, as you might imagine, my suspicions are aroused when a man of Godey's background and experience sends his own ward to seek the help of the man who sent him to prison. It is not in my nature to believe the tiger has lost his stripes."

"What about revenge?" I asked. "Under the circumstances, might that not be a reasonable fear?"

Holmes scowled. "I would not say 'fear' is the correct word, Watson, but I do intend to be most circumspect until I have learned more. I refuse to draw a conclusion based on incomplete information.

"There is a third factor that compels me to take up this puzzle, and that is the charity gala in Berkeley Square. I have been aware of it for some time, and I have been most curious as to why Lady Armstrong is hosting it."

"True," I said, "I would never have considered her a champion of the working man. What is the name of that charity?"

He handed me the card.

"Ah, yes: The Working Man's Christian Improvement and Grace Abounding Benevolent Society of Newcastle Upon Tyne. There's a name that 'falls trippingly,' eh? Didn't her family make its fortune from the manufacture of munitions and armaments?" I asked.

"Quite," Holmes said. "Lady Armstrong took over the family's enterprises when her husband died. His absence left the factories teetering, and she walked in and ran the entire operation. It was almost as though she willed it to prosper. And she did so while establishing herself as the doyenne of Newcastle. In her day, Lady Armstrong truly was someone to reckon with. I doubt that age has diminished her."

"Indeed," I said.

"Yes. And there's this little fillip, Watson. You may recall the last time that considerable public attention was paid Lady Armstrong . . . "

Holmes stopped speaking, walked briskly over to his shelf of commonplace books, and ran his long fingers over the bindings. "Let me see . . . '87, '86, ah, here, '85 . . . nearly five years ago, I think."

He flipped through the pages of the scrapbook quickly, found what he was looking for and read, tracing his finger up and down the columns of newsprint as he went.

"Aah. Yes. Mm-hmm. Mm-hmm. Yes. The occasion was

her becoming the owner of an immense and priceless ruby called the 'Blood of Punjab.' "

"I do remember the accounts," I said. "The jewel was said to be as fine a stone as any among the Crown Jewels. In fact, if memory serves, the newspapers said the gem was even more spectacular than some of those in the Tower, no?"

"Correct, Watson," Holmes said. "Now, let me see. I should have a . . . Yes!"

He pulled a small pamphlet from the same commonplace book and waved it aloft.

"Here are some details, Watson. The Blood of Punjab is the biggest double-star ruby ever found. It weighs 2,209 carats."

"Incredible," I said.

"Quite," he said. "It is a cabochon cut 'double star.' Color is described as beautiful deep red, bringing to mind ripe pomegranates with a slight purplish tinge. Known in the trade as pigeon blood. Only the finest stones are so described."

"Double star?"

"Oh, yes," Holmes said. "Most peculiar. Owing to some unique aspect of its makeup, the stone has twelve distinct rays . . . are you interested in the particulars of its internal structure, Watson? I do know something about this."

I shook my head, relieved to have been spared what undoubtedly would have been an exhaustive scientific explanation.

"Well, perhaps it is enough to note that those who have seen the precious gem say that in the proper light, the rays seem to dance inside it. Six rays in a good stone is a rarity, but twelve in a flawless gem of that size is unheard of. It is nearly four inches long and almost half that wide. It is nearly priceless."

"And it was unearthed in the Punjab of northern India, obviously," I said. "Hence the name."

" 'Obviously'?" Holmes repeated, his eyebrows drawn up into arches. "The only thing that is obvious here, Watson old fellow, is that you are quite mistaken, although I suppose it's a reasonable enough surmise."

I expected that Holmes would continue his narrative. Instead, he returned to the clippings with which he had been preoccupied before our visitor arrived. He snipped another article from the newspaper and let it fall atop the pile by his chair. Our visitor, in the meantime, had curled up on the divan and was fast asleep.

"Well, for heaven's sake, Holmes!" I blurted out. "Where does the stone come from?"

"What? Oh. Burma. Here, Watson," he said, handing me the pamphlet. "You can read about it yourself."

So I did. These were the salient points:

The stone came into British hands some time during the winter of 1845–1846 after one of four especially bloody battles between British regulars and the Sikhs. A wounded, fatigued soldier, Lieutenant Alfred Cochran of Bristol, was seen half running and half walking through the battlefield, saber in one hand, bayonet in the other, slashing and jabbing wildly at anything in his way. He had bravely distinguished himself that day but was badly wounded, exhausted and parched.

Cochran's mates weren't in much better shape, but they went after him. From a distance, they saw him atop a small knoll and shouted. He turned toward them and stared, not comprehending. Then a jet-black stallion, a magnificent riderless war horse, materialized between them. Its bridle was gold, its harness was woven strands of silver, and on the horse's magnificent broad head was an ornate battle hood made of rich tapestry interwoven with golden threads. And fastened tightly into the center of the battle hood was an incredible double-star ruby.

The magnificent horse had suffered a mortal wound and was dying. It turned toward Cochran, faltered and fell. The soldier tried to comfort the dying beast. He had seen the extraordinary ruby, for it gleamed in the sun, but still he tended to the horse; he managed to tip what was left of his entire day's ration of water down its throat. By now the soldier's friends were standing beside him, watching in silence. Moments later the horse died, and at the very instant of its demise, the horse disappeared, leaving behind the stone we know as the Blood of Punjab.

"Holmes, this story is preposterous," I said. "What rubbish!"

I handed the pamphlet back to him, and he carefully tucked it into his book.

"Surely, you don't put any stock in it," I declared.

"All four soldiers testified under oath that it happened in exactly that manner," Holmes said.

"Yes, but even so . . . "

"Would you care to postulate what really happened, Watson?"

"Do you know?" I asked the detective.

"Absolutely not," he said. "I have never really given it much thought, to tell you the truth, precisely because, as you noted, Watson, it is such a fantastic tale."

"Well, my guess, Holmes, would be that Lieutenant Cochran and his compatriots came by the ruby illicitly, and when they were caught with it, Cochran made up the story and they all swore to it."

"Watson, I must say I am impressed," Holmes said with a look of bemusement. "That is quite logical."

"Well, really, old man," I said. "I've never heard precisely that story, but there were always comparably wild tales circulating among the regiments, even in the thickest of it. 'Inja, exotic land of a million mysteries' and all of that. A lot of men got thoroughly caught up in it. Me? I couldn't wait to be shut of the entire subcontinent."

"The problem, Watson, is that nobody ever did figure out where the stone came from, and when all was said and done, Cochran did have possession of it."

"So to this day nobody knows where the ruby came from?"

"Or the solid gold bridle, silver harness and the rest of the battle raiment."

"What?"

Holmes smiled.

"Oh yes," he said. "You may visit them at the Royal Museum, but only by appointment. Eventually, Cochran donated them. Without all of those items, his story would have been laughed at outright. But with them—and the gem, of course—it had a certain . . . believability. The story has only added to the value of the ruby."

"Why, it must be worth hundreds of thousands of pounds," I said.

"Quite so," Holmes said. "Whatever the market will bear."

"Amazing," I said.

"Now you understand why owning the Blood of Punjab affirmed Lady Armstrong's position as one of the wealthiest women in England. I suspect that is why she instructed her agents to acquire the gem. The status it confers is worth a great deal to someone of her social position.

"The size of the stone rather militates against its use as jewelry," Holmes said, "but that did not prevent Lady Armstrong from having it incorporated in a necklace almost immediately."

"She's a Philistine then," I said.

"Actually, Watson, the Philistines—oh, never mind."

The boy yawned loudly, stirred and stretched and turned toward the back of the divan. Holmes and I lowered our voices to a whisper.

"As I said, I am intrigued that Lady Armstrong is hosting this charity affair," Holmes said. "And then there is this Giacomo Famiglietti."

"You have misgivings about him?" I asked.

"As I do about nearly every aspect of this event, Watson."

"Such as . . . ?"

"One: Why does the wealthiest woman in England want this particular dirty-faced urchin as her guest? There are thousands just like him loose all over London."

"Granted," I said. "And two?"

"Ah, that should be even more obvious, Watson. You tell me."

"Why is a man like John Godey so upset at such a prospect that he would court his jailer for help?"

"Just so!" Holmes said. "Just so! Why, indeed?"

Chapter 5

Asleep with his head resting atop his folded arms, the boy looked even younger than his years.

"I can't help but wonder what fortune awaits him," I said.

"Who's to know?" Holmes asked. "If he doesn't fall victim to one form of contagion or another, he'll probably turn to crime."

"Well, perhaps we can help this one," I said, "though I had hoped to pass the holidays rather less involved in intrigue than usual."

"Maybe a trip to Covent Garden will boost your spirits."

"John Godey?" I offered.

"Precisely," Holmes said.

We decided that I would go to Covent Garden early tomorrow, before Tommy would expect me, and keep an eye on him and his uncle and especially their customers.

I turned to the boy. "Tommy," I said. I shook his shoulder gently and then spoke louder. "Tommy. Wake up, son. You've got to be getting home."

I poured him more tea, for he was groggy when he finally awoke.

"Tell me, young man," Holmes said, "where do you and your uncle John spend the nights usually?"

"At the 'ope Settlement 'ouse over on Long Lane," he said.

"That's the one near Aldersgate Street?" Holmes asked.

"Aye," Tommy said. "It's east of the Smit'fields Markets it is, on the north side 'o the road. A right good place, too. I ain't 'ad flea bites more'n a year now. Places we used to sleep, Uncle John and me, if 'ere was a mattress, 'ere'd be so many fleas 'oppin' all over the tickin' you didn't want to bed down if you could 'elp it. Some nights, fleas'd be so bad I'd sleep in the vegetable cart."

Listening to the boy, I suddenly realized I was having a hard time resisting the urge to scratch myself. I am not an overly fastidious person, nor am I squeamish, but just the thought of fleas was quite enough to make my skin crawl.

"Then do you also keep your cart at Hope Settlement House?" I asked, trying desperately to change the subject.

"Aye, we do."

"Has it always been just you and your uncle?" Holmes asked.

"Long as I know," the boy said. "Me ma 'n da, 'ey both died almost right after I was born. Killed in a 'splosion at the gas works in Bet'nal Green, they was. Uncle John, 'e's me ma's brother, 'e's the only kin I got."

"And when did your uncle John begin to get sick," Holmes asked.

"Early last winter, I think," the boy said. " 'E started losin' 'is weight 'bout then. He used to be a strappin' guy, an' a boxer. Why, I seen 'im 'it a bloke so 'ard once on 'is chin, 'e come right up offa the street and laid flat out in the air, 'e did, and when 'e 'it the ground 'e was out cold.

"Now Uncle coughs sump'n terr'ble," the boy said, and the excitement left his voice. It was replaced by a sadness made all the more palpable by his diminutive size and young age. "Sometimes when 'e 'as a spell, 'e can't stop it and it just doubles 'im up. 'E's 'urt his sides so much 'e don't stand up straight no more. An' he goes on the drink. It's 'cause 'o the pain an' all."

"Does he sleep at Hope Settlement, too?" I asked.

"Aye, 'e does," Tommy said, but he sounded a bit tentative. Holmes noticed it at once.

"What is it, young man?"

"Well, Mr. 'Olmes, 'e always checks to see I'm snug, an' then he writes in his journal. 'E says it 'elps him get to sleep. Sometimes, though, when I wakes up in the night, he ain't about, an' I worry. But come dawn, 'ere 'e is, right 'side of me. I don't know where 'e goes, but I don't ask. I 'spect it's not my bid'ness."

"That's a very good way to look at it, young man,"

Holmes said. "He does always come back, as you say, and that is what matters."

"Aye, Mr. 'Olmes," the boy said.

"Well, Watson," Holmes said, "we should get him a hansom cab before his uncle gets worried."

"Mr. 'Olmes?" Tommy asked.

"What is it?"

"Well, it's like this. . . ." As the boy struggled to find the words he needed, he looked down to the floor and put one foot behind the other, then alternated the order. I think he was trying to decide which of his pitiful shoes needed hiding the most.

"I don't want to wear no fancy clothes like a toff, or go nowhere I don't belong. What's the point o' that? They'll only be laughin' at me. I don't talk like 'em. I talks plain, I does, not fancy. An' those bloody clothes won't be no good to me, now will they? Why, I'd look like a li'l organ grinder's monkey goin' to work in Covent Garden like 'at, wouldn't I? Well? Wouldn't I?"

"Oh, I don't think so," Holmes said, "but you could give them away, or leave them in a charity bin . . . or sell them if you didn't want them."

Tommy brightened.

"I think there are some good things about this that you should take into account," Holmes said.

"An' what'd they be, then?" the boy asked, his curiosity slowly rising.

"Well," Holmes said, "there will be a lot of good food for you to eat. In fact, I am quite certain there will be more good food there than you or I or Dr. Watson or your uncle John could possibly eat in a week."

"An' sweets?" Tommy asked.

"Oh, you may count on it," Holmes said. "You don't suppose that all of those grand people would get dressed up in their fine tuxedos and evening gowns, and pay a lot of money to attend an event like this, if they were not going to get some sweets in return, do you? Unless I am badly mistaken, there will be one silver charger after another piled high with sweets and fruits, more than you could possibly eat."

The boy's expression changed so dramatically, and his eyes went so wide, that I had to laugh.

"For true?" Tommy asked.

"Most certainly," Holmes said. "And you know, I don't think I would worry so much about how you'll fit in."

"No?"

"You are quite a good mimic," Holmes said. "In fact, you are very good. If you think of this little undertaking of ours as a bit of acting, you will be fine, especially with a little coaching."

"You mean, I don't have to change who I am, just sound like 'em?"

"And act like them," Holmes said. "That is very important. But listen, if you can arrange to come here with some regularity between now and the day of the dinner, Dr. Watson and Mrs. Hudson will help you with that. They will teach you what you need to know. As far as the actual event, well, I intend that Dr. Watson and I will be there right in the same room with you for the entire time. So what do you thank, lad?"

The boy's eyes lighted up and a smile spread across his face. He stood and stuck out his chin at Holmes.

"I like it very much, sir," he said, with the clearest of diction and in the most refined manner. "I think this endeavor shall suit me quite nicely. I will tell Uncle that I have elected to attend the banquet, and that I expect to have a jolly good time. Thank you again, sir."

With that the boy bowed quickly. Holmes smiled and nodded. I clapped enthusiastically. There was little doubt that with some guidance and support, the boy could pull it off. We bade Tommy a good night, put him aboard a hansom cab, and paid the fare to Shoreditch and the Hope Settlement House.

Tommy waved excitedly from the window, until the cab was nearly out of sight.

"Tomorrow I shall see to it that we are invited to the party," Holmes said as we were going up the stairs to our rooms. I knew better than to ask how he intended to accomplish such a feat. For a man who sometimes seemed to have nearly no concern for polite society, he also had the most extraordinary entree into it.

He poured a brandy and handed it to me, and then poured one for himself. Over our nightcap we reexamined all that we knew about John Godey and the boy, and came up with an appropriate plan.

Chapter 6

I set off for Covent Garden at first light—such as it was.
The air was cool and the streets were hung with fog, which
was common given the time of year. This one was not the
diaphanous coverlet of light and ethereal mist that always
seems to hover in selective memory. This fog was thick. It
was inordinately wet. It was brownish-yellow. And it stunk,
though I cannot say that it slowed me down.

After all of those years in London, I had grown accustomed to unclean and noxious air. Malodorous vapors arose
from cesspools and sewage outfalls from thousands of
houses and tenements. The stench was augmented by fresh
manure from countless well-fed horses, and the poisonous
offal of countless factories and foundries. Broad plumes
and deep pools of industrial and chemical wastes sat reek-
ing at the city's core all along the River Thames, where
they were ceaselessly deposited and too slowly carried off
to sea. And over all of that lay a pall of acrid wood smoke
and sulfurous gas from the soft coal that burned in number-
less parlor heaters, on fireplace hearths, in kitchen stoves
and deep inside countless factory furnaces. Their stacks
protruded from every horizon like dark and ominous fingers jabbing the sky.

The air was a foul mixture of scents, indeed, and it was
only worsened by the unseasonable warmth that had dawned
after a crisply cold December night. Every surface of every
leaf on every tree, every gray cobblestone and granite settle,
every black wrought iron fence and every soot-darkened
and brown-smudged stone building wept with droplets of
oily moisture. There was no wind, not so much as a soft
light breeze to dry the damp. The sun was out, of course,
but that early in the day it lay so near the horizon that its

light could not reach far. At least the day did not threaten to host one of those "London particulars" that we all dreaded. On those days, the air by noon was charcoal gray and so thick and impenetrable as to stop all commerce and traffic. This was, however, very close. The fog softened all of the city's edges and dampened and altered all of its predictable and familiar sounds. What was near sounded far away, and what was far away sounded farther still. It was only with the greatest difficulty that I was able to discern neighborhood landmarks that yesterday would have been as familiar to me as our own rooms.

I walked slowly down Baker Street and had to stop at every crossing. As I passed Portman Square, I peered cautiously around and poked all about me with my walking stick until I was sure that I had my bearings and could turn east on Oxford Street with a measure of certainty and safety. I did not want to become one of those horrible accidents in the city's newspapers. Invariably, on the morning after one of these fogs would come a published report that some poor woman or youngster had stepped off a curb too quickly and was run over and crushed or crippled by a private carriage or public conveyance. The muted clang of warning bells sounded from the trams that moved slowly and steadily along the city's streets. They mingled with the shouts of drivers calling out warnings from atop their hansom cabs. "Traffic here! Step lively, now! Traffic here!"

On the grounds that it might, in fact, be wiser to be in a hansom cab, I considered trying to hail one, but I did not see how I might do so safely, so I resolved to stay afoot. I moved cautiously along Oxford Street, stopping periodically to check my navigation. Once past Oxford Circus, I counted seven blocks, and I knew that I should be at the junction of Charing Cross Road. I turned south and then, about four blocks later, east again onto the top of Leicester Square, an old haunt. I had passed many a memorable night there at the Empire Music Hall, and not a few at Daly's or, for that matter, The Alhambra, but I could not see these venerable establishments through the murk. Having little time for needless exploration and no time whatsoever for pointless reverie, I pushed east, knowing that I had to be nearing my mark. In the gloom I needed considerable diligence to safely traverse St. Martin's Lane, but I managed. Scant moments later I found myself, all appendages intact, confronting an unfettered and reverberating barrage of new noises and simultaneous, commingled shouts that I was certain could only arise from the immense colonnaded *piazza* of my destination. Nowhere was commerce more visibly and viscerally present than in Covent Garden.

"Turnips here! Nice purple-tops. Good turnips here."

"Cabbages a'plenty! Old Tom's got cabbages a'plenty!"

"Spuds I've got! C'mon now, guv! Paddy's got potatoes here! Big clean potatoes!"

Once in a while the sharp flat voice of a newsboy yelped for attention: "Latest news here! All the winners here. Get the latest news."

"Chard and beets now! While we got 'em! Chards and beets here!"

"Greens, all fresh 'n' ripe! Greens here! Get 'em fresh!"

And there were flower sellers, usually old women, or bedraggled young women, calling out in singsong voices so soft that they could barely be heard by anyone passing beyond a dozen feet away. "Buy a posy? Fresh flowers for your missus, sir? Nice flowers! Fresh this morn! Flowers. Fresh flowers."

There was no sequence to any of the sounds, nor any rhythm; they seemed to play off one another all at once. The tram bells still chimed out their warnings in the background, but the cries of the nearby costerman made the bells seem considerably more distant than they actually were.

Many of the carts and wagons in the immense market were lighted up by naphtha flares that gave off a sharp and sickening gas. The torches yielded an unnaturally intense but limited white light that made the fog itself seem brighter and yellower. The flares also created a strange intermediate range of shadows, and within this layer the costermen and newsboys and flower sellers all scuttled about, talking, shouting and working; the effect was dizzying. I had hoped that the heavy fog might help me remain unseen while keeping an eye on John Godey and his nephew. But it occurred to me quite clearly now that while the fog would diminish their ability to see me, so would it affect my ability to see them.

For well over an hour I pushed, poked, prodded, squeezed and clumsily sidestepped my ways all through the broad and teeming *piazza*. I was bumped repeatedly and jostled so regularly that I knew at once it would be prudent to keep one hand inside my coat and on my billfold at all times. And I was right, for mere moments after I had done so, I felt the velvety brush of fingertips on the back of that hand.

I jabbed my walking stick where instinct dictated and was paid with a startled "Oww! Bastard!"

I turned sharply toward the cry and saw the would-be thief clearly. He had fallen to his knees, not five feet distant, clutching both hands to his chest, for that, apparently, was where my cane had hit him. He was a bony little weasel of a man with a tight dark woollen cap pulled down almost to his eyebrows. His lips were curled in a pained and angry grimace that revealed darkened and broken teeth. He glared at me and uttered a string of curses and meaningless guttural noises even as he stabbed his hand into the pocket of his jacket. It was clear that he was reaching for a knife or a sap or worse.

"Oh, no, you don't," I said.

I took two quick steps forward and swung the stick again, straight down this time as hard as I could with my right arm, which is quite hard, indeed. With a loud crack the cane caught him a glancing blow on the side of the head. He screamed in pain, stumbled backward with his right hand spread hard and flat against the bloodied side of his head, and then fell to his knees again. But this time he rolled to the side, got to his feet and ran off into the murk. The entire incident lasted much less than a minute, I am certain, and it caused no particular commotion, for though a few people may have heard the tussle, even fewer saw it.

I regained my composure and pressed on. As any man so accosted would, I felt good about having properly defended myself. I was rather lost to my musings for a few minutes, but a scruffy, dirty-faced young girl returned me to the street with a start. She was a bold young thing, and she angled her way toward me through the crowd. She wore a shabby, rust-colored shawl pulled tightly about her shoulders. She held the ends of the garment together in her small fist, which she kept clutched to the middle of her bosom. The girl put her free hand on my arm, and the instant I stopped, she stood on her tiptoes and whispered softly in my ear that she had "comfort" to offer.

"I've a room nearby," she said.

I brushed her away, but not roughly.

"Off with you," I said. I shook my head from side to side in what I hoped was gentle reproach. I probably would have chided her had I not, at that very moment, thought I heard Tommy's voice. I had grown somewhat more accustomed to the fog's distortion of distance, so I knew he was close by. I forgot about the girl and turned in the direction from which the voice had come. I angled myself forward, and took two more steps while peering straight ahead into the gloom.

The boy and his uncle, John Godey, were only about fifteen feet from me, just to the right of a couple of old flower sellers.

"Leeks 'n' onions," Tommy called out. "Leeks 'n' onions, over 'ere at Uncle John's. Just pulled. Fresh this morning. Leeks 'n' onions, right over 'ere. Leeks 'n' oni— Doctor! Dr. Watson! It's me, Tommy."

I feigned surprise; so much for being inconspicuous.

"Tommy!" I said. "I wasn't sure I'd find you in this nasty weather."

"You're early, Doc."

"What—? Oh, yes. I guess I am." I presumed that the broad-shouldered man who stood beside and just behind Tommy was John Godey. He was appraising me carefully as we spoke.

"Yes," I said, "I was with a patient, but I finished earlier than I had expected. Would this gentleman be the Uncle John of whom you spoke so fondly?"

"Aye," the man himself said with an uncertain smile. "I'm the only one in this market'll answer to that."

John Godey moved toward me with a half smile on his face, but he was cramped up and bowed over as if carrying a load of rocks on his massive shoulders. He was hunched over at an acute angle to the ground, and when he moved, he walked almost sideways, like a crab. It hurt to watch him. It was obvious that Tommy's uncle was in a good deal of pain most of the time, perhaps all of his waking hours. The pain contributed, substantially I am sure, to the gray-white pallor of his complexion. John Godey looked up at me and extended a right hand that was very nearly twice the size of my own. His eyes were a hard dark brown, but there was a softness in their expression that gave the lie to his gnarled exterior.

"I am Dr. John H. Watson," I said. "It is my pleasure to meet you, Mr. Godey. Your boy, Tommy here, is a fine young lad. He's a credit to you, sir. Very much a credit, I would say."

" 'E is, 'at's for sure," Godey said. "That's a right kind thing to say, an' I thank you for it."

"Only the truth," I replied. "Only the truth. He's a good boy, and it is abundantly clear that you have done right by him."

He turned to his ward.

" 'Ere, Tom," he said, "whyn't you go sit a spell, or visit wi' somebody while I speaks with the doctor here? 'At's it, run along for a few minutes."

Every breath that Godey took was a tight dry wheeze. It was unsettling to hear.

"I've tried to do right by him, Dr. Watson," Godey said, "I have, indeed. 'E's all I care about in this life, but—"

And then the coughing began, one slow, deep and powerful rattling cough after another that came so hard on the tail of the one preceding it that his face turned bright red and he sucked in air greedily with a great gasping sound and then it started all over again. In several minutes, when the spasm was over, Godey was left with barely enough breath to remain upright. The poor man's entire frame shook so mightily with the wracking coughs that every attack moved him some little distance backward.

"Good God, man," I exclaimed. "How long have you been like this?"

"Late last winter, I 'spect," Godey said. "Aye, that'd be about right."

"You should be in bed, maybe even in hospital. There

could be any number of things at work here, Mr. Godey, none of them good, I'm afraid."

"Aye," Godey said. "Well, Doctor, none of us gets promised an easy time of it now, right?"

I disregarded his bravado. "You must tend to that cough," I told him.

Godey stepped closer and crooked his finger, motioning me to lower my head so he could speak more quietly.

"Aye, I'll tend to me cough, but you listen, Doctor," he said. "I ain't got much longer 'ere, an' I know 'at. 'Ere's not much can be done, an' I knows 'at, too. You give it whatever fancy name you want. Maybe bad ague or sump'n' brought in by 'em bloody foreigners. I don't know. Could be the 'sumption. Don't take long for 'at to go through a man, whittle him down to a stick. I seen it before. I prolly already lasted longer wi' it 'n most, wouldn't you say, now?"

"I wish I could argue with you, sir," I said.

"Well, I see you be an honest man, Dr. Watson. I 'preciate 'at. I do. 'Ere was a time, 'course, when I was just the opposite. No damned good I was."

"I understand you have a . . . a past," I said.

He laughed at my euphemism. The sound was much like a snort.

"Aye," Godey said, "a 'past' is what I 'ave, all right."

"Sherlock Holmes sends you his regards, Mr. Godey," I said. "I am to assure you he bears you no ill will. He figures you probably paid whatever debt you owed society."

Godey was frowning and nodding as I spoke. His eyes were cast downward at a point about midway between us, as though he was concentrating on every word.

"Holmes also said that I was to thank you for sending Tommy to us with this little mystery. Holmes is most intrigued, as am I, and we are willing to do what we can to help him prepare for the outing, presuming, of course, that it is your wish that he go. We intend to go with him if he does."

"'At's right kind, 'at is," John Godey said, looking directly at me. "Right kind o' 'im—an' you, too, Doctor, 'tickly since you don't owe me and the boy nothin.' Spirit o' the season, must be, eh?"

"Oh, perhaps a little," I said. "The truth is, Tommy's a good bright lad, and I've taken a liking to him. And Holmes' curiosity is aroused."

The man smiled, and I suddenly felt uneasy. His expression seemed sour, as if he were smiling only begrudgingly.

"S'pose I knew at'd be the case," Godey said. "I knew once 'Olmes got wind o' this, 'e wouldn't like the smell."

"About that, exactly, Mr. Godey . . ." I said. "Can you explain your misgivings a bit more fully? On the face of it, there doesn't seem much to be alarmed about. Tommy seems somehow to have drawn the notice of a wealthy patron. Through the ages, that sort of thing has been rather commonplace. Why, some of the great painters of Europe had—"

"You ain't serious, are ya, Doc?" Godey asked. "You must be 'avin' me on. 'At's it."

"Not at all," I said. "Not in the least."

Godey's thoughts were not delivered in a steady, modulated voice. His emotions were too strong for that; they seemed almost to overpower him, and as a result, his words spilled and tumbled out like prisoners breaking free of their restraints.

"Listen, Doc. I don't mean no disrespect, but I'm too many years on to start believin' in fairy tales. Folk like 'at rich old toss-pot Lady Armstrong don't just reach down from their golden t'rones and do the likes o' us good turns without there bein' somethin' in it for theirselves, somethin' big's my guess. Now, I don't know just what that sartin thing'd be in this 'ere case, though I could make some smart guesses, but whatever it is, it means them usin' my Tom somehow, an' I won't have 'at! I won't."

"Then, Mr. Godey, keep the boy home. Are you not asking Holmes and me to protect him? Isn't that what's at the heart of this? You think that boy is in danger, fancy dinner or no. Isn't that right?"

The man's answer told me clearly what I had already surmised, that behind the costerman's misshapen exterior lay an intelligence of deceptive depth, and despite his wretched physical condition his faculties were not in the least bit blunted.

"Aye," he replied quickly. "My Tom's been singled out

now, hasn't he? That's the heart of it," Godey said. "Somebody out there's got a fix on my boy. So I'm arrangin' for you and Mr. 'Olmes to protect him, just like you'd protect a reg'lar client . . . An' fer yer trouble, you and Mr. 'Olmes gets one o' them mysteries to puzzle on. I figger the two of you are 'trepid 'nuff to take on a job like 'at as a matter of . . . Oh, fair trade, we'll call it. An' like I said, Tommy'll be safe and sound," Godey said, "because . . ."

"Because you can no longer protect him," I interjected. "Isn't that right?"

My abruptness brought the man up short.

He snapped his head sharply toward me and looked straight into my face. There was a suggestion of a smile on his chapped lips, and his rheumy eyes were opened wide.

"Oh, aye," Godey said. " 'At's it, entire, it is. I see now why you've been pairin' up wi' Mr. 'Olmes: Yer near's smart as he is."

I was not flattered. "Listen," I said. "In order to properly prepare Tommy for New Year's Eve, we'll need you to allow him to visit us in Baker Street several times, beginning at your earliest convenience. Is that possible?"

"Aye, Doctor," Godey said, " 'at's fine so long as the two of you see he's back and forth safe an' sound."

"You have our word on it, Mr. Godey," I said. "Now, I have brought you something." I reached into my jacket pocket and withdrew an envelope with Godey's name written on it in Holmes' hand.

"Sherlock Holmes sends you this," I said, placing it in his hand. I have to admit, I was curious as to its contents.

Godey scowled at me with an air that was so uncertain as to be nearly apprehensive.

"It's all right," I said. "Really."

He opened the envelope and fanned his thumb across the top of several large notes of currency. He looked up at me as if in question, clearly not comprehending, then withdrew a folded note from the detective and read it carefully.

Tears came to Godey's eyes and they were genuine. He snuffled a bit, cleared his throat and then wiped the back of his coat sleeve across his face. He shook his head steadily from side to side, and encountered some difficulty speaking. He handed the note to me. It read as follows:

My dear Mr. Godey,

 When you can, bring the boy around to Steadman's, the clothier on the Marylebone Lane, and ask for Mr. Arnold, who will be expecting you. He is to help select new warm clothing and proper shoes for Tommy. And you may plan to have the boy fitted for new clothes there at the start of each season.

 I have arranged payment, but mind: Where the boy is concerned, the clothing and shoes—and anything you may choose to do with the additional modest funds I have given you here—are to come from you, just as they must have in the past, in better times.

Presuming your agreement,
I remain most sincerely yours,
Sherlock Holmes

 " 'E's a real gentleman, Mr. 'Olmes is," Godey said softly. "I don't . . . I don't know 'at to say, Doc," he said. "I'm touched, I am, an' I thank you. I thank you, sir. 'At's all I can say, I guess. Thank you, and God bless the both of you; 'at's it. You tell Mr. 'Olmes I said 'at. 'God bless 'im,' I says."

 Then Godey let out a sudden short laugh that seemed to announce a sharp change of mood.

 "God bless even 'at long left jab o' his. 'At's what landed me in the docket and then off to old Newgate: 'at long left jab o' Mr. 'Olmes's. 'E tell you about that, Doc? I'd a paid to see 'at fight we had, if I hadn't a been in it, and on the losin' side at that. I seen many a fight in my day, I did, an' I saw some fighters was mighty good. Jem Mace I seen. An' Tommy Sayers, an' Tom King an' lots others in my time. I used to watch the prize fights at Wonderland and Blackfriars an' a few other places, an' I was pretty fair myself, I don't mind sayin.' I made some good money in some of them smaller clubs, I did. But you believe me, Doc, when I tell you that Mr. Sherlock bleedin' 'Olmes was just about as good there ever was. Maybe still is, for all I know.

 "I laid there in me bunk at old Newgate sometimes wit'

me eyes shut, an' all I could recollect o' that cursed night down in St. Giles was Mr. 'Olmes' left fist. 'At's all I could see, that left fist o' his. Him flickin' it hard at me face like the tongue of a viper snake wi' a rock on the end of it. An' 'e's hittin' me over 'an over 'an over till I couldn't see straight for all the blood in me eyes, an' the pain from me broke nose, an' it was clear I was gettin' the worst of it, see? My nose was broke in two places. Two, mind.''

The more Godey talked, the more animated he became. He had bent over in the unorthodox half crouch that he must have used as a boxer. Now, keeping his feet stationary and using only his hips, he bobbed left and right. Then he weaved back and forth and, despite his ruined frame, managed to mix up all four moves so that not a single one was predictable as part of any succession. The rationale, of course, was that an opponent would find it difficult to hit a target that was constantly in motion. And when Godey started moving his feet, the difficulty was increased dramatically. Then he brought up his two big gnarled fists, and it seemed for all the world as if he had stepped back in time, straight through his years in prison and on the streets of London and back into his fight that night with Sherlock Holmes in the darkened hellhole that was St. Giles.

"Then he comes shufflin' in on me, Mr. 'Olmes does. I let's 'im 'ave a good hard one in the gut wi' me right. Like this: Pow! It was a good punch. It was all I had left and then some, but it wasn't near good enough. Mr. 'Olmes, 'e takes it like it was a love tap, and he nails me right in the beezer wi' two fast combinations. Like this: Bang; babang! Bang; babang! And then two more jabs. Like this: Bang! Bang! And then the one 'at did me in come next.

"It musta been somethin' to see, Dr. Watson. Truly. Mr. 'Olmes 'its me wi' this overhand 'ookin' right cross of his . . . Boom! . . . 'At punch, it musta came down from somewhere's up in the bloody Tower, 'at's how powerful it was. A real Jem Mace finisher. 'E always said, old Jem Mace did, he always said the only time to use a big right was when it was time to end it, an' 'at's what Mr. 'Olmes did. 'At punch was somethin.' Wham! An' it was all over for old John. 'At was 'at. I was a goner.''

Godey straightened up as best he could, and let the fight

slip back into the past, but then he was beset again by the wracking cough, and it was a few painful minutes before he spoke again.

"Cor, 'at's awful," he said shaking his head. "But you know, Doc? I forgive Mr. 'Olmes after a time, I did. I truly did. Ain't nothin' in this life 'at'll ruin a man's insides faster 'n' 'atred, Doc. Might 's well eat a bucket o' lye as 'ave yourself a diet o' 'atred. You remember 'at, Doc. At's what Mr. 'Olmes taught me, 'e did, an' it's a lesson I'm better for knowin'.

"So, bless 'im for 'at, and now for this gift you've brought us. Me and Tommy's a right lucky pair o' gents, seems to me. So God bless 'im, I says. An' you, too, sir. An' I ain't never meant it more."

Chapter 7

John Godey took my right hand in both of his and shook it vigorously. I do not have a small hand, but compared with his, mine might as well have belonged to a toddler. I cleared my throat and nodded to him as a signal of my understanding. I told him I would be sure to send some laudanum back with Tommy after his first visit, and with a tip of my hat I stepped backward two paces into the fog. As soon as I believed I had been swallowed up in it, I turned and circled around until I could hear the voices of Tommy and his uncle again and could be sure that I was this time directly behind them.

I insinuated myself into a tight alcove that I had spotted while talking with Godey and remained there for quite some time. However, precious little that happened for the rest of the afternoon was worth noting, certainly nothing untoward or suspicious.

With half of my attention I watched and listened, and with the rest I reviewed my conversation with Godey. I could appreciate Holmes' dilemma where the man was concerned. There was something slightly sinister about Godey, but he was otherwise an engaging and likeable fellow. I reasoned that if I knew nothing of his history, I would be inclined to take him at his word, so I resolved to let Godey's actions speak for or against him.

The day dragged on, and when the hubbub of noise and sales activity finally seemed to rise again, I realized the dinner hour was drawing near. By the time Tommy and his uncle John were out of vegetables, darkness was closing in and rain had begun to fall. It was light at first, little more than a mist, but simultaneously the coolness of the day had rapidly turned to a chill, and what had been a slight breeze now sharpened into gusts that had some bite.

As I trailed after Tommy and his uncle, the fog began to dissipate. I worried that my task would be made more difficult, for regardless of his surroundings John Godey regularly turned and looked back over his shoulder. I thought that this was more a habit born of a hard and uneasy life than of any specific awareness of my presence, but nevertheless, if I was not extremely careful it could prove to be my undoing. I pressed on, keeping a good distance behind, trying all the while to devise a believable explanation for my presence. Within a few blocks I came to the conclusion that apart from the truth there could be no believable, or even vaguely acceptable, explanation, and I began to despair at that.

Just as quickly, however, I realized my fears were groundless, for the night's unsavory elements conspired to help me. The wind picked up, and the rain began falling more heavily. Tommy and his uncle were forced to move ahead bent into the rain, their heads down and pulled into the collars of their jackets.

I had followed the pair out of Covent Garden and up Russell Street, across Drury Lane, over to Chancery Lane and then east on Cursitor Street, where the rain suddenly came down in torrents. I was drenched and cold and suddenly very tired, too, I have to say. I thought for sure that John Godey and Tommy Rogers, whose day had been considerably longer and harder than mine, would have to stop in a moment. But they did not. I cursed my luck; if only I could dry my face so I could see them clearly. In exasperation I tucked into a sheltered doorway for just long enough to rub my face dry with my handkerchief. I emerged in an instant, but nowhere could I see Godey and the boy. I quickened my steps, and at the junction of Fetter Lane thought I spied two figures in the distance and determined not to lose them again.

At Holborn Circus, the rain abated and I realized I still had my proper quarry in view. I followed them up Charterhouse Street to the square and the Hospital of St. Bartholomew the Great, and then to Aldersgate Street. There I hid in the shadows of a broad oak tree and watched

Tommy and his uncle as they entered Hope Settlement House.

Once I stopped, I realized that besides being cold, thoroughly soaked and tired to the bone, I also was so hungry that I felt almost faint. Too many hours had passed without sustenance of any kind. I didn't want to leave my watch, but under the circumstances felt I had little choice. I reasoned that if John Godey was going out again that night, he probably would not do so until he could be certain that Tommy was in bed and sound asleep. It seemed reasonable to think I might leave for a bit, find some nourishment and, with even a modicum of luck, return to my post without missing much.

One hour, I told myself, no more. I walked hurriedly back to Charterhouse Square and in the familiar shadows of old St. Bart's seated myself at a small table in the corner of a busy tavern that I knew served good fare. I ordered brandy to push away the cold. By the time I was halfway through my drink, the white-aproned waiter returned with a bowl of thick and piping-hot lentil soup, a small loaf of crusty bread and a dinner plate piled with pieces of cold roast pork. I distinctly remember thinking that it had been a very long time since I had welcomed such a simple meal as earnestly. I checked my pocket watch, ordered another brandy and dug in.

"Beggin' your pardon, mate," came a gravelly voice. "Would ye 'ave a light there?"

I was so hungry and so engrossed in my meal that I had not noticed anyone approaching my table, and the voice so startled me that I spilled my spoonful of soup.

"Sorry there, mate," came the voice again. I looked up to see a grizzled sailor looking down at me. He was tall, rather gaunt, and he was holding out an unlighted briar.

"Me lights got soaked in that downpour," he said by way of explanation.

"Oh," I said. "Oh, certainly. That is, if my own aren't too damp."

He was polite enough for a rough-looking customer. He wore a heavy dark woollen pea coat and a watch cap from which strands of disheveled curly hair poked out. His hair was red, as was his short rough beard, and even in the dimly lighted tavern I could tell that he used his facial hair to mask a field of pockmarks. He stood waiting patiently while I fished matches from the inside pocket of my vest.

"Never mind, mate," he said. "Barkeep'll have some."

"No, no," I said. "I know I have matches. I'll be wanting them pretty soon myself anyway. Might as well find 'em now as later, Mr. . . . ?"

"Nat," the sailor said.

"Mr. Nat," I said.

"No," the man said. "Just Nat, s'all."

"Ah, yes. Well, Nat, I'm John. Good to meet you," I said, and held out my hand.

"Aye," the sailor said, and gripped my hand firmly.

"Soup as good as it smells?" he asked.

"Yes," I said, still looking for my matches. "I've got to say it hits the spot. Uh, would you care to join me for a bowl?"

"Nah," the sailor said. "I've et, thankee."

"Ah," I said, finally laying hold of the matches, which surprisingly seemed quite dry. "Here they are."

He grunted in acknowledgment, flicked a match into flame with his thumb, lighted his pipe and then exhaled a small cloud of acrid gray smoke.

"I ain't seen you around here before," he said.

"Just passing through," I told him. "This foul weather slowed me down."

"Aye," Nat said. "It'll do that."

"Are you just back from a voyage, Nat?"

"Aye," he said, a trace of curiosity in his voice.

"Ah, I knew it. Salt stains on your coat."

"You're a mite nosy, ain't you?"

"Good Lord, no," I said. "Don't be offended. Really. I'm not prying. It's just sort of a habit from—"

"Bad habit, mate."

"Oh, come now, Nat. Here. Sit down. Sit down. Waiter, bring us drinks, would you? Another brandy for me. My friend here will have a . . . ?"

"Double whisky," Nat said loud enough for the publican to hear. Our waiter went to the bar to get the drinks.

"Mebbe you kin tell me where I shipped to, then," Nat said. His voice still had a slight edge.

"Well," I said. "I don't know. Let me think for a moment." I looked at Nat and thought to myself what Holmes might say in just such a circumstance. I looked the sailor up and down. I figured Nat would presume I was looking for clues to the correct answer; in fact, I was—but I also was buying myself some little time in which to think.

Our drinks arrived. Nat tossed his back at once, cleared his throat and set the glass down with a decisive thump.

"Well?" he asked, a slight smile evident behind the red beard.

"No," I said. "Having no telling visual clues and no other basis on which to form a sound judgment as to your seaward comings and goings of late, I have to say, I do not know where your travels have taken you recently."

Nat smiled.

"Now, John," he said. " 'At's right smart, 'at is. Man should always recognize the limitations of his situation. 'At's gotten me through many a tight spot, it has."

Nat rose from his chair. "Well," he said, "thankee again."

"Don't mention it," I said.

He walked off and I regretted seeing him go. It had been a long day, and company, however briefly encountered, was welcome. I looked at my watch, and seeing that I had been away from my post for nearly an hour, I paid the bill, pulled my collar up about my chin and left the tavern. I returned to my oak tree on Aldersgate straightaway and resumed my watch of Hope Settlement House. Immediately, I found myself wishing that I had not left my post at all, for I had no way of knowing for certain if Godey was still inside.

I gave it an hour—an hour filled with self-recrimination, I might add—and when the man did not emerge, I prepared to leave. I filled the bowl of my pipe, tamped it tightly and lighted it for the long walk home. I moved away from the shadows and had turned up the street when I heard a distant cough. I turned, and who should I see coming out of the side door of the settlement house but John Godey; there was no mistaking the bowed stature and crab-like walk.

I followed him from a safe distance, and again I quickly

grew attuned to the timing of his habitual looks backward; it was every forty steps, no more and no fewer. So at precisely those intervals I ducked off the sidewalk for the briefest of moments, counting his steps all the while, for Godey never stopped moving, and then stepped back onto the trail. It was dicey work, made all the more so by the rain's having stopped some time ago, thus improving visibility somewhat. Light, wispy patches of cold fog had begun to settle in, and I was thankful for that, for midnight was drawing close, and the few people left on the streets were very noticeable, indeed.

Godey seemed to be headed back toward Covent Garden. I followed him westward on Charterhouse Street, but instead of crossing Holborn Circus and heading south onto Fetter Lane, he crossed in a westerly path that put him straightaway onto High Holborn, and that worried me, for I knew well where that road might lead. With every step I grew more certain of it, and with every step I wished more fervently that I had brought my handgun.

Before I knew it, I had followed Godey into the knot of streets known as St. Giles, an area that was known in every corner of London as a haven for thieves and cutthroats. Its heart was the proximate terminus of seven streets, where atop a tall column once stood an odd, seven-faced clock that gave the neighborhood its name: the Seven Dials. There were many other parts of the city that were about as rough and dirty as this one, but none were much worse. The place stunk of rotting garbage and human waste, and it was said that a man could die in the gutter here with a knife in his back and not be moved until the rats carried him off or devoured him where he lay. I suspect that was an exaggeration, but I did not know to what extent.

The actual Seven Dials clock was long gone, having fallen victim well over a hundred years earlier to a rumor that the big timepiece actually marked the site of buried treasure. Excavation had yielded nothing but dirt, however, and in disgust the clock was removed from the area altogether and given a proper home somewhere in Surrey—Weybridge, I believe.

I dearly wished that I were there now. I held my scarf over my mouth and nose in a futile effort to fend off the

stench that permeated the area, but while I did so, I kept
my eyes trained on Godey. I saw him enter what appeared
to be a public house or social club of some kind; I could
not tell which, for the sign board had been torn from the
exterior brick wall of the place. Its original site was clearly
marked by a rectangular discoloration on which someone
had scrawled the single word ALE in black letters. Greenish-
yellow light shone through the entrance, which appeared
to be unencumbered by a door of any kind, despite the
inclement weather.

Godey stood in the doorway for a moment, stopped
dead, bathed in the light. From my vantage point, he
looked more like a stationary black cutout, a silhouette on
a lamp shade, than a real person. But then he straightened
up somewhat, gave a glance backward over his shoulder,
walked inside and was approached immediately. The
stranger was a man; I was sure of that much, for he wore
a flat cap set at an angle. I was not close enough to discern
his features, so I waited for a few minutes and then moved
out of the shadows. I had taken but a few steps in the
direction of the pub when two men appeared directly in
front of me. I had no idea where they came from, but like
Godey, they, too, were outlined by the light from the entrance to the bar, their features obscured, intentionally, I'm
sure. The man on the left was very wide and so extraordi-
narily tall he might have had a natural place in a freak
show. The thug on the right was wiry looking and about
my size, but next to the giant he appeared very short.

The tall one spoke first.

"Where you goin', guv? Doncha know 'is ain't no fit
place for a toff?"

The shorter man laughed, a hollow noise that was exaggerated and artificial and carried an undisguised malevo-
lence. He was an echo, not bright enough to even originate
his own nasty thought: "Doncha know 'is ain't no fit place
for no toff?" I could see the glint of a long steel blade in
his right hand. My breath caught in my throat.

They stepped toward me as they talked, their design obvious. There was no hope of escaping them, so I raised my
cane as though it were a sword. I intended to do as much
damage as possible, not by swinging wildly with the stick,

but by jabbing with it. If I could quickly catch one of the men in the solar plexus with a hard thrust, I stood to at least even the odds. I straightened my arm, cane at the ready, as though it were a razor-sharp sword, for which at that very moment I would have paid most handsomely.

But then a deep voice, full of gravel and hard intent, spoke loudly from the darkness between the buildings to my right.

"Aaay . . . What gives 'ere, gents? This don't look fair to me, it don't. No, sir. I think it be best 'at you two blokes shove off for some other 'arbor."

It was Nat, the redheaded sailor I'd met at the tavern near St. Bart's. I couldn't believe my good fortune. He stepped out of the darkness and into the street.

"Bugger off, you," the shorter man snarled. He still held the long-bladed knife in his hand, but now it was well below his waist and parallel to the ground, ready for use. He crossed the street in a few quick steps and ran directly at Nat.

The sailor ran, too, but not, as might be expected, in the opposite direction. He ran straight at his attacker, side-stepped the man's lunge with his knife and kicked him hard in the groin. The blade dropped from the man's hand, and he doubled over in pain. The sailor hit him with a fast left hook and then quickly followed that with a hard right hook. The punches rocked the cutthroat's head back and forth so sharply that I wondered if the blows would break his neck. Before the assailant had a chance to focus again, Nat hit him four more times with left jabs that were so hard and flawlessly exact that they seemed almost mechanical, a precisely machined piston shooting straight out from the sailor's shoulder, exploding, retracting, extending, exploding—each time with a sharp splat as Nat's knuckles connected with some part of the man's face, over and over and over again.

The man jolted backward every time he took a punch. I marveled that he did not go down. And when Nat stopped, the man staggered directly at him, which was his final mistake. Nat jumped backward so quickly that his movement seemed like some sort of dance step. But he was only making room for a spinning, whirling kick that was as fast as it was painful to witness. It caught the thug square in the face, and he went down hard and decisively.

His immense companion, had he been a smarter man, or at least a more experienced fighter, would have rushed into battle at his comrade's side. As I reflect on the incident now, I think the big fellow never expected he actually would have to fight. Most likely, he was accustomed to scaring people off, and on those few occasions when his chosen victims didn't run, his friend with the knife undoubtedly was able to handle the night's business. From beneath his coat he had drawn a cudgel of some sort, and when his friend went down, he started toward us from the opposite side of the street. At first his dark unshaven face bore a rather surprised look, but when he decided to move on us, the look quickly turned to rage. The gigantic man swore at us repeatedly and rapidly and at the top of his lungs. His oaths were black and bloody promises. His curses were unintelligible and fearsome bellows intended to confuse and frighten, in much the manner of an ancient Celtic warrior charging into battle. There was no time to think, only to move, and in that moment of recognition I heard Nat the sailor shout, "Now, Watson!"

His voice suddenly sounded different, more familiar, but I had no time to give it thought, no time to wonder why. I think I was probably dimly aware that Nat had used my surname, though I could not recall using it when we were together back at the tavern. I realized moments later, of course, that Nat the sailor actually was Holmes in disguise, but at that very instant I was far more concerned with getting out of St. Giles in one piece. This wasn't a scrum at Blackheath; this was for real, and I was oblivious to anything but the engagement at hand. We were halfway home. One man down. One man left in the way.

We hit the big man together. I rammed the top of my head hard and straight into his lower gut and drove the air out of him in a painful, explosive burst. Simultaneously, he swung his sap straight down at me. I caught it on the top of my right shoulder. I felt a dull pain, but I knew he was getting the worst of it, for Holmes had launched himself feet first and struck home.

The detective had run hard at our quarry and closed the

final gap parallel to the ground, the hard heels of his boots trained straight at the big man's head and upper torso like battering rams. One of Holmes' boots cracked flat into the big man's nose; I could hear the unmistakable and sickening sound of bone snapping. A split second later, Holmes' other foot hit him square in the chest. The three of us went over together in a pile.

I got to my feet quickly, rubbing my shoulder. Holmes was already upright and peeling off his red hair and bushy mustache.

Our big target lay on his back groaning loudly. His partner was still out cold, not six feet away.

Holmes turned the smaller cutthroat over, pulled the knife sheath from the back of the man's belt, slipped the long blade inside, and put the weapon in the pocket of his pea coat. Then he turned to me and said, "It is time we left this place, Watson. There are many more where these two came from."

"After you, old man," I answered, and we fairly flew back into the night.

Chapter 8

It would not be an exaggeration to say that Holmes saved my life that night in St. Giles, and it was not the first time that he had done so. And I am proud to say that in the course of our long association, I was able to return the favor on a number of occasions, largely because I was never slow to use my trusty service revolver.

Holmes, however, considered all violence a lamentable failure of reason. He preferred to rely on his wits, and only when force was a necessary and unavoidable last resort, his physical skills; the former were becoming legendary, and the latter, while not normally associated with a man so well known for his intellect, were remarkable on several fronts.

Though he was a tall, rangy man, Holmes was possessed of surprisingly great strength. One villain several years ago tried to warn us off a case with a show of brute strength that merely served to amuse Holmes. The man picked up the long steel poker that stood beside the fireplace in our Baker Street quarters and, in a furious burst of strength, bent the heavy rod into the shape of a horseshoe. Then he cast it aside and left in a huff, sure that he had intimidated Holmes; of course, he had not. Had the blackguard stayed he would have seen Holmes, almost laughing, pick up the poker and straighten it with a sudden flex of his wrists.

It was Holmes' remarkable concentration and stern discipline that magnified his strength. For years he had been a student of the ancient Japanese martial art of baritsu. Having watched him practice many times, I knew that he had an uncanny ability to defend himself, almost a sixth sense that came to the fore only under extreme pressure. And when he had to, he could attack with deceptive speed and deadly accuracy, just as he had tonight.

With equal diligence and determination, Holmes applied those very same attributes to other martial disciplines. He was quite a good archer. He was a master of the single stick. He had proven himself to be a deadly swordsman and one of the best boxers for his size and weight anywhere in London. All of which served to make him a compleat, if unlikely, warrior.

He took manly pride in his abilities, of course, but never was he boastful. In fact, he was inclined to think of his physical skills as practicalities.

"Without them," he said, "some part of my consciousness would always be devoted to steering clear of danger, and I am not willing to reserve any part of my faculties for that. I cannot afford to do so, Watson. I need all of my concentration, all of my sensibilities and skills, if I am to deal successfully with the complex little problems that come our way. Physical prowess simply buys me the freedom to do so.

"Besides," the detective said, "if I were every bit as much the wizard of detection that you seem determined to impose on the reading public, I would not have to be concerned for my safety; we would never find ourselves in harm's way. I would be able to solve almost any mystery without ever having to stray very far from our quarters. In that, I would be merely the equal of my brother Mycroft, and I regret to say that, at least in that regard, I am not. You see, Watson?" he had said. "I am more modest than you sometimes take me for."

I was mulling over that conversation as I sat trying to get warm before our fireplace some time after the trouble in Seven Dials. I had wrapped myself in a heavy woollen blanket. With one hand I held its edges tightly together; with the other I held a small snifter of brandy.

"Your intervention was most timely tonight, Holmes," I said. "Thank you."

"Not at all," he said. "Had I been any slower in leaving that damnable pub, it might be you lying back there in the gutter right now."

"Nat, indeed," I said. "I should have known at once that it was you, Holmes. I have to say, by not identifying yourself when we met, you made me feel like the fool."

"Don't be silly, Watson," Holmes said. "If you had seen through my ruse, it would not have been a very good one, would it?"

"I suppose not," I said, "but . . . "

"And if my disguise was not effective enough to fool even you, old fellow, you who above all others knows me so well, then I might have found myself vulnerable when I could least afford it, no?"

"I suppose that's one way of looking at things," I said. "Yes."

"It is the *only* way of looking at it, Watson. The *only* way. In the most honest manner possible, you vouched for the effectiveness of my disguise. Thus ensured and fortified, I was able to apply my modest powers to good result. You probably saved *my* life, Watson. It is I who am indebted to you."

He was barely able to keep a straight face as he led me through his tortuous reasoning.

"All right, Holmes, you've made your point," I said, "but tell me, what was it, exactly, that brought you out?"

"There, too, I was slow," Holmes said with a sigh of disgust. "It did not occur to me until late afternoon that you might not have taken your service revolver with you. I took the liberty of checking your room, and when I found your Webley Double Action in the bureau drawer where you usually keep it, I decided I might prove more useful in Covent Garden. Not that it was at all clear that you would need my help, Watson. But I thought to myself, 'Well, just in case . . .' As it happened, I arrived just as Tommy, John Godey and you were leaving. Eventually, I broke off and went ahead to the pub."

"Before I forget, Holmes, why did you stop to take that thug's knife?"

"Impulse, I suppose. I haven't given it much thought. I didn't want him to spring to his feet and bury the weapon between our shoulder blades, either; he did not go down easily, that one. Perhaps I simply had doubts about whether he was going to stay down. Who knows?" the detective said. "I suppose not everything demands keen analysis. And I do have a good knife now, don't I? Perhaps I should learn to use it."

"Now that you mention it, Holmes, the knife does seem to be one of the few weapons to which you have never paid much attention."

"You're right," he said. "The knife is such a common-place item." Then almost to himself: "Maybe I *should* give it more heed, out of principle, if not practicality, I mean. Although, I can't say that I understand the dynamics of it."

"Dynamics?"

"Well, yes, Watson. I don't understand what particular knowledge or skill must be brought to bear in order to ensure that a thrown dagger arrives at its mark point first. Why doesn't the end of the handle hit the target first? It's obvious that considerable skill and a good deal of practice must be involved. I just never gave it much thought."

It struck me that Holmes looked especially weary, as well he might be after the earlier events of the evening. I was about to comment on it when he said, "Tell me, what did you make of John Godey? A lesser fellow would be mired in anger and bitterness, I suspect, especially in light of his poor health, don't you agree?"

"I do, Holmes," I said. "I thought he responded appropriately to everything I had to say . . . and to your note as well. The man cannot be blamed for wanting to protect Tommy, even if the actual extent of the boy's endangerment appears uncertain. Godey seemed as convinced as you that something is seriously amiss."

"Mmmm, yes," Holmes said. "Yes, he did. What do you suppose it was that he was holding back?" As he asked the question, Holmes struck a match and relighted his briar.

"Holding back?" I asked, fanning the burst of white smoke out of my eyes.

"Of course, Watson. Of course. You hear, my good man, but I'm afraid you do not always *listen*. It was a poor man at his cynical best. Godey said he believed people like Lady Armstrong—he called her an old toss-pot, I think—couldn't possibly do anything nice for people without their being something in it for themselves.

"And then, Watson, then Godey said he could make some 'smart' guesses what that certain something might be. I was hoping you would seize on that statement; it was nearly an invitation. When you didn't, I had to bite my tongue to keep from crying out."

"I'm sorry, Holmes, I—"

"There were too many points to keep track of," Holmes said. "Still, what do you suppose our Mr. Godey was referring to?"

The detective answered his own question: "Some bit of intelligence about Lady Armstrong's charity dinner; it had to be. I think he kept it to himself because he had no reason not to. We had already made it apparent that we were in. Had we responded differently, he might have used the information as a last resort."

"Shrewd," I said.

"I do not know, Watson. Perhaps. There was a time when the implication of slyness fit John Godey perfectly, but I do not know whether that is still the case. I think that for now we must give him the benefit of the doubt. Until we know otherwise, let us presume that Mr. Godey was merely being circumspect."

"Well, if he was all that circumspect," I asked, "why would he be going to a hellhole like St. Giles so regularly?"

"Watson, you do surprise me sometimes," Holmes said. "Finally, after all of this discussion, you bring us to a nattering little point that is very near the heart of things: Why? you ask. The simplest of all questions."

Now he was being pedantic and almost petty, but he was right. I knew it and said so begrudgingly.

"Well, Holmes," I said, "what is the answer? Why *does* John Godey make periodic visits to such a place as St. Giles?"

"I have no idea, Watson."

"But you clearly implied that—"

"No, Watson. You inferred that I had the answer when in fact all I had was the simple question. And that's still the case, unfortunately. We need more information.

"Meanwhile, we have a visit with Lady Armstrong to look forward to," he said. "She has consented to see us at Planetree tomorrow afternoon." Holmes put special emphasis on the word "consented," as if to imply that Lady Armstrong was behaving rather badly.

"Aha," I said. "I see. And you are worried for some reason?"

"No, I am not worried," Holmes said. "I am annoyed. I am apprehensive. I do not like this woman, and I do not look forward to dealing with her. Everything that I know of her suggests that she typifies the worst of her sex, Watson. Domineering. Manipulative. Venal. Unpredictable. Not to be believed or trusted."

"She must be quite something," I said.

" 'Quite something,' " the detective repeated. "That's a delicate way of putting it, but yes, Watson, so I am led to believe. I am tired at the moment, and just the thought of our impending interview with the woman is enough to put me in a foul humor."

Holmes' assessment proved to be well founded. In fact, he could have called Lady Mirabelle Llewellyn Armstrong a witch, and I still would have considered him well spoken—perhaps even overly polite.

Chapter 9

Lady Armstrong posed problems from the very outset.
Holmes and I alighted from our hansom cab, paid
the driver and walked up the broad stone steps of Lady
Armstrong's magnificent home. It rose three stories over
the classically elegant and carefully manicured Berkeley
Square, long a favorite address of the upper orders. "Planetree" was a somewhat less than inspired appellation, though
it certainly was accurate and descriptive; the house was bor-
dered on three sides by huge specimens of that well-known
tree with the mottled gray-green bark.

Over the massive bright black front door was a large
swag of evergreen boughs bound up for the holidays in a
brilliant red ribbon and carefully dotted with lovely dried
rose blossoms of white, yellow, peach, pink and red.

"Isn't that beautiful, Holmes?" I remarked, pointing over
our heads.

"Yes, quite," he said without looking. He was about to
raise the large brass knocker on the door when the portal
opened noiselessly. A tall and muscular "butler" stood before us in livery, staring. According to Holmes, he was Lady
Armstrong's personal attendant, her manservant and guard.
He offered neither a smile nor a salutation. Instead, he
glared at us, sniffed the air with a nose that was already
slightly upraised, and asked, "Are you expected?" The man
was being needlessly rude and impertinent, I thought, and
so, apparently, did Holmes.

"Expected?" Holmes said loudly. "Of course we're expected." He stepped boldly through the door, and probably
would have ground his boot into the diffident butler's
brightly shined shoes, despite the man's size, had not the

fellow shown the good sense and agility to quickly move aside. I followed Holmes.

"Tell Lady Armstrong that Mr. Sherlock Holmes and Dr. John H. Watson are here," Holmes said sharply. "Now, if you please. And take your ludicrous pretensions with you . . . Cuthbert."

The transformation wrought by Holmes' aggressiveness and then his pointed use of the man's name was stunning. The butler's face blanched. His entire frame sagged, and he tilted his head downward at the brightly polished white marble floor as he spoke.

"Yes, sir," he said. "Immediately, sir." He gestured to his left while barely raising his head. "Please follow me."

In merely a few steps, we found ourselves in a small, well-appointed reception room just off the large foyer.

"I will tell Lady Armstrong that you are here, gentlemen. Won't you both please be seated?"

The butler bowed curtly, his left forearm and hand bent straight across his waist. With a simultaneous sweep of his right arm he indicated a pair of uncomfortable-looking chairs set companionably behind a large tea table.

"You will please excuse me," he said, and left the room.

We did not bother sitting.

On a table in the corner was a Christmas tree decorated with gilt-edged ribbons, gaily colored bows and shimmering gold-colored garlands. Over the fireplace mantel was a precise replica of the holiday swag we had seen over the front door, but it was decidedly smaller, almost a miniature.

"Holmes," I said, pointing at the decoration, "that swag is even beautiful at about a quarter of the size. You really have to appreciate the work that goes into such a thing . . . not to mention the artistry."

"Mmmm," he said. "Not to mention." Again, he was paying no attention whatsoever.

I noticed that electric lamps, still rather a novelty, were set up on other small tables. One of the lamps had been turned on. I walked over to look at it, and marveled aloud at the convenience of it.

Holmes was not terribly impressed, however.

"I suspect, Watson, that if electrical lighting were all that reliable, the gas service to the house would not have been allowed to remain simultaneously intact." He opened a valve on one of the dormant wall lamps, and there was an immediate hiss, as if to prove his point.

"Well, it makes sense to have an alternative at the ready in case any of these lamps burn out," I said. "I'm told that the filaments don't last very long."

Holmes grunted as if to say he was neither surprised nor very interested. I changed the subject.

"How did you know that dreadful butler's name, Holmes?" I asked.

"From inquiries and my 'background' reading," he said, rather smugly, I thought. "I found him in my files: Cuthbert Wilson, one more bit of nasty business from Shoreditch. He was in and out of trouble with the law for years, and then resurfaced about seven years ago, somehow all painted over with respectability. His barking and snarling is intended to intimidate all but the stoutest of hearts."

"If the man were my butler," I said, "I would dismiss him at once."

"Only if he did not do what you wanted him to do, Watson."

"Do you mean he . . . ?"

"Of course," Holmes said. "Lady Armstrong is well known as a tough manager. Even a Cuthbert Wilson would dare do nothing on his own. I suspect that he always does exactly what Lady Armstrong wants him to do. I suspect that her attitude is, if a caller can't—"

Holmes was stopped short.

"Allow me to finish that statement," came a woman's thin and strident voice. In the doorway a figure materialized that could only have been Lady Mirabelle Llewelyn Armstrong.

I had guessed that she would be in her dotage, but never did a guess appear to be more off the mark. A sense of her history suggested that she had to be in her sixth decade, but whatever her true age was at the time of our meeting, she remained an imposing figure of a woman and the very picture of vitality. She moved quickly, but with a natural and unassuming grace. She was nearly as tall as Holmes, and her face was almost as angular, but in a pleasing and entirely feminine way. Her frame was shapely, her eyes the clearest blue. Her skin was as white as polished alabaster and no less smooth. Her hair, done up in a chignon, obviously had been jet black at one time, but now included plentiful strands of white, which added an aura of sophistication to her features—not that she needed it, for this was a compelling woman, one with a bearing to rival royalty.

If Lady Armstrong also had possessed a warm and disarming smile and a pleasant voice, I would be compelled to recall her as beautiful. I must report instead that her smile was quick and so mechanical that it barely caused her pale lips to part, and when they did they revealed teeth that were unnaturally small and sharp-looking and as yellowish-brown as the city's fog. And her voice was a fright; I shudder to think of it. The sound she made in what for her was normal conversation was high-pitched, nasal, sharp and shrewish, and she must have been nearly deaf, too, for she spoke in a tone so unnaturally loud that even the memory of it makes my head hurt.

" 'If a caller can't handle Wilson,' " she reiterated, " 'he certainly is not worth Lady Armstrong's attention.' Is that roughly what you had intended to say?" she asked Holmes. "I presume that you are the illustrious Baker Street detective we have been hearing so much about recently."

"I am Sherlock Holmes, Lady Armstrong."

Holmes' voice, compared with hers, was downright melodious. It was well modulated and rather soft, but firm and exceptionally clear.

"This is my friend and colleague, Dr. John H. Watson," he said with a sweep of his hand toward me, "and yes, that is approximately what I would have said."

"Good," she retorted without a smile. "At least you are not a liar. That's something in your favor, I suppose."

Holmes' lips twitched in the briefest suggestion of a smile. The woman was standing unfashionably close to him, and I realized at once that my supposition about her near deafness had some validity. I was certain of it a moment later, when I noticed that as soon as Lady Armstrong finished a sentence, she noticeably shifted her focus from the person's eyes directly to his lips in anticipation of a response. Only when the person finished talking did she elevate her gaze again.

Holmes stood squarely before Lady Armstrong. Both of

his hands rested atop the head of his walking stick, which was planted firmly between him and the woman. His legs were spread apart so as to concentrate his weight somewhat forward on the balls of his feet, angling his torso even that much closer to our hostess. He was the very picture of implacable determination.

"You leave me no alternative but to be even more direct than is my custom, Lady Armstrong. So be it; I did not come here to curry favor. I am—"

"Arrogant," the woman said.

Holmes snapped at her before she could add to her insult.

"I will not be drawn out," he said loudly, "and I most certainly will not be browbeaten. Not by you, Lady Armstrong, not by anyone. You will listen to what I have to say. What's more, you will respond to my questions in a manner that would be recognized as civil anywhere in the monarchy or we will depart at once. If we do, then you will be left to wonder how it came to be that you finally had met a worthy foil and then failed to measure up."

The woman's eyes widened and her lips moved and her mouth opened and closed several times, revealing her ugly teeth. All the while her features reddened noticeably. When Lady Armstrong finally found the words she wanted, she spat them out.

"Why, you impudent—"

Holmes cut her off again. This time he said sharply, "Come, Watson!"

He was already moving. I followed. We brushed so close to the apoplectic and startled Lady Armstrong that she staggered backward slightly. We were out of the room in an instant. Into the foyer we went, and through the massive front door, which Holmes had flung open as quickly and easily as if it were a cupboard door in a lowly pantry. The door swung back against the wall with a most indelicate crash that reverberated through the foyer.

Lady Armstrong's voice rose above the noise.

"All right!" she shouted. "All right! Wilson. Wilson, you shiftless fool. Stop those two. Bring them back here this instant. Wilson!"

The big butler came around from behind one of the

plane trees, his arms outstretched from his sides, as if to show the absence of a weapon.

"Mr. Holmes," he called. "Mr. Holmes."

The detective turned toward him. Wilson lowered his voice.

"I think you've won, sir," he said. "You have her attention, at least for now."

"Do you think so?" Holmes asked. "We shall see." We turned and walked briskly back up the steps and into the house. The butler was directly behind us.

Lady Armstrong met us in the foyer with a wry smile upon her lips, which thankfully remained closed. It was as if a vicious storm had passed and a better part of the day had dawned. I would not say that she actually became charming, but she was suddenly pleasant enough to undercut any anger that remained on our part.

"Come with me, gentlemen . . . Please," Lady Armstrong said. She tilted her head slightly and offered us a demure smile; it was coquettish of her, clearly calculated to give us a glimpse of unattainable and long-forgotten beauty.

"Wilson," she said softly, "tell Sarah that we will have tea now, and do ask David to join us when he can. He is in the east wing, I would imagine."

The butler nodded and walked off briskly, but without a sound.

Lady Armstrong led us into a magnificent, immense rectangular room that was part library and part gallery. The two walls that formed the ends of the room were lined from floor to high-vaulted ceiling with shelves of books. Only the door through which we had entered broke the expanse of books on one wall. The focal point at the opposite end was an enormous gilt-edged fireplace of white-veined black marble. It was flanked by more bookshelves. The opposing long walls were hung with so many fine paintings that I cannot possibly recount them all. There was at least one large Caravaggio, and a Venetian scene that I took to be a Canaletto. There was a painting by Ingres, and two by Seurat. Holmes appeared drawn to a Vernet. I noticed at least two Rossettis and several paintings by Lord Frederic Leighton. I am sure there were a good many others whose creators I did not know or cannot now recall. The overall effect was stunning.

"Doctor?" Lady Armstrong said inquiringly.

"Oh, I'm sorry," I said. "I was lost in your collection."

"Indeed, Lady Armstrong," Holmes said. "You have a fine eye."

"Thank you," she said. "Would that I could claim much credit for it. My late husband started the collection so many years ago that I would hesitate to even tell you when. Our son, David, seems to have inherited his good taste. He has expanded our collection considerably."

"I particularly enjoy Lord Leighton's work," I said. I was looking directly at a rather large, horizontally oriented oil titled *Idyll,* in which a shepherd, seen from the back, played a flute for two forest nymphs. "Isn't this the one for which Lillie Langtry is rumored to have posed?" I asked.

Holmes frowned at me. I knew we had an agenda to follow, but I could not help myself.

"It is no rumor," Lady Armstrong said. "That young woman, the more scantily clad of the two, is Miss Langtry; I know that for a fact. Freddy Leighton is an old friend. Deliciously scandalous, don't you think? I suppose the woman's proclivities are not to be admired, but her talent and courage certainly must be respected."

I nodded. Holmes remained silent.

The maid, Sarah, entered with a service of tea and an assortment of biscuits. She guided us to a proper table off to the side of the room, and after she poured for us and departed, Holmes addressed Lady Armstrong.

"I have two—no, three—immediate questions," he said.

Lady Armstrong nodded.

"A young man of my acquaintance, a street boy, seems to have been singled out for invitation to your holiday banquet and concert, and I must ask why."

"And the second question?"

"Unless I am grievously mistaken, Lady Armstrong, and I do not believe that I am, your name usually is among the least likely to be publicly associated with charities."

"That is not a question," she said.

"I beg your pardon?" Holmes replied.

"That was a statement, Mr. Holmes, not a question."

The impatience in her voice was clear, as was her flash of anger; it was as though the first, arrogant and combative Lady Armstrong was still there, lying in wait for provocation.

"I would have thought the question was implicit," Holmes sniffed.

"Oh, very well," Lady Armstrong said. "If you insist. I won't press the point, but—"

"Oh, Mother. Really." A gently reproving voice from the doorway interrupted her in mid-sentence, something not often done, I suspect.

"You are much too contentious."

So saying, Lord David Armstrong entered the room. He was a rather short and pudgy man, about five foot three inches tall, and he seemed dwarfed by the cavernous library. He had a ruddy, lightly pockmarked face and an unfortunate nose; it was narrow and abruptly hooked, somewhat like a hawk's beak. He was in his early forties, prematurely bald, and I would have guessed that he was not very active among the ladies were it not for the striking young brunette whose white-gloved hand was draped most comfortably over his left arm.

As Holmes and I rose, Lady Armstrong made the introductions. The young woman was Miss Jane Ryder of Chicago. She was sylphlike and so willowy as to suggest a form drawn in liquid. She exchanged pleasantries with everyone.

"Miss Ryder came here with her brother, John, to vacation and tour and thereby combine some pleasure with a bit of business," Lord Armstrong volunteered. "Their family made its mark in silver mining two generations ago, and then, more recently, in meatpacking and wholesaling—government contracts and such. Jane and her brother came here to scout out new investment possibilities. Now her plans have changed . . . rather permanently, I would say. Haven't they, my dear?"

Miss Ryder turned her gaze toward the floor, pursed her lips ever so slightly and murmured, "David," in a mock reproach that paid considerably more homage to convention than was necessary.

"Miss Ryder has consented to be my wife," Lord Arm-

strong declared with obvious pride. "I will make a formal
announcement on the eve of the new year."

As soon as we had offered the couple our congratula-
tions, Holmes turned the conversation back to the Armstrong family's curious involvement with a charity.

"Oh, yes," Lord Armstrong said. "The question you
asked of Mother. How rude; forgive me. Well, you were
quite correct when you noted that our family's name never
was associated with charitable works—I really couldn't help
but overhear part of your conversation. The point is, I have
been trying to change that cold perception of our family. I
do not believe Mother will be offended if I claim credit for
establishing the Working Men's Christian Improvement and
Grace Abounding Benevolent Society of Newcastle Upon
Tyne, but in truth, it never would have been possible without her."

So saying, Lord Armstrong turned in his mother's direction, as if to say, "Now it is your turn." His movements
and gestures all seemed oddly specific and exaggerated, the
sort of decorous theatricality one sees only among perform-
ers and drunks. Regardless, Lady Armstrong had been
properly cued, and she responded.

"In the past five years, Mr. Holmes, our charity has
raised and distributed a small fortune exclusively in behalf
of the lower orders," she said. "We also have contributed
to the support of other charitable organizations as well, so
it becomes quite impossible to say accurately just how
many of the poor unfortunates we have helped to clothe,
feed and house."

The instant she stopped speaking, Jane Ryder spoke.
"It's so truly noble to help the poor," she said quite needlessly. She turned her gaze to her betrothed, who returned
it with fawning affection. "It makes me proud just to be a
friend of Lord Armstrong's," she said. He responded by
placing his free hand atop the delicate-looking, white-
gloved appendage that had remained hooked through his
arm all of this time. I stole a glance at Holmes and noticed
that his mouth was curled into an odd expression, as though
he had sunk his teeth into a succulent ripe apple and bitten
a worm in half.

"And Master Thomas Payton Rogers?" Holmes asked. "The street boy of my acquaintance?"

Lord and Lady Armstrong looked at each other blankly.

"He means nothing to me," Lady Armstrong said.

"Or me," Lord Armstrong said.

"Then, with all due respect," said Holmes, his voice now tightly controlled, "how does he come to have been invited to your soiree?"

"He has?" Lady Armstrong asked. "Who is he?"

"An orphan who has been in the care of his uncle for nearly all of his life, about eight years," Holmes replied.

"Ah," Lord Armstrong said, "he must be one of the poor children the improvement society came up with. A dozen such children were selected at random from the rolls at various of the settlement houses and, of course, the Salvation Army."

Holmes pointedly raised his eyebrows and asked, "At random? Really?"

Lord Armstrong seemed startled by Holmes' persistence.

"Why, yes, Mr. Holmes," he answered. "Of course. I mean, what reason could any of us possibly have for singling out any one of these unfortunate children?"

"My point entirely," Holmes said. "What reason?"

Lord Armstrong inhaled so deeply that his chest suddenly puffed up and he seemed for a moment to grow taller; the effect was lost when he exhaled. "Oh, dear," he said. "With all due respect, Mr. Holmes, I do not think there is any reason to think that our selection of your little friend is anything more than a coincidence."

"No," Holmes said. "There is no coincidence here at all, Lord Armstrong. You see, neither Dr. Watson nor I knew the boy before the invitation was extended. It was the invitation that brought him to our door . . . literally."

"Still," Lord Armstrong said, "your suspicion is misguided. We thought that it would be appropriate to have on hand some of the very people who will most benefit from the society's work. I say, 'we,' but I must give all of the credit to my dear Jane, for it was her idea."

Miss Ryder smiled demurely and nodded her head once.

"Indeed?" Holmes asked.

"Well, yes, Mr. Holmes," Jane Ryder said softly. Only

after she spoke the detective's name did she raise her eyes and look directly at him. Her gaze was penetrating and so clearly and frankly appraising that it seemed for the moment in the cavernous room that only she and Holmes existed.

"I thought the poor children would love a fine holiday meal," Jane Ryder said, "and I thought that perhaps exposure to fine music as well might make their dreadful lot a bit more palatable . . . if only for a short while."

Holmes looked at her and said nothing. For what seemed a particularly long and uncomfortable moment, he appeared to be deciding whether to accept or reject Jane Ryder's explanation.

"I suppose, too, Miss Ryder," Holmes said abruptly, "that the proximity of such children during the heart of the Yuletide season might also serve as a rather keen inducement to their benefactors."

"The children might have that effect, Mr. Holmes, but would that be necessarily bad?"

"That isn't the description I would use," Holmes said, but before she or anyone else could ask which description he *would* use, the detective forged ahead.

"It certainly will be interesting to see the children's response to such a fine violinist as Signore Famiglietti," he said.

"Do you know his work, Mr. Holmes?" Miss Ryder quickly asked.

"Regrettably, no," he said, "but I believe I may know the name."

"Do you really?" the young woman said. She looked mildly startled, as though it would be surprising that anyone outside of her small and fashionable circle of intimates could possibly know anyone as renowned as Giacomo Famiglietti.

Holmes picked up on her response at once. "I have long been a student of the violin," he said.

"I see," the young woman said. "Yes, of course. John and I first saw him in concert in New York, and we really were quite taken. Just two months later, when we were at home in Chicago, we attended another of his concerts, and it was then we decided that we simply had to meet him.

"Well, the three of us became fast friends almost at once. As fate would have it, there was such a marvelous response to Signore Famiglietti's two scheduled performances in Chicago that he was asked to extend his stay, and John and I hosted him for the duration. We could not believe our good fortune when we realized his European itinerary would put him in London during the holidays."

"Then it is your friendship that brings Signore Famiglietti to Planetree?" Holmes asked.

Lord Armstrong chimed in. "Oh, yes," he said, "Jane and her brother are far more knowledgeable in the realm of music than I." He tapped the right side of his head and said, "Tin ear, what? I enjoy music very much, but I have to confess a lot of it sounds very much the same to me."

"John and I thought that a concert by a famous virtuoso would be the perfect complement to the Society's gala," Miss Ryder said

"My dear, I rather suspect that his performance will be the highlight of the evening," said Lady Armstrong, "rather than merely a complement to it."

"I quite agree, Lady Armstrong," said Holmes. He had stood listening quietly, his eyebrows knitted together so tightly as to make him appear totally engrossed, if not fascinated, by everything that was being said. He nodded often.

"I quite expect that Signore Famiglietti's mere presence at Planetree will make him the talk of London," Holmes said, "quite apart from his playing, which I am sure must be almost magical. Do you suppose he will include any of Vivaldi's concerti in his repertoire? I do love them. And, of course, there's *The Four Seasons*."

"Twaddle!" I thought to myself. I realized that I was struggling to make no visible response to the little scenario that Holmes was playing out. The truth was, he intensely disliked Vivaldi, and I knew it. In fact, though *The Four Seasons* was universally recognized as one of the composer's greatest works—and one that I greatly admired—the piece could not be played within Holmes' earshot without its eliciting some gratuitous and disparaging comment. "There is a technical perfection to the work that cannot be denied," Holmes would say, "even by me, and it is accessible by even the most casual of listeners, which is all to the good—I suppose. But parts of the composition are so mawkishly emotional as to be well, trite, Watson. Really. And the finer the musician, and the more august the accompaniment, the more unbearably trite the work becomes."

It was abundantly clear to me that the unabashed enthusiasm that Holmes professed for Signore Famiglietti and his concert was merely calculated to secure us an invitation, but I also suspected that he was having me on as well. An instant later, I was sure of it.

"In fact, Dr. Watson and I have often discussed the technical perfection of each of Vivaldi's *Seasons,*" Holmes said, turning his head to look directly at me without so much as a glimmer of a smile, "not to mention the simple and yet deceptively sophisticated elegance of the overarching composition. Isn't that so, Doctor?"

"Not to mention," I managed to say.

Finally, from the increasing depths of this deception, Lady Armstrong rose to Holmes' bait. The poor woman really had little choice at this juncture; it was the only polite alternative Holmes had left her.

"I wonder, Mr. Holmes," she said, without much enthusiasm, I thought, "I know this is rather short notice, but do you suppose that you and Dr. Watson might join us at the Society's benefit next week? Of course," she hastened to add, "if either of you has another commitment, I am sure we will not be offended. 'Tis the season and all, so if—"

Holmes cut her off quickly.

"I would love to," he said, "and I'm sure that I speak for the good doctor as well."

I nodded and smiled as graciously as possible.

"Of course," Holmes said, "as guests we would expect to make a charitable contribution to the Society. We would insist . . . wouldn't we, Watson?"

He had taken me by surprise, and not pleasantly, I might add, for my financial resources were far, far more limited than his. I had no choice but to mutter something that by its tone alone could be taken as an agreement.

In the corner of my eye, I noted that Miss Ryder had craned her lovely white neck toward Lord Armstrong's ear and was whispering to him rather excitedly.

Before Lady Armstrong could demur or invent some

other reason why we might not accept the invitation, Lord Armstrong interrupted.

"Mother, I do not wish to embarrass anyone, but I think we must postpone the invitation to Mr. Holmes and Dr. Watson until we can speak with Jack—uh, John. Excuse me, gentlemen, Jane's brother, John Ryder—Jack to his friends—is in charge of seating, Mr. Holmes, and when we spoke, which was only yesterday, he had grown very concerned lest we find ourselves unable to accommodate the crowd.

"It seems, Mother, that we have had many more acceptances than we had anticipated."

"I see," Lady armstrong said, her demeanor somewhat brighter. "The Society's popularity seems to have at least one unfortunate aspect, after all. I do hope that Mr. Holmes and Dr. Watson will under—"

Lord Armstrong interrupted her.

"I know what we can do," he said, turning to Holmes and me. "Jack will be at the club tonight. He loves to gamble . . . Well, who at the Aurora doesn't, eh, Jane? My point is, if the two of you would join us for drinks, I'm sure we can get to the bottom of this seating thing." He stopped abruptly. A look of exaggerated surprise came over his face.

"Oh! Ha-ha. I did not mean for that to be such a double entendre: 'The bottom of this seating thing . . . ' Oh, Lord! Isn't that funny, though?" His words must have seemed that much funnier to him when they were spoken again, for Lord Armstrong loosed a peal of laughter that echoed through the library with a bone-jarring resonance.

Miss Ryder affected a light empathetic laugh and clapped her hands together in approval.

With Lord Armstrong caught up in paroxysms of laughter, Lady Armstrong took three steps toward us, which had the effect of consigning her son and his fiancée to the background for a moment. She must have been embarrassed, but it was not apparent. She remained imperturbable, playing on as though our strange meeting were unfolding instead with the utmost propriety.

"Mr. Holmes?" she asked.

"Yes, Lady Armstrong?"

"The third question?"

"Oh, yes. Thank you," he said. "I wanted to ask, Lady Armstrong, if you intended to wear your most famous gemstone to the New Years' Eve festivities."

"You refer to the Blood of Punjab, I presume?"

"None other," Holmes said.

"Well, of course, Mr. Holmes," Lady Armstrong said with a smile. "Do you think that I would pass up such an opportunity? Really, Mr. Holmes, a lady must have some fun in life. Don't you agree?"

Holmes said nothing, merely smiled quickly and turned toward Lord Armstrong, whose laughter was subsiding. The man caught his breath and mopped his brow with a handkerchief. He said to Holmes, "Well, sir, will you join us tonight, then?"

"This is most kind of you, Lord Armstrong," Holmes said. "I hope this is in no way an imposition." His ingratiating manner was so out of character I feared that in another instant he would appear ludicrous, but then I reminded myself that I was the only one present who really knew Holmes. To them, I suppose, his response was only appropriate.

"No imposition at all," Lord Armstrong said. "None whatsoever. Do you know the Aurora Club?"

"I believe it is on St. James Street," Holmes said, "but I've not been there."

"It's more modern than many of the others," Lord Armstrong said. "It takes a bit of getting used to, but it's quite nice, really. Shall we say eight o'clock?"

Holmes nodded and smiled.

I smiled.

The charming Miss Jane Ryder smiled.

Lady Armstrong smiled, though not as broadly as everyone else.

Only Lord Armstrong's toothy smile seemed genuine. I suspect the poor fool was the only completely honest person in the room.

Chapter 10

It was late afternoon by the time we returned to Baker Street. We enjoyed a leisurely supper, changed into proper evening attire and hailed a hansom cab for the Aurora Club. It was a cold night. Stiff winds and great swooping gusts pushed and pulled the fog through the city in billows and drifts, all to an odd effect, for it created a landscape that seemed to stutter and flutter across my vision. A row of buildings would be clearly visible, their facades and entrances clear and bathed in gaslight in one instant, then swathed in fog the next, then clear again an instant later. It was a strange, disorienting sideshow even somewhat dizzying.

We traveled south across Oxford Street, east to Bond Street, then south again and down to Piccadilly. We crossed onto St. James Street and then rode south down into the very heart of the city and the epicenter of what has been popularly dubbed "Clubland."

Throughout London there were countless numbers of bars, public houses, wine rooms and saloons, but every neighborhood also supported goodly numbers of social clubs. Districts such as Whitechapel and Spitalfields and Stepney and St. George's-in-the-East, and Shoreditch and Bethnal Green seemed to have more than their share of them. "Working men's clubs" they were called, but some of the roughest and rowdiest dens imaginable were included among their number.

Our properly heeled West End had no fewer clubs, but they differed in class distinction. The proper neighborhoods of the upper order, districts such as Mayfair and Westminster, St. Marylebone, Soho and Belgravia, were home to the most prestigious of all the clubs in London. The very best held out the promise of true exclusivity, the satisfaction of a rarefied belonging. Some clubs would not even allow their members to entertain guests or visitors on the premises. Other clubs consigned visitors to small and spartan anterooms. And in a few cases the club's toilet and the visitors room were one and the same!

With the West End clubs so firmly ensconced in the social landscape of the city, it followed, quite naturally, that membership in one or more was practically mandatory for anyone who hoped to move comfortably in society. There was a formal club for virtually every category of interest, from traveling, theater and literature to golfing, sailing and political and philosophical pursuits. There was even a club for the most unclubbable of people, such as Holmes' older brother, Mycroft. He was the most prominent member of the Diogenes Club on Pall Mall, one of the oddest (and most sanctimonious) of all of the London clubs. Not only were members of the Diogenes Club not allowed to speak to one another, they were not even supposed to acknowledge one another's presence; the only exceptions took place in a single small room off the foyer in which visitors were allowed.

Regardless of the orientation or shared interests of their members, however, some things about the clubs were predictable. One could presume that membership was predominately male; that beer, ale, wine and liquor, if not being drawn or poured constantly, would at least be readily available; that smoke from pipes, cigars and cigarettes was omnipresent; and that regardless of one's preference—whether it was cards, dice, board games, racing or billiards—sporting activity was always to be found.

It had been a while since I had spent time in a proper club, and I was looking forward to our visit. I sat back against the worn leather seat of our cab and listened to its steel-rimmed wheels click across the shiny and damp cobblestones of the city's streets. The hooves of our horse made a rhythmic clacking noise in counterpoint, and every once in a while, for no reason that I could divine, the driver would cluck at the noble beast, as though it would stop dead in its tracks were he not to urge it forward. The cab's big leaf springs must have been spent because it tended to sway. I felt as though I were being rocked to sleep. I would begin to doze, look up to see a row of town houses emerge from the fog, close my eyes briefly and reopen them just in time to see the same facades fall back into the night as the next cloud bank gusted in.

Over supper, Holmes and I had talked at length about our visit to Planetree. I thought he had concluded that the best part of the meeting with Lady Armstrong was that it was over. Now, however, with no apparent prompting other than perhaps his suspicion that I was about to fall into a deep sleep in the hansom, he chose not only to resume the discussion but to do so in that disconcerting way he had of abruptly letting me in on a conversation that was already well under way inside his head.

"On the other hand," he announced with no preamble whatsoever, "one never really knows."

"What?"

"Oh. I was just thinking, Watson, that it is always difficult to know what lies beneath such hardened veneer as what Lady Armstrong presents."

"The woman is unbalanced, in my opinion," I said. "She is a Janus. One face is arrogant and insulting, and the other is cordial, even engaging."

"Surface, Watson. All surface."

"My point exactly," I said. "Your characterization of her was most apt. The woman's a troll, Holmes. Not to be trusted. Did you notice her teeth, those small pointed things? And brown, besides. Probably dried blood."

Holmes made a huffing sound that I took to be a laugh; I could not see his face clearly in the darkness of the cab's interior.

"What do you make of Lord Armstrong?" I asked. "He seemed like a decent enough fellow."

"But?" Holmes prodded.

"What do you mean, Holmes?"

"The tone of your voice implied a 'but,'" he said.

"Well, you wouldn't know that he's cut from his mother's cloth, now, would you?"

"Indeed not," Holmes said. "And? Do I detect an 'and' in the air?"

"And," I said with resignation, "it is difficult to see what that young woman, Miss Jane Ryder, sees in him." I felt petty and cruel as soon as the words were out of my mouth; my distaste must have been evident.

"Just so, Watson. She does not fit with Lord David Armstrong, and that's the cruel truth of it," the detective said. "One must never feel bad for speaking the truth. What's more, my friend, this woman also seems like a conniver. I would be surprised if Miss Ryder's brother proves to be much different. We shall see very soon."

Holmes' timing was perfect, for no sooner had he uttered his final words in the matter than the hansom pulled to the curb on St. James Street directly in front of the Aurora Club. Two large brass lanterns flanked the doorway. A servant in elegant livery of the deepest claret greeted us and examined the cards of introduction Lord Armstrong had provided.

"Ah," he said, "you are expected, gentlemen." With a pleasant, if practiced, smile he motioned us inside a long and large dark-paneled foyer that felt every bit like the sanctum that it was supposed to be. St. James Street, manicured and architecturally elegant though it was, suddenly seemed crass and miles away. The room was so preternaturally silent as to suggest whispers. At the far end, off to the right, appeared to be a hallway, and I thought that I could see immense double doors at the far end of it.

A white-jacketed steward was standing nearby. The butler summoned him with an economy of movement that was every bit as practiced as his smile, though no less elegant for that.

"Alan," he said, "show our guests to Lord Armstrong's table."

"Follow me, please," the man said. He led us down the corridor in silence and stopped before the double doors, his back to us. He gripped the brass door levers with both hands, turned them up and outward at the same time, pulled both portals open wide, then moved abruptly backward also as to let the doors swing fully open, and slipped inside, leaving Holmes and me suddenly framed in the entryway. While Alan the steward sought out Lord Armstrong, we took advantage of our window on the Aurora Club.

Nearly all of the best West End clubs comprised several elegantly appointed rooms of different kinds, dining areas, gaming rooms, billiard rooms, bars, lounges, studies and parlors, and a good many offered sleeping accommodations for their members as well. The heart of the Aurora Club, however, seemed to be a single immense room, much the way I have heard the main floor of casinos described, but with at least some of a traditional club's accoutrements.

Gaming tables filled the room from one wall to the other, and anywhere from four to eight players were seated at each one; many tables were girded by a single, and sometimes double, row of standing onlookers, bent on watching the play. Some of the gaming areas were contiguous. Some were flanked by billiard tables where two men or four were playing. Situated all over the immense room were small tableaus—parlors without walls, if you would—in which members of the Aurora Club sat and read books or newspapers, conversed with friends, or enjoyed a small meal. White-jacketed stewards moved quickly among the members, taking orders, serving drinks and whatever else the members required.

Occasionally, the steady thrum of voices was punctuated by a loud laugh or the sharp thin "pock" of a hard maple cue stick striking a billiard ball. The air that washed over us was a current of odors and aromas, complementary and contradictory, heavy and grayish-brown from tobacco smoke, and fulsome with the aroma of hops and an overlay of cloying sweetness, undoubtedly from brandies and liqueurs. I detected a trace of licorice, too, and realized that it had to be absinthe. Some of the members also were enjoying hearty teas, from the scent, and others were sipping rich coffees.

But it was the lighting in the room that was so startling. The entire cavern was encircled by three rows of lightly hissing gas lights. Their flames danced, twinkled and sparkled, and each movement was captured and reflected back into the room countless times by the innumerable pendants of six huge, rather quickly revolving, cut-glass chandeliers that hung from the club's ceiling. The constant turning of the great chandeliers was doubtlessly explained by some hidden system of gears and pulleys and weights and counterweights, but I didn't care how it was done, because the effect was, in short, too bizarre. The constant movement of the myriad, endlessly refracting pieces of cut glass multiplied and seemed to intensity the reflections, so that light seemed to dance and play constantly across the surface of every object in the room, regardless of where one looked. It was positively garish. And the effect it had on human faces was downright bizarre. One instant a face appeared normal, the next misshapen.

"I don't like this place, Holmes."

"It feels like a fancy bordello one instant," he said, "and a freak show the next. Wouldn't you say so?"

"Not having been in either a fancy bordello or, for that matter, a freak show, I really wouldn't know," I replied. I expected Holmes to demur good-naturedly or at least rise to my implicit query, but he did neither.

"Trust me, Watson," he said. "It does."

I furrowed my brow in question.

"Another time, perhaps," he said, half looking at me, half watching the steward, Alan. He was standing beside Lord Armstrong, who was seated with other men at a gaming table in a far corner. Our host rose from his chair and began making his way toward us, which was not as easy as it would have been were he sober.

I looked at Holmes. "Much too early in the evening for this," I said under my breath.

The detective nodded. Lord Armstrong bumped into an empty chair, nearly toppled over it, righted himself rather comically, looked in our direction with an eager expression and continued toward us on his privately charted course. I was thankful he did not shout out our names in the process, for even at a distance Lord Armstrong's hunger for friendship was pathetically obvious.

"Mr. Holmes. Dr. Watson. So glad you could make it. Isn't the lighting rather a panic? It's as though you get to shee people as they sheem to be for one instant, and then in the next, as they might be beneath their shkins. Do you shee? Come. You musht meet Jack Ryder. Heej a good friend of mine. A dear boy. Come. Come. Right thish way. Jusht follow me."

"Perhaps we should not interrupt your game, Lord Armstrong," Holmes said. "We could visit another time."

"Nonshense, shir," he said. "I sheem to be loojing anyway, aj alwaysh."

We followed him across the room, and I suddenly felt pity for the man. The harder he tried to appear sober, the more obvious his problem became.

We reached the table and he directed his attention to one of four men who had remained seated. "Jack. Jack," Lord Armstrong said. No one at the table bothered to look in Lord Armstrong's direction.

"Shee here," the drunken man said. "Theej are the two gentlemens I waj telling you about." It was clear that proper introductions, though they were Lord Armstrong's to perform, were out of the question.

The seated man, who obviously was John Ryder, sighed in exasperation and waved Alan the steward to the table.

"I think our noble benefactor needs some coffee, Alan."

Lord Armstrong looked blankly at Ryder, and then just as blankly again at the steward and back again to Ryder, still not comprehending.

"Be a good fellow, David," Ryder said. He was addressing the man by his first name, which was clearly condescending and contemptuous given Lord Armstrong's title. The other men at the table snickered. I was getting angry quickly, and in another second would have thrust myself into the sickening little tableau in Lord Armstrong's behalf had not Holmes' right hand suddenly clasped my wrist like an iron cuff, a clear warning that I was to hold my temper.

"Just go with Alan," Ryder told Lord Armstrong. "He'll take care of you. Be a good little boy now, David."

Ryder turned to the steward and frowned darkly. "Alan," he said in a deep voice, "you be damned certain that it's strong coffee. Do you understand? This sot will need a gallon of it, I think."

The men at the table snickered again as the steward led Lord Armstrong off through the crowd. Ryder smirked at the men seated around the table, obviously satisfied with himself.

Holmes rapped his walking stick on the table top so hard that I was surprised when the stick did not splinter. The noise was sharp and flat, and it reverberated like a gunshot. The men at the table recoiled in surprise and confusion, but not Ryder. He sat calmly, his eyes trained not on us, but downward at the tabletop. Holmes waited for a couple of seconds as patrons at other tables began to turn our way, and then he struck the tabletop again, even harder this time, and then, in a voice filled with anger and contempt, he spoke so loudly that he was very nearly shouting.

"Lord Armstrong led me to believe that the Aurora was a club for gentlemen," Holmes said. "Obviously, he was mistaken."

The men at the table suddenly looked as if their mothers had caught them pinching candy—all, that is, except Ryder. His face—what I could see of it, for it was still cast downward—wore a smug look of bemusement. He slowly moved his gaze across the table and with purpose that was so obvious as to be almost theatrical, he brought his head upward and looked directly at Holmes for the first time.

The gazes of the two men locked. The impact of it rippled out into the room the way a stone causes ripples along the surface of a lake. One by one, games of poker and hazard stopped. Cue sticks rattled to a rest across billiard tables while their users stopped to watch the drama unfold. Dishware and silverware stopped rattling and clinking, and talking ceased. The stewards stopped moving.

All eyes were cast toward Ryder's table. Holmes stood before it, his hands resting one atop the other and both upon the head of his cane, which he had planted squarely in front of him in much the same way that he had braced for his battle of wills with Lady Armstrong earlier in the day. The detective's lips were set in a tight, firm line. His jaw was thrust slightly forward, teeth clenched, though not hard enough to move or knot the muscles along the sides of his face. Holmes' gray eyes were set wide open, unblinking, and they were hard and unreadable.

John Ryder rose to his feet without taking his eyes off Holmes. Ryder was perhaps two inches shorter than the detective; he was heavier, too, but the weight was all bone and hard, lean muscle. His cheekbones were pronounced, almost sharp. His skin was fair. His eyes were dark, but his thick, shiny black hair was darker still, and it was combed straight back off the broad expanse of his forehead. He wore a mustache that was not much more than a pencil line above his full lips, and his jaw was so perfectly squared off that it seemed sculpted. Ryder would have been considered handsome by most standards, but the moving lights of the Aurora Club made his face look severely angular and rather unnaturally sinister.

"I have heard of you, Mr. Sherlock Holmes," Ryder said with an odd half smile, "even before you met my sister today, and you are quite correct, sir. I was not behaving like the gentleman that I truly am. Please forgive me; I assure you it is not representative . . . though I cannot vouch for the behavior of these other rascals."

His last remark was intended to inject levity into the tension, but nobody laughed.

"It is not I who is owed the apology," Holmes said. His voice had a prim sharpness to it, and his eyes bored relentlessly into Ryder's.

The American's gaze narrowed. He stared back at Holmes in silence, but only for a moment. It was clear that he had expected Holmes to blithely forgive his rude behavior.

"You are correct again, sir," Ryder said. His jaw was tight. His words sounded as though they were cramped and flat. This was a man who angered quickly. "I will apologize to Lord Armstrong tomorrow," he said. He looked down at the table, expecting Holmes to respond.

The detective remained silent, unwavering, merciless.

Ryder looked back at him. "I give you my word," he said. He spoke the words slowly. His voice was measured, very low and tight; drawn down any harder, it would have broken.

"Very well," Holmes said, and he offered his hand. Ryder looked at it, took it in his own, and the two men shook. Tension seemed to rise from the table and dissipate like fog running before freshening air. With it went the silence. Almost at once noise in the room rose to its former levels.

"Allow me, Mr. Ryder, to introduce my good friend and companion, Dr. John Watson."

"My pleasure, Dr. Watson," Ryder said. "I hear that you tell a good yarn, sir."

"Thank you," I said, "but make no mistake. They are not yarns. Not a word is fiction."

"Truly?" Ryder asked.

"Truly," I answered.

"Well, you fellows are pretty daring, then."

"Oh, not really, Mr. Ryder," Holmes said.

"Call me, Jack, please."

"I think not, Mr. Ryder. I very rarely use first names without surnames. It always seems so familiar and disrespectful. My custom. Don't be offended."

"Aha," Ryder said. "Well then, I shall not be offended. In America, you see, we are considerably less formal in most circumstances than you people. But I am not in America at the moment, so . . ."

I noticed that his voice, reinforced by his mannerisms—a raised eyebrow here, a smirk there, or a questioning tilt of the head, a dismissive or suggestive flick of the wrist—always seemed to have an edge to it or a trace of sarcasm. The overall impression was that for every straightforward statement, there lay another beneath it that was purposely unspoken. As a result, one could never be quite certain who or what one faced in the person of Mr. John "Jack" Ryder.

Holmes smiled and nodded.

"Now, where were we?" Ryder asked. "Oh, yes. Dr. Watson's stories. They do make the two of you appear quite intrepid. Am I to understand from your comment, Mr. Holmes, that despite Dr. Watson's explanation, the reality behind the stories is different, that perhaps you sometimes shy from the fight? That would not do in America, you know."

"Nor would it play here," said Holmes, "regardless of what anyone may infer from Dr. Watson's stories, which quite rightfully seem to be enjoying considerable popularity, I am proud to say."

This last comment, a rather rare bit of praise, took me aback. In fact, Holmes usually complained that I emphasized drama and narrative at the expense of the science and logic that he so rigorously employed in deduction and detection, but never, at least to my knowledge, had he volunteered as much publicly. Sherlock Holmes was a gentleman and my loyal friend, and even though he was being disingenuous, his high public compliment caused my chin to rise ever so slightly.

"I do detest violence, Mr. Ryder, but this agency is always prepared to do whatever a case requires. So far we have been up to the challenge."

"In that case, gentlemen, I applaud you both," Ryder said. "You have a most commendable attitude. It is unfortunate but true that one must always be prepared for trouble, especially today. One must go about his business with the awareness that there is always someone watching and waiting who is better."

Holmes laughed. "Oh, I would never concede that, Mr. Ryder."

"Really? And why not?" the American asked.

"Because it is not true," Holmes said firmly, the trace of laughter gone. "Any number of people may be watching at any time, and for any number of nefarious purposes, I'll grant you, but not one among them is my better."

"And you believe that?" Ryder asked. "All braggadocio aside now?"

"I would not have said it otherwise," Holmes said.

"Well," Ryder said, "for your sake, Mr. Holmes, I hope you are correct. Either way, you certainly are a gamer. In our American West not so very long ago, you would have been a town tamer, and there'd be gunnies from all of the territories on the lookout for you, eager to try their hand against yours."

"But not so in your Chicago?" Holmes asked.

"Not in that way, precisely. Chicago is much more . . . civilized. Some ruffian might be inclined to call you out in an alley and then beat you to within a thread of your life, or a gentleman might be inclined to brace you—"

"At a private club?" Holmes asked.

A quick and thin smile formed on Ryder's lips. He looked directly at Holmes and nodded his head. "Quite possibly at a private club," Ryder answered, "but then we're just speaking hypothetically, are we not?"

"Yes," Holmes said. "Quite."

I thought I could best be of service by changing the topic

quickly. "Mr. Ryder," I asked, "did Lord Armstrong have a chance to discuss the reason for our coming here tonight?"

"He did not," Ryder said. "In fact, I was trying to think of a polite way that I might ask."

The man might have been telling the truth specifically, but he was lying generally, though I had no idea why. Ryder had already made it clear that his sister had spoken to him about us, and it would have been most unlikely that she had failed to tell him that we were looking for a proper invitation to the New Year's Eve benefit.

"Directness usually seems to work best," Holmes said, "though some people do take offense."

"I'll try to remember that," Ryder said, sarcasm obvious in his voice.

"Dr. Watson and I came here this evening because Lady Armstrong invited us to the Society's benefit without knowing precisely how large the guest list already is. Lord Armstrong suggested that you might be able to adjust the seating to accommodate us."

"Oh, I see," Ryder said. "But I'm afraid that's out of the question, Mr. Holmes."

"Really? That is most unfortunate," Holmes said. "Watson and I had intended to make a generous donation, too. Say, a hundred pounds each."

That amount of money was more than twice what most people donated at charitable functions. Ryder paused and then smiled at Holmes.

"Are you a gambling man?" Ryder asked.

"On occasion," Holmes said, though I never knew him to gamble so much as a farthing.

"Fancy this, then," Ryder said. He clapped his hands several times to draw everyone's attention back to the goings-on at his table. Then he turned his face upward, as though he were speaking to the juncture of ceiling and wall at the far end of the room, which, as it turned out, he was. Following his gaze to that spot, I noticed a small gallery where two men sat overlooking the floor.

"Stop the lights!" Ryder shouted to the gallery. "Stop the lights, please. There. Thank you. Now, my good friends," he said loudly to the members of the Aurora Club, "I am wagering two invitations to Lady Armstrong's New Year's

Eve benefit against Mr. Sherlock Holmes' marker for two hundred pounds that he cannot beat me at a hand of Chicago cut."

There was some laughter and a murmur of enthusiasm, and members from all over the room arose and pushed toward our corner in anticipation of the contest.

"What is your game, Ryder?" Holmes asked curtly.

"This, Mr. Detective. You will draw the ace of spades from a fresh deck of playing cards. You will replace it in the deck anywhere you please and then shuffle the deck as much as you want for as long as you want. Regardless of what you do, though, in one move I will cut the ace of spades."

"And if you fail to do so?" Holmes asked.

"Then I will personally deliver the invitations you seek," Ryder said.

"Not good enough," Holmes said. "If you lose, you must also cover our two-hundred-pound donation."

Ryder smiled and flicked the air dismissively with the back of his left hand. "No matter," he said. "Consider it done."

Holmes quickly withdrew a cheque pad from his jacket, scrawled his legal name and the amount tendered, and dropped it before Ryder on the green felt of the gaming table.

The gambler motioned to a steward, and the man brought Holmes a sealed deck of playing cards. The detective held the deck out in front of him for all to see. He broke the seal, emptied the cards in his right hand and fanned them out face up in an arc on the table.

Holmes quickly located the ace of spades and removed it with his left hand. With his right he collected the fan of cards and stacked them in a tight pile. He turned to face the members and raised both of his arms. He held the deck in his right hand, and with his left carefully inserted the ace of spades into the middle, making certain that the action took place where everyone could see it. Holmes shuffled the cards for a few moments, long enough so that it was clear to everyone that the ace of spades had been thoroughly mixed into the deck.

Holmes then set the deck down squarely in front of Ryder.

"Is that it, then?" Ryder asked loudly. "You may shuffle the deck some more if you wish."

Holmes shook his head. "That will suffice," he said politely.

"Very well, then," Ryder said, and his words had no sooner left his lips than they were followed by a sudden shout, like an exhalation, and a lightning-like movement that put him quickly on his feet. With his right hand Ryder had drawn a long razor-sharp dagger, apparently from behind the collar of his jacket, and in a sort of arcing, windmilling motion had driven the knife straight down through the deck of cards, which now lay pinned fast to the green-felt–topped table. He stood, hunched over it, his hand still clutching the handle.

"And thus," Ryder announced with a flourish of his hand, "is the ace of spades cut." He turned to his audience with a broad smile and announced, "And thus is the great Sherlock Holmes undone."

The club members began to laugh. Ryder stared at Holmes in obvious derision, his lips curled into a sneer. I could not believe the audacity of the man!

"And I," Ryder said with a loud laugh, "am two hundred pounds to the good." So saying he reached across the table for the cheque Holmes had written.

But just as his hand neared the slip of paper, a claret-colored playing card fluttered across his fingers and landed face up on the green felt. It was the ace of spades, and it didn't have a mark or cut on it.

"On the contrary," Holmes said loudly. "You lose."

Some men shouted, for they had seen all of the play from their vantage point near the table.

"Holmes took out the ace of spades."

"The ace is uncut!"

"Holmes beat him! He palmed the ace."

The turn of events quickly became clear, and as it did the laughter began anew. This time, mixed into it were shouts of amazement and laughter. A good many members of the Aurora Club applauded and shouted, "Bravo! Bravo! Good show! Bravo! He showed you, Jack!"

Ryder was enraged. He stood opposite Holmes, doing his best to control himself; the effort was barely working.

Though a thin pale smile was painted like a slash across his face, he glared at Holmes and it was apparent that his efforts at control were leaving him as taut as a bowstring. Cords of sinew stood out on the side of his neck, and his hands trembled.

He moved closer to Holmes, and by instinct I immediately reached into my coat pocket as though I had brought my trusted revolver along. I hadn't, but there was no need.

Ryder inclined his head toward Holmes with a broad smile, obviously intended for public consumption, and said in as low a voice as possible, "You cheated me."

Holmes smiled, too, and under his breath replied, "It was a cheater's game from the start, and you know it. I simply evened it up, Mr. Ryder. Let me repeat, 'You lose.'"

Ryder jolted backward with his arms outstretched and turned in a semicircular motion to quickly address the roomful of Aurora Club members.

"Now . . ." Ryder said, "now you all understand why Mr. Sherlock Holmes is the very best of his rare breed. I think we all owe him a hearty round of applause to show our appreciation."

Ryder made a great show of leading the ovation, which was thunderous.

Holmes smiled, bowed politely and said to Ryder, "The address is 221B Baker Street. I will expect the invitations to be delivered no later than noon tomorrow."

"And so they shall be," Ryder said from between grinding teeth.

Holmes turned from the table as if to leave, and then turned back to Ryder.

"And, oh yes," Holmes said, "I will check with Lord Armstrong tomorrow afternoon to be sure that he has received the donation in our names . . . and that you have properly apologized for having been so churlish."

"I told you that I would do so!" Ryder said, his muffled voice even more strained now. "I gave you my word."

"I know, Mr. Ryder," Holmes said. "I know."

So saying, Holmes picked up the cheque he had written and tore it into four pieces. He held them in his fist outstretched above the gaming table. He paused for effect, turned slowly in a complete circle so that he had the attention of the club's patrons, and then opened his fist. The pieces of paper were nowhere in evidence. Instead, Holmes' calling card fell flat upon the green felt.

The club members were still laughing and applauding, and some even were stamping their feet and cheering when we passed through the door and out into the hallway. I could tell from the reflections on the wall that the chandeliers had begun revolving again.

We collected our overcoats and walked outside into the cold night on St. James Street.

"A walk home might do us good, Watson."

"Very well," I said, and we strode up St. James Street.

"How the devil did you do that, Holmes?" I asked.

"Do what?" he asked.

"You know very well what I mean."

"The ace of spades?"

"Yes, of course."

"Practice," Holmes said. "A good bit of dexterity—fortunately, I have long and nimble fingers—but mostly a good deal of practice."

"How did you know what he was up to?"

"I didn't exactly," Holmes said, "but I had heard enough about the Aurora Club to know that it counts high-stakes gamblers and even some old-fashioned sharps among its august members. But Ryder himself gave it away."

"Really?"

"The way the man said, 'Chicago cut.' It was clear that he intended a double entendre. Some of the club patrons laughed rather too knowingly when he said it, and that cinched it."

"Well, you certainly got the better of him," I said. "That should keep him in his place, I would think."

"I'm afraid not, Watson," Holmes said. "I suspect that it will have the opposite effect. It's one thing for a gambler to lose straight up. As unpleasant as that might be, it is at least acceptable. But it's entirely another matter to be outsmarted, out-gambled, if you would. And that really was the situation. He called out the game so all of his friends would know, and then I shamed him at it. That is a grievous wound, a professional insult, you see."

"Then we have made an enemy tonight," I said.

"No," Holmes said. "Ryder was already our enemy. He was lying in wait. The question is, why."

"Do you expect that he will pay the two hundred pounds?"

"I'm rather afraid he will," Holmes said.

"I don't understand, Holmes."

"Well, Watson, if he chooses not to pay, however ungentlemanly that might appear, it would at least be an understandable display of anger, and I would be inclined to let it lie. Ryder is probably a good enough judge of character to know that."

"By not paying, Ryder would be able to simply wash his hands of the entire evening's business?"

"That is correct," Holmes said.

"And if he does pay?"

"Ah. Yes. If he does pay, Watson, he will be acting as though cunning and deceit are parts of a fair game; all that matters is the winning."

"The end justifies the means, in other words?" I asked.

"Precisely," Holmes said. "And having been beaten at a 'just' game, an equally just debt is owed and must be paid, when in fact both the game and the debt that arose from it are spurious."

"I don't know, Holmes. I think you are reading too much into this."

"Only if I am misjudging our man's intelligence, Watson, and I don't think I am. No, if Mr. Ryder pays his debt to me, he might as well be announcing that even though we are not sure how it began, or why, or even precisely what it is, the game is still afoot."

Chapter 11

Ryder's draft for £200 arrived at 221B Baker Street the next day, precisely one minute before the noon deadline. At the sound of a knock on the door to the ground floor, Holmes quickly arose from his chair, checked his pocket watch and announced, "Right on time. I do admire that, especially in an adversary."

The detective poked his head out of our parlor door and hollered impatiently down the stairs: "Come in! Come in! It's all right. Come in!"

I heard the door open and feet clomp up the stairs.

"Mr. Sherlock Holmes?" said a young voice I didn't recognize.

"Yes," the detective said. "You have an envelope for me, I presume."

"Yes, sir," the voice said. "It's from Mr. John Ryder, sir."

"Come in, then."

The voice belonged to a messenger boy dressed in the claret livery of the Aurora Club.

Holmes signed for the envelope and handed the boy a coin.

"I see from your coat that it's snowing," Holmes said.

"Thank you, sir," the messenger said. "Yes, sir. It is snowing. It's jolly, I think. I mean, just in time for Christmas. And maybe it'll still be on the ground for Boxing Day, too."

Holmes frowned. "One can only hope," he said. "Well, thank you. Good day, now."

"G' day, sir, and have a good holiday, sir."

"I shall try," Holmes said. The detective called out as

the messenger reached the foot of the stairs, "Oh, young man . . ."

The boy turned and looked up toward Holmes.

"Sir?"

The detective reached into his trousers pocket and flipped another shiny coin into the air high over the stairway. The boy tracked the progress of the coin as it fell, end over end, spinning in an arc. The light from the open doorway caught its shining sides in flight so many times that the bright silver coin looked like a Christmas bauble dancing on the snowy breeze from the open door.

The boy reached out deftly with his right hand, snared the coin and clamped his fist around it.

"Good catch," Holmes called down. "You have a good holiday, young man."

"Thank you, sir," the boy said. "I shall. Thank you again."

Holmes waved him out.

"Be sure to close that door tightly," the detective called, but too late. The boy was gone. The door was ajar, and the wind quickly blew it wide open again. More cold winter air rushed in, followed by more blowing snow. And something new—voices . . . singing. I heard them at once. Ah, of course, carols! Not that I had forgotten the holidays; I truly had been aware, but not as keenly as I might have been; we had been so damnably busy.

I do love the season, which is why I was so delighted to hear the song. And this particular one, a relatively new composition as carols go, for it was not yet fifty years old, was "Good King Wenceslas." I am not a religious man, but the story of the Good King was poignant and inspiring. I knew all of the words, and being able to pick up the simple tune, I quickly found myself singing along.

". . . Mark my footsteps, my good page;
Tread thou in them boldly:
Thou shalt find the winter's rage
Freeze thy blood less coldly.

In his master's steps he trod,
Where the snow lay dinted;

Heat was in the very sod
Which the saint had printed . . . "

I must have been singing rather loudly, because on his
way downstairs to fasten the door, Holmes called back to
me, "Oh damn, Watson! Must you, really? I am doing my
best not to be a curmudgeon about this infernal season,
but I swear, that song is enough to send me leaping into
the abyss."

"Really, Holmes? I think it is a fine carol," I said. "And
I am not alone. It is very popular."

"It is too popular," he said. "I hear it once and I want
to scream, and this time of year it is everywhere. I hear it
on every street corner. I hear its unctuous strains wafting
up from every choir loft in every church regardless of the
denomination. I mean, it is so . . . so syrupy, so woefully
sing-song:

". . . Where the snow lay dinT—ED;
Heat was in the very sod
Which the saint had prinT—ED . . . "

He sang the carol in a falsetto, which gave his low opinion of the song even more of an edge, which made me
angry.

"Oh, stop it, Holmes!" I said. "It's a popular song. I like
it very much, and so, it seems, does most of Christendom.
I think you might take that into account before you—"

"Oh, yes, yes, yes, Watson. You're right. You're right. I
do not hesitate to say so. Take no offense. I am so preoccupied with this Armstrong business all of a sudden that I
find every distraction maddening."

I would not be placated, however.

"Be that as it may, Holmes, in truth, you hated that song
last Christmas, too."

"I simply dislike the tune, Watson. It seems to encapsu-
late all that's wrong with the season."

"Just what would that be?" I asked. "What's so dreadfully wrong with this season? In all seriousness."

"Nothing, Watson, it is a grand and glorious season.
Even for someone like me, who is not of a particularly

religious bent, the season is, at least philosophically, full of wonderment and fine fellow feeling and good intent. I just believe that the celebration of it should not be . . . well, mandatory. One ought not to have celebration and well-wishing thrust upon him as though it were an obligation."

"And you feel somehow put upon?"

He paused. I think he was taken aback to think that anyone might find such an attitude the least bit peculiar.

"Well . . . yes, Watson, I do," Holmes said finally. "I am loath to say so because it must make me sound like some self-centered and petulant crackpot. But I can say it to you, old friend, because you know that I mean no harm by it."

"I do know that," I said, "but what was going through your mind a few minutes ago when you tossed an extra coin to that messenger boy? Was that not in keeping with the spirit of the season? Boxing Day isn't until the day after Christmas, and here you are already giving alms to someone in service."

"Yes," the detective said. "It was in keeping, I know."

"But . . . ?" I prodded.

"'But . . .'" Holmes replied, "I felt as though I had to, not that I really wanted to. Don't you see the difference?"

"Well, Holmes. Of course I see the difference. But by fastening on this one aspect, you are missing the point of it all."

"Indeed?" He had brought yesterday's late edition of the newspaper up from the foyer and was flipping through it indifferently as we spoke.

"Why, yes," I said. "The season is supposed to bring out the generous best in people—you included. So what if, for a brief time, you feel importuned by it, old fellow? If the season causes you to act in a more humble and brotherly way than you might at any other time of year, then it is working its charm quite effectively, thank you very much— and fulfilling its purpose, too, I might add."

"And you and all the rest of the world would have me simply bear it," Holmes asked, "even if it is profoundly against my will?"

"Or be as damned as Dickens' Scrooge," I said. "Yes. It is the one time of year, Holmes, when even you must put others ahead—"

"Aaargh!" Holmes shouted and leaped to his feet as though he had been scalded.

"Really, Holmes. It isn't all that bad. Get a grip on yourself, man."

"Blast! Confound it all!"

"What on earth is wrong?"

"Look at this, Watson! Will you look at this?"

He turned the newspaper toward me, folded it roughly and quickly in half and held it out in his hand so that I could see.

On page twenty-six of *The Daily Telegraph*, set in a fancy bold type that completely filled the lower right quadrant of the page, was this message:

Good people of London,
In this, the most hallowed of seasons,
May you and yours find blessed joy,
And may the poorest among you find eternal peace.

And it was signed,

Merry Christmas,
Sherlock Holmes.

Chapter 12

I always believed that some of the great detective's instincts and senses were gifts that providence bestowed only rarely because their possession ensured either genius or madness. Holmes lived, and prospered, in the difference, and sometimes I wasn't quite sure which extreme he was courting. His response to the odd Christmas notice in the newspaper was just such an instance.

"What is this all about, Holmes?"

"Well, how would I know, Watson?"

"Why would anyone do this?" I asked. "I mean, it's not as though it's a harmful thing, it's—"

"Not harmful?" Holmes shouted. "Good grief, Watson! There is always harm in such a thing. Here I am being singled out before the entire city, and I have no idea why, or by whom, or for what true purpose. We are more often hurt by the things we do not know than by the things we do know, Watson, and something like this could not happen innocently. There has to be a larger purpose behind it."

He had thrown the newspaper down onto the table and was stabbing his long index finger at it as he spoke.

"But what larger purpose, Holmes? And please stop shouting," I said. "We will puzzle it through."

"Humph!"

"Well, maybe someone did it as a favor," I offered. "Perhaps when all's said there's some good intent behind it."

"A favor? What favor? What good intent could there possibly be?" Holmes' words were snapped off like so many rapid drumbeats, and his voice was somewhat lower, more tightly controlled.

"Well," I said, "and this is purely conjecture, let's say that someone of your acquaintance wanted you to be seen as something other than the hardworking professional detective that you are, someone who's more, let's just say, uhm . . . outgoing, than people might think. What better way to do it than to use the occasion of the Yuletide to have you wish everyone well? Holmes, you're glaring at me! Please stop. This isn't any of my doing, after all."

"All right, Watson. All right. But I think your suggestion as to motive is entirely unworthy. It's preposterous. It makes no sense whatsoever."

"Well, perhaps it is some kind of practical joke, Holmes, a trick played by someone who is taking delight in being . . . I don't know . . . ironic."

"Oh," Holmes said. "In other words, Watson, it is, in fact, hysterically comical to suggest that I am outgoing and compassionate enough to publicly wish everyone a Merry Christmas?"

I tried to answer him honestly and evenly, without the merest suggestion of criticism.

"Well, Holmes," I said, "I wouldn't put it quite that way, but if there was not a modicum of truth in that supposition, you would not be quite as upset now, would you?"

The detective said nothing. He turned his back to me abruptly, thrust both of his hands into his trouser pockets and looked down at our rather threadbare carpet. He removed his hands as though he didn't know quite what to do with them. He crossed his arms, tucking his hands into his armpits. He took deep breaths and slowly walked over to the fireplace, as if suddenly searching for something with which to occupy himself.

Holmes reached into the coal scuttle, where he kept cigars and the dottles of shag tobacco that he knocked out of his briar pipe whenever he cleaned it. I found his habit of saving old unburned clumps of pipe tobacco an annoying and miserly eccentricity. He put a couple of the dottles in his pipe, tamped them down and lighted it, drawing the hot smoke in deeply and exhaling loudly and completely so that in what seemed like an instant, a layer of grayish-white smoke hovered just below the ceiling.

Holmes always was difficult to read, and this moment was certainly in keeping; I had no idea what would come next. He looked at me, clenched the pipe between his teeth and let his words tumble somewhat awkwardly out from around the stem.

"No one else would dare say such things to me, Watson. I should be thanking you."

"Think nothing of it, Holmes," I said. "We'll get to the bottom of this, don't worry."

"Ah, that's just it, Watson: I am afraid *not* to worry. I trust my instincts, and my instincts tell me there is more at stake here than we know. I cannot shake the feeling that this is the start of deeper trouble.

"Look at this ad again, Watson. Wait, let me read it aloud to you; perhaps that will make a difference. This part: 'May you and yours find blessed joy . . . ' All right. Nothing much there. It's not original, and it is a bit unctuous, but harmless enough. Then comes this line, Watson, '. . . And may the poorest among you find eternal peace.' There! Does that not sound ominous, or eulogistic?"

"I think it is quite innocent, Holmes. Really. '. . . And may the poorest among you find eternal peace.' I think you have to stretch a good distance to come up with something foreboding in that. This *is* the Christmas season, Holmes. Perhaps if the backdrop were darker I might react differently. I just do not see it."

"I disagree, Watson, but no matter. Until I can discern some more information that sheds light on the subject, this is all conjecture. So . . ."

He grabbed his hat and overcoat with a sudden alacrity and clarity of purpose, turned up the collar, wrapped his long gray woollen scarf tightly about his neck and, taking up his walking stick, announced, "I am going to visit our friends at *The Daily Telegraph*. Somebody paid a pound or two for that advert, and I intend to find out who."

So saying, Holmes threw open the door and stepped out. He took one step and charged directly into little Tommy Rogers. The collision left the boy seated on the landing looking up at the detective.

"Are you all right?" Holmes asked.

"I'm okay, sir," the boy said. "Did you notice my new clothes Uncle bought—?"

Holmes paid no attention. Before the boy could finish

his question, the detective was halfway down the stairs, his long scarf trailing after him.

"Watson," he called back sharply, "the boy is here. See to him, will you? Mrs. Hudson!" Holmes hollered. "Mrs. Hudson?"

I heard the door to her rooms creak an instant before Holmes pulled open the front door. The sounds of the street blew in with snowflakes and another freshening breeze.

"Where is . . . Oh, there you are," Holmes said. "I'll be out late, Mrs. Hudson. Don't hold supper for me. Thank—"

The slamming door cut off his words.

Chapter 13

I know that Holmes never would have intentionally hurt the boy's feelings, but that did not change the effect of his indifference. Though I understood it and accepted it as, well, his way, it made me angry, nevertheless. I determined not to show it, however.

"Hello there, Tommy," I said, trying hard to sound chipper.

"Hello, Doc," he said.

"Say, don't you look fine! Aren't those new clothes? And new shoes, too, if my eyes don't deceive me, eh?"

"Yes, sir. Thank you, sir. I thought Mr. Holmes might notice, but he di'n't. Did I do something, Doc Watson? Is he tired o' me, 'cause I can . . . you know, I don't have to go through wi' this, really."

"Don't be silly, Tommy. Why, Holmes was saying to me just last night how pleased he is with your progress."

The boy perked up noticeably. I was lying, of course, but in a good cause; Holmes had said nothing one way or the other.

"Did 'e now, Doc?"

"He most certainly did . . . Master Tom. He most certainly did. Uhm, listen. Mr. Holmes can be, well, sort of abrupt sometimes, because he gets so caught up in one problem or another. And that can make him seem like he's somewhere else, even when he's right there in front of you."

"Aye. Yer sayin' e's too busy, right?"

"Well, perhaps too busy for his own good sometimes, yes. But then we all are now and then, aren't we?"

"Aye. There's truth in that, Doc. I see how busy me and

Uncle John are wi' just our workin' wi' the vegetable cart, and I just shakes my head sometimes."

"Well, there you go, Tommy," I said, thankful once again that despite his youth and disadvantage the boy caught on to everything very quickly.

"Now, here's the point," I said. "You just can't be too quick to get upset when people don't behave quite the way you expect them to. They're only people, after all, no matter how much we like them, and everyone is different. And where Mr. Holmes is concerned, well, I think sometimes the more intelligent somebody is, the more different and, well . . . quirkier they are. And Mr. Holmes, he's brilliant, as we all know, and so he has peculiar ways. You just have to trust him. And that's how it is. Does that makes sense to you?"

"I guess so."

"Very well. Ah, I hear Mrs. Hudson coming up the stairs now, so we can start with the day's lesson."

I rose from my chair to admit our landlady, and it was a good thing I did because she was carrying a full tray of silverware, bowls and a steaming tureen of rich beef barley soup. It smelled so good that I found myself hungry at once.

"Good grief, Mrs. Hudson, you might have called to me," I said. "I'd have come down to help you."

"No bother," she said, "but if you would bring up the tray of fresh bread and butter that I've set on the foyer table, that'd be appreciated."

"She's a strong 'un, ain't she?" Tommy whispered.

I looked down at him reprovingly. "That's disrespectful, young man." I said it quietly, so Mrs. Hudson would not hear, but I was having a difficult time not smiling. For her diminutive size, our landlady was, in fact, a strong woman, and this was hardly the first time I had come to that realization.

"I'll go down and get the bread tray, ma'am," Tommy said, and he was out the door in a flash, trying to redeem himself, I was sure.

"Don't you spill it, now," Mrs. Hudson called after him.

"He's a good boy, that one, Doctor. Don't you think so?"

"I do, indeed," I said.

"Mr. Holmes left in a hurry today, didn't he, Doctor? I'll bet it's about that ad, isn't it? Mr. Holmes never would have done such a thing now, would he? I was surprised myself. Then I realized it had to be some kind of holiday trick. That brought a smile to my lips, I don't mind saying."

"So it did not strike you that there was anything foreboding about the ad?"

"Heavens no, Doctor," Mrs. Hudson said. "How on earth could there be foreboding in a Christmas wish?"

"Well said, Mrs. Hudson. My feelings precisely, but Holmes seemed to think . . . Ah, here's Tommy with the tray. Good job, young man."

Mrs. Hudson set the table, and the three of us sat down to dine. Tommy quickly identified the soup spoon and, after spreading his napkin on his lap, picked up the spoon and tackled the soup. With every spoonful he made an awful sound.

"You must not slurp your soup, young man," Mrs. Hudson told him. "Just remember not to suck it up. Take the side of it in your mouth, and tip the spoon. Like so. But first, before you get the spoon anywhere near your lips . . . watch." She held her left hand on her lap and, taking the spoon in her right, demonstrated how to partake of the soup in a proper fashion.

"You see," Mrs. Hudson said, "a gentleman knows that he moves the spoon away from himself, like so."

"Aye," Tommy said, "but that don't make no sense, ma'am . . . beggin' your pardon."

"And why not?"

"Well, if the idea is to get the soup up to yer lips and down yer gullet, then why would yer be increasin' the distance between you and the soup by headin' the spoon off to the opp'site shore? It don't make no sense to me at all, ma'am."

"It doesn't make *any* sense," I interjected.

"There," Tommy said, "Doc Watson agrees with me. See Missus Hudson?"

"That wasn't what I meant, Tommy," I said.

He looked at me, puzzled.

"It doesn't *have to* make sense, Master Rogers," Mrs.

Hudson said. "It is etiquette. It is the way people with proper breeding behave."

"Aaw, bugg—"

"Tommy!" I said sharply. "None of that. Do as Mrs. Hudson says if you don't want people at that banquet thinking you're ill-mannered."

"Oh, aye," he said.

"Tommy," I said. "Remember what Mr. Holmes said? Maybe it will help here, too. When you are dining, keep in your mind's eye a picture of people seated in a nice restaurant and eating properly. You have seen that many times, haven't you?"

"Aye, Dr. Watson."

"Well then, pretend that you are one of the people in that picture, that's all. You don't have to understand why they are doing things in a particular manner. You just have to remember precisely *what* they are doing. You are acting, remember?"

"Aye, Dr. Watson," Tommy said. "Just like Mr. Holmes said before. I remember."

He finished the soup at a reasonable pace and in the proper fashion.

"You have remembered what Mrs. Hudson told you about courses and utensils?"

"Aye, sir."

"What is the purpose of the fork that is larger than the salad fork but smaller than the dinner fork?"

"At'd be for fish, sir. I see that and I'll be presumin' there'll be a fish course."

"Very good," I said.

"And when in doubt about which fork to use, remember that you always . . . "

"Work from the outside of the setting in toward the plate," Tommy said.

"And remember, young man," Mrs. Hudson said, "no matter how hungry you might be when you sit down to a proper meal, you must never eat in such a way as to announce that fact."

"I'm not sure—"

"Never attack your food like some ravenous animal," I said. "You must always take your time."

"That's right," Mrs. Hudson said. "A gentleman always shows restraint."

"Well, you mean that even if I ain't had nothin' to eat all day, not even s'much as a crumb, I ain't s'posed to let on?"

"Not by your manners, no," Mrs. Hudson said.

"Well, then manners is a pretty dishonest thing, I guess, huh?"

"What do you mean?" I asked.

"It seems to me, Doc, that the whole point of havin' these manners is so that you can cover up some of the things that make you different so people will figure you're just like them in every way."

"Well," I said, "I don't know that I'd put it in quite that way, but in a sense, I suppose, yes. Society imposes a kind of conformity."

"But they know 'at's not the truth, right? They know 'at when everybody's lookin' and talkin' and dressin' and eatin' all the same, that underneath all that there's real different people."

"Well, yes," I said. "Of course."

"Then, what's the point?" Tommy asked.

"Well, it's polite society, Tommy. It's just the way things are. It's the way people are. It is civil. If people want to get to know each other beyond formal appearances, then they make a concerted effort to do so, to develop an association or a friendship and then learn more about the other person. You know that."

"Well," the boy said, "I guess I do. I still don't see the point. I mean, if everybody didn't feel like they had to act in a certain way and do a certain thing in just such a way, like everybody was bein' watched all the time, then people would probably get a better idea of how that person really is. Then gettin' to be a friend and such wouldn't be so much work. Wouldn't be no big deal, at all, 'cause you wouldn't have to pretend nothin'. Don't you see what I mean, Doc? Mrs. Hudson?"

I did see what he meant, and the unadorned simplicity of it made me smile to myself. Would that the world were as simple and straightforward a place, and the people in it as honest and unprepossessing as Tommy would have them.

"I must go downstairs now," Mrs. Hudson said abruptly. "I expect I will see you tomorrow, young man?"

"Aye," he said. "Thank you, ma'am."

"How are you feeling about this, Master Tom?" I asked.

"Well, pretty good, Doc. I think it might be kinda fun, really. Playactin' like 'is."

"That's my boy," I said. "That's exactly the way to look at it. And remember, you'll have me and Mr. Holmes there looking out for your best interests."

"Aye," Tommy said. "I'm countin' on 'at, sir."

"I don't suppose you've had much time to get your uncle John a Christmas gift, now, have you?"

"No sir. I never 'ave money for such. I mean, he don't expect me to."

"But you would like to get him a little something, wouldn't you?"

"Aye, sir. I would. Yes."

"Well, what might that be?"

The boy scrunched his eyebrows together in a moment of hard, concentrated thought. When he suddenly popped his eyes wide open and a smile came to his lips, I knew he had hit on it.

"Gloves," he said. "Uncle John needs gloves real bad. 'Is got ruined a while ago, and 'e's been wantin' a good pair ever since. Always. 'Is 'ands gets wet an' cold, and then they dries out and the skin on 'em cracks and split open, an' 'e's in pain all winter, 'e is. 'E don't ever complain, but I know it. 'E 'asn't 'ad the money to replace 'em"

"Well," I said, "perhaps we can find him a good warm and sturdy pair." Then I lied to the boy again, but once more in a good cause. "Mr. Holmes and I were talking about it last night," I said, "and we thought it might be a good idea if we helped you pick out something for your uncle."

"You'd do 'at?"

"We would," I said. "As a favor and sort of a gift to you. That's from Mr. Holmes and me, even though he's not here right now to join us."

" 'At's great, Doc. What're we waitin' for?"

"What are we waiting for, indeed, young man? Let's go."

Chapter 14

Moments later Tommy and I we were out on the pavement of Baker Street confronting the day. The winter air was even dryer and crisper than I had recalled, and it was laden with blowing and twirling flakes of light and downy snow that tickled when they brushed by. But all in all, it was a pleasant sensation. Carols were still drifting our way from some street corner, distant but still well within earshot. Nearer, judging from the relative clarity of the sound, were the steady and distinctive ringing of hand bells. I knew at once that the sound came from the Salvation Army workers, for not a holiday season passed now but that the brethren didn't appear all over the West End soliciting donations for the poor. They deployed into the neighborhoods, fanned out silently, set up their small encampments early and then stayed out late, regardless of the weather. And the volunteers seemed to be everywhere. A pedestrian could not go far in any direction without being forced to choose between indifference and charity.

My affection for young Tommy caused me to reflect on how necessary was the work of the Salvation Army and the charitable trusts, civic associations and religious organizations that were working in behalf of the poor. There were many shelters now, and a good number of settlement houses, too, all over the city, and yet there were not nearly enough of them. Countless children were consigned to a wretched existence by their circumstances, living in dirty "gardens" of red brick, their rooms little more than vermin-infested warrens, blackened holes off filthy alleys that emptied into paved courtyards littered with garbage and trash.

It was an abominable situation, and it was widely recognized as precisely that. It was little wonder that most of the upper tier these days lived in fear of widespread social unrest. Personally, I think it was that very same fear, and not any innate beneficence on our part, that accounted for the general increase in charitable activities.

My shopping mission with Tommy, of course, was not nearly so noble and grand an effort, but I knew I would be content if it made even a small difference in the boy's Christmas. I hailed a hansom cab for us, and a few short minutes later, we stepped out in front of a leather goods shop I had frequented some time ago, Hazelton's on Bond Street. Despite the rather lofty address, the shop had always enjoyed a reputation for high-quality items at fair prices. While I did not believe John Godey needed, or for that matter even would want, gloves of the finest kid leather, he certainly did need gloves that were warm, durable and a proper fit. The latter point suddenly gave me pause.

"Tommy, your uncle has very big hands, does he not? I mean, *very* big."

"Oh, aye, Doc, 'e does that. I mean, 'at's why 'e don't 'ave no gloves."

"I beg your pardon?"

"Well, he ain't never been able to find any 'at fit 'im, leastwise any he could afford."

"Oh," I said. "Well. Good grief, lad, maybe we had better set our sights on something else. I mean, after all, if he couldn't—"

"Well, let's just look, Doc. Who knows? Maybe we'll find somethin' just right."

"Very well," I said. "After you, Tommy." So saying, I ushered him through the door and into Hazelton's.

"What a great smell, 'at!" Tommy said, rather too loudly, I thought.

"It is, isn't it?" came a distinctively reedy voice that I thought I recognized. "I have worked here ten hours a day six days a week for more than twenty-three years, and I have never tired of it. It's so earthy and rich. I just love it."

I groaned inwardly. I recalled that the man was a chore, well meaning enough, for sure, but annoying and odd, and he always seemed to have all the time in the world, which I never did. Suddenly, his name came back to me.

"Mr. Weatherbee, isn't it?" I asked. "I haven't been in the store for more than a year now."

"Charles T., yes it is," he said. "Well, I guess there's nothing wrong with your memory, is there?"

He moved from behind a counter at the side of the floor toward the front center of the shop, where Tommy and I stood, but he had to feel his way by moving rather slowly and touching the tops of the counters as he walked.

"Your voice is familiar, but my eyesight isn't what it once was," he said, "even as recently as a year ago. Something with my blood, I'm told. Leads to complete blindness eventually. Probably not too long now."

Indeed, Charles T. Weatherbee wore steel-framed glasses with lenses so thick that his eyes appeared magnified to several times their normal size. They seemed much too large for his face. In truth, he looked rather like a bug, and I could not help but feel sorry for him.

"Dr. John Watson, Mr. Weatherbee. You probably don't remember me. I was with my friend and companion, Mr. Sherlock Holmes, when we came in last."

"Oh, I do," he said, clapping his hands together in front of him. "I most certainly do remember. Yes. Yes. Yes. But where is Mr. Holmes? I can still make out shapes, you know. And this short one here is not Mr. Holmes, unless in the past year he has had worse luck than I. Has he shrunk?"

"No," I had to laugh. "Holmes hasn't shrunk. He's off on business," I said. "We're very busy, you know."

Weatherbee didn't seem to be listening. He bent over and put his face close and square up to Tommy's. The boy looked frightened, I thought, or startled at least.

"Now, don't be bothered, young man," Weatherbee said. "I don't bite. I only look as though I might. It's these glasses." He lowered his voice conspiratorially and put his mouth nearer to Tommy's ear.

"Don't you think they make me look like an insect? Really?"

"Oh, no, sir," Tommy said.

But as he was speaking, Charles T. Weatherbee was raising his hands, palms outward, on either side of his head. He looked straight at Tommy, wiggled the fingers of both hands vigorously and stuck out his tongue.

Tommy laughed loudly.

"See, young man?" Weatherbee said. "An insect, just like I said."

He laughed at himself and said, "Now, Dr. Watson, how may I help you?"

"We need a good pair of gloves for—"

"Did you have a color in mind?"

"Uhm, no," I said.

"Suede perhaps?"

"I shouldn't think so."

"Most men like a suede at one point or another," Weatherbee said. "Suede has a leisurely look about it, not exactly elegant, but still . . ."

"I don't think suede would hold up very—"

". . . refined," Weatherbee said, not hearing a demurring word that I had uttered. "That was the word I was looking for," he said. "Refined. Right there on the tip of my tongue all the time." He angled his head toward Tommy and stuck out his tongue.

He pointed at it with the index finger of his right hand and ordered Tommy: "Ook."

The boy stood on the tips of his toes and peered at the man's outstretched tongue.

"I don't see nothin', sir," Tommy said. " 'Cept'n your tongue, I mean."

"No other words out there on the tip that I might be needing?" Weatherbee asked. "Better look again." He stuck out his tongue again, even more insistently this time.

Tommy laughed.

"I think I saw a word, but it fell off on the floor," Tommy said. "Watch where you're walkin', now. You find it, you better not be puttin' it back on there wi'out a washin', sir. Floor's dirty, you don't mind my sayin'."

It was Charles T. Weatherbee's turn to laugh, and he laughed so hard he found it necessary to remove his thick, heavy glasses and dry his eyes.

"You're a quick one, you are, young man. So, Dr. Watson, what color suede do you think our friend would favor?"

"Not suede, sir," I said quite pointedly. "I tried to tell you that. Given that the recipient of the gloves is—"

"Oh, this is to be a gift, is it? And why did you not say so?"

"Well," I said, "I hardly think it matters, really. I—"

"Well, of course, it matters," Weatherbee said. "Mr. Holmes would not wear suede of any sort, and—"

"It isn't for Holmes," I said.

"Oh," Weatherbee said, raising his voice a full octave. "I see. Then these gloves are for another . . . friend of yours? Another . . . man?" he said softly, almost secretly. "I don't mean to be indiscreet, sir. Really, I don't. But . . . A professional man, like Mr. Holmes?"

"The recipient," I suddenly found myself shouting now, "not that it is really any of your concern, is this boy's uncle, Mr. Weatherbee."

"His name is Weatherbee, too?" the clerk asked. "You don't say? What an odd coincidence!" As he said this, he cast his eyes toward the ceiling, opened his mouth wide and put the palm of his right hand against his cheek in mock surprise. He did it so quickly that his hand slapped his face and the impact set his big glasses awry at a sharp angle, making his much magnified eyes appear crooked. Had the glasses not caught on the edge of his nose, they would have fallen to the floor.

Tommy laughed so hard, he doubled over.

Despite my growing impatience, I had to laugh, too, for it was clear now that the clerk was having us on.

The heavy glasses fell.

"Oh," I said. "I hope they're not broken."

Tommy reached for them quickly.

"Oh, it doesn't matter," Charles T. Weatherbee said. "I don't really need them anyway."

"You don't . . . "

"No. It's just a little game I like to play with the customers. It's pretty boring otherwise. Sometimes I come out all bandaged up and on a crutch. Sometimes I dress as a woman; that really startles 'em."

"I'm sure that it does," I said. "Been playing these little game of yours for a while, have you?"

"Just since last year when I bought the place from old Mr. Hazelton. He went bonkers, you know."

"Really? I'm so sorry to—"

"Mmm. Yes," Weatherbee said. "Most days toward the end, he couldn't recall his own name. He'd just sit over there in the corner, that very corner there, staring off into nowhere. He used to drool quite a bit. We had to put a bib on him, right over his suit jacket. We kept him out of the customers' line of vision. Had to, you know? Bad for business, that."

"Yes, well . . . Listen, Mr. Weatherbee, I—"

"Call me Fritz," he said.

"But . . . Your name is Charles, is it not?"

"Yes, Charles T. The T is for Thornton. But I've always liked the name Fritz."

Tommy made a noise that was much like a gasp. I turned to him sharply, but he looked away.

"Oh, for the love of . . . No. No. Don't say anything. Listen to me, Charles T. Weatherbee, or Fritz, or whatever you call yourself . . . " I was talking very loudly, not hollering, but it was clear that I was frustrated. "I came here to buy a good pair of gloves for this boy's uncle. They can be black or brown; it doesn't matter. They must be strong and well made and supple, but not suede and fancy. And no raised welts. And they must be big. He has an exceptionally large hand."

"Just one?" Charles T. Weatherbee asked quickly. "That's too bad, really."

"Two, of course," I said, refusing the bait now.

"Well, you never know," the clerk said. "Always pays to ask."

"I'm sure," I said. "Perhaps we should look elsewhere, Tommy."

"Is there a problem here?" It was another voice, older but strong and firm. I turned to see a man in his late sixties, thin but not at all fragile-looking, bald with a tonsure of white hair and a warm earnest smile. He wore half glasses and he was peering over them at Charles T. Weatherbee.

"Perhaps you should tend to the stock now, Weatherbee."

"Yes, Mr. Hazelton."

Tommy made a noise. I must have looked stunned.

"Are—are you the owner, sir, uhm, Mr. Hazelton?"

"I am, and proud of our leather products, too."

"And you were not terribly, uhm, sick last year?"

"I have been blessed with wonderful health for my entire life, nearly seventy-five years," Hazelton said. "Why on earth do you ask?"

"Oh I thought that . . . Never mind, sir. It's really not—"

"Are you interested in purchasing gloves exactly like those you were describing for Weatherbee? Don't judge Hazelton's by him, please. He's always been a bit odd, and he doesn't seem to have improved with age. He has become unpredictable. I never know quite what to expect of him anymore. I'd have let him go years ago if he weren't my son."

"Your son? But he said his name was . . . Never mind. Never mind. Yes. The gloves. Please."

"I think you will find these very much to your liking, sir."

I was dazed. Hazelton laid a pair of black gloves on the counter. I picked one up, turned its cuff over for a look at the hide, which was quite thick and brushed soft. My hand was lost in it.

"What do you think, Tommy? These are very good, it seems to me. How about the size?"

"They're the largest we have, sir, and they represent what I would hold to be an excellent value, sir. Excellent."

"I think they'd be just right, Doc," Tommy said.

"If they are not," Mr. Hazelton said, "if they should prove too large, or for that matter, too small, you may return them. Providing that they are not soiled and can be resold, I will refund your money."

"Well, that certainly is fair," I said. "We'll take them, then."

"Very good, sir. That will be ten pounds and sixpence, then."

"What?"

"It's a lot of glove you've got there, nearly twice the leather in it as any other glove in the shop, sir. And a very good choice, sir," Hazelton said. "Very good, indeed. A most perceptive choice, and tasteful, too, if I may say so. Those gloves can be worn with anything. Did I mention that the price includes a pair just like it for the young man?"

"Wow!" Tommy exclaimed. "Thank you, sir. Wow! 'At's swell. Thanks, Doc."

"Don't mention it," I said. I paid my money, and tried very hard to stare straight through Hazelton's eyes all the way to the back of his head. But if my baleful look bothered him, he didn't show it.

"A wise purchase, sir," Hazelton said with a smile. "Very wise."

Tommy put on his new gloves and smacked his hands together a couple of times as if to test the leather's strength. Old Mr. Hazelton, meanwhile, put John Godey's new gloves in a box with some tissue paper and put the box in a black paper sack that had the name of the store on it in gold-colored letters. He tapped the name with his index finger and smiled at me.

"Don't forget us, sir."

"Now, how could I do that?" I asked, and we turned and walked outside. I closed the door on his cheery "Merry Christmas, now."

"I would just as soon walk back, Tommy," I said, pulling my collar up, for the chill wind was up again. "The air's cold, but the exercise will do us good. What do you say?"

"Sure," he said. "Do you go there very much? Those people are pretty strange."

"I hardly noticed," I said.

As we walked, I mulled over the past half hour that we'd spent in Hazelton's. I felt odd, as though the bizarre little visit had somehow sucked all normal sensibility out of the afternoon.

We stopped at the corner of Vigo Street while a tram passed, and quite unintentionally I found myself listening to the conversation of two men behind us at the curb.

"So what's becoming of that Holmes fella, eh, Freddy?"

"Hard to figure, isn't it? I never took him for a bleedin' Father Christmas, Alfie. Let me see that page again."

I turned around, first looking past the two men and moving my head from side to side impatiently, as though straining to see around them. When they turned their gaze in the same direction as my own, I looked down quickly at their newspaper, which I presumed would be yesterday's *Daily Telegraph*. But it was not. It was *The Times*. Today's edition.

"Good Lord," I exclaimed to no one. "What on earth is

this about? Excuse me. Excuse me," I said. I pushed my
way back through the small throng of pedestrians and shop-
pers. "Tommy. Tommy, come over here, please." I stepped
back and away from the crowd and reached into my pocket
for some coins.

"What is it, Doc? You look upset."

"Here, Tommy. When the street clears a little, I want
you to cross to that corner and get us today's copy of *The
Times*. Okay?"

"Done, Doc." With that, the boy took off for the news-
stand. I took a cigar from my jacket pocket. I cut off the
end with the pocket knife I had taken to carrying. I turned
my back to the wind, cupped my hand over a match and
in its sharp and sulphurous heat lighted the cigar and then
puffed on it intently.

Tommy returned in a moment, out of breath.

"Here y'are, Doc."

"Mmmph," I said. I took the newspaper in both hands
and flipped its pages quickly one by one. I used my tongue
to push the cigar to the corner of my mouth, so I could
talk more clearly.

"Thank you, Tommy," I said.

On page twenty-six of *The Times* I found what I was
looking for. Another advertisement; it read:

Good people of London,
I give you a new verse for an old song this holiday season:
God rest ye, merry gentlemen.
Let nothing you dismay,
Despite what ever fortune
Be yours this holiday.

And it, too, was signed: Sherlock Holmes.

Now I was worried. The rhyme even mimicked "Good
King Wenceslas," the carol Holmes despised.

"I'll be hanged," I said. "Maybe Holmes was right, after
all."

Chapter 15

While Tommy and I were being entertained by Charles T. Weatherbee and old Mr. Hazelton, Holmes was assaulting *The Daily Telegraph*.

"I wish to see the advertising manager," he announced to the receptionist.

"That would be Theodore Winchell, sir. Down that big hallway to your right. Third door on the left, sir."

Holmes nodded in thanks and walked briskly down the wide dimly lighted corridor, passing among a number of newspaper employees, all of them rushing about, seeming as purposeful and mysteriously directed as bees in a hive. Holmes stepped straight between two men; one of them did not see the detective coming and got jostled so hard that the man stopped and stared after him, but Holmes paid no attention. He reached the third door on the left and opened it straightaway. He did not knock. He simply turned the door handle and walked in.

The office was plain and much smaller than one might have expected of a prominent manager for a major newspaper, and it was cluttered with books, stacks of newspapers, crumpled sheets of foolscap and stacks of pencil sketches and line drawings. In the middle of the flotsam was a large rectangular, flat-topped oak desk, and behind it sat Theodore Winchell. He was a wide and corpulent man with eyes like small raisins and a youthful and unlined face so red and perfectly round that it seemed to have been heated under extraordinary pressure.

"Who the devil do you think you are, barging in here?"

"I am Sherlock Holmes."

"Oh . . . " he said. "Mr. Holmes. Yes, I guess I remember

you. If you had knocked, sir, I would have been happy to see you in."

Holmes glared at him. "What do you mean, you remember me? We have never met."

"No, no," Winchell said. "I'm quite sure we have. Just the other day, when you came into this very room to make the arrangements for your ad in yesterday's editions. A nice bit of work, it was, too. The calligraphy was just right, don't you think?"

"You say that I was here? We transacted business?"

"Well, we must have, Mr. Holmes. How else would your advert have appeared?"

Winchell paused. He looked at Holmes, then looked away and turned back to the detective. "Is this a prank of some kind?" he asked. "If it is, sir, I should warn you that I am not—"

"No, Mr. Winchell, this is no prank, I assure you. And let me also assure you that until a few moments ago, I had never set foot in this building."

Winchell turned his eyes to the green blotter on his desk.

"If you say so, Mr. Holmes." Winchell looked up toward the detective, then past him and out into the corridor where people still were passing by. "Uhm, excuse me for just a moment, sir . . . Brooks! Hey, Peter Brooks! Come in here for a bit, will you?"

A small and wiry little man, in his late twenties or very early thirties, wearing a wool suit of loud black and white houndstooth check, stepped into Winchell's office.

The young man identified Holmes at once. "Say now!" he exclaimed. "You're Sherlock Holmes, aren't you? I'll be. I heard you were in the building recently, Mr. Holmes, and I cursed my luck to have been out at the time. I'm glad I'm here now."

Brooks looked furtively at the palm of his right hand. Seeing that it was smudged with black ink, he tried to rub it off on the leg of his pants. He again looked quickly at his palm and, this time apparently satisfied, stuck it straight out at Holmes.

"It is a great pleasure to meet you, sir."

Holmes shook Brooks' hand and smiled politely.

Winchell cleared his throat for attention and then interrupted. "Brooks, we seem to have some sort of mystery here."

"How so?" Brooks asked. Without taking his eyes off Holmes, and with an economy of movement that was as unobtrusive and nearly unnoticeable as it was practiced, the reporter took from his trousers rear pocket a small pad of paper, and from his jacket pocket, a small pencil. With one item in each hand, he stood poised to take notes. Neither Holmes nor Winchell tried to stop him; this was a newspaper, after all.

"Well, Brooks," said Winchell, "you are aware of the advert we published yesterday over Mr. Holmes' name?"

"Indeed," Brooks said. "A nice sentiment it was, sir."

"It was not my own," Holmes said.

"I don't understand," the reporter said, jotting notes on his pad without looking.

"Quite simple, really," Holmes said. "Someone disguised as me presented himself to your Mr. Winchell and paid for the ad."

"No!"

"Oh, yes," Holmes said. "Yes, indeed."

"Winchell, why did you believe the man was Holmes?" Brooks asked.

"I'm looking at him, same as I did that day," Winchell replied.

"You mean, they looked alike? Someone was masquerading as Mr. Holmes?"

"If this man is to be believed," Winchell said, "yes."

"Oh, I am to be believed, Mr. Winchell," Holmes said sharply, "and may I suggest that you either accept that fact here and now, or we will have trouble."

Winchell's face turned an even deeper shade of red. He put both hands palms down flat atop his desk so hard that they made a loud slap, and with considerable effort pushed himself straight up from his chair.

"Don't you threaten me," he told the detective.

He was half upright when Holmes flipped his walking stick in an arc and brought it to an abrupt stop at one of the creases that marked the end of Winchell's neck and the start of his left shoulder. He had not hit the man. He had simply put his stick where Winchell would see it. The man slapped it hard with one hand, but the stick did not so much as quiver; it was as though the shaft were held fast in a steel vise.

"Mr. Winchell," Holmes said. "I never threaten; I was merely explaining reality. And I very much resent being called a liar."

"Well, I, uhm . . . first, I did call it a mystery, didn't I?"

"Indeed, you did," Holmes said.

"Winchell," Brooks said, "are you absolutely certain the man who paid for that advert was this gentleman standing here right now?"

"Well, he looked much like him, yes."

" 'Much like him,' " Brooks reiterated, but with a trace of disgust. "Then you are no longer sure?"

"He might have been a little heavier, less wiry-looking."

"As tall?" Holmes asked.

"Maybe an inch shorter, now that you mention it. Maybe two inches shorter."

"Two inches shorter," Brooks repeated. "Winchell, you are sure that the visitor was a man, I presume."

"Please," Holmes said. "Mr. Winchell, you did not ask for any identification?"

"Well, there was no reason, was there? The man dictated what he wanted in the advert, and—"

"Did he dictate placement as well?" Holmes asked.

The reporter looked at Holmes and then at Winchell, but never stopped his note-taking.

"He said the advert had to be on page twenty-six, yes," Winchell said. "I told him that if the space had to be guaranteed, the cost would be twenty percent more."

"Twenty percent?" Brooks said. "Bloody Mary, you blokes are thieves!"

"Come, come," Holmes said. "Mr. Winchell, your 'Mr. Holmes' was insistent that the advertisement appear on page twenty-six? Is that correct?"

"At first I said it was impossible. I told him the space was accounted for."

"And was it?" Holmes asked.

"Certainly," Winchell said. "A bit of news there and a much smaller advert."

"And how did our visitor respond?" Holmes asked.

"He said, 'Good day, then. I'll take my business elsewhere.' That's when I offered him the twenty percent deal."

"You were willing to move or kill the story? And the smaller, and I presume less costly, advertisement as well."

Winchell grinned slightly. "Business is business, as they say."

"Yes," Holmes said, "unfortunately for us all." Then, without even a slight pause, he spoke rapidly so as to not give Winchell time to entertain a rejoinder. "And how did our man respond, exactly?" Holmes asked.

Winchell was stung; it was obvious in his small black eyes. But he answered Holmes' question. "The man said, 'No matter.' He dismissed the extra cost. Then he paid it."

"How did he dismiss it, Mr. Winchell?" Holmes asked.

"Well, with his hand. You know. How else?"

"I do not know, sir," Holmes said. "I was not here. That is why I asked."

"All right. All right. Well, he said, 'No matter,' and he flipped his wrist sort of backward, like he was flicking off a fly that had landed on the back of his hand."

"His left hand?" Holmes asked.

"Yes, his left hand . . . I think . . . " Winchell paused. He moved both of his hands as if to imagine the position of his earlier visitor in relation to him, and then said, "Yes, I'm sure; it was his left hand . . . not that it matters."

"Of course it matters," Holmes said. "It may seem a mere trifle to you, Mr. Winchell, but I assure you that in the final analysis such details matter a great deal."

"Humph! You're the detective," he said.

"Thank you for that," Holmes said. He turned to the reporter and asked, "Brooks, why do you suppose our man insisted that the advertisement appear on page twenty-six?"

"Lucky number? The fellow's superstitious, maybe? Who's to know?"

"Who, indeed?" Holmes said. "Who, indeed? Well then, I will take my leave. Good day, gentlemen."

Winchell made an indecipherable noise, much like a grunt.

"Can I walk out with you, sir?" Brooks asked. "I'd like to ask you some more questions."

"If you must," Holmes said, "but I will only answer you if it suits my purposes."

"And what might those be?" Brooks asked. "Your purposes?"

"To clear up this mess," Holmes said sharply. "What else?"

In the lobby, as the two men neared the main entrance, Holmes stopped. "Brooks," he said, "is that young lady the same receptionist who would have been working when our man came in?"

"Let's see. That was . . . No. It was another person."

"You're sure?"

"Yes, sir. Very sure. My turn."

Holmes said nothing. He looked at Brooks and waited.

"When did you first become aware of the advert in question, Mr. Holmes?"

"Earlier today. I was with my companion, Dr. John H. Watson, in our rooms in Baker Street."

"That's 221B Baker?"

"It is," Holmes said.

"The message seems innocent enough," Brooks said. "Why were you upset?"

"Wouldn't you be?"

"I'm sorry, sir. I wouldn't want to put words in your mouth."

"No, of course not," Holmes said. "Well . . ." He explained his misgivings, and the reporter dutifully wrote his words on the notepad.

"Excuse me, Mr. Holmes," Brooks said, "but do you suppose this is related to something else you might be working on right now?"

Holmes seemed taken aback slightly, but not unpleasantly.

"A good question, young man. I suppose it is possible, but I rather doubt it."

"Why?" Brooks asked.

"Because it seems unlikely," Holmes replied curtly.

"Well, what other cases are you working on now, sir?"

"You do not really expect me to answer that, do you, Mr. Brooks?"

"Be right nice if you were to do so," he said with a sheepish smile.

"But not likely," Holmes said.

"So you've got no idea?" Brooks asked.

"If I did, young man, it would not be my habit to divulge it," Holmes said. "I would need to be certain as to its reasonableness, number one. I would have to take into account the effect of my discussing it in public, number two. I would have to have eliminated all other possibilities, no matter how outlandish or improbable, number three."

"All right, Mr. Holmes. All right. I get the point," Brooks said. "So I suppose you've also got no idea who passed himself off as you?"

"That is what I said."

"You are baffled?"

"At the moment, yes," Holmes said.

"Perplexed?"

"Yes, for the time being."

"Vexed? If I were to describe your present attitude as vexed, Mr. Holmes, would that be accurate?"

"More so by the second, yes. If that's all you have to ask—"

"Oh, say . . . here are today's other papers," Brooks said.

"Ah, the competition," Holmes said. He picked up a copy of *The Times* and paged through it in the rough and haphazard manner that was his customary first look.

"Truth be told, Mr. Holmes, we aren't really much competition for *The Times,* but it always pays to know what the other blokes are doing."

Holmes looked at the page of the newspaper in his hands and blanched. He had reached page twenty-six and found the second ad.

"I suppose that you will make a story of this, too, Mr. Brooks?"

The reporter read the consternation in Holmes' face, then looked at the page to which the detective pointed. "And you didn't put that advert in the paper either, did you, sir?"

"Of course not," Holmes said.

"I had to ask."

"I know," Holmes said.

"I'll treat you fairly in my story."

"See that you do," Holmes said.

Then the detective turned and walked out the door.

Over drinks late that night, Holmes was telling me the details of his visit to the newspaper when sharp knocking sounded on the downstairs door.

"Nothing good ever seems to come of a late-night visit," I said.

Holmes said nothing, but he slipped his pistol into the pocket of his dressing gown before we went downstairs.

I opened the door to find a young man in a garish suit standing there with his hat in his hand.

"What do you want, Brooks?" Holmes asked curtly.

"I am very sorry to call on you so late, Mr. Holmes," the young man said, "but I must ask you a couple of questions."

"No," Holmes said, "and furth—"

"Please, sir," the young man said. "In the interest of fairness, I must speak with you."

The detective frowned and said nothing, but he opened the door and motioned the reporter inside with a sigh of resignation.

Holmes introduced me to the reporter quickly and said to him, "I do not wish to be unnecessarily rude, Mr. Brooks, but I would appreciate it if you would get on with your business. It is very late."

"It is, indeed, Mr. Holmes," Brooks said. "I promise I'll be quick. First, the number twenty-six: Do you suppose it is significant that both advertisements appeared on page twenty-six of their respective newspapers?"

Brooks had his notepad in one hand and a pencil in the other, poised and ready to write.

"What do you think?" Holmes asked.

"I'm sure I wouldn't know, Mr. Holmes," Brooks said, "and it wouldn't matter if I did, not really. It wouldn't be right to be quoting myself now, would it?"

"That wouldn't stop too many of your confreres."

"Don't judge me by their actions, sir."

"Very well," Holmes said, and so it went for at least another few minutes or so; just how long, I don't know because I excused myself and retired. I was sure I could read about it in the morning, and I was right.

Chapter 16

I arose late the following morning. Holmes had been up for quite some time, judging from the scraps of food that had dried on his plate at the breakfast table. On his chair lay the morning's edition of *The Daily Telegraph,* which was already thoroughly rumpled and roughly folded. Holmes was no respecter of neatness, and I was hardly a fastidious person myself, but I did find it annoying that most of the newspapers I got to read looked as though they had been passed around on a train.

I yawned and reached for the edition. Holmes' voice startled me.

"It seems generally even-handed to me," he said. He was sitting by the window, looking out over Baker Street, sipping a cup of tea.

I raised my eyebrows.

"Oh, sorry, Watson. I thought you had caught sight of the story already. It's on the front page. I folded the newspaper so you'd see it first off. Tell me what you think."

I mumbled something like "Good morning, Holmes," and tried to focus my bleary eyes. The headline was "Noted Detective Gets Mystery for Christmas." The story was quite long, but it seemed uncommonly fair and thorough, and I said so.

"I quite agree," Holmes said.

"But I was surprised to read that you put no stock whatsoever in the use of page twenty-six of the newspapers."

"As well you might be, Watson. I was forced to prevaricate. I believe the use of page twenty-six is a bald reference to the twenty-sixth day of December."

"Boxing Day?"

"What else *could* it be, Watson? No other interpretation is reasonable."

"But what *about* Boxing Day, Holmes?"

"I have no idea," he said, "but I think there will be trouble of some sort."

"What can we do?" I asked.

"Probably nothing," Holmes said, "which infuriates me. I am convinced there will be trouble, but I don't know what kind, and I don't know where. So I am left to wait. That is what frustrates. The waiting. And not knowing for what."

As we talked Holmes had picked up the dagger that he had taken from the cutthroat in St. Giles. It was a nasty-looking weapon. The handle was short, as though made for a small hand, and it was nearly as flat as the blade, which was strong, rather heavy and exceptionally rigid despite its long taper, and it appeared to be made of an uncommonly good steel. The hilt was so small as to be barely discernible, and both edges of the blade were razor-sharp.

Holmes was flipping the knife end over end and catching it in his hand. The first few times he did it, the knife made one complete revolution and the handle landed flat in his palm. But when that no longer seemed a challenge, Holmes flipped the knife a bit harder and a bit higher, so that it made two complete revolutions before landing handle first in his palm. He did this several times with his right hand, then several times with his left.

"You're making me nervous, Holmes," I said.

"Nonsense, Watson . . . Ooops, look out!" Holmes had flipped the knife higher, but not quite high enough for it to make three complete revolutions, so as it neared his outstretched palm, the knife was coming down point first. Holmes moved his hand just in time. I moved my foot. The dagger hit the floor point first and stuck straight in with a dull but unmistakable twang.

"What do you make of this knife, Watson?"

"Are you serious, Holmes? It's a knife. A long, sharp and pointed one, and I would like to note that it very nearly landed on my foot."

"Aside from that?"

"What are you smiling about, Holmes? You very nearly

make a pincushion of me, and you think it's funny," I said. "I did move pretty fast, though, didn't I? The reflexes are still good, eh?"

"Seriously," he said.

"Seriously? Well, I guess it reminds me of the dagger that Jack Ryder used to stab the deck of playing cards that night at the Aurora."

"I thought so, too, Watson. Yes. But mostly because of shape, not any specific marking or anything of that sort. Yes?"

"I'd agree," I said.

"Knives are interesting, Watson. Each has only one or two specific uses. In this case, the one is obvious; the other, I think, perhaps less so."

"Stabbing," I said. "It has two sharp edges, not merely one."

"The obvious use, yes," Holmes said.

"And the other?" I asked.

"Throwing," he said. Holmes took the small handle of the dagger between the thumb and forefinger of his right hand, brought his arm quickly back and threw the knife very hard straight at the main door to our parlor.

"Holmes!" I shouted, startled.

The knife hit the door point first with a hard *Thwaack!* The noise reverberated for a moment as the steel blade thrummed with the impact. The tip of the dagger was stuck deep into the middle of the large stile that separates the door's raised vertical panels.

"Aah!" Holmes said, obviously pleased with his marksmanship. "See how perfectly balanced it is? I never could have done that with a lesser knife. I haven't the skill. Oh, don't worry, Watson. I'm certain that I locked the door this morning. I wouldn't want to impale anyone before lunch."

No sooner had he finished speaking than there came a quick knock on the door. It opened almost instantly and Mrs. Hudson walked straight into the room. I rolled my eyes to the ceiling and turned to the bookcase, away from our visitor.

"Ah! Good morning, Mrs. Hudson," Holmes said. "I presume by your obvious agitation that we have a caller downstairs of some prominence."

"Indeed we do, sir," Mrs. Hudson said, her bright eyes wide with interest. "Uhm, what was that loud noise I heard when I was coming up the stairs?"

I answered quickly. "I dropped a large book," I said. "No harm done, Mrs. Hudson."

Holmes nodded appreciatively, but discreetly, in my direction.

"Oh," she said. "Well, yes, Mr. Holmes, prominent, to be sure."

Our landlady looked down at the beige calling card in her hand, and read: "The Lady Mirabelle Llewellyn Armstrong, Mr. Holmes. The wealthiest woman in all of London, and she's come to see you, sir. Imagine!"

"Indeed," Holmes sniffed. "And why wouldn't she? Well, please do show her in, Mrs. Hudson. Come, come. We mustn't keep the gentry waiting."

"Oh no, sir. Very good, sir."

As Mrs. Hudson hurried out the door, I walked to the outer edge of the damask curtains that straddled our window on Baker Street, and parted them delicately so as to spy on the thoroughfare. In the street directly below me stood Lady Armstrong's brougham. It was a beautiful coach, lacquered a bright and glossy black with gilt edging. The Armstrong family coat of arms adorned each door, and an elegant brightly polished brass lamp gleamed at each of the coach's four corners.

Her liveried driver sat atop the coach, top hat in place, whip in hand, staring straight ahead, all business, as rigid as a Beefeater on horseback, and eternally devoted to one purpose and one purpose only: to safely ferry her ladyship wherever she wished to go.

On the pavement, standing at attention precisely an arm's length from the door of the brougham, stood Cuthbert Wilson, Lady Armstrong's personal attendant. He was as lifelike as any wax figure at Madame Tussaud's but somewhat stiffer. No lamppost on the street stood any straighter. It made me downright uncomfortable just to look at him.

Behind me, our visitor swept in amid a soft rustle of elegant fabrics. A small cloud of light, undoubtedly expensive rose perfume trailed after her. Even outside of her own milieu, Lady Armstrong had all of the presence of royalty, though none of its charm.

Holmes was leaning casually against the sideboard when she arrived.

"Lady Armstrong," he said. "How nice. May we get you tea?"

"Thank you, no," she said. "I shan't be long."

"I see. Very well. Won't you have a seat, at least? Now, how may we be of service?"

"I must speak with you in private," she said primly.

"Anything that you would say to me, Lady Armstrong, you may say to Dr. Watson. I assure you, he is the very soul of discretion."

"I must insist," she said sharply, her thin, reedy voice honed to a keen edge.

"Then good-bye, madam."

"I beg your pardon?" she said, looking startled.

"I do not wish to be discourteous, Lady Armstrong," Holmes said softly, "but really, we can do no business. You are wasting my time, and you are wasting Dr. Watson's time."

So saying, Holmes walked to the door and opened it wide. With a slight bow, a wave of his arm and a simultaneous questioning lift of his eyebrows, he bade Lady Armstrong to leave.

She did not move. She looked at me indignantly. She glared at Holmes, but said nothing. She remained perfectly still, and she remained seated.

"Very well, Mr. Holmes," she finally said. "Perhaps I forget myself. If you would close the door again . . . please."

The detective nodded. Lady Armstrong turned to me and said, "I am sorry, Dr. Watson. My desire for . . . confidentiality is really only that. It should not be taken personally."

I said nothing. The room was silent. The moment grew awkward.

"Doctor," she said, "I do not often apologize."

"Forgive me, Lady Armstrong," I said. "Yes. Of course I accept your apology."

She smiled but did not part her lips. "I think perhaps I would have some tea if that is still possible, Mr. Holmes."

"Of course," he said.

I have long suspected that Mrs. Hudson knows more about people, how they are likely to behave and what their needs might reasonably be in any social setting, than any seer possibly could divine. No sooner had Holmes opened the door to call her than in she marched with fresh tea steaming from a full silver service.

"There's plenty more, Mr. Holmes," she said, setting the service on the sideboard. "Just give me a call."

"Thank you, Mrs. Hudson."

She walked to the door and stopped briefly to stare at the dagger that was still stuck in the middle of it. She shook her head and left.

The instant the door clicked shut, Lady Armstrong arose from our couch, walked to the sideboard and took charge of the tea.

"Why don't you gentlemen sit down? I will serve," she said.

Any words that I might have used to express my shock at her behavior were lodged tightly in my throat, so I did as she suggested and said nothing.

Holmes was quiet, too. He bowed his head slightly, ever the gentleman, and sat. For more than thirty minutes, we discussed politics and pleasantries and holidays past, and through it all Lady Armstrong was gracious. She was solicitous. She was engaging. She was warm, agelessly feminine and almost coquettish. I can accurately report that by the time Lady Armstrong finally got down to business, I was quite charmed, though I still disliked the woman, and I certainly didn't trust her.

"Well," she said, "I suppose I must come to the point."

"Whenever you are ready," Holmes said. He had positioned himself directly across from our visitor, his elbows resting on the arms of his comfortable chair, the tips of his fingers tented together and supporting his chin.

"I have come here to hire you, Mr. Holmes," she said. "I believe I need your services."

"And why is that?" the detective asked.

"Because I am worried about my son, David, Lord Armstrong," she said. "Mr. Holmes, it is only with very great difficulty that I say this. David is my only child. He is all I

have in this world, really, and he means a great deal to me;
you must understand that despite the . . . despite the nature
of what I have to say to you."

She paused as if waiting for an answer.

Holmes nodded solemnly.

"Mr. Holmes, David is sincere to a fault, and he is loyal
and public-spirited, and he always has been willing to
work hard."

Holmes sighed, as if to signal his boredom.

"But David is a weak man, Mr. Holmes." The detective
stirred noticeably. "And, though I am loath to say it aloud,
sir, David is a drunk. By mid-evening he usually has rendered himself totally insensible, often for the second time
in the same day. Sometimes I find myself wondering if he
is ever completely sober. His condition has become more
and more noticeable as time has passed, so I suspect that
what I am saying comes as no shock."

Neither of us said a word.

"David also lacks physical presence, and I suspect that I
am merely stating the obvious when I add that he is not
especially good-looking. What's more, Mr. Holmes, I also
regret to say that he does not possess much more than a
very average intelligence. Please understand that however
unkind my remarks may seem, they are only observations."

"Lady Armstrong," Holmes said, "you have no need to
justify your remarks. You may trust that we see them as
they need to be seen. Pray, continue."

"Very well. My point is this: David is of a marriageable
age, but he is not a terribly appealing sort of man. And yet
I am supposed to believe that he somehow commands the
sincere love and devotion of that beautiful young creature
you saw him with earlier this week."

"Miss Ryder," Holmes said without stirring.

"Yes," Lady Armstrong said, "Miss Ryder. I do not like
her, though for David's sake I have tried to hide my real
feelings."

"Might you also be afraid that if Lord David marries,
you will be left dreadfully alone?"

"You need not remind me of the fact," Lady Armstrong
said flatly. "David is my son. I would miss him."

"Of course," Holmes said impatiently. "Of course. Let

us consider Miss Ryder apart from your son. Why do you dislike her?"

"She is an opportunist, Mr. Holmes. In plain language, a tramp. I believe she looks at my son and sees only the great wealth which, as my only child, he surely will inherit upon my demise. She is not to be trusted, Mr. Holmes, and neither is her brother."

"And why not, pray?" Holmes asked idly.

"His coarse actions betray him. I think he is a rogue. Lord knows, he is a gambler. I do not approve of gamblers."

"Gambling is not a crime, Lady Armstrong, and your dislike of the Ryders notwithstanding, I was led to believe that they do not need your fortune or anyone else's," Holmes said. "Are they not quite wealthy in their own right?"

"I am told so, yes . . . by them," Lady Armstrong said.

"I see," Holmes said. "Then allow me to come quickly to the point. If you were certain the Ryders are exactly what they appear—wealthy, self-absorbed young Americans on holiday—would you feel differently about the marriage?"

"Enough," Lady Armstrong said curtly. "I want you to find out the truth, Mr. Holmes."

"Ah, the truth," Holmes said. "But what if the truth proves to be other than what you suspect?"

Lady Armstrong had stiffened visibly as her words had grown more strident, and now, as she spoke, her back no longer touched the divan on which she was seated.

"Do not test me, Mr. Holmes. I do not like it." She paused, as if she was carefully considering what to say next. "I fully expect that my personal suspicions should have nothing whatsoever to do with your conclusions. You must reach them on your own," Lady Armstrong said.

Holmes clapped his hands together sharply and arose quickly from his chair, which startled me and left our guest blinking her eyes.

"Excellent!" Holmes exclaimed. "Excellent. We shall endeavor to help you, Lady Armstrong. And I have every reason to believe that we will be able to do so in a relatively brief period of time. But mark my words, I will hold you to your insistence on having the highest regard for the truth, regardless of the cost. Which brings me to my fee . . ."

"I expect that it will be high, Mr. Holmes. Else your time would not be worth mine."

"As you wish, Lady Armstrong."

"Then good day, gentlemen," she said. "It has been my pleasure." She stood as if to leave.

"One moment," Holmes said. "Is it still your intention to wear the Blood of Punjab at the benefit on New Year's Eve?"

"Is there some reason that I should not?"

"I am somewhat concerned for your safety," he said.

"Nonsense," she said. "That is why I have guards. They have proven their worth."

Holmes raised his eyebrows. "Really? When last?"

"April, if memory serves."

She started to walk to the door, but Holmes had not finished.

"One moment, Lady Armstrong . . . Please," he said. "What were the circumstances?"

"I don't see that it would have any . . ."

Holmes motioned her back to her seat on the divan.

"Oh, very well," she said. She sat down but with a deep sigh, as if she was tired of the discussion.

"There was a burglary at Planetree, but nothing came of it. Wilson saved the day . . . inelegantly but nevertheless. At the time he was staying in a room on the first floor not far from my study, which is where I keep the ruby. It is locked away in an especially sturdy wall safe, as you can imagine.

"Wilson awoke during the night and thought he heard noises downstairs. He grabbed his pistol, threw open the door to his room and ran out into the hall. An umbrella stand had been set in his way, and he upset it, making quite a racket. Then he noticed an eerie sort of light coming—"

Holmes fairly leaped at the word. He raised his right arm quickly, the palm of his hand facing Lady Armstrong.

"Eerie in what sense, pray?"

"Oh, he said the light seemed to be growing, somehow."

"In intensity?" Holmes asked, his eyes wide now.

"Why, yes," Lady Armstrong said. "I believe so. Yes."

"Ah, very good," Holmes said. "You may continue."

"Wilson said the light seemed to be coming from the study, or very near it. But when he tried to run down the stairs, he caught his ankle on a wire that had been wrapped around the base of the newel posts. Wilson tumbled headlong down to the ground floor. He was fortunate not to break his neck. When he came to his senses, the burglars were gone."

"The safe was intact?" Holmes asked.

"Yes," Lady Armstrong said. "They got nothing."

Holmes raised an index finger as if to remind the woman of something. "But they left a noxious odor in their wake, did they not?"

"Why, yes," she said. "The room was absolutely suffused with it. I had to throw open the windows just to . . . But how did you—"

"It is my business to know such things, Lady Armstrong," Holmes said. "Was there anything else? Say, a ragged burn mark of some note on the floor . . . or a carpet perhaps? Rather near the wall safe?"

"Well, both actually. Yes. I did notice a dark spot on the floor, and some time later I found a series of ragged holes in the carpet some distance away," she said. "Now that you mention it, the carpet holes were rather near the wall safe, but I didn't associate that with the burglary though. I just—"

"Ah," Holmes said, obviously satisfied with himself. "But previously the carpet had not been in disrepair? No moth damage, for example?"

"Of course not, Mr. Holmes," Lady Armstrong said with a slight edge to her voice.

"No, of course not," Holmes said. "Then the damage most likely would have been caused by a vial of spilled acid. The sudden racket made by your guard caused the intruders to spill it. Well, it serves them right, eh? No matter now, I suppose. The thieves were foiled, and all's well that ends well."

"Precisely," Lady Armstrong said. "The castle proved impregnable, the treasure unattainable. There's been not the merest spot of trouble since. So as you say, Mr. Holmes, 'All's well that ends well.' And now I really must go."

Holmes nodded once and arose at the same time as our guest.

"Happy Christmas, Mr. Holmes, and to you, too, Doctor."

We returned the sentiment, and she turned once again toward the door. She paused briefly to look at the dagger protruding from it.

"How very odd," she said without looking back. The closing of the door wafted her scent, a delicate suggestion of roses, across the room. It swept over us lightly, and she was gone.

I peeked through the window down into Baker Street again and watched as Lady Armstrong stepped into her brougham. She had been with us for well over an hour, and in all of that time, neither her driver nor her guard, Wilson, appeared to have moved at all. She climbed into the coach and closed the door behind her. Wilson pulled himself up beside the driver, and in a moment the rig pulled noiselessly out into the street.

"What a strange story," I said.

"Wasn't it though?" Holmes replied.

Chapter 17

I went about my business and then, some time later, noticed Holmes standing by the window staring pensively out into the street.

"Holmes?"

"Oh, yes. I was just thinking about Lady Armstrong's story."

"The burglary?" I asked.

"So-called, Watson, yes. Never was a priceless gem in less danger of being stolen than under those circumstances."

"I don't understand," I said.

"Elementary, really. No cracksman with any degree of sophistication would try to use acid on a stout and well-made wall safe, for one thing. And only an exceptionally good cracksman—and a bold one, I might add—would even consider taking on such a job in the first place. And if he did, he would want to finesse his way in. Acid would be an insult to his sense of professionalism. Furthermore, acid simply is not practical. It's messy, and Lord knows, it's dangerous. And how does one get the acid deep into the locking mechanism where it needs to do its work? Were they going to burn a hole through the safe? They would have needed a barrel of acid, Watson."

"Well, why would they have brought acid with them at all, then?" I asked. "For that matter, Holmes, why did you even suspect it?"

"I was trying to think of chemicals that stink that also might be associated, however erroneously, with cracking open a safe. Acid was a possibility."

"Ah," I said, "the noxious odor Lady Armstrong mentioned? . . . The acid eating through the carpet!" I exclaimed.

"Possible . . ." Holmes said.

"Indeed," I said.

". . . but not likely."

"Oh."

"The odor permeated the study, Watson. I think 'suf-fused' was the precise word Lady Armstrong used. A splash of acid would not have that effect. No, the source had to be something else."

"But what?" I asked.

The detective did not answer my question. Instead, he mused at Lady Armstrong's mention of an "eerie glow."

"I'd almost forgotten about that," I confessed.

"Mmm, yes. We must not," Holmes said. His brow was furrowed, his lips pursed together.

"Holmes," I said, "do you suppose the light and the nox-ious smell are tied together?"

"My good man," Holmes said with a sudden cheer-fulness, "I don't 'suppose' that is the case, I am certain of it. What's more, I know what caused it. But I dare not say until I can deduce just what happened in Lady Armstrong's study that night last April."

"It is so important?" I asked

"It is, indeed," Holmes said. "In fact, I would say that what happened in the study that night is crucial to our understanding of this entire affair. Well, I will have some-thing to grapple with as I go about my work this afternoon. The boy is coming over, is he not?"

"Yes," I said.

"Good. Good. Well, tell him I am looking forward to our Christmas dinner together, will you, Watson? I've barely spoken to him these past couple of days. I hope he understands."

"I'm sure he does," I said, which was a lie. Tommy didn't understand at all what Holmes was up to, but for that mat-ter, neither did I.

"Tell him I am going to an important meeting, Watson. It is only the truth."

"With whom?" I asked.

"John Godey," Holmes said, "but you had best not tell Tommy that."

Chapter 18

Holmes took Godey completely by surprise late that afternoon. The costerman was in Covent Garden wiping down his empty cart. Holmes walked up behind the man in silence.

"John Godey, isn't it?" he said, still walking. The costerman was startled beyond explanation. He wheeled around in the direction of Holmes' voice, the detective an apparition looming suddenly through the fog. Godey balled his huge right hand into a fist and brought it back past his ear, ready to unload a punch. Holmes stood directly before him now, his hands resting atop his walking stick. He smiled at Godey.

"We went through that once, if memory serves," Holmes said.

"Who the . . . ? Well, now," Godey said. "As I live an' breathe, if it ain't Mr. Sherlock 'Olmes!"

"It's been quite a long time," the detective said.

"Aye," Godey replied. "It has at that. Let me shake yer hand."

The two old combatants took each other's hand in a tight grip, and tried each other's strength for a lingering moment. Godey stared up into the detective's gray eyes and said, "I ain't what I was, Mr. 'Olmes." And then he let go of the detective's hand.

"What brings you here?" Godey asked. "It ain't Tommy? Tommy's all right, ain't he? If anything's 'appened—"

Holmes quickly held up his hand and nodded.

"The boy is fine," the detective said. "Just fine. I expect that he is having tea and biscuits with Dr. Watson and Mrs. Hudson even as we speak."

"Aach, that's good. I was worried for a moment there.

'At boy's been a blessin',' 'e has. I don't know what I'd do, anything 'appen to 'im. I . . . Oh, seein's 'ow I got the chance here, Mr. 'Olmes, I want to thank yeh fer the help with Tom's clothin' an' all."

"I was glad to do it," Holmes said.

The two men stood in silence, looking at each other. The noises of the market rose and swirled about them like the day's dank, oily fog.

"Uhm, so 'ave yeh got business here today, Mr. 'Olmes?"

"Just with you," Holmes said. "I thought it might be best if we met outside the house before tomorrow's dinner. Less awkward for both of us, no?"

"Aye. I been sort of wonderin' 'ow it'd go 'tween us," Godey said. "You know I don't blame you for what happened way back."

"A lesser man might," Holmes replied.

"Oh, well, that's nice of you, 'at is," Godey said. Then he gave Holmes a hard, inquiring look. " 'At ain't all yeh got on yer mind, though, is it now?"

Holmes responded with a tight and quick smile and looked quite pointedly at the top of Godey's right hand, which bore an unusual spider web of scar tissue.

"I judge from the redness of that scar, Mr. Godey, that it was received not too long ago. Say, last spring?"

Godey touched the scar with the fingers of his left hand, as if reminding himself of it.

"A nasty burn by the looks," Holmes said.

"Aye," Godey said. "I still 'urt to think on it. Melted lead's what did it."

"Really?" Holmes said.

"Aye. I was 'elpin' a friend who was makin' 'imself an anchor for a skiff he keeps. Some of the melt slops out of the mold when 'e's pourin' it. I told him, I says, 'Tink, you got too much melt there.' Tink Walters, it was. I says, 'Pour some off,' but he don't listen. And to top it off, when he does pour, he pours it too fast, and it slops and spatters an' it burns right through my gloves, it does."

"Mmmm," Holmes said distractedly, as though he hadn't been paying much attention to Godey's explanation. "You were fortunate not have been burned even more badly."

"Aye, 'at's a fact," Godey said.

They were silent, and then Holmes spoke quickly, and in a voice that was hard and thin.

"I'll be blunt about this," he said. "I think there is much going on here that you've not been forthright about from the very start. I believe you know a good deal about a botched burglary at Lady Armstrong's home last April. Furthermore, I think her prized jewel is still a target, and I think you know something about that, too."

"Think all yeh want, Mr. 'Olmes," Godey said, "but even if all 'at was so, I'd not be one to rat out anyone. I'd a figgered you'd know 'at."

"I do," Holmes said, "and I respect it. But that's not the point, is it? Not really." Holmes took a step forward and the costerman moved backward quickly.

"Let's get down to the hard nub of it, shall we, Mr. Godey?"

Holmes was talking faster now, although his voice, just as suddenly, was lower. He moved nearer to the costerman as he spoke, but this time Godey didn't back up.

"You don't give a fig what happens to you," Holmes declared. "No, you don't. It's all such a chore sometimes that you'd just as soon be done with it anyway. If they'd only come at you straight up and head on, you'd fight back as best you could and let the devil take the hindmost, eh? That's not hard to understand. It's no great mystery, not to me. Do you think I know nothing of such things? Do you?"

Godey's eyes were wide, not in fright but confusion, for he didn't know what to make of Holmes' outburst. The detective was so close to him that the costerman was bent slightly backward over his cart. Holmes jabbed his index finger into the costerman's chest.

"There's a hole in there; isn't that right, Godey? No doctor could ever find it, but it's there, eh? Just as sure as we're standing here."

Holmes backed up a step, looked down at the wet paving stones of the market, and took a breath so deep that it made his shoulders rise and fall. John Godey straightened up, too. He looked at the detective apprehensively.

Holmes' voice was little more than a whisper, and it was filled all at once with sadness and sympathy and a brilliant shining anger.

"They used the boy to get to you, didn't they, John? That's a hard thing for men like us to accept, hmm? If you dare to hold anyone dear, you become vulnerable. That's how they've pulled you in, isn't it? Isn't it?"

Godey lowered his head.

"Yes," Holmes said softly, the word trailing off like a serpent fleeing the light. "You're in it up to your neck."

"Don't you judge me, Mr. 'Olmes," Godey said. There was no anger in his words, and his eyes were downcast.

"I am not judging you," Holmes said. "Not at all, and I've already agreed to do what I can in the boy's behalf. I'll not go back on my word. But for his sake, if not your own, you had best watch your step. These are deep waters."

"Don't I know it," Godey said. "Don't I know it."

Holmes turned away, walked two steps and turned back to the costerman.

"Dinner tomorrow?"

"Aye," Godey said.

"You will bring the boy?"

"Aye."

Holmes nodded and turned to leave.

" 'Ey, wait."

Holmes turned and looked at Godey.

"You ever think back on 'at night at Seven Dials?"

"Many times," Holmes said. "What about it?"

" 'Aaw, 'at was some good fight, 'at was. I thought I come awful close," Godey said.

He raised his big fists, jabbed at the shadows and started moving his feet in a quick little shuffle.

"I thought I almost 'ad ya."

"So did I," Holmes said. "You were very good."

"Acch!" Godey exclaimed. "I knew it. Almost had yeh, eh? Real close, wasn't it? Cor, I thought so! Lucky thing you uncorked that big right just when you did, eh? I'd a 'ad yeh fer sure. I knew it."

Godey hooked his left fist at the air a couple of times, fighting the shadows. He winked at Holmes and nodded, and then threw a right cross.

The detective smiled wistfully, nodded, and walked back into the darkening fog.

John Godey didn't watch him go. He was busy with his shadows.

Chapter 19

Christmas morning dawned bright, sunny and sharply cold. I put on my heaviest robe and slippers and went, half awake, into the parlor. I found Holmes sitting in a veritable cloud of blue-gray smoke, which told me much. The detective sometimes measured the complexity of a problem by the number of pipefuls he smoked en route to a solution.

"Merry Christmas, Watson," he said.

"And to you, old man," I said, but could not help coughing even before I had gotten the words out. "Holmes, it's stifling in here. Have you been up all night?"

"What was that, Watson? Oh, yes. Quite. I have been working on our little problem."

"How many pipes does this one merit?"

"Oh, I lost track some time ago, I'm afraid."

"You won't mind if I open a couple of windows?"

The detective was so lost in his thoughts that he did not hear my question. I opened two windows and the cold winter air began flowing freely in through one, straight across the room, and right out the other. The smoke disappeared quickly, but by the time I could close the windows, I could see my own breath and I was beginning to shiver. I pulled my robe more tightly around me, but Holmes remained unaffected all the while.

"What time is Mrs. Hudson seating us?" he asked.

"I believe dinner is at two," I said.

"And our guests?"

"Tommy and his uncle will arrive about one o'clock, or perhaps half-one."

"Very good," Holmes said. "I must go out and tend to a couple of chores and—"

"Chores, Holmes?" I said sharply. "It may interest you to know that nearly all of the shops are closed on Christmas Day. So are the banks. And the apothecaries. And tobacconists. Clothiers of every stripe. I should think you will find it quite impossible to do chores today because everything is closed. Why, there probably will even be fewer hansom cabs to be had today."

I continued in this vein for some minutes. Holmes sat quite still, as unmoved by tirade as he had been by temperature.

Then, finally, he interrupted. "Are you quite finished?" he asked.

"Quite!" I said. I rather forcefully tamped some of my Arcadia mixture into my own well-worn briar pipe and lighted it.

"Telegraph offices, you may recall, are open on Christmas Day," Holmes said.

"Quite," I said again, though this time feeling like quite the fool.

"Now, if you would be so kind," Holmes said, "please open the door for Mrs. Hudson. I believe that she is at the top of the stairs, and judging from her footsteps, she is carrying something heavy."

I opened the door to find Mrs. Hudson bearing a serving tray so large that she could barely reach the far edge of it even with her arms stretched straight out to their very limits.

"Good Lord, don't drop it," I said. "Here, let me help you."

I carried the tray to the sideboard, but when I turned around Mrs. Hudson was coming back into the room bearing another, and it was no less full than the first.

When I had helped her set out the meal, what sat before us was a table fit for royalty. There were two different dishes of eggs, toast, scones, marmalade, bacon, a variety of sausages, ham steaks, a smoked haddock and rice dish that had a name I could not recall, a meat pie of veal and ham, juice and tea.

Mrs. Hudson normally was the most modest of women, but her pride was rarely disguised where her cooking was concerned.

"Holmes," I exclaimed, "will you look at this? What a feast Mrs. Hudson has got up for us!"

"Will I look at it?" Holmes said. "I can't take my eyes away . . . Mrs. Hudson, is that kedgeree you've made? You shouldn't have; I'm sure smoked haddock has been dear of late. Really, you have quite outdone yourself."

"Oh, be off with you," she said, obviously pleased with Holmes' praise. "I've got much too much to do before dinner to be wastin' more time with the likes of you two. Lord, it's freezing in here! Did you leave the windows open all night?"

Mrs. Hudson heaped more coal on the fire, shook down the ash, and waited briefly as the heat began to come up.

"I swear, you would freeze up here," she said, more to herself than to us. She hurried toward the door. From the hall, she called back, "Merry Christmas . . . and don't be late."

As soon as she had left, Holmes walked over to the fire and spread the coals out to the corners of the hearth, away from the focus of the heat. He was trying to slow the rise in temperature that Mrs. Hudson had made inevitable.

"I have no idea why Mrs. Hudson enjoys such impeccable good health, Watson. She works constantly. She seems to live on tea and scones and the occasional biscuit. And she is always cold. There are cadavers in the teaching surgery at St. Bart's with better circulation, I swear."

"Well, Holmes," I said, "by the time I could close those windows I'd opened to get rid of the smoke in here, I was freezing, too."

"Seriously?"

"Yes, Holmes. It was nearly as cold in here as it was out in the street. You didn't notice?"

"I'm afraid that my concentration was elsewhere, Watson. I have to say that the matter at hand has me somewhat . . . confused."

"Well, I can't understand why you are confused, Holmes. I mean, think about it for a moment. Let's just look at the pieces, shall we?

"We have a poor street boy becoming a guest at one of the season's most talked-about soirees, needing us to protect him, though we are not yet certain just what it is or who it is we are protecting him from. Let us not forget that the boy's guardian is someone you helped send off to prison many years ago, but who seems to have since turned himself into a reliable citizen."

"Hmmm," Holmes said. "By all means, continue."

"Now, that business really should be an end in itself," I said, "but it turns out that it is not. Why? Well, because the hostess of the benefit, who is one of the wealthiest women in the entire country and who is, let us not forget, the proud owner of a legendary gemstone that many men would kill for, has simultaneously hired us.

"And why? Because she fears something is amiss with a beautiful young woman from America who has fallen for her son, who, while he may be a nice fellow, also is something of a toad and an inebriate.

"And if that scenario should not be enough to put it all on a music hall stage, Holmes, consider that off in the wings we have the young woman's brother. He bears looking at, too. He is a wealthy businessman, but also an amateur gambler of some local repute and a decidedly peevish sort of fellow, who quite possibly is something of a rogue in his own right.

"Now, let us not forget that somewhere in the background we have a roving Italian violinist who appears to be well known to most of the civilized world, and who is going to grace us all with his presence and a concert. But before that happens, an imposter shows up and causes a spot of bother by placing Christmas messages in your name in two of the city's biggest newspapers . . . Lord only knows why.

"And you call this confusing, Holmes? I wouldn't call it confusing, old fellow; I would call it bizarre, maddening, nightmarish perhaps, but confusing really doesn't do it justice, do you think?"

Holmes smiled.

"You really have been paying attention, haven't you, Watson? A very apt summation, I think. Unfortunately, it is all every bit as strange as you have cast it."

He sat silently for a moment staring at the floor.

"Perhaps this will raise your spirits," I said. I reached into my pocket and withdrew a small wrapped box.

"Merry Christmas, Holmes," I said.

"And Merry Christmas to you, Watson," he said. As he spoke, he walked over to his bookcase and reached for a leather-bound book. For a moment I feared that my gift was to be a study of Etruscan history. Instead, Holmes reached behind the book and withdrew a wrapped box that appeared to be nearly the same size as the one I had given him.

We caught each other taking note of the similarity, but said nothing. We opened our presents at the same time.

"A new briar," he said, looking at his gift. "Thank you, Watson."

"A new briar," I said, looking at my gift. "Thank you, Holmes."

We looked at each other and shook our heads, for the two pipes appeared identical: a medium-sized bowl, an oblate shank encircled by a narrow band of gold and a good black bit.

"I think that sometimes neither of us is blessed with much imagination, Watson," my friend said.

"Not so, Holmes," I said. "Closer examination will reveal that your pipe is different."

"Indeed?" Holmes said. "Let's see." He studied the two. "Ah, yes," he said, "the stem of mine is decidedly longer."

"As is appropriate for someone of your height," I said. "I have noticed that you prefer a long stem. You will note, Holmes, that sometimes I see and, in fact, I also observe . . . contrary to the oft-delivered opinion of a certain detective."

"I stand in awe of your powers of observation, Watson," he said, bowing slightly, "and of your impeccable taste."

"Our impeccable taste," I said.

"Indeed," Holmes replied, "and, by the way, I meant to commend you for seeing that young Tommy had a chance to buy a present for his uncle John."

He tamped a small amount of tobacco into the bowl of his new pipe and waited for my reaction.

"How did you know that I, uhm . . . that we had bought gloves for John Godey? I don't recall telling you that I had done so."

"The receipt must have fallen from your coat pocket," Holmes said. "I have it."

"How did you know what it was for?" I asked.

"Well, it was from Hazelton's, and while gloves are not all that they sell, it is the product for which they are best known," he said. "Neither of us seems in need of gloves, which raised the question, 'Who would be?' The price seemed exorbitant to me, even for the finest leather in that store, so I concluded that it had to reflect the uniqueness of the item. That suggested an outsized hand. It was not awfully taxing to go from that point to John Godey, you see."

"They threw in gloves for the boy," I said.

"They should have thrown in gloves for us, too, at that price, eh?" Holmes said. "But I am not caviling; you made a good choice."

We talked good-naturedly through our fine breakfast and then fell silent. I could hear carolers in the street.

"The spirit of the day seems to have lifted your mood, Holmes."

"Perhaps it has, Watson. Perhaps it has. And that being the case, sir, I think I had better take advantage of my good mood and get out and about before it changes. I'll be back in ample time for dinner, Watson. Don't you fear."

"As you wish, Holmes," I said. "I think I shall do the same myself in a few minutes."

And I did just that, and for longer than I had planned. For nearly two hours I strolled leisurely through the West End, listening to carolers and church bells, stopping briefly to admire innumerable town house doors and entrances that had been fancily decorated with long garlands of bayberry and ivy and evergreen boughs. There were swags and wreaths made from spiky deep green hollies or full branches of soft, lush yew. There were fragrant boughs of spruce, hemlock and pine and shiny sprigs of boxwood. Invariably, they were all carefully and creatively bound up by colorful wide holiday ribbons of every color imaginable: bright green, gold, silver, red, pink, yellow, white, even a blue here and there, and plaids, too. I could see gaily decorated Christmas trees in the windows of some homes. In all, it was a grand and cheerful day, and I was not alone in thinking it so. I was wished an enthusiastic "Merry Christmas" by no fewer than twenty other strollers, men, women and children alike, in just the first half hour of my sojourn. I returned the salutation in kind and stopped counting after that.

I returned to Baker Street with my spirit renewed and my disposition better than it had been in weeks. Holmes had returned. We gave Mrs. Hudson her gifts, a fine woollen shawl and a silver brooch with an unmistakable thistle done in filigree. She was so taken with them that tears welled up in her eyes. We pretended not to notice and instead lavished considerable praise on her household decorations—and with just cause.

The Christmas tree, a well-shaped little spruce, was placed in a stand and set atop a table in the window. The tree was decorated with colored ribbons, foil-wrapped candies, paper flowers, shimmering garlands of gold tinsel and unlighted white candles. A long full and fragrant garland of bayberry leaves was carefully draped over the fireplace mantel. The sideboard was covered with what I knew to be Mrs. Hudson's hand-woven holiday linen. The large dining table was covered with a crimson coverlet over which had been laid a tablecloth of fine Irish lace. The centerpiece was beautiful, too: fresh flowers, small sprigs of evergreen and a spray of red and gold ribbons. Everywhere I turned, Mrs. Hudson had set a bowl of candies, nuts or fruits.

"Holmes," I whispered, "she must have been up all night, what with the cooking and decorating and all. And look at the tree, will you!"

"She was," Holmes said in an equally low voice. "I can attest to that. I heard her working."

"But it was fun, you see, so it did not matter," Mrs. Hudson said, for no sound ever seemed to escape her notice.

She was suddenly startled by three hard raps from the brass knocker on the front door.

"That must be our guests," Mrs. Hudson said, "and right on time they are."

"Permit me," I said, already walking toward the door.

Tommy and John Godey chimed out a loud and hearty "Merry Christmas" in unison at almost the instant I opened the door. They said it so forcefully that I was startled, and I stepped back. The look on my face must have been comical, because both of our visitors immediately set to laughing. I joined them, returned the greeting and shook their hands as I closed the door behind them and took their coats.

"We are right on time, Doc Watson," Tommy chirped.

I pulled out my pocket watch and opened it. "So you are. Exactly half-one," I said.

Next thing I knew, Tommy was quite ceremoniously studying the face of a new watch that he had pulled from his own pocket.

"It is that," he said. "Exactly. It's just now half-one."

"Well, Master Tommy," I said, "someone seems to have a fine new watch. May I see?"

I opened it and noted the inscription: "For my boy Thomas P. Rogers, with love, Uncle John. 25 December, 1889."

"Well, what a fine gift, young man," I said.

"I've never had no watch of my own," Tommy said.

"Well, you certainly have one now," I said. "A fine one. Take proper care of it, and it should last you forever. Say, Mr. Godey, are those new gloves?" I asked.

"Indeed they are, Doctor. Tommy got them for me for Christmas. Ain't they fine, though? Best gloves I've ever 'ad, I'll tell you."

"Well, good for you," I said.

Holmes, who had been leaning against the sideboard watching us greet each other, suddenly came forward with a smile on his face and his arms spread wide in a welcoming gesture.

"Merry Christmas to you both," he said, "and thank you for joining us. Mr. Godey, it is a pleasure to meet you. Tommy has spoken of you so often that I feel as though we already know each other."

Holmes extended his hand, and as Godey took it in his own, I saw the detective wink at him ever so quickly.

"Aye, Mr. 'Olmes," Godey said. "It does seem that way."

Mrs. Hudson brought us cups of hot mulled cider. The boy presented her with a red holiday candle set into a varnished piece of silver birch and decorated with dark English ivy, and some sprigs of yew dotted liberally with small red berries.

" 'Is is for you, ma'am," he said, holding the gift up to our landlady with both hands. "It's from me and my uncle John here. It's not much, Mrs. Hudson, but we wanted to say thanks for invitin' us today and for all the help you've been givin' me, with the lessons and all."

"Aye, ma'am," John Godey said. "I wish things 'as so we could do more, you've been so good with the boy an' all. But thank you. Thank you kindly, ma'am."

I don't think I have ever seen Mrs. Hudson more at a loss for words than she was at that moment. She tried to speak but stopped, swallowed visibly a couple of times, cleared her throat and took two breaths that were so deep her shoulders shrugged. When she did speak, her voice sounded brittle.

"Well," she said, "aren't you the pair, the two of ya, to be bringin' me such a wonderful present. Would you look at this? I don't think I've ever seen its likes. Have you, Doctor? Mr. Holmes? It will serve nicely right here on the sideboard, in the middle of all of the pies and sweets here. Isn't it beautiful? Now when the holiday's over, I'll be packing it up carefully so I can set it out again next year, and the year after that, and the year after that. And every Christmas it'll remind me of you both."

Tommy nudged his uncle, as if to say, "See, I told you she'd love it." Godey nodded in assent. Mrs. Hudson went off to the kitchen, and the four of us spent a few minutes in pleasant conversation remarkable only for its lack of gravity and import, for that was exactly what the day called for.

Mrs. Hudson's dinner was one of the best I had ever seen, let alone eaten. I had always thought her to be a good cook, but this was truly wonderful. The heart of it was a Christmas goose, filled with a peach, apricot and cornbread stuffing and cooked to a delicate caramel brown. On its own, it was a grand sight and the centerpiece of a wonderful meal, but flanked as it was by a roast beef and a large glazed ham, it was nothing short of spectacular. There were brussels sprouts, carrots, nested onions, sweet potatoes, seasoned mashed potatoes, three different breads, rolls, sillibub, compote, cranberry sauce, a full-bodied red wine, a delicate white wine, milk and tea.

Mrs. Hudson served us a fine rich Christmas pudding with a thick cream topping and all aflame in brandy—as I said, spectacular. Tommy, wide-eyed and eager, dug his spoon into the pudding and promptly scooped out, to his obvious surprise, a silver coin.

"A crown!" Tommy exclaimed, his eyes wide with excitement.

"'At means sartin' luck for you, it does, Tommy me boy," John Godey said.

"Who deserves it more?" I asked.

"Here. Here," Holmes said.

"Ooh," Mrs. Hudson said. "You are the lucky one."

Tommy's smile spread from ear to ear. He wiped the crown clean on his napkin and, without thinking, raised it toward his mouth, but stopped short with an embarrassed look. He knew the coin was real. It was inconceivable that anyone present could lie to him. He put it in his pocket, and a look of befuddlement appeared on his face.

"Beggin' your pardon, Mrs. Hudson," he said, "but who do I thank for my crown?"

"Why, Father Christmas, I suppose. Old St. Nick," she said. "Who else might it be?"

"Well, I didn't know but what you . . . Well, I don't know, Mrs. Hudson, but . . ."

"'T wasn't me, young man," she said, "and don't you go thinking it's so, either. I don't have so much money I can afford to go leavin' it around in the pudding, do I now?" The tone of her voice was serious enough, but anyone who knew the dear woman would have recognized the playful light that danced in her eyes. As it happened, though, she was telling the truth. I had seen Holmes slip the coin into the pudding, and I had heard him show Mrs. Hudson which of the five dishes was to be served to Tommy.

"Father Christmas, eh?" Tommy asked. "I see. Well, Father Christmas or St. Nick or whatever your proper name is, Thomas Payton Rogers thanks you kindly for his gift." He looked at each of us in turn as he spoke. "And if you present yourself tomorrow at his cart in Covent Garden, you've a bag of fine turnips coming to you. Oh, not tomorrow, seein' as it's Boxin' Day, but the day after'll do. So you be sharp and look us up."

We all laughed, but John Godey's laugh turned suddenly into a long, low and deep cough that rumbled and rattled inside his chest.

I watched the poor man handle it as best he could, and out of the corner of my eye, I noticed Mrs. Hudson. The instant Godey's cough had begun, she had taken the linen napkin from her lap and clenched it so tightly in her fist that the skin across her knuckles turned white. Her fist was pressed against her mouth, as if to keep from crying out. The color had drained from her face, and I could see in her eyes the strain of desperate panic.

I stood quickly and went to her side.

"Mrs. Hudson," I asked, "are you quite all right?"

She pushed me away, dabbed the linen napkin at her eyes and stood. She walked to John Godey's side, put a firm hand under his elbow and nudged him to get out of his chair.

He looked at her questioningly, helplessly, as the coughs continued to shake his body, in one wave after another. He managed to rise, however, and with Mrs. Hudson's assistance slowly walked out of the room.

"We're going to have us some tea in the kitchen," she called back over her shoulder. "We'll be fine. You help yourselves to the dishes on the sideboard. I didn't do all that baking so as to give it away now."

We had been so taken by the main meal and the day's pleasantries that we had barely noticed the spread of sweets that she had set out for us. The sideboard was filled with fruit pies, mince and cherry tarts, biscuits and a rich Christmas cake.

"Tommy, do you see anything there you might still have room for?" Holmes asked the boy.

"Oh, aye, sir," the boy said. "I'd have some apple pie if I could."

"Are you doing the honors, Holmes?" I asked. "Because if you are, then perhaps you would be good enough to serve me a small piece as well. Can't have our guest here eating alone, can we?"

"I should say not," Holmes said.

Mrs. Hudson later told me in detail what transpired in

the kitchen. She sat John Godey at her kitchen table and poured him some of her "medicinal tea." I don't know exactly what was in the concoction, but I recall from personal experience that it is strong, dark, sweet, decidedly alcoholic and served just short of the boil.

"You shouldn't be fussin' over me, ma'am," Godey said. "You've gone to enough trouble today."

"Don't give me any of your nonsense, John Godey. We'll talk plain. When last I heard a cough like that, it was my husband's. You'll forgive me for sayin' it, and on the Lord's own birthday, too, but my John's been dead many a year now, God rest his soul. And as long as I draw breath I'll never forget the sound of that cough. That's what I heard in you just a minute ago, a dead man's cough, plain enough."

"Aye, ma'am," Godey said. "I've know'd it for a while. You'll excuse me for sayin' so, but the 'sumption could 'ave me buried before you get to yer point . . . No offense, now."

"None taken," Mrs. Hudson said. "My point is this, sir: That's a fine boy you've raised there, Mr. Godey, and I want to know . . . Well, sir, have you made provisions for him? What will become of the boy when you're gone?"

Godey's eyes had never left Mrs. Hudson's face. He sat slumped back in his chair, weak and unsteady from the coughing fit, but when Mrs. Hudson asked her question, Godey did his best to sit up straight, as if he were a student unexpectedly called upon to read aloud in class.

He leaned forward, set his mug on the table and with obvious pride said, "Tommy will be all right, Missus Hudson. You can bet I've made plans for him. Truth be told, speakin' in money terms, he'll be a far sight better off when I'm gone. Not right away, mind, but later. I've seen to 'at in no unsartin' terms."

"Really?" Mrs. Hudson said.

"Oh, aye," John Godey said. "Don't you worry, ma'am. But I thank you all the same." Then he fell to coughing, harder and longer this time.

Mrs. Hudson opened the new silver brooch that held her shawl closed. She removed the garment, gently spread it across Godey's broad shoulders and tugged the ends gently down around his neck for warmth. And they sat together like that until the man's coughing at last subsided.

Chapter 20

(John Godey had long ago established the practice of recording his thoughts and activities in a daily journal, and I have drawn from that homely chronicle in preparing the following part of the narrative. I have supplemented it, of course, with the results of numerous interviews and, where necessary and appropriate, my own deductions and observations. I am confident that it is as accurate a representation of the day's events as any man might assemble.)

John Godey awoke at first light on Boxing Day. False dawn, some call it, those dead quiet minutes of heather gray half-light that precede the winter sun. He lay in his bed with his hands behind his head, listening to the small noises rising from the downstairs kitchen. The noise was reassuring, he thought, oddly warming somehow, like listening to the clanks and groans of the radiators when the pressure in the pipes was uneven or rising.

It had been a nice Christmas day; in fact, he was hard pressed to remember one better. He replayed every moment of it, and had already recorded it in his journal, lingering on the images and impressions that he found most pleasing: the look on Tommy's face when he'd given him his new watch; the boy's obvious pride and satisfaction when it became clear the new gloves he'd bought his uncle fit just right; the surprise on his face when he found the lucky coin in his Christmas pudding. The more John Godey thought about Tommy, the happier he became.

You couldn't ask for a better boy. Lord, wasn't he in a hurry to get there yesterday. And who'd blame him? The smells of Mrs. Hudson's fine rich cooking seemed to fill every corner and crevice of the Baker Street house. And

how about that old girl? Hmph! It was a marvelous thing
that he should be so comforted in his pain, and by a
stranger, no less. Such a surprise, this feeling accepted in
that house—in Sherlock Holmes' house, no less—and
maybe even valued. It occurred to John Godey that in most
ways his life had never been better. And it struck him that
it was odd and, in a way, cruel that that should be the case
now, to think that he should find such comfort and simple
pleasure just as his days seemed to be slipping away. It was
enough to make a weak man bitter, but he was not a weak
man, at least not in that way.

Godey got out of bed, went down the hall to the bathroom and then walked downstairs to the day room, the big
room where everyone took their meals. It was a room of
windows—more windows on one long side of the room, in
fact, than there were on the entire opposite side of Hope
Settlement House. The room was long and rectangular and
it was divided in two by a huge fireplace with back-to-back
hearths. At one end was a big larder. The kitchen ran the
full length of the inside wall, and at the other end, smack
in the center of the bank of windows that formed the end
wall, stood a marvelous Christmas tree, a fully adorned
spruce tree that easily rose twelve feet high. The children
had all had a hand in making and hanging the decorations
and draping the long silver-tinsel garlands. It fell to the
older ones to decorate the top of the tree, because the job
had to be executed from the top of a tall folding ladder.
But when it came time to choose who would set the winged
angel atop the tree this year, all of the children drew straws.
And Tommy had won.

Two of the bigger boys locked their legs around the ladder to anchor it. Tommy, who was not at all fond of heights,
swallowed hard, tucked the big angel under his left arm,
and with his right steadied himself as he slowly climbed the
ladder. From the very top step he had just barely been able
to touch the tip of the tree. He reached over the tip and
gingerly lowered the angel down over it. When he took his
hand away, all of the children cheered.

The angel sat a bit crookedly on her perch now, but
looking at her made John Godey smile. And he had to
laugh aloud when he looked at the base of the tree, for

spreading out a good ten feet on the floor around it was a sea of boxed gifts at least two layers deep and all sealed up in gay holiday wrapping, with colorful ribbons and big bows.

Godey was old enough to remember when Boxing Day was known mostly as St. Stephen's Day, when all of the churches in the city opened their alms boxes and doled out the contents to the poor of their parishes. While the alms boxes were still emptied for the poor, it had become more the custom, especially for those in service, to bring an empty box to their regular customers and patrons, who would fill it with small gifts. And increasingly it was the preferred custom for the rich to bring gift boxes to the poorest of the poor. Hence, the display that spread out from the base of the tree. The gifts had been dropped off at Hope Settlement over the past few days, and the house staff had dutifully positioned each one. Every box was tagged, but only to indicate suitability for a boy or girl, man or woman.

John Godey returned to his room, dressed and stood for a moment at the window, lost in his thoughts, surveying the brightening dawn. He bent over, put a big hand on his nephew's shoulder and said, "Wake up, Tommy, m'boy. Wake up. It's Boxing Day, lad. You don't want to miss out, do ya now?"

The boy sat up in his bed, rubbed the sleep from his eyes and stretched.

"Mornin', Uncle," he said, a big smile spreading across his face.

"Get movin' now, Tom," Godey said. "You don't want to be late."

"Aye," Tommy said. A scant few minutes later, he was walking into the big day room with his friends, easily more than three dozen of them, and most of the roughly fifty adults who were Hope residents, too, for they enjoyed surprises and gleeful spectacle as much as anyone.

The event was always a little raucous, and from the opening of the first gift, a lovely doll with a complete change of dress, this year's was no different. Cups of hot cocoa got slurped and spilled, and the littlest children, as always, argued over candy and who had popped open a Christmas cracker already and who hadn't yet taken a turn. At the edge of it all, two of the matrons tried their level best to lead a disheveled assemblage of carolers in a spirited rendition of "Good King Wenceslas."

John Godey was right up front, torn wrapping paper swirling all around him and two other adults as they handed out gifts to the children.

"My turn, Uncle," Tommy called out. He ran around to the front from behind a knot of children who were considerably taller and somewhat more aggressive than he.

"Uncle John. Over here," he said.

Godey looked at the boy and then down at the pile of gifts. He spied a rich-looking box wrapped in gold foil with a red ribbon. It was about a foot square. He picked it up and was surprised at its heft. He held it in both hands, wondering for an instant why this gift box seemed somehow different from the dozens and dozens of others he had been handling so quickly in the past few minutes, and then it was gone. Tommy had run up and grabbed it, laughing. The boy took four running steps and sat down hard with the box on his lap. He tore at the paper quickly. Godey was still bothered, still curious. He walked over to his nephew just as the boy tore the gold paper and lifted the top off the box.

They both looked inside at about the same time, but Godey was still several feet away. The contents didn't register with the boy. It was a box of metal pieces and nails and junk, and then a little wisp of smoke curled up out of it and . . .

John Godey screamed. It was an unearthly and terrible sound, because his voice was the voice of a grown man, but it was as loud as any scream could be and it cut through the holiday mayhem. It hung in the air and reverberated off the hard walls and ceiling and floor and all of the glass as though it were its own undying echo: "Nooooooo!" And no one who was there ever forgot the sound or what happened inside it. "Nooooooo!"

And then John Godey, gnarled and bowed by his years, threw himself headlong at the box, hitting Tommy in the shoulder and kicking him over hard and onto the tile floor of the day room. "Nooooooo!"

The box skittered ten feet out onto the floor and Godey, hunched over, his arms reaching out, his big hands moving, stumbled after it, still screaming, "Nooooooo!" Then he had the thing in his hands and he ran as hard as any man could straight for the door at the back corner of the room.

The explosion was hard, sharp and deafening. It left stinking white smoke in the air, and it blew the heavy door, intact, straight out into the yard. It punched a big hole in the huge windows of two adjoining walls, and all of the glass around the hole split into pieces and dropped onto the floor and split again into thousands of shards that licked out like gleaming little razors into the stunned crowd, where men and women and boys and girls already were crying and screaming. Suddenly many more were bleeding. Some were cut by the glass, and some were hit by the small jagged pieces of metal and sharpened horseshoe nails that had given the bomb its lethal weight.

John Godey lay crumpled and broken on the floor, the holes in the walls gaping wide behind him. He had lost fingers from both of his big hands. Part of his left side had been blown away, exposing a hideous white curve of rib bones. There were cuts on his face and a deep gash across his forehead, and pieces of metal and sharpened horseshoe nails were embedded in his throat. By rights, he should have been dead before he hit the floor. Instead, he hung on, pawing at the bright red oxygenated blood that burbled obscenely from his throat.

Tommy ran through the smoke and the havoc and fell to his uncle's side. He put his small hands over the bloody hole at John Godey's throat, trying in vain to stop what was happening.

"Uncle! Oh, Uncle John! No. You can't die, Uncle John. No. Please, don't leave me. Uncle John."

The man's voice, if it could still be called that, was low and wet and ragged, and Tommy could barely make out his words.

"Be . . . strong . . . love . . . you . . . Tommy."

And then John Godey exhaled, just one rough gasp and his pain was mercifully over.

Bitter cold winter air poured into the room through the holes in the walls. The shrieking of the wounded had turned to cries and moans. The blood all over the boy's hands and clothes suddenly felt sticky. Tommy jumped to his feet, crying, gasping, making sounds that were not words, frantically wiping his hands and arms. Then he stopped and was silent. He wiped his eyes and his nose across the back of his shirt sleeve and walked over to where he had fallen to the floor with the box in his lap.

He saw a big piece of the embossed gold wrapping that had enclosed the bomb, and he bent over and picked it up, as though seeing it for the first time. In all of the excitement and in his eagerness to open this fancy Boxing Day gift, there was something he had not noticed before; it was taped to the wrapping. Tommy tore it off and examined it, turning it over in his hands, still awash with blood, and then in shocked disbelief he crushed it in his fist and screamed out, "Nooooo!" at the top of his lungs exactly the way his beloved uncle John had screamed. He could hear people running and he could see the matrons coming to him, "Noooo!" and he started to run, but backward, tripping "Nooooo!" and stumbling and falling and the boy cracked his head sharply on the tiled floor and for a moment all he could see was tiny lights on a darkening field and then the entire room seemed to close in on him.

Chapter 21

I had just set out for a walk and was less than a block from our rooms on Baker Street when I heard the news-boy hawking an emergency edition of *The Daily Telegraph*.

"Extra! Extra! Settlement house bombed in East End. Hero gives own life to save l'il 'uns. Extra! Boxing Day bombing. Hope Settlement House. Extra!"

"Here, boy," I said, handing him a coin. I read the broadsheet and couldn't believe my eyes.

"Good Lord!" I exclaimed.

I ran back to our quarters and raced inside and up the stairs. I threw open the door to find Holmes standing in the middle of the parlor with his arms folded across his chest, waiting for me with a pained and angry expression on his face.

"I heard noise in the street and cracked the window," he said. "I could just make out the headline, but I have the gist. How many were killed, Watson?"

"One . . . John Godey."

"And Tommy? What of the boy?"

"I judge from this account that he is all right, thank God."

The next thing I knew, we were hailing a hansom cab and promising the driver a half-crown gratvity if he got us over to the East End in a hurry, which he did; we arrived at Hope Settlement House in a matter of minutes.

The entrance was blocked by a uniformed police officer whom neither of us had met before. He was a tall, broad-shouldered man with a bushy mustache and eyes that were dark and lifeless.

Holmes handed him his card, and while the officer looked at it, he said, "This is my companion, Dr. John H. Watson."

"I think I've heard of the two of you," he said. "I'm Constable Ridley Thompson. No disrespect, but I'm under strict orders not to let anyone in."

"Surely, Mr. Holmes is an exception, Constable," I said.

"No exceptions," he said stiffly. "Sorry. Those is my orders."

"I understand completely, Constable Thompson," Holmes said. "Perhaps if you would be good enough to tell whoever is in charge—"

"I can't do that, sir. I'd have to be leavin' my post now, wouldn't I? Inspector Lestrade would have me badge, 'e would. And I am under the strictest orders, sir—"

"Yes," Holmes said. "So I have divined. Let me explain it this way, Constable. Dr. Watson and I have very often solved—we have sometimes been of considerable help to the good inspector. In fact," Holmes said, raising his voice, "we have been of *so* much help that I daresay Lestrade will be more angry that you have kept us from the scene of this crime than if you were to leave us standing here before a locked door for a moment while you sought his advice."

Holmes was running out of patience quickly, and it was clear that Thompson was getting angry. In fact, I don't think the man actually was listening to Holmes' request. He seemed instead to have fastened on the fact that Holmes dared to challenge him. By the time the detective had finished speaking, the constable was tapping his night stick against the side of his leg.

"Now you understand this, Mr. Detective, *sir*. I don't care for your fancy attitude, *sir,* and I am not about to—"

The door opened behind Thompson; Lestrade interrupted him.

The hatchet-faced inspector nodded at us. Thompson turned to look at him.

"Is there a problem here, Constable?" Lestrade asked.

"These two blokes—"

"These two are not 'blokes,' Constable. I'm sure they have properly introduced themselves. They are friends of the Yard."

"Sir, you told me—"

"I know what I told you, Constable," Lestrade said with

exaggerated patience. "I should have told you to let them in the instant they arrived. My fault. Are we clear on this, Thompson, or do you want me to repeat it?"

"Very good, sir," Thompson said. "Thank you, sir."

"Any time, Constable."

Thompson turned rigidly and looked at us. And then, quite pointedly, he looked beyond us, obviously angry that we had bested him.

We followed Lestrade into the day room and stood there surveying the wreckage. It was like looking in on a walled battlefield. An emergency surgery had been set up to one side, and settlement house matrons and three nurses and two doctors who had come running from a nearby clinic were busy with patients. I took off my coat and rolled up my sleeves.

"Holmes," I said, "these poor people need me more than you do. I'm going to volunteer my services for a while."

"Of course," Holmes said.

"Inspector," I said, nodding to Lestrade.

Holmes—as always—later filled me in on the conversation exactly as it transpired.

"I don't mind telling you, Mr. Holmes, this is one of the nastiest bits I've ever seen. What's it all comin' to when some fiend can explode a bomb in a poorhouse? And on Boxing Day, no less! Half the city will be screaming for us to bring this one in. And I, for one, won't be blamin' 'em! It makes me sick to my stomach, it does. I'll have the bastard who's to blame for this, Mr. Holmes. You wait and see if I don't, sir."

"I hope you do, Lestrade. I knew John Godey."

"Really?"

"Yes. So did you, but it was years ago." Holmes shook his head at the scene before him. "Look at how the poor devil died."

"Aye," Lestrade said. "Best I can figure, he not only saved his boy . . ." Lestrade looked down at his small note-pad and flipped pages until he found what he wanted. "Well, not *his* boy, the matron tells me, his late brother's. It'd be his nephew, Thomas Clayton Rogers."

"Payton," Holmes said, "Thomas Payton Rogers. And

'his boy' is an accurate enough description. He raised the boy as if he were his own."

"Oh," Lestrade said. "Uhm, you know them both, Mr. Holmes?"

"Yes, Lestrade. In fact, they were our guests yesterday for dinner."

"Maybe you had better explain, Mr. Holmes."

"Very well," the detective said, and he quickly apprised Lestrade of our involvement.

The medical personnel had been more than happy to receive my services, meanwhile, and I was glad to see that that while many of the wounds were quite serious and demanded immediate professional attention and careful cosmetic suturing, only a few threatened to have lasting effects.

Holmes saw that I had finished my work and called me over.

"Tommy is upstairs," the detective said. "The matron says we can see him for a couple of minutes, but not until tomorrow."

"I thought he was not injured," I said.

"The matron says he screamed several times after the bombing, but he's not uttered a word since. She says he is in shock."

Chapter 22

Holmes was up earlier than usual the next morning. When I came in for breakfast, I found him, as I so often did these days, seated before the window, staring out over Baker Street.

"Have you given up sleeping, Holmes?" I asked.

"Good morning, Watson. No, I slept some. I have been mulling over this business for the past couple of hours."

"And?" I asked.

"It is as I had feared, Watson. In fact, it is far worse. We're caught up in an evil that I should have surmised from the very start. I may yet be proven wrong. I hope that I am. We will know soon enough, I think."

"Tommy is going to need help, Holmes."

Mrs. Hudson knocked twice on the door and entered carrying our breakfast on a tray.

"Good morning," she said. Her voice was hoarse, and it was clear that she had been crying.

"Mrs. Hudson, please sit with us," Holmes said, rising to offer her a chair at the table. "Come. Sit."

"It's just so sad, Mr. Holmes," she said, taking a seat. "Mr. Godey was a bit of a character, I suppose, but I think he was a good man, and—"

"Mrs. Hudson, you will get no argument from us," Holmes said.

"I don't think he had too long to live, with his condition and all," she said.

"His health was precarious," I agreed.

"But still . . ." she said.

"Yes," I agreed, "still . . . Let me pour you some tea," I offered. "I was just saying that Tommy will need help, and—"

"Oh," Mrs. Hudson said, "I think that's been taken care of."

"I beg your pardon?" Holmes asked.

"How so?" I asked.

"Well, Mr. Godey told me he had made provisions for the boy."

"Really?" I said, for I was quite startled; I had presumed Godey was utterly without means.

"Aye, Dr. Watson. On Christmas, when we were down in the kitchen, we talked."

"Was he more specific than that, Mrs. Hudson?" Holmes asked.

"That's all I know, Mr. Holmes," our landlady said. "Mr. Godey said he had made provisions, and that eventually the boy would be well taken care of, but he didn't say how and he didn't say by whom."

"That was the word he used, 'eventually'?"

"That was more the sense of it," she said.

"Maybe the boy himself knows," Holmes said. "When he's up to talking, we'll have to inquire."

Shortly after noon, Holmes and I presented ourselves at Hope Settlement House and were immediately referred to Mrs. Edna Phillips, the matron in charge. She was relatively new to the job, but carried herself with all of the confidence born of vast experience. It helped, I am sure, that she was a tall and comely woman. Her uniform was every bit as white as any snowfall I had ever seen, and her hair, which appeared to be prematurely white, was done up at the back of her head in a tight bun. An unmistakable aura of severity surrounded her. In fact, she presented about as stern and unyielding a demeanor as any first sergeant I had ever soldiered with. We took seats in her office. She sat behind her desk, folded her hands on the blotter and gave us what I am certain was, for her, a generous smile; her bloodless thin lips barely parted.

"The boy was up at dawn on his own," she said without preamble. "He was quite hungry and he seems to have all of his faculties about him. In fact, I would say the indications are that as horrible as it must be, he recalls everything that happened to him. As you probably are aware, that is sometimes not the case among victims of severe trauma.

Young Thomas, however, was asking about some of the other children. It was clear that he was aware they had been hurt. And he asked about the funeral plans for his uncle, poor Mr. Godey."

"Tomorrow, I presume?" Holmes said.

"Yes."

"Who has the body?" I asked.

"Wilfred Hutchins and Sons."

I wrote the information on the notepad I keep in my jacket pocket.

"May we see the boy?" Holmes asked.

"Yes, but not alone," Mrs. Phillips said, "and before we go upstairs, I must ask you what gift it was that you brought here for Boxing Day."

As she asked the question, Mrs. Phillips tilted her head back and raised her chin just a bit, all the while never taking her eyes off Holmes. Her posture was accusatory.

"I beg your pardon?" Holmes replied.

"Your gift," she repeated stiffly. "The one you brought to Hope Settlement House for Boxing Day."

"I brought no gift," Holmes said. "I have never been here."

"Come, come," Mrs. Phillips said. "You were noted during the evening of Christmas Day. Mrs.—"

"I will not permit you to call me a liar," Holmes said.

But the woman continued. ". . . Carstairs, one of our cooks, told me yesterday that she recognized you as the man who came to the door Christmas night and left off a gift wrapped in fancy Eaton foil. And the whispering around here, Mr. Sherlock Holmes, is that the bomb was what you delivered. It is a fact that the infernal package had been wrapped in gold foil!"

Holmes sprang to his feet, glowering at the woman. "You dare accuse me? Who do you think you are?"

I stood, too. And with both of us bent down toward her, staring intently, the matron pushed her chair away from the desk, as if to give us room, but not much. She was only digging in, for she glared right back at us, her jaw set.

"We came here to see Tommy," I said, "not to be interrogated by you or to be made the target of some inane accusation. I insist that we be allowed to visit the boy."

"Well, I—"

"Now!" Holmes said. His voice was strident, and his attitude as imperious as any I had ever seen him employ. "And if there is more questioning to be done," Holmes said, "it will not be done by you."

The matron suddenly gave in, but I sensed that it was a calculated response.

"Very well," Mrs. Phillips said. She sniffed the air hard once, like a hound looking for a scent. The matron rose, straightening her starched white skirt, and stood behind her desk.

"Come with me," she said, and stalked out of the office.

We followed her through Hope Settlement House but at a distance.

"There's something very wrong here," I quickly said in a low voice.

Holmes nodded. "She had made up her mind about me before I arrived," he said. "Just now she was taking the measure of her enemy."

"I don't understand," I confessed.

"Neither do I, completely, Watson, and I am afraid it's going to get worse soon."

We had neared Tommy's room. The matron opened the door and stood to the side, her arms folded across her chest in the manner of a guard, waiting for us with a hateful stare.

The boy stood on the opposite side of the room from the door, standoffish and apprehensive. We walked up to him at once.

"I am so sorry, m'boy," I said. "I truly am. He was a good man, your uncle."

Tommy nodded. He looked sad. His eyes were dry, cried out, I supposed. "Thank you for coming, Doc," he said.

I realized then that Tommy was going out of his way not to look at Holmes. He was not even acknowledging the detective's presence. I could feel Mrs. Phillips' eyes on our backs.

"I am happy that you are safe, Tommy," Holmes said. He had bent down on one knee, in an effort to create a sense of intimacy. "You know how we felt about your uncle John, and how—"

The boy turned on Holmes fiercely.

"Don't you say 'is name, even!" Tommy spat out the words. His face was no more than a foot from the detective's. I was taken by surprise; I did not know what to say. It was obvious that Holmes didn't either. Shock registered on his face.

"I don't ever want to hear you say 'is name!" Tommy shouted. "Or mine either! Ever again. Bugger you! I 'ate you. You leave me alone." The little boy raised his right arm to Holmes and made a fist. "You already done enough. I 'ate you! I 'ate you! You leave me alone." And so saying, Tommy punched the detective in the mouth as hard he was able. Holmes could have stopped him, but he did not. He did not move. He did not flinch. The sound of the boy's blow seemed to reverberate in the small room.

Tommy sobbed and ran between us, past the matron and out the door.

I handed Holmes my handkerchief; he didn't seem to understand why. His expression was nearly blank and unreadable.

"Your lip, Holmes," I said.

He absently touched his fingertips to his lips and, seeing blood on them, took the handkerchief.

"Thank you," he said. I made it a point not to notice his upset.

"Let's get out of here, Holmes."

Mrs. Phillips had remained in the doorway all the time. The incident had caused her to elevate her chin a good ten degrees. She kept it there, trying her best to look down on us as we walked past her in silence.

She smirked but said nothing—which was wise, I thought.

Chapter 23

The incident with Tommy had left Holmes much more upset than I anticipated. We spent most of the evening in silence. I read another sea story, and Holmes got caught up on his cataloging of newspaper clippings. But it was a kind of busy work for him. In fact, he did not seem able to get around the unpleasantness with the boy, and he was not yet prepared to solve it, so he was stuck, as lost in a fog as a hapless vessel in one of my sea stories.

Several times during the evening I looked up from my book to see Holmes absently touching his swollen lip or looking off into space or staring silently into the red-orange glow of coals on the fireplace hearth. I knew that he was going over and over the confrontation with the boy. I was so lost in my own thoughts, however, that when Holmes did finally speak, his voice startled me.

"Watson, there has to be something else that accounts for Tommy's reaction to me today."

"Logical enough," I said, "but what?"

"He is a smart boy, yes? Perhaps not in the conventional sense of the word, but innately smart, naturally savvy. So he sized us up pretty quickly—you, Mrs. Hudson and me—and I think that virtually every involvement he had with us must only have served to reassure him. Would you agree?"

"Yes, of course," I said.

"Well, that being the case, Watson, don't you think the boy also would have a pretty keen fix on the likes of Mrs. Phillips and whoever this cook is, this Mrs., Mrs. . . . What the devil's her name?"

"Carstairs," I said.

"Yes, this Mrs. Carstairs. Is it not likely that he would see their dose of poison . . . this business about my being seen delivering a suspicious package as . . . as unlikely, or at least something that he would confront me with, give me a chance to explain?"

"Holmes," I said, "I think you are asking a lot of that boy. I don't think you can expect him to get his bearings that quickly."

"I overestimate him?"

"No," I said. "I think you underestimate the effect of what he is going through. I think it's going to take some time, and—"

"But we do not have time, Watson. None. Mark my words: This is all moving too fast. And there is this piece, this thing we do not yet know about that has turned that boy against me. There must be something else. There has to be."

"Holmes, I think you're exhausted. I am going to turn in, and I think you should, too. We have Godey's funeral first thing in the morning," I reminded him. "It doesn't promise to be the best of days."

I could not possibly have known how much of an understatement that would turn out to be.

Chapter 24

The bombing of Hope Settlement House had captured the attention and anger of the city, and the newspapers had mined the circumstance for all it was worth. I have to say, however, that neither Holmes nor I believed that they had done so unfairly. The bombing was a sensational event, and I use the word in its most legitimate context. The travesty was made all the more horrible by the fact that it was perpetrated during the holidays, when goodwill and fellow feeling is presumed to be at its peak. All the newspapers had to do was tell the story, and this they did.

Reporters had found out rather quickly that John Godey had spent time in prison; I'm sure police tipsters had taken care of that. But to the newspapers' credit they had fastened most tightly on the man's redemption, on how he had served out his jail sentence for youthful misdeeds and paid his debt to society, and how in the years that followed he became a loyal guardian to his young nephew and as near to an honorable man as any costerman ever could hope to be. And all of the stories, most of them with great imaginative flourishes, told of how the quick thinking and selfless actions of "this simple man of the streets" had saved the lives of a good many poor and homeless children that day.

Within forty-eight hours of his awful death, John Godey was a full-fledged hero, and thousands of Londoners turned out for his funeral, the substantial cost of which was willingly and quietly borne by the benefactors of Hope Settlement House. Decidedly little was made of Godey's not having been a churchgoing man; the settlement house directors simply announced that they would be honored to have Wilfred Hutchins & Sons arrange for services to be conducted for "the martyred John Godey" on the premises that had been his home.

The Daily Telegraph paid for Godey's casket, a beautiful creation of fine polished mahogany with gleaming brass handles, and then featured prominent illustrations of it alongside the news coverage. The front parlor of the shelter had been set up as a viewing room. The casket was front and center, flanked by lighted candles and banks of flowers. It took the better part of the morning for all of the well-wishers to file by. Tommy stood off to one side, red-eyed, looking dazed by the outpouring. At his side stood the head matron, Mrs. Phillips, severe and dry-eyed through it all. Her response to us was insulting. She stepped back a full pace, let out a loud huff of exasperated air and looked sharply in the opposite direction.

Holmes bent over to whisper in Tommy's ear. "You must trust me, Tommy. No matter what anyone else thinks. We are going to need your help to bring down your uncle's killer."

The boy gave no sign that he had heard anything the detective had said.

Holmes moved off rather dejectedly, and I took his place.

Tommy looked up at once. "Thank you for coming, Doc," he said. "Uncle John liked you a lot. And Mrs. Hudson came earlier, 'e liked her, too."

"And we all liked him, Tommy," I said in as soft a whisper as possible, "but now, listen to me . . . Please, boy. The way you're treating Holmes is wrong. He is your friend."

He looked up at me with tears welling in his eyes. His lips quivered as if they were trying to form words but could not get started. It broke my heart to see him so. The boy threw his arms around me—around my waist, to be exact, for he was short—and I bent over and hugged him and held him close to me while he cried. I whispered softly in his ear that his uncle John had been very proud of him and that he was looking down this day watching the goings-on for sure, and because of that Tommy had to bear up as manfully as he could.

"You'd best get on," said a loud strident voice. "There's others want to pay their respects." I looked up to see Mrs. Phillips glaring at me.

Before I could reply, a woman with red hair, dark eyes and a deep raspy voice stepped from the front of the queue and walked directly toward the matron, speaking loudly as she came.

"You lave it be, yeh cow! And don't go pooffin' up yer udders like you kin have the better of me, if that's what yeh be thinkin.' I'd like to see yeh try! I'd just as soon be settin' yeh on yer fat arse right here and now. Me Johnny'd look down on it and t'ank me, he would. You lave this boy alone. Now! Get off with yeh!"

By the time the woman had completed her verbal assault, she was less than a foot from Mrs. Phillips' face. It was clear the matron did not know what to make of this. She seemed frozen between anger and fear, her hateful stare locked on the woman's eyes. The matron must have seen something raw and impressive there, because she couldn't hold her gaze. It was suddenly clear that Mrs. Phillips was not about to call the woman's bluff. She turned and walked out of the viewing room without another word.

" 'Scuse me, if'n you don't mind, sir," the woman said to me, "I'd like to see Mr. Tom, 'ere."

"Certainly," I said.

The woman bent to one knee—with some difficulty, I thought—and took Tommy's hand in both of her own. Her raspy voice caught with emotion as she spoke.

"Tommy, I'm Polly McGovern. Yer uncle was me friend fer a good long time, and 'e spoke of yeh so much 'at I feel like I've know'd yeh all yer life. I'm 'ere payin' me respects, but I'm keepin' a promise I made to yer uncle, too. So when you feels up to it, lad, you come see me. We got things to talk about, you and me."

Then she looked at me and smiled. "Maybe 'is toff 'ere'd help yeh find yer way. St. Giles not bein' the finest neighborhood exactly. Come durin' the day, mind."

Tommy nodded.

"Yeh won't be forgettin' old Polly now?"

The boy shook his head.

The line was pushing impatiently through the doorway, so Polly McGovern and I said good-bye to Tommy and joined Holmes outside.

I introduced her to the detective. The two exchanged

pleasantries, and then the woman frowned and stepped back from Holmes. She looked him up and down, literally, in what seemed to me to be quite a brazen appraisal, but the frown stayed frozen on her face all the while.

"I can't fer the life o' me say why, but I'd be willin' to bet I seen you 'afore, Mr. 'Olmes. Do you s'poze that's likely?"

"I don't believe so," Holmes said.

"Fer sure?"

He nodded.

"Somethin' about the eyes," she said. "Brings me in mind of a fellah I see'd around. Ned or Nick or somethin' like 'at. Ah, who knows?"

Polly McGovern looked at Holmes coyly all of a sudden. She had strong white teeth and a smile that melted away at least ten of what I guessed were her sixty-odd years.

"I'm sooch a ravin' beauty, you'd not be forgettin' if you'da met me, eh?"

"My very thought," Holmes said with a smile.

"I know it was you 'at put my John away some years back, Mr. 'Olmes. We 'ated you then, and it's safe to say there's still plenty out there who does, but when John got out, 'e was a changed man, and 'e . . . well, 'e's changed me, I don't mind sayin', and for the better, and to his way of thinkin', you was the agent of that, too, y'see. But I guess 'at's not news, eh?"

Holmes smiled politely. "I am sorry for your loss, Miss McGovern. Dr. Watson and I both think a great deal of Tommy—despite his current low opinion of me."

"Oh, 'e's upset, is all."

"It's more than that, I fear, but . . . Miss McGovern, I must ask you about the provisions Godey made for the boy. How was he able to do so?"

"Is 'at last part so important?" she asked.

"Ah," Holmes said, "I was rather afraid . . . Let us just say that if the police thought for a moment that some ill-gotten gain, say the proceeds of some burglaries in the distant past, had somehow been used as investment capital . . . One of them was quite big. Lord Cedric Atkinson's home. The loss created considerable hardship and . . ."

"Go on," Polly McGovern said.

"On second thought, I suppose the police have to have a way to ascertain the exact source of the funds," Holmes said.

"Aye," she said. "That they would."

"And it's probably more than reasonable to presume that the swag from the heists disappeared long ago."

"Reasonable, as you say," the woman said.

"And, of course, no one could look at the way a simple costerman—or his close friend—passed their days for years on end and have any reason to think that they ever had any money of their own."

"If they even had cause to look," Polly McGovern said. "Y'see, some people, they reach a point in their life, money don't matter, 't'all. It ain't what's important. Yeh are what yeh are; money don't change 'at. 'At boy, Tommy—and me, too, I'm kinda proud to say—we was about all 'at mattered to John."

"I gather there are terms that apply to the boy's fortune?" Holmes asked.

"Aye, 'e needs to be eighteen," the woman said. "I aims to give Tommy—and only Tommy—the name of the solicitor what's in charge of it."

"A trust, I presume," Holmes said. "Excellent."

"I don't know what they call it."

"Well, Tommy's future would appear to be secure. I'm rather more worried about his situation at present."

"Oh, I 'spect this business'll get better in time," she said.

"That's the problem," Holmes said, looking over my shoulder at something that had caught his eye. He nodded in its direction, and I turned just as the elegant ebony funeral coach of Wilfred Hutchins & Sons pulled up to the front of Hope Settlement House. "Much like Mr. Godey," the detective said, "I'm afraid that I am out of time."

What a perfectly macabre thing to say, I thought; but at that very moment, who should come into plain view very near us but Inspector Lestrade?

"Mr. Holmes," he said, "could I have a word with you, please?"

Chapter 25

I suspect it was not coincidence that Polly McGovern quietly took her leave just as our old acquaintance from Scotland Yard arrived, but if Inspector Lestrade was the least bit curious about her, he gave no sign.

He did seem rather awkward and preoccupied, though, which wasn't like him.

"Nasty business, this," he said to Holmes.

"It is, indeed," the detective replied.

"I was off to the side of the viewing room there, and I couldn't help but notice that you and the boy don't seem to be getting on too well," Lestrade said, the question to Holmes implicit.

"We appear to be mired in a misunderstanding," Holmes said.

"You had met the matron, Mrs. Phillips, before today?" Lestrade asked.

"Yes, Lestrade," Holmes said with a quick smile. "A charming woman."

"Charmin'," Lestrade said in a mocking tone. "You'd do well to watch your back when you're near her den."

"Quite," Holmes said. "She believes I am the bomber of Hope Settlement House. I presume you know that, Lestrade."

"Of course," the inspector said. He looked away from Holmes, first in one direction, then another, as though concerned that we were being watched; perhaps he was just uneasy with the sudden turn in the conversation. I know I was.

"The cook, one Estelle Carstairs, says she saw you with a package that turned out to be the bomb, but it's not clear to me that it was really you she saw."

"You seem to be trying hard not to smile," Holmes said. "Was she comical?"

"Well, let's say she wouldn't be much of an eyewitness," Lestrade replied. "I'm not too sure what's going on there. I think maybe she sees whatever her boss, matron Phillips, tells her to see, but as it happens, Mrs. Carstairs' eyesight's very bad. She does a right good job of hiding it, but I doubt she could tell a cucumber from a carrot if they weren't different colors."

"I can't say I'm sorry to hear that," Holmes said. "May I also presume you know that someone has been doing business in my name?"

"I do." Lestrade opened his notebook and read:

"December 22. Page twenty-six of *The Daily Telegraph*:

" 'Good people of London,
In this, the most hallowed of seasons,
May you and yours find blessed joy,
And may the poorest among you find eternal peace.'

"And then the next day, December 23. In *The Times,* but also on page twenty-six.

" 'Good people of London, I give you a new verse for
an old song this holiday season:

God rest ye, merry gentlemen.
Let nothing you dismay,
Despite what ever fortune
Be yours this holiday.'

"Someone might take 'This holiday' to mean Boxing Day, eh, Mr. Holmes? I mean, in light of the most recent events and the fact that both were positioned on page twenty-six, as in December 26."

"Someone might arrive at that conclusion, yes," Holmes said. The detective paused for dramatic effect, and when he continued he raised his voice and spoke rapidly, all the while punctuating his words with gesticulations and flourishes that required the use of both hands. "But only if he was a complete nitwit, Lestrade. Come now, Inspector! Really! Do you suppose that if I were to perpetrate a crime such as this, or for that matter, *any* crime, that I would be apt to leave a set of clues that any ninny could follow? A—"

"Mr. Holmes, please," Lestrade said. "People will hear you."

The detective paid no attention.

"A—a two-part riddle, for God's sake! It's preposterous, Lestrade! In the parlance of the morons you manage to arrest, Inspector, 'This is a bleedin' frame-up.' It's the work of some plodding amateur. It's . . ."

I don't believe I had ever seen Holmes quite so obviously upset in public. I grabbed his forearm and locked on hard.

". . . pedestrian and un—"

"Enough, Holmes!" I said. "Stop it, man."

He looked at me in startled and angry disbelief, and for a moment I thought he would punch me. Instead, he shook his head as one might shake off water, and then he closed his eyes for a moment.

"Forgive me," he said, but his voice was flat and bitter.

"I am only one person at Scotland Yard, Mr. Holmes. There's a lot of 'em that's looking at this case, and they're a damned sight higher up the chain than me. You had better understand that."

"I see," Holmes said, very quietly, I thought.

"And there's something else," said Lestrade. His voice was low and taut. It was clear that he was upset and trying hard not to show it. "Your callin' card was found at the scene of the bombing."

"What?" Holmes was ashen. "That's preposterous, Lestrade."

"It was attached to the gold-colored paper that the bomb came wrapped in, Mr. Holmes."

Holmes was incredulous, and he raised his voice again.

"Why didn't I just have my portrait painted and attached to the package as well?"

Lestrade raised both of his hands, palms turned outward toward Holmes, as if to stop the detective's renewed onslaught. It gained some ground for the inspector, and he stood firm on it.

"There's them at the Yard that would say that sometimes

your criminal element does such things out of sheer cocki-
ness and arrogance," Lestrade said. "It's a way the smarter
ones have of spittin' in the eye of the law, y'see."

Holmes fell silent. He took several deep breaths and
looked around and then back at the policeman.

"You have seen my card, Lestrade? You are certain that
this is so?"

"We have it, Mr. Holmes. Yes. The matron took it from
the boy, brought it in yesterday."

"Tommy had it?"

"Aye. He found it in the day room at the Settlement
House right after the bombing. When Mrs. Phillips came
into headquarters, she was still angry that he hadn't given
it to her straight away. Said she had to twist his wrist good
and hard until he opened his hand; I told her in no uncertain terms what I thought of that. And I told her that for
a while I'd be sending a man around to check on the boy
without any prior notice, and that we had best find him
well."

"Good for you, Lestrade," I said.

Holmes nodded but was otherwise silent for a moment.
Then he said, "Inspector, I mentioned to Watson earlier
that I was surprised I had not heard from the Yard sooner."

"The funeral, Mr. Holmes." Lestrade looked over the
detective's shoulder and then over mine, too. "It was decided that a low profile was to be maintained."

"And that the trail should grow cold, meanwhile?" Holmes
asked. "There's not a lot of wisdom in that, Lestrade."

"Well, it's not entirely my call, is it?" the inspector
said heatedly. Then he took a step closer to Holmes and
said, "Ask me, we'd have had a presence at these here
services and continued with the investigation, meanwhile.
Not them. They figured, first get 'im in the bleedin'
ground all polite like, and then, seven, eight hours after,
it's back to business."

Holmes nodded as though he suddenly was very tired.

"Well," Lestrade said suddenly, "we'll be seeing you."

Lestrade was barely looking at either of us when he
tipped his hat and walked off.

I should have understood at once what was going on, but
I regret to say I did not.

Chapter 26

Save for the occasional scrape or clink of our utensils at supper, the only sound in our rooms was the soft low hiss of the gaslights and an occasional huffing of the winter wind across the top of the chimney.

"You're quiet, Holmes," I said.

"Oh," he said, temporarily roused from his distraction. "Yes, I've been caught up with our puzzle, Watson. I keep moving the pieces around, but I can't make them all fit. Well, we shall see. What time do you have?"

"Half-six, exactly."

He took a cigar from the coal scuttle, lighted it and was instantly enveloped in smoke. I opened the nearest window, and lighted a cigar of my own. The change from my pipe was refreshing. Holmes walked to his bookshelves, took down an unused commonplace book and, setting it on his knee, began writing furiously.

I, meanwhile, turned to the late edition of *The Daily Telegraph* and was soon engrossed in the front page. I became vaguely aware of some movement in the room a few minutes later, and when I looked up Holmes was donning his overcoat and hat.

"I'm going out for a walk, Watson. A little solitude in the brisk night air may help me puzzle through this mess."

I nodded and didn't think much more about it until roughly an hour had passed and Holmes had not returned. That worried me immensely. One night last winter when he had disappeared, it turned out that he had been taken prisoner by the so-called "Monster of St. Marylebone." We had needed time, good fortune and all of our wits and then some to close that book with our skins intact, and I didn't much relish the possibility of being in similar straits again.

"You're being foolish," I chided myself aloud. There was no one to argue the point with me, but I needed to hear a voice just then, even if it was only my own.

"Holmes' being gone but one hour of a winter's night does not exactly constitute his being missing."

I shook my head as if to laugh at myself, but it made me feel rather odd to be talking as though I were an actor on stage before a silent and unseen audience. I went to the sideboard and poured myself a tumbler of good scotch, added a small amount of carbonated water from the gas-ogene, stirred, took a nice hearty draught, and savored the warmth and richness of it. I brought the tumbler to my lips and would have had another good swallow had not an assault of sudden sharp and insistent knocking—no, pounding—on the front door startled me to such an extent that my role in the play ended abruptly and I almost dropped the glass.

"This *is* déjà vu!" I muttered. I set the glass down hard, slopping some of the amber liquid on the sideboard. I threw open the door to our rooms and rushed to the top of the stairs. Mrs. Hudson was already at the front door.

"Hold on there!" she said, throwing back the bolt and opening the door, which was filled immediately by three large men. One of them was a rather elegant but stern-looking fellow in a long dark wool coat, a police official of some rank, I presumed, because he was flanked by two uniformed constables, one of whom I recognized as the eminently disagreeable Ridley Thompson.

"Scotland Yard," the leader announced to Mrs. Hudson, as though she had not already divined as much. "Step aside now. Where is Mr. Sherlock Holmes?"

"He is not here," I said. I shouted from the top of the stairs. "What is it you want?" I realized instantly, of course, that these men had come to arrest Holmes.

"You must be Dr. Watson," said the police official. He began walking up the stairs toward me, removing his gloves as he spoke. He smiled, and as he reached me on the landing, he extended his hand, as if in friendship. My arms were folded across my chest, and they remained that way. I looked down at his extended hand and then quite pointedly looked him in the eye instead.

"He is not here," I said. "I have nothing else to say to you." I turned and walked into the parlor. I took up my drink from the sideboard and then walked over to the fireplace mantel, leaned against it and took another swallow.

The policeman followed me and stood in the doorway. "Very well, then," he said. "Have it your way. I am Inspector Miles Wallingford. Those constables downstairs are Ridley Thompson and John Comerford. Excuse me for just a moment, Doctor."

He left the doorway, walked to the top of the stairs and called down to Mrs. Hudson:

"My men must search your house. I regret that we must do so, ma'am, but I trust you will not impede them in any way."

As he spoke, I emptied my glass, which was fortunate indeed, because through the bottom of it I noticed what appeared to be a new piece of correspondence pinned to the mantel with Holmes' penknife; this was his preferred way to temporarily file unanswered letters and such. I moved closer and saw that the paper seemed to be a page torn from a commonplace book, undoubtedly the one in which he had been writing earlier. I started to reach for it, but hearing Inspector Wallingford come back into the room, I turned the reach into a stretch to the floor, from which I plucked some imaginary bit of paper and flicked it at the fire.

I had heard of this Miles Wallingford. He had a reputation as a dogged and ambitious man but, despite his elegant appearance, rather an unimaginative dimwit who would be lost without his book of rules. It followed that he was not a very effective criminalist, and he was too proper and too much of a social climber ever to have made any real mark as an investigator, not that he could. One more administrator obviously less competent than the men under him, and given the ineffectiveness of Scotland Yard much of the time these days, that was damning indeed.

When Wallingford turned from the stairs, he looked at me appraisingly and pursed his lips together as though pondering something. He put his hands behind his back, canted slightly forward and, without taking his eyes off me, walked into the parlor. I presume his hard-eyed and penetrating official police stare was intended to unnerve and intimidate me. It did neither. In fact, his attitude served only to help strengthen my resolve not to cooperate in any way.

"So where is he, Doctor?"

"He's not here."

"You have already said that."

"And it is still true," I said.

"You won't tell me where he is?"

"I have no idea where he is," I said.

"Come now. You don't really expect me to believe you."

"I don't expect anything of you, Inspector. You asked me a question and I gave you an answer. It happens to be the absolute truth. Whether you choose to believe it is entirely up to you."

"I don't much care for your attitude, sir."

"Really? Well, Inspector, I don't much care whether you do or not," I said, somewhat surprising myself. Perhaps it was the scotch; I don't know, but it felt good to let go a bit, so I continued.

"Furthermore, sir, I don't much care for you," I said. "You come barging into our house with a pair of your uniform hounds and you want to arrest Sherlock Holmes, my friend and companion. Do I need to remind you how many times that man has quietly and selflessly come to the rescue of your supposedly skilled investigators? Why, the best you've got were so befuddled they didn't know which end was up, and most of the time, after he had pulled their chestnuts out of the fire, he even was willing to let them take most of the public credit for what was largely his work. And this is how you repay that debt?"

My back was to the fireplace hearth. He took two steps toward me, and if he was any closer he'd have been in my vest pocket. He was taller than me by a good ten inches, so he was able to look down at me. I had all I could do to resist the urge to jam the heel of my boot into the top of his instep. I was quite certain that would only land me in jail. So instead I jumped up on my toes, fast, slightly forward and with a slight twist at the same time, which had the effect of driving the top of my forehead quite neatly straight into his nose, which hurts quite a bit from what my patients have told me.

"Oww!" he shouted.

"Oww, damn!" I said, continuing to twist away from him toward the hearth, pretending not to realize what I had done. I was too busy vigorously fanning the seat of my pants as though they might burst into flames at any moment.

"Oww," I said. "Lord, it must have been a spark or an ember or something. I very nearly set myself . . . Oh, Inspector." I tried not to notice that he was glaring at me in a combination of rage and amazement.

"Now, how did that . . . ? Oh, good Lord," I said. "I must have banged into you when the fire . . . I'm sorry, sir. I am *very* sorry. I really am most embarrassed, Inspector. I had no idea that I had—"

"You struck me."

"Well, I suppose I *bumped* you, sir," I said earnestly. "I don't think I would say struck you. No, no. That would imply intent, you see, sir, and—"

"You deliberately butted me with your head."

"Oh, really, Inspector, I . . . Oh, perhaps we should get some ice on that. It's swelling up pretty quickly. Is your nose starting to bleed? Oh, too bad. Here, here. Sit down on the ottoman there. Let me get you a hand towel from the sideboard."

"I've half a mind to arrest you for assaulting an officer of the law."

I returned with the cloth, thinking to myself, "Half a mind would be somewhat of an exaggeration," but I think I managed to look directly at him with as much innocence as believability might require.

"Oh, really, Inspector," I said, pretending not to take him seriously when, in fact, I suspected he was quite serious. "You must have better things to do. Now, I can only apologize so many times. Really. And about that head-butting reference. I did play rugby for Blackheath, sir, so I do know a head-butt when I see one, and well, quite frankly, Inspector, that was not a respectable head-butt, well . . . Excuse me, sir. Would you be offended if I offered you a small drink? It's just the wrong end of the day for the both of us, if you know what I mean, and I think I could use one, even if you couldn't. Excuse me, just . . .

"Oh, your nose is still bleeding. Here. Take your index finger and put it at the top center of your upper gums. No, not actually in your nose. Under your upper lip, between the inside of your lip and the gum. That's it. Now press as hard as you can and hold it there. But tip your head straight back. Straight back. Close your eyes. Straight back. Not too far; you'll fall over. Look straight up at the ceiling. I guarantee that will stop the blood in just a moment."

That was true, of course. I had him cutting off the flow of blood to the bruised area, but while he was doing that, I turned and ripped the note from Holmes off the mantel, cleared my throat to cover the sound of the paper's being crumpled in my fist, and stuffed it in my trouser pocket. I walked to the sideboard trying hard not to smile, for I had, in fact, given the officious policeman a good crack in the nose, managed to confiscate the message from Holmes and seemed to be getting away with my misdeeds. I was quite pleased with myself, though I was determined not to show it.

I made my drink and was about to turn back to Wallingford when he said, "A small one. No more than three fingers."

"Three," I thought to myself. "That constitutes a small one?" "Very good," I said in response. "And would you care—"

"Neat," he said, his voice a bit muffled by the hand towel I had given him.

"Yes," I said, telling myself to be less solicitous now. Polite should do nicely. "I'll hold your drink, Inspector. Just keep your finger there for a bit longer. When you want to, open your eyes and put your head back up straight, but do it slowly or you'll feel faint."

In a minute, the policeman was back in order, or as close as he was ever likely to be, and I handed him his drink.

He did not thank me.

"You do not know where the detective went?"

"No, I do not. He said only that he was going out for a walk. He said he thought a little solitude might help."

"With what?"

"Why, with this business at Hope Settlement House and the death of our friend John Godey."

"Friend, you say? Humph," Wallingford said. "It was Holmes who actually collared—help collar—the man and then watched him go down for ten long. He was no friend of John Godey's."

"At the time of the arrest, that certainly was so, but not of late." I made it a point to speak matter-of-factly, so that I might keep the edge out of my voice. "People do change, Inspector."

"Not in my experience, they don't."

"Then you believe the tiger always keeps his stripes, eh?"

"I do," he said. "I most certainly do." He handed me his glass. "I'll have another. Same."

"Certainly." I was more than happy to oblige. Another half hour of this and he'd be liable to forget who he was. Then his two accomplices barged in.

"Beggin' your pardon, sir. 'E ain't anywhere's downstairs," Thompson reported.

"And you checked the cellar, of course?" Wallingford asked without turning around to his men.

"We'll report back directly, sir."

"Don't be all night about it."

"No, sir," Thompson said. "We won't, sir. It ain't likely to be that big, sir."

"I didn't—never mind. Never mind. Get it done or I'll have the two of you walking Drury Lane by this time tomorrow."

At the mention of one of the dreariest streets in the city the two constables nearly tripped over each other getting to the stairs.

"This place have an attic?" Wallingford asked.

"I suppose," I said. "Now that you mention it, I don't believe I've ever been in it. There must be something there between the ceiling and the rooftop."

"He's not here, is he?" Wallingford said.

"With all due respect, Inspector, no. I have no idea where he is. He went out for a walk"—I took my watch from my vest and opened it—"well over two hours ago."

"My guess is that your friend could have felt the noose of the law closing on him, and he decided to take it on the lam. I don't think he'll show his face back here tonight. Of course, if he does, we'll be on the lookout for him, you can bet on that."

"Well, I don't see how he could possibly slip by you, then," I said.

He looked at me, not sure if I was making fun of him or not.

"What I meant," I told him, "was that if he returns to the house and you are lying in wait for him, well, of course, you should have him."

"Aren't you curious why Lestrade is not in charge of the investigation, Doctor?"

"Not particularly, no," I said. "A lot of public attention has been drawn to the bombing. I figured it was the sort of highly visible case that might demand the services of the top man."

"Well said, and that's true," Wallingford said. "Put your best out front; that's the way the thinking goes. But if your friend Mr. Sherlock Holmes does not return tonight, it will be because he has been warned off. He knew in advance that we were coming for him. That points to his friend Inspector Lestrade. I had him taken off the case, and if I can prove that—"

"I hardly think Lestrade qualifies as a friend, Inspector," I said. "By virtue of the cases we have been involved in, we are acquainted, to be sure. The same can be said of others, Tobias Gregson, for example. Or Carter Horn. Or William Osgood. Simon Gallatin . . . I could go on."

"And they are on my list of possibles, too, and don't think they're not," he said sternly.

"Or, Inspector," I said, "maybe it was you who warned off Holmes."

"What? How dare you—"

I raised both hands, as if to fend him off. "No, no. Hear me out. Is it not entirely possible that he was returning to our quarters and he saw the three of you? Your carriage is still out front, is it not?"

"Well, yes. I suppose it's possible," Wallingford said, "but my guess is that Lestrade—or one of those others you mentioned—tipped him off to us."

"You have to follow your instincts," I said. "I suppose

when all's said and done, that's still what closes the case, eh?"

"Right!" Wallingford said. "Instinct, pure and simple. I see that despite the company you keep, you're one who understands the true nature of good detective work. Instinct is what wins out every time. Every time."

"Oh, to be sure," I said. It was clearer than ever that the man was not only a fool, but a dangerous one, the sort of police official who was eminently capable of making life-and-death decisions purely on the basis of whim, professional bias, popular prejudice or some unique combination of the three. The facts are nice, of course, but only if they're a convenient fit. Fortunately for London, there were at least a few in Scotland Yard who didn't share this fool's beliefs.

Thompson returned, the ever silent Officer John Comerford by his side, and reported that there were no fugitives hiding in the cellar. Holmes and the Crown Jewels, too, could have been stashed in the attic, about which I had boldly lied; the attic housed an ample storage loft and we used it often. It also was possible that Holmes might have been sound asleep in either of our two bedrooms. Inspector Miles Wallingford hadn't seen fit to check any of those possibilities—instinct, pure and simple, I suppose.

The three policemen turned as one and left without offering so much as a good night. It was much too late for that anyway.

Chapter 27

Through the side of the drapes that were drawn across our front window, I watched the three policemen get in their coach and drive off, and only then did I take Holmes' hastily written, now crumpled, note from my pocket. I flattened it against the sideboard, smoothed out a couple of creases and read:

Watson,
Unless I am gravely mistaken, by the time you read this note some of Scotland Yard's finest probably will have tried to arrest me for the death of John Godey and the bombing of Hope Settlement House. I believe that was the purpose of Lestrade's meeting with us this afternoon; more than anything else, he was trying to warn me: seven, eight hours grace after the funeral . . . I hate to say it, but I believe I am in his debt.

You must be asking yourself why I was not forthright about my plan. Quite simply, I needed to be sure that if the police came to arrest me, you would be able to respond in your usual honest manner. Your capacity for deception, my old friend, is practically nil, which, as I have pointed out before, is to your inestimable credit. I won't belabor the point; just be assured that my actions in no way reflect on the depth of my trust in you. Quite the contrary, for there is much work yet, and much of it falls to you.

You must win Tommy back. He needs to understand that we are still on his side. Tell him that if he can bear to trust us, and me in particular, for the next three days, then the murder of his uncle John may be avenged. I have a plan, but its success depends on the appearance of normalcy. That includes Tommy's being present at the benefit dinner on New Year's Eve.

I expect that Lady Armstrong will be quite upset by these developments. If the opportunity presents itself, assure her that I am working in her best interests even now, and that I will continue to do so.

Be careful, my friend. The Yard will be watching, so be circumspect.

Meanwhile, I must play the chameleon in order to continue my work.

I will be in touch; you may count on it.

The note also included specific instructions for me and a list of miscellaneous tasks that had to be undertaken before the benefit dinner. I read the note again to be sure that I had missed nothing, and then stooped to the hearth and laid it on the hot glowing coals. The paper burst instantly into flame, then curled and puckered to a thin brittle black ash and broke apart. The draft carried bits of it up the flue. I had a vision of Holmes' fate, like his words, being sucked out of the chimney and carried to oblivion on the cold night wind, but I put it out of my mind.

We had been in tougher spots, I told myself. Then I repeated my words until I believed them.

Chapter 28

I did not fall soundly asleep until shortly before daybreak, so I was not at all pleased when I was awakened by some sort of ruckus on the ground floor, even if it was mid-morning. I threw on my robe, slipped my revolver into my pocket, and opened the door to find Mrs. Hudson standing atop the stairs, hands on her hips, her jaw clenched tightly and staring down at none other than Lady Mirabelle Llewellyn Armstrong.

The wealthiest woman in London, a newspaper folded under her arm, was poised midway up the stairs, glaring at our landlady. As I opened my door, I saw Lady Armstrong's guard, the ever imposing Cuthbert Wilson, coming through the front door. He ran to the foot of the stairs and took two steps upward before he saw me. By then I had moved well to the side of Mrs. Hudson and had my hand-gun aimed straight at him. When I was certain he saw me, I cocked the hammer.

"Far enough," I said.

Wilson froze.

"This is unacceptable," said Lady Armstrong.

"I will decide that," I said. "What is the problem here?"

Mrs. Hudson spoke first, addressing her words to Lady Armstrong.

"You may be the grand dame of this city," Mrs. Hudson said, "but that gives you no right to barge in here like you owned my house. I'll not put up with the likes of that."

Lady Armstrong's bosom rose and fell quite noticeably a couple of times, and then she said, "You are quite right, Mrs. Hudson. I—I am sorry."

There was prolonged silence as Mrs. Hudson looked at the woman.

"Well, you're in time for tea," she said finally.

"This is getting tedious, Lady Armstrong," I said. "You seem incapable of dealing with people without causing some sort of uproar."

She gave me the oddest look; I'm not even sure how to describe it. She twitched her head a bit to one side and used her lips and eyes to affect a sheepish sort of look. It was a kind of facial shrug, I suppose, as if to say, "I did it again, didn't I?"

I shook my head in exasperation and uncocked my revolver. Wilson tipped his cap, and I swear he winked at me before retreating through the front door to assume his customary post by Lady Armstrong's carriage. Mrs. Hudson stepped aside, and the woman slowly came up the stairs.

We were silent for a couple of minutes. Mrs. Hudson entered with tea. Lady Armstrong nodded in thanks; my landlady acknowledged it and left. As soon as the door closed, Lady Armstrong put the morning edition of *The Daily Telegraph* on the table and pointed to the headline over the lead story by Peter Brooks, I presumed: "Sherlock Holmes Flees Arrest for Hope House Bombing."

"Well," I said, "they wasted no time."

I read the story quickly. I was impressed, once again, by its fairness. Brooks used the information he had garnered during his earlier contact with Holmes to round out the background of the story. He also had been scrupulously fair in trying to put Scotland Yard's thinking—to the extent it could be called that—into an understandable perspective.

. . . Inspector Miles Wallingford insisted that Holmes' disappearance suggests the detective is guilty of the crime.

"I want to take this opportunity to urge Mr. Holmes to turn himself in," Wallingford said. "We will track him down if we have to, but it will go easier if he comes in of his own accord.

"I am not at liberty to go into the details that we already have at our disposal," he said, "but if Sherlock Holmes had nothing to hide in this dastardly affair, he wouldn't have run, now, would he?"

There's that remarkable instinct at work again, I thought.

"This is a terrible situation," Lady Armstrong said.

"I assure you it would be much worse if Holmes actually had been arrested," I said. "I am in touch with him, Lady Armstrong, and he specifically told me to assure you that he is hard at work on your case even now."

"I'm sure you mean well, Doctor, but I rather suspect that Mr. Holmes' own well-being is taking precedence over his efforts to resolve my problem."

"I repeat, Lady Armstrong, he said to tell you that he is hard at work on your problem even now. How? I do not know. Where? I don't know that either, and if I did, with all due respect, I would not say. Holmes must be left to his own devices in these things. If he needs our assistance, he will let us know, I am sure. But, meanwhile, you must trust him. There really is no alternative."

"Are you forgetting that Lord Armstrong is to make his marriage intentions known at the benefit, Doctor? I must know whether to countenance this union or find a way to prevent it."

"You must do what your conscience dictates, Lady Armstrong. Meanwhile, be assured that Holmes is well aware of the situation, and is doing whatever needs to be done."

"I don't intend to let anything stand in the way of my benefit dinner and concert," she said.

"Good," I told her. "I am looking forward to it myself. I expect that it will be a momentous occasion."

"Momentous? What an odd choice of words."

"Not at all," I said. "Fine food and drink in one of the city's finest homes. A gracious hostess. A showing of the Blood of Punjab. A concert by a fine violinist. All for a most noble cause and at the very peak of the holidays. It doesn't seem to me that 'momentous' is an inappropriate description at all m'lady."

She eyed me thoughtfully.

"Well," she said, "we shall see."

"So we shall," I said.

"May I trust that if I am needed before then . . ."

"We will contact you at once, of course."

"Good day, then," she said.

I am glad to report that the woman left Baker Street

with considerably less fanfare than she had arrived. From the parlor window I watched her coach pull away from the curb. No sooner had the carriage moved beyond the periphery of my vision than I caught sight of a broad-shouldered man who seemed to be staring quite brazenly at our premises. I knew that it couldn't be Holmes in disguise, for this man was easy to spot. He wore a dark coat, matching bowler hat, and was leaning casually against a lamp post down the opposite side of the street. One of Wallingford's men, I was willing to bet.

I told Mrs. Hudson that I would be going out for a while and that she should be careful to not let anyone in the house whom she did not know and trust.

Chapter 29

With the discreet help of Inspector Tobias Gregson as intermediary, I arranged a quick meeting with Lestrade at an out-of-the-way table near the back of Simpson's-in-the-Strand. We ate a hearty lunch of steak and kidney pie and drank a couple of pints of ale. I paid, and I let him know that Holmes and I believed we were much in his debt for standing by us.

Lestrade was never a brilliant investigator, but the Yard didn't have many who were better. What Inspector Lestrade did have was a refined sense of fair play and a keen sense of honor, and that derived purely from the fact that he was immensely proud to be a policeman. More than anything else, it was what, I think, made it impossible for him to flatly acknowledge, even to me, even now, that he had warned Holmes of the impending arrest; part of him would forever regret that he had compromised the Yard.

I didn't push. Instead, I simply asked if he would like to have a direct hand in solving the bombing of Hope Settlement House and the murder of John Godey and, in the process, who knows what else?

"That's not the toughest question you've ever asked, Doctor," Lestrade said.

"I know," I said. "Is there some way that you could spirit Tommy back to 221B Baker Street for a while this evening?"

"It'd be irregular," he said. "And I'd be putting my neck out some, you realize. If Wallingford finds out . . ."

I sighed in disappointment. "You're right, Lestrade. I shouldn't even have asked. This is just such a bloody mess all of a sudden, and Holmes needs some—"

The inspector cut me off.

"Well, I did tell the cook, that Mrs. Carstairs, that I might need to speak with her again. And now that I think of it, this might be a good time. Maybe in the process I could sort of make it a point to say hello to Tommy Rogers."

"Can you get him here?" I asked Lestrade.

"That won't be a problem," he said. "Wallingford never tells his men anything. The investigation will be over before most of them realize I'm not even supposed to be on the case. If any of his cronies asks what I'm about, I'll say that we need the boy to identify some evidence found at the scene. That's reasonable, I think. I'll bring him to my office at headquarters, just for a quick visit, and then we'll come over here . . . so we can compare the evidence with items in Mr. Holmes' possession."

Tommy went along with the charade, and at about seven o'clock that night, Lestrade brought the boy to 221B Baker Street and then went out for a long walk through the West End.

"Thank you for coming tonight," I said. "How are you doing, lad?"

"Everywhere's I look, I 'spect to see Uncle John," Tommy said.

"I know, my boy," I said. "It is always that way, no matter the circumstances, and no matter who you are. Death always comes too soon to people we love. It is always hard."

"I'll never forget 'im," Tommy said. "I know'd 'bout 'im bein' in jail and all, an it didn't matter none, not to me."

"I am glad to hear that," I said. "I wasn't sure you knew."

"Oh, aye. 'E wanted me to know. 'No bad secrets 'tween us,' Uncle said, 'not s' long as I can 'elp it.' 'At's 'ow 'e wanted it."

The little boy was dry-eyed and sad, and his voice was matter-of-fact, nearly monotone. It was as if some of his youth and vitality had been taken from him in one horrendous blinding flash. I hated to see it.

"I ain't ever goin' to forget 'im, Doc, no matter what."

"Of course, you won't, Tommy," I said. "Who ever said

you were supposed to? You're not. What will happen is, eventually you will—"

"That policeman, that Inspector Wallingford, he said that a man learns he has to put such things out of his head. 'Just bite down an' march on,' 'e says."

"Well, you do have to get on, that much is true, Tommy, but not so the rest. I'm afraid the inspector isn't one to be giving advice on very much."

Mrs. Hudson had brought us some tarts and scones and a steaming pot of hot tea, and I poured each of us a cup.

"What I started to say, Tommy, was, what will happen to this awful sorrow you have, you'll find a place for it eventually, but it's a place that's inside you, not something apart from you. And that's where your uncle John will always be, right there. After a time the good memories you have will sort of fill the emptiness that's there right now. But it takes some time, and you have to give it a chance to happen. You go about your life as best you can, and after a time, well, that hole fills in bit by bit, like a wound that takes a long time to heal. Does that made sense to you?"

"Aye, Doc, an' you be sayin' it, I know it's true. But Mrs. Matron Phillips, she said about what that Wallingford bloke did: 'You have to forget him,' she says. 'Get on wi' it. 'Sides, 'e was dyin' fast anyway,' she says."

I am always startled and angered by the brutality that adults visit upon children. Sometimes it is intentional, sometimes not. Sometimes it is physical, sometimes not, but the effect is always the same.

"Was 'e, Doc? Dyin,' I mean. Fast, like Mrs. Matron Phillips said?"

I sighed and looked the boy in the eye.

"He was dying, Tommy," I said. "Yes. There's not much doubt of that."

"You knew."

"I'm a doctor, Tommy. It's my business to know."

" 'E din't tell me, and you din't tell me."

"It wasn't my place to tell you . . . and besides, Tommy, you already knew, didn't you? I think you knew it when you asked me to examine him and then for sure when you saw how much laudanum I sent him."

The boy's eyes filled with tears, but he wiped them away as though they were an annoyance; I suppose it seemed more important just then to talk.

"I have no idea how much longer your uncle John had, Tommy. Three months. Six months. A year? I don't know."

"Did he know, then? You tell 'im?"

"I didn't have to tell him. A man knows these things. Here, have a scone, lad. They're still warm."

He talked around half a mouthful of the fresh biscuits. "Just like Uncle knew about Mrs. Matron Phillips. 'E knew she was no good. 'E 'ad no use fer the likes o' her. Din't matter to him, she looked swell like she does. 'E said, 'What matters' 's what's inside,' and Uncle John says, what's inside her is dead."

"Well, I don't know about—"

"Oh, you don't have to pretty it up for me, Doc. She's just a—"

I cut him off sharply. "Keep a civil tongue, young man. Think what you want, and don't ever lie, but if you keep a civil tongue in your head, you'll be accepted in polite company. Is that clear?"

"Aye," the boy said with resignation. "But, Doc, if Uncle was dyin,' why didn't he talk to me about it?"

"And what would he have said, Tommy? 'I'm dying, my boy, but I don't know when, just sooner than later. Now, don't you worry about it, and don't you start being sad or treating me different.' What would he have said?"

"I guess you're right, Doc, as usual."

"Well, I am right, but not 'as usual.' You can say that about Mr. Holmes, nearly all of the time, but not me."

"I don't say nothin' 'bout him."

"Tommy, I'm not going to beat about the bush where this is concerned, because we're two honest men, but Holmes was set up; he had nothing to do with the bombing."

"Din't 'e 'ate Uncle John?"

"Lord, no, Tommy. Why would he?"

"Well, 'at's what that Yarder said. That Wallingford. An' Mrs. Matron Phillips, she was sittin' right there, and she agreed wi' 'im, an'—"

I held up my finger. "Back up a moment," I said. "How

much time have the two of them spent talking to you about this?"

"It's just that when I see her, the Mrs. Matron Phillips 'ese days, she's usually wi' 'im. They're real friendly like, an—"

"Was he there when Matron Phillips twisted Mr. Holmes' card out of your hand?"

"She din't," Tommy said. " 'E did, Doc. 'E did it, said he'd wring my hand right off, I didn't open it up and let go the card. It was her, I'd a' kicked her shinbones in two, she laid a bloody—"

"Aah, aah! A civil tongue, I told you. Listen, Tommy. You didn't hand over that calling card immediately because down deep, you knew there was something wrong there; you knew Mr. Holmes couldn't have done such a thing as bring that bomb to the settlement house—any more than I could have. And now you have to be man enough to act accordingly."

"I guess I do know it," Tommy said, and the tears started to flow as though he had been holding them back forever. Five minutes. Ten minutes. I do not know. It took a while for the well to run dry.

"You think Mr. 'Olmes 'll forgive me?"

"If I know Mr. Holmes, Tommy, he already has."

"Really?"

"Yes, really," I said. "But now it's time to put that behind you. If you want to help Mr. Holmes, and me, too, and in the process maybe get justice for your uncle John, we've got to put our heads together and get busy. The question is, lad, are you up to it?"

He looked straight at me and stuck out his hand. I shook it and then called down to Mrs. Hudson for some more tea and biscuits. She didn't bring in the service, though; Lestrade did. He was smiling, wearing a clean white apron and, over his forearm, a waiter's white linen towel.

"A nice touch," I said.

"Aye, that's enough out of you," he said, with a wink at me. "I'll thank you not to be acting so familiar with the help."

I smiled and said, "That reminds me, Lestrade: Tommy tells me that Inspector Wallingford has been spending quite a bit of time alone with the head matron of the settlement house. But then, I suppose that with the investigation and all . . ."

"Of course," Lestrade said. "He's running the thing."

For the next hour, Lestrade and Tommy and I ate biscuits and drank tea and made our plan, or as much of it as we could without Holmes' direct involvement, which I hoped would come soon, somehow.

Then without any preamble, Lestrade turned the conversation back to Wallingford.

"He's a married man, you know," the inspector said.

"What are you . . . ? Oh, Wallingford. You don't say?" As if I had not suspected as much. "Wouldn't it be too bad for him if the commissioner's office got wind of it?"

"Oh, yes," Lestrade said. "It surely would."

He tried hard not to smile but didn't quite manage.

Chapter 30

I had been right in supposing that the man I had seen leaning against the street lamp yesterday was one of Wallingford's, for a new person took up the job roughly every ten hours, which approximated the average work shift at Scotland Yard. It seemed silly of the police to be so obvious, but then I realized that the police spy had assumed the one vantage point from which all avenues of entrance and egress at our house could be monitored. It was clear that the Yard was determined to take Holmes into custody should he set foot anywhere near 221B Baker Street.

Oddly enough, however, it became quickly apparent that the same vigilant public servants possessed no real understanding of the ease with which the detective could exchange one complete identity for another, because at first the police showed a complete lack of interest in any visitor to Baker Street who did not appear at once to be Holmes. And thus it was that for about the first day and a half of surveillance, Lestrade and Tommy and Mrs. Hudson and I—not to mention a small contingent of deliverymen, tinkers and tradesmen—were able to come and go from our quarters with about as much freedom as we might normally have enjoyed.

That changed rather abruptly by the end of the second day, however. Our watchers' superior officers, who would have been too numerous to count, must have quite forcefully explained Holmes' penchant for drama and disguise, because the Yard's neighborhood emissary suddenly seemed suspicious of anyone who so much as glanced at our front door. By day's end the policeman had accosted postmen and dairymen, a baker or two, a flower peddler, an old Italian costerman selling fresh roasted chestnuts and a couple of innocent pedestrians who had merely happened into each other and tarried by Mrs. Hudson's door to exchange pleasantries.

At four o'clock, however, the policeman's job turned hopeless, for it was at precisely that hour that an unruly knot of citizens came marching down Baker Street, stopped at 221 and threatened to storm the house in search of "the devil's own detective"—that, at least, was the impassioned if somewhat overwrought reference to Holmes employed by the Reverend Dwayne Tisbury. He claimed to be the chief prelate of some obscure church that was five names long and boasted a profound commitment to fight social injustice in all of its sundry and insidious forms.

Truth be told, Tisbury was a hell-raiser and a rabble-rouser, and man of the cloth or no, that was how he was best known by most of Scotland Yard. The preacher and his friends were apt to show up outside a St. James Street social club on Monday evening inveighing against "demon drink," only to be found later that night deep in their cups at one of their favorite taverns in the East End. Tuesday might find them in Hyde Park trying to stir up sentiment against immigrants, and on Wednesday they'd be marching along the Marylebone Road launching verbal assaults against the "repressive" attitudes and policies of the Metropolitan Police. And so it went. Few people ever paid them much attention; fewer still took them seriously.

But owing largely to personal flair and a singular gift for theatrics, Tisbury generally could be counted on for some form of entertainment, and this appearance on Baker Street proved no different. Flanked by about ten of his associates, the fevered preacher boldly took a stance before Mrs. Hudson's front door, raised both hands to the sky as if he were a Moses beckoning Pharaoh's army to its doom, and unleashed a barrage of vitriolic and sanctimonious rhetoric. Tisbury's voice boomed; it was clear and resonant, and commanded attention, if not respect.

"All of you inside this house, in the name of decency and the common good and all that is right and just and holy, we call on you to hand over this Sherlock Holmes, the devil's own! The devil's own detective! Yes, he is! He is a creature of caprice and malice and unholy intent. Say amen, my brothers and sisters."

Tisbury seemed to swivel at the hip, first left, then right, taking in all of his cohorts, his arms still upraised.

"Brothers and sisters, say amen," he ordered again. And a reedy chorus of "Amens" came back to him. Thus fortified, Tisbury continued. The spying policeman, meanwhile, had left his station by the lamp post and was nervously watching the goings-on from about half the distance.

"He has slaughtered our friend Mr. John Godey. Mr. Godey, a man of the people. Mr. John Godey, the hero of Hope Settlement House. Say amen," Tisbury intoned. The faithful obliged. A few passersby had joined them, more out of curiosity than allegiance, I presumed.

"He has attempted the murders of the impoverished. He has warred against the infirm. He has raised his hand against women and children, against the blessed of the Lord. Say amen."

"He has been an agent of Satan. Say amen. He is an evil thing sent up from the blackest recesses of the infernal abyss. He does the dark lord's bidding. By helping him, all you in this house, you countenance his misdeeds and—"

The breaking of glass forced Tisbury to interrupt his tirade. Someone in his company had thrown a rock through the window of the front parlor. I heard Mrs. Hudson scream. I ran downstairs and rushed into the room. Outside, whistles were blowing and I could hear people running and shouting. I presumed that the man watching our house had called for reinforcements to deal with Tisbury and company.

"Are you all right?" I asked Mrs. Hudson.

"Oh, yes," our landlady said. "It just startled me. I don't think it was thrown very hard," she said. "The glass didn't fly far. Now, don't be making a fuss."

"You might well have been hurt, all the same," I said. "What was thrown?"

As I asked the question, I scanned the carpet for signs of the missile and found it quickly, a rock the size of a lime. I bent over to pick it up and found a note wrapped around it and tied in place with a white cotton string.

"Eleven tonight. Aurora Club. Bring Holmes. This could just as easily have been another bomb," the note said.

I had no sooner read it than an arm reached in over my shoulder. I could tell from the sleeve that the long arm belonged to one of the officers with the Metropolitan Police.

"I'd best take that," a deep voice said.

"See here," I said, turning quickly around as I spoke, "you've no right to—"

Uniformed policemen were coming into the house, and already before me, not a foot away, stood a man in uniform wearing big mutton-chop sideburns. He was scowling at me from under a shelf of bristly brown eyebrows. Because I was standing so close to him, I could not take in his entire frame or take stock of his stature or overall features. Up close, it was his eyes that gave him away: cool heather gray.

"Holm—" I blurted, and then turned the detective's name into a well-rounded cough, followed by a clearing of the throat.

He winked. "I guess I'll see you at eleven," he whispered. "Take the third hansom cab outside Paddington Station." Then he stepped into the background, ostensibly to examine the broken window.

"You, sir," another policeman called to me. "Was it a rock they used to break the window?"

I nodded and handed it to the man, a police lieutenant, who kept on talking. "They're lucky no one was hurt, 's'all I've got to say. I'm right tired o' this bunch," he said. "We'll see this time if we can't fix it so's they'll stay to home more."

"Very good," I said. "I'm sure they'll get what's coming to them."

By now, of course, Holmes was gone. He must have anticipated that there would be some movement in the case today; there was no other way to explain his presence, certainly not by coincidence. Although it wouldn't be out of the question for him to have stirred the pot himself, so to speak: maybe he had somehow even suggested the day's protest to Rev. Tisbury, especially if it was the only way Holmes could get near the house in safety.

And posing as a policeman, that was a stroke of genius.

If anybody had cause to ask questions, they would find that the unidentified policeman was most readily distinguished by his big bushy sideburns; of course, that was entirely the point. Good disguises often deflect attention to some spurious feature; it's a major element of the costume, and one that Holmes, of all people, knew how to exploit to grand effect.

I learned only much later that Ryder had hired a street Arab to throw the rock and the message through Mrs. Hudson's window. The transaction was witnessed by Holmes himself.

I marveled at the man's nerve; little did I know just how much more of it we both would need.

Chapter 31

After supper I poured myself a whisky and read for a while. I was looking for a comfortable way to pass some time before my appointment with Holmes and our visit to the Aurora Club, but there was none. I could not force myself to think of anything else. Our progress in the case had been stalled and then diverted, and now I was eager to have us back on track.

I finally gave in to my restlessness; I disassembled my faithful Webley Double Action revolver, meticulously cleaned, oiled and loaded it, and then slipped the gun into a shoulder holster that I had recently bought. Too many times the protruding hammer of the revolver had snagged and torn my coat pocket. I figured it was only a matter of time before my luck ran out and the lack of a proper holster cost me and Holmes that which we could not spare, and I was determined to give providence a helping hand. I was pleased to find that the holster was comfortable and discreet, too. I put a handful of extra cartridges in my coat pocket and laughed to myself: "Just in case we have to fight a war, I suppose." Then I set out for Paddington Station.

It was a black night. No moon. No stars. Just darkness like ink, broken only by surreal glowing pockmarks of orange-yellow lamp light, and air so cold that it felt like a knife in the lungs. I put my head down, tucked my chin into the upraised collar of my overcoat and walked quickly. I was at the station in a matter of minutes. It was busy for a late night, which was fortunate; I didn't have to wait long for the third hansom cab in the row to present itself for occupancy. When it did, I got in. As soon as the door closed, I realized I was not alone.

"It's good to see you, Watson," Holmes said.

"And you," I replied.

"You brought your revolver?"

"Of course."

"Good. Let's hope we don't need it."

"Holmes, I have no idea what we are doing."

"I'm not surprised," the detective said. "The pieces have all come together at once."

"You must explain," I said.

"All right," Holmes said. "The Aurora Club is not far, so we don't have much time. Let us begin with the obvious: Jack Ryder is a most worthy adversary."

"Are you certain it is Ryder?" I asked.

"Who else could it be? His intention and his involvement have been daringly forthright almost from the start. I told you: When he paid me the two hundred pounds he lost, he might as well have challenged me to break up his game. If I remember correctly, Watson, you suggested I was reading too much into his actions."

"Well, he did not appear to be that sophisticated," I said. "Then, was it also Ryder who posed as you in order to place the adverts?"

"It had to be, Watson, yes. You will recall that he is rather like me in some physical respects."

"I still don't understand why we're meeting him like this."

"We have no choice."

"Holmes, the man is a blackguard, and if he is to blame for this mess, then he also is a cold-blooded killer. We could be riding to our deaths tonight."

"I hardly think so," Holmes said.

"And why not?"

"Killing me now would spoil his fun."

"His *fun*," I said sharply. "John Godey is dead. Tommy is orphaned again. Jack Ryder has framed you for a murder. A share of the public wants your head, as do the police, and the man has threatened to set off a bomb in our house. If I get the chance, I'm going to—"

"Calm down, old friend," Holmes said, and I caught the edge in his voice. "I didn't say *I* was having fun. I said Ryder is having fun, and he doesn't want it to end. Make no mistake, Watson. I intend to stop this scoundrel, if not tonight, then soon. Very, very soon."

"And this so-called meeting?"

"He wants me out of the way."

"So you go walking right into his lair, big as life, and he shoots you dead. Case closed. Excuse me for saying so, Holmes, but that doesn't appear to be much of a plan."

"No, no, no. You don't understand. Ryder is a thief and a killer, but above all he is a player of games, a gambler. The bigger the game, the better, but the play is the thing."

It seemed obvious to me that Jack Ryder was not alone in his love of the game, but there would have been no profit in criticizing Holmes; he could not change that aspect of his nature. The hansom cab slowed and then stopped.

"Well," Holmes said, "let's not keep him waiting. After you, Watson."

We alighted from the cab quickly and walked straight to the darkened front door of the Aurora Club, which was closed between Christmas and New Year's. We didn't have to knock. The door opened and Jack Ryder stood in the entrance with his arms folded across his chest. He was wearing a black wide-brim Stetson with a low crown, and it made him look a bit like an outlaw from the old American West. He fixed us with a sardonic smile.

"How good of you to come, gentlemen," he said.

"How could we refuse?" Holmes replied.

"Exactly," Ryder said. He turned, walked to the double doors of the huge gaming room and opened them. Most of the room was in shadows; it was as silent and foreboding now as it had been noisy and chaotic when we were there last.

"I trust you would not object to joining me at my table?" Ryder asked Holmes.

The detective was silent; he extended his arm toward the table. Ryder smiled, proceeded across the floor, and we followed. He took a seat at the gaming table where we had first encountered him, and we sat opposite.

"You have proven resourceful, Mr. Holmes," Ryder said. "I had rather hoped you would be moldering in one of your fine British jail cells by now."

"Sorry to disappoint you, but if anyone is bound for jail, it is you," Holmes said.

"Oh, I don't think so, Mr. Holmes. I really don't."

"We shall see soon enough, Mr. Ryder. Now, pray get to the point of this meeting before I lose my patience."

"And wouldn't that be a shame, now?"

Holmes rose to his feet so quickly that he startled me. Instinctively, I reached for my revolver as I got to my feet. Ryder was half out of his chair; in an instant he had tipped off his Stetson, pulled a pearl-handled derringer from it, cocked and aimed it. By the time he rose to his full height, the pistol already was at arm's length and aimed directly at Holmes' head. I am proud to report, however, that by then I had thumbed back the hammer on my Webley, leaned sharply across the table and brought it to bear directly on the center of the gambler's chest. The end of the gun barrel was no more than two feet from him.

The gambler and the detective were locked in each other's stare.

"I could kill you," Ryder said.

"And die in the process," Holmes said.

Ryder's response was a sardonic smile.

"All right," he said. The gambler raised his small pistol toward the ceiling; I backed off the hammer on mine.

"This is not the American West," Holmes said. "You are wasting my time. We're leaving, Watson."

"Wait," the gambler said. "There are two large canvas sacks beneath my chair. I'm going to reach down and pick one up, then put it on the table." I kept my revolver in my hand as he did so.

"I want you out of the game, Mr. Detective," Ryder said. "I am prepared to buy your hand. Open the bag."

"Ryder, you are boring me," Holmes said. "If you want that bag opened, then do so yourself."

Ryder frowned, lifted the bag over the table and pulled on its drawstring. Stack after stack of counted and bundled bank notes toppled out. He shook the bag and more fell out. By the time the second sack was empty, the entire top of the table was covered with bundles of money, two and three layers deep.

"That's half of what a hundred thousand pounds looks like, boys."

Holmes' reaction startled me. His mouth opened slightly, but he said nothing. He sat down and stared at the piles of currency. He appeared transfixed, numb, like a man who had just received horrible news. I could not understand what I was witnessing. Holmes' numerous successes as a detective had left him well off, but money always had been incidental, always far more a by-product of his work than the reason for it. Always. In fact, he had never seemed to care one iota about wealth, his or anyone else's. It seemed incongruous for him to be captivated by this display, but captivated he was, and there was no mistaking it.

I looked at Ryder and hated the smug, thin smile that I saw on his face.

"I seem to have finally gotten your attention, Mr. Holmes," the gambler said.

"What do you want?" Holmes asked, his voice flat and lifeless.

"Nothing," Ryder said. "You see, that's the irony. I want you to do . . . nothing." In his annoying, entirely self-satisfied way Ryder was playing now, trying to be coy, and he was not very good at it. "You may leave here right now with all of the money that you see before you; let me remind you there is another identical sack of it on the floor.

"One of the club's cabs is at the curb; just tell the driver where to take you. However, this does presume, of course, that tomorrow, Mr. Holmes—and you, too, Dr. Watson—the two of you will simply stay home. You may enjoy a quiet New Year's Eve counting your fortune and devising ways you might spend it."

"You mean, neither of us is to attend Lady Armstrong's affair?" Holmes asked.

"That's correct," Ryder said. "I have plans, you see."

"I know," Holmes said. "I've known for some time."

"You have not known, Mr. Holmes; you have suspected," Ryder said. "There is a difference, eh? Tell me, what have you suspected, Mr. Holmes?"

"The stone, the Blood of Punjab. That's what you want."

"Terrible to be so predictable," Ryder said, "but yes, if you were to fill ten of these tables with money, the value would not be nearly as great as what that single stone is worth." Ryder's voice changed, subtly perhaps, but noticeably all the same. His tone was stronger, less playful. His words came faster.

Ryder slammed his fist onto the piles of money. "I want that stone," he said. "You will not stand in my way." The man was obsessed with the Blood of Punjab.

The detective had not been looking at Ryder; now he did.

"I may simply take the money and . . . and leave?" Holmes asked.

"That's right," Ryder said.

"What is to prevent me from taking your money and then finding a way to interfere with your plans tomorrow night?"

"Why, sir, your word as a gentleman," Ryder said. "What else? What greater security could I have than the word of the great Sherlock Holmes?"

"I accept your compliment for what it is, Mr. Ryder, which is to say meaningless," Holmes said, "but even so, you realize that are gambling with one hundred thousand pounds, no?"

"Of course," Ryder said. He gave out with a loud coarse laugh. "I am a gambler, after all. And if the stakes weren't high, and the game a little . . . dangerous, shall we say?— it wouldn't be worth my time, now, would it?"

"A valid point," Holmes said. "Well then, Watson, if you would be so kind as to help me refill this bag . . ."

I looked at Holmes, and the disgust in my eyes must have registered, for he did not look directly at me when he handed me the empty sack. I was tempted to refuse, but I did not. Instead, I crooked my arm like the end of a croupier's stick and swept the money toward me into the waiting maw of the sack.

Holmes helped by eagerly pulling more bundles of money toward us with both hands. Ryder watched, a smug grin on his face. He took a watch from his pocket, opened it and announced, "That took us less than thirty minutes. See how easy it was?"

I tied off my bulging sack. Holmes opened the second bag, removed a bundle of bank notes and examined the bills carefully.

"Oh, Mr. Holmes," Ryder said. "You don't trust me? I am so disappointed."

"No," Holmes said with an air of resignation. "I do not trust you. It turns out that you are not a worthy opponent, after all, and I sincerely regret that. I thought you had some mettle, but it turns out that you are hardly worth my time. Allowing us to see that watch was supremely arrogant, Mr. Ryder, and stupid."

The pocket watch was still open in the palm of his hand. As Ryder looked down at it, I took note of the timepiece for the first time, and clenched my teeth so hard that I made an audible clack. It was Tommy's gold pocket watch, the one John Godey had given him for Christmas.

"Oh, this little trinket," Ryder said. He raised his head and stared hard at Holmes. "You may consider it my hole card," he said.

Holmes didn't flinch. He glared at the gambler and spoke words that were hard, flat and so utterly devoid of humanity that it was frightening.

"You have lost this game, Ryder," Holmes said. "The boy means nothing to me."

"Is that a fact?" Ryder asked. "Well, then I guess it also won't matter too much how he's treated until this is over, will it? All the same, Mr. Holmes, just in case you're running a bluff, I think we'll keep him safe and healthy a while longer. Whether the runt lives past New Year's Eve is still going to depend on how you play your cards. If you and the good doctor stay home and count your money, maybe the boy'll live to a ripe old age."

Holmes said nothing. He hoisted the sack to his shoulder, turned and walked away in silence; I did the same.

We were halfway to the door when Ryder called out, "Mr. Holmes."

We stopped but did not turn around.

"Don't be so hangdog. Every man has his price. We just agreed upon yours, that's all." We continued walking. "At least it's quite a lot of money."

Ryder broke into a long rolling peal of laughter. It echoed through the cavernous room. We closed the double doors behind us and I could still hear the sound. It stuck in the air the way a foul deed sticks in the conscience.

Chapter 32

I let my canvas sack fall to the stone landing at the top of the stairs to the Aurora Club.

"Holmes," I said, "you had better tell me that this is some kind of ruse."

He smiled at me. I did not smile back.

"Have a little faith, Watson, will you? Come. We've got to put this in a safe place."

I had all I could do not to argue, not to demand to know at once what Holmes thought he was doing by taking a fortune in blood money from that murderous scoundrel in return for not cleaving him in two, but then I shook myself, took a deep breath and shouldered the sack. "A little faith," he had said. Through all manner of danger and travail, I always had trusted Holmes implicitly, and on balance, he had never let me down. I decided this was not the time to change my habit.

"The Diogenes Club," Holmes told the driver.

Holmes' brother, Mycroft, was out of town briefly, but one of his friends, a charter member of the club who actually lived on the premises, let us in. Phineas Cobb was well into his eighth decade. He was a skinny, wrinkled little fellow with a scant few strands of hair on the left side of his head; these he kept plastered in straight lines extending straight across his bald scalp. I had no idea what his profession had been, but he had been associated with London's oddest club for so many years that his name was nearly synonymous with it. More to the point, he embodied all that it stood for, which was not much. Phineas Cobb always was silent, therefore his virtue was never challenged.

"Phineas, Mycroft is out of town, but I need to store these sacks for a couple of days," Holmes said.

The old man nodded, turned and, after closing the door behind us, walked up the stairs to the second floor. He led us down a long corridor to stairs at the back of the building that led to a third floor. We followed dutifully. At a small closet midway down the corridor, Cobb stopped and unlocked and opened the door, which was, I noted, exceptionally thick. Boxes and sheaves of papers filled the lower two shelves, which were about four feet deep, but the top shelf was empty. Holmes threw both sacks onto it, pushed them toward the back, took boxes from each of the lower shelves, and put them in front of the sacks, and then shut the door. Cobb locked it and then gave Holmes the key.

"I need to stay the night, Phineas."

The old man nodded, guided us back down to a room on the second floor and left. It was a lavish bedchamber, outfitted with every comfort one could wish for. A small bathroom adjoined.

"I won't exactly be roughing it, will I?" Holmes mused.

"I should say not. Now, tell me what's going on, Holmes. Please."

"I was worried that you might raise a fuss back there," he said. "I am glad that you didn't."

I nodded. "But I have no idea why you took the money."

"I need Ryder to think that he has very nearly won. The power of money is one of the few things he knows and understands. His fatal flaw is his inability to accept that others can be indifferent to it. The pile of money told me precisely how high the stakes are."

"Yes, a hundred thousand pounds," I said.

"No, Watson. That's just the amount he's actually willing to lose. He stands to gain much, much more than that, so much more that he needed insurance. That's why he took the boy."

"If we show our faces at the charity dinner," I said, "he'll know we're trying to stop him from stealing the gem, and he'll kill Tommy, or have him killed."

"That's what he wants us to believe," Holmes said, "yes."

"You were bluffing about not caring for the boy, weren't you, Holmes?"

"Of course, Watson. I don't think I fooled Ryder in the

least about that. What Ryder doesn't know is, I did not intend to."

"I don't follow you."

"As long as Ryder saw through my bluff, Watson, he will be thinking that we won't interfere with his plans—out of fear for the boy's life."

"But, of course, we will interfere," I said.

"We have to. He's going to kill the boy. In fact, we can count ourselves lucky that he has not done so already. We've got to get Tommy out of Ryder's clutches before he completes his play tomorrow night."

"Damn him," I exclaimed. "If he wants fireworks, Holmes, let's give it to him. We're wasting time."

"No, Watson, we can't. He is prepared for us to move against him between now and the start of tomorrow night's festivities. And if we were to do so, he would kill Tommy. I could not take such a risk."

"What are we supposed to do? Just let Ryder make his play and hope that he turns Tommy loose out of a sense of fairness? Not bloody likely, would you say?"

"No, of course not," Holmes said, "unless . . ."

"Unless what?"

"By thunder, that's it, Watson. You said it a moment ago: 'If he wants fireworks . . .' That's it. Yes. Once again, Watson, you have struck on it."

"What are you talking about, Holmes?"

"Watson, didn't you set off fireworks at that reunion with your old comrades from the Northumberland Fusiliers?"

"Yes," I said, "but what's that got—"

"The rockets that were left over. Are they still stored in the cellar?"

"Uhm, well, yes. How did you know? I didn't want . . . I mean, if Mrs. Hudson were to know I had explosives in the house . . . So I packed them—"

"Yes, yes. I know. I know. Can they be seen or heard from a long distance, a very long distance?"

"Well, yes. One in particular, it's a monster, must be nearly three feet long and a good six inches in diameter, and it— Holmes, what are you laughing at?"

"If Mrs. Hudson knew you had a fireworks shell that size in her cellar, you'd be out on the street, and me with you."

"I suppose that's why I hid it."

"Indeed," Holmes said, still laughing. "All right, all right. Here's what we must do . . ."

We spent the next couple of hours developing and refining the plan. By the time I returned to Baker Street and climbed into bed for a few hours of long overdue sleep, I was fairly convinced that what had seemed unimaginable now seemed merely impossible. At least it was a step in the proper direction.

Chapter 33

The decade was ending on a night in which the London air was so cold and clear and sharp that it actually felt clean. Berkeley Square was alive with merriment and anticipation. Garlands of lush evergreens were wound about every street lamp, and each was ablaze in gaslight. Candles glowed in every window of every grand house that faced the square. Small torches lighted the brick and stone walkways to stately entrances that had been specially decorated for the occasion. Knots of well-dressed carolers strolled up and down the streets, filling the air with song and goodwill and, with every exhaled breath, a sharp little burst of fog.

Planetree was twice as gay and bright as any town house on the square. A steady stream of broughams and carriages and coaches pulled up to the pavement at the home of Lady Mirabelle Llewellyn Armstrong, where a battalion of people took over the cumbersome task of handling traffic. Small countries had been invaded with less organization and planning, I'm sure.

A liveried footman helped each couple alight and then assigned and directed their driver to one of several nearby side streets that had purposely been cleared and, for convenience' sake, blocked off at their far ends. At the top of every side street stood a traffic manager whose job it was to record which couple's conveyance was parked where. When the street was full, the manager brought his "census" back to the captain of valets, who was strategically stationed by the front door, and then quickly returned to his post at the top of the street.

A couple who was taking their leave of Planetree would be announced to the valet. The valet consulted his census and, if all was working well, he would know at a glance which traffic manager needed to be hailed. The valet dispatched a runner to the proper manager at the top of the proper street. The manager then summoned the proper carriage, and mere minutes later, Lady Armstrong's guests would board their carriage and head home out of Berkeley Square.

That, at least, was the theory, and were it not for the effects of copious holiday drinks and New Year's toddies on drivers, managers, runners and valets alike, the system probably would have worked quite well. Unfortunately, the drinking began quite early, probably in honor of the cold weather. And then there were the difficulties posed by more common folk. Costermen selling hot chestnuts, or bangers with peppers and onions, or strong coffee came into the side streets from the blocked-off far ends. And with them came throngs of Londoners of all stripes, all eager to see the toffs and their ladies. Mixed into this melange of humanity, of course, were pickpockets and toughs and a good many prostitutes. By the time Lady Armstrong's guests had been served their preprandial drinks, a good many of the drivers were already ringing in the New Year inside their lordship's coaches with their trousers down around their ankles.

Naturally, where there were so many people, there needed to be police to keep a semblance of order; but it was also New Year's Eve, and whether the lords and ladies on Berkeley Square thought it quite right or not, the police were not about to spoil everyone's good time. Despite that, they managed to mediate arguments, break up fights, scare off an occasional ill-tempered lout or mollify a foul-mouthed lady of the night. They kept the peace and maintained a measure of goodwill, despite the fact that their job didn't get any easier as the night wore on.

Inside Planetree, of course, the cream of the upper orders were enjoying themselves immensely, which is to say with studiously polite and invariably meaningless conversation that was liberally sprinkled with venomous innuendo and self-conscious double entendres, most of them bawdy. Looking in at these people, peering in through the high-wall French doors, was like watching a private theater of the absurd. One grotesque after another, some of the biggest names on the city's large social register, flitted by the glass doors en route to one more overeager handshake, or perfunctory kiss on a heavily powdered, cloyingly sweet-smelling cheek. It was a world that depended on its own hypocrisies for validation; without masses of impoverished people for contrast, how would the rich know they were well off? It was not a world of which either Holmes or I were terribly enamored, though it was, in fact, the one in which we lived.

When at last Lady Armstrong entered the large banquet room, it was with her guard, Cuthbert Wilson, nearby and discreetly watching all of the time. On her own, especially at a gathering such at this, Lady Armstrong was a vital presence, but with the storied Blood of Punjab atop her décolletage, she was stunning. She knew it, of course, and savored every moment, every proffered hand, every insincere kiss, every insipid, cooing smile and every graceful and grateful touch. It was luxurious to be envied, regardless of the reason, and the Blood of Punjab offered a great one.

In any light, the large deep red stone was a fantastic thing. It was set in a field of glistening blue-white diamonds, each worth a small fortune, but none so fine as to compare with the gem at their center. It was perfection. Every facet of its ample surface seemed to feed on light, capturing it, pulling it in, devouring it, turning it around and around each of its twelve distinct rays, drawing it in deeper and deeper and deeper, as though the stone itself had no bottom, only a blood-red, measureless depth that reflected light back to the surface and out into the world again, as if the priceless jewel were truly just the shining of an immortal captive star. Under the bright new electric lights with which the banquet room was equipped, the gem seemed wonder. No wonder Jack Ryder was obsessed by it.

The American entered the room well behind Lady Armstrong. He was flanked by his beautiful sister, Jane, and Lord David. Each carried a drink and smiled pleasantly. They seemed to know everyone, or rather, everyone seemed to know them, which, of course, was better.

To properly present the sumptuous meal that was one of the evening's highlights, it took nearly as many waiters and servants as there were guests. No heads of state ever dined better than did the guests at Lady Mirabelle Llewellyn Armstrong's New Year's Eve dinner to benefit the Working Man's Christian Improvement and Grace Abounding Benevolent Society of Newcastle Upon Tyne. It would be talked about for years to come.

Every table had a complement of two children, a boy and a girl served up directly from the streets of London or one of the city's settlement houses, workhouses or orphanages. They had been washed, dressed, coached and rendered just as presentable as any of the suckling pigs, filleted salmon or steamship roasts of rare red beef that graced their tables. I was suddenly glad Tommy was not a part of the display.

Midway through the third course, at 9:23 P.M., the electric lights slowly dimmed all over the room. The crowd murmured in awe, to which Lady Armstrong smiled appreciatively. She, of course, was at the head table with some of the most notable members of the peerage clustered around her. Directly behind the head table, the corner of the room by the immense French doors lay in darkness. Lady Armstrong's ever present guard stood in the light just beyond, surveying the room constantly.

As if from nowhere, the room was suddenly engulfed in music, a violin concerto, commanding and energetic one moment, softly melodic and infinitely melancholic the next. The music continued for perhaps four or five minutes. Then light began to illuminate the darkened corner near Lady Armstrong's table, and in it was the source of the music, a violinist who had to be the famed Signore Giacomo Famiglietti.

The light grew brighter and brighter until it seemed that he was playing at the center of the sun. His face appeared to be deeply lined and bearded, but it was hard to tell because he was half turned to the windows, away from the harsh white light. In the distance a crimson red spot exploded against the clear black sky. It caught the attention of the diners nearest the window; they pointed and smiled, but the violinist kept their attention. His fingering was nearly maniacal in its speed, and his bowing was extraordinary. It was delicate and precise, and as capable of infinite nuance and subtlety as it was possessed of great narrative

power. The piece he played was obscure, but that did not
seem to matter. His fingers flew over the frets of his beautiful instrument with impossible speed. His bow was possessed. The crowd responded eagerly. Some of the diners
pushed their chairs from the table and rose to their feet,
applauding all the while and shouting, "Bravo! Bravo!"

Then the entire room was plunged into darkness. The
music stopped abruptly. The crowd was startled and confused, immobilized. Some chairs scraped on the floor. There
were footsteps, some running, then a woman's shriek, as
sharp and thin as a wire. It fell away as quickly as it had
arisen. For the briefest of moments, the big crowded room
fell eerily, frighteningly silent, and then it erupted in chaos
and pandemonium.

Chapter 34

I, meanwhile, was in another part of the city. Holmes had calculated that I would have about ninety minutes in which to rescue Tommy and execute our plan. By then, having not been confronted by Holmes, Jack Ryder would feel free to attempt the theft of the great double-star ruby. It came down to this: I had to get the boy to safety shortly after the start of the dinner at eight o'clock. Then, at about half-nine, with Signore Famiglietti's performance under way, I was to signal Holmes that Tommy was safe.

"If I know the boy is beyond harm, one way or the other," Holmes said, "then I will do whatever needs to be done to stop Ryder. But I must know, or I will take no action."

I sat back on the ride across town to the East End, thinking about our conversation and the plan we had devised. I was headed for Hope Settlement House, and not just because that was where Tommy lived.

"He's in the hands of that harpy, matron Edna Phillips," Holmes had said. "She's one of the puzzle pieces we've been missing, Watson. One of the cable inquiries I made on Christmas Day went to my old friend Pinkerton in the United States. He reported back only yesterday that our man Jack Ryder is not related to Chicago's socially prominent Ryders. It sounds as though the man may have traded on the family's name for a while, using it as entree until representatives of the family chased him off.

"No shock there," Holmes said, "but what did surprise me was the fact that while Pinkerton knew quite a lot about our gambler, he had no idea who this Jane Ryder might be; she did not fit the description of the woman normally in Ryder's company, his wife, Emma. Pinkerton described her as tall, strikingly attractive, prematurely gray hair, physically imposing, and notably austere."

"The matron?" I asked.

"Just so," Holmes said. "It fits. She is relatively new to Hope Settlement House; she started there late last spring. I feel certain Tommy is in her clutches. I don't think Ryder would entrust the boy's fate to anyone else. In fact, I am sure of it."

"She would hurt him, you think?"

"Watson, she was in the day room watching the festivities and waiting for the bomb to go off. She may even have carried the device into the building. I think she'd kill the boy in an instant."

"Doesn't Ryder need a way to signal her, though? He has to tell her whether to let him go or . . . I see," I said. "There's no way for him to signal her, is there?"

Holmes shook his head.

"Then the boy could be dead already," I said.

"It's possible, Watson, yes. But I suspect not. The odds are at least in his favor. I don't think the Ryders will decide what to do with Tommy until they are sure the game is over."

"I hope you are right, Holmes."

"So do I, Watson. For now, we have no choice but to presume that I am. You just plan to get Tommy out of there shortly after eight o'clock."

"I'll do my best, Holmes," I said.

I had gone to the offices of *The Daily Telegraph* and sought out the reporter Peter Brooks.

"I need your help, Mr. Brooks," I said, "but in return, by virtue of the events that should unfold, you will have a sensational story."

"Indeed?" the young man said. "And what might the headline on it be, if I may be so bold?"

"How about this? 'Holmes Surfaces, Nabs Killer of Settlement House Hero John Godey' "

"On the level?" Brooks asked.

"Absolutely," I said, "but it could get a bit nasty."

"I'm your man," the reporter said.

"There's one other thing."

"What'd that be, gov?"

"We're going to need one of those *Daily Telegraph* delivery wagons, one of the smallish ones that you see all the time dropping off newspapers at the stands—with some newspapers in it, just for authenticity's sake."

"I suppose you'll be wantin' a horse, too," the reporter said.

"I'd rather thought that would go without saying," I told him.

"You're bloody well serious, aren't you, Doc?"

"We don't have much time, young man," I said. "If you can't help me, I'll manage some other way." I tried to sound confident, but I wasn't. There was no other way.

"If the boss gets wind of this, it'll be my head for sure," Brooks said. "Oh, what the bleedin' hell! Let's do it."

"Very good, Mr. Brooks," I said. "Very good, indeed. I will be looking for you at 221B Baker Street in one hour."

"I'll be there," the reporter said.

He was as good as his word, and right on time. I came out of our house trying to look inconspicuous while carrying an eight-foot length of chain and an outsized explosive skyrocket wrapped in newspapers. I put the package in the back of the wagon, beside the bundle I had asked Brooks to bring, threw in the chain and went back into the house. A moment later, I came out with four three-foot lengths of rigid stovepipe. I added them to the cargo, pulled a canvas tarpaulin over it and got up next to Brooks.

"What's that, Doc?" the reporter asked with a laugh. "You bringing your own fireworks to this party?"

"I am, indeed, Mr. Brooks," I said. "That's exactly what I'm doing."

The reporter didn't know what to say. "Hey, Doc. You know, I was kidding."

"I wasn't," I said. "Let's go."

En route, I explained what I was going to do.

"That's not much of a plan, Doc," he said. "Did you play a lot of rugby, by any chance?"

"Quite a lot, in fact," I said. "Why do you ask?"

"You must have been something out there," Brooks said. "Just waded into 'em, didn't you?"

"I see your point," I said with a chuckle. "Yes, I did."

It was nearly eight o'clock when we pulled into the small courtyard of Hope Settlement House.

"Step lively," I told Brooks, "we have very little time." I handed him the length of chain and said, "If anybody tries to stop us, you swing that chain like you were driving moneychangers from the temple. Let's go. And stay close."

We ran up to the door, and I knocked hard and kept knocking until I heard footsteps and a voice.

"Hold your horses, there. I'm coming. I'm coming."

I was convinced that the key to making the rescue work was speed and brute efficiency, but I was not comfortable with the knowledge that, in all likelihood, I would have to treat a woman roughly. That is not in my nature; nor is it in Holmes'. I was determined, however, that if that was the only recourse, then I would do whatever needed to be done, no matter how unsavory, especially if Tommy's life depended on it. "Work fast," I told myself. "Don't give them room to think. And don't stop. Maintain the offensive. Don't stop. Just don't stop."

I backed away two steps as the knob on the front door to Hope Settlement House turned. When the attendant opened the door a crack, I hit it hard with my shoulder and kept going. The door caught the poor man in the side of the head, and by the time he hit the floor Brooks and I were well past him, heading straight down the ground-floor corridor for the matron's office. Most of the living quarters for staff and tenants of the settlement house were upstairs or out toward the back of the building, and that worked to our distinct advantage, particularly on a night when people could be counted on for revelry and merriment. I was relieved that while there were such noises, they emanated from more distant parts of the house, not here.

There was no one in the hallway. I walked up to the door of the matron's office, withdrew my pistol from its holster, and kicked the door open; it flew back on its hinges and hit the adjoining wall so hard that it almost bounced shut again. The response from inside the office was a scream—rather mild, I thought—and a muffled sort of shout, which was odd. I ran into the room, Brooks by my side, and then I understood. It would be a gross understatement to say that we had surprised Mrs. Emma Ryder, for she was busy entertaining her guest, none other than Inspector Miles Wallingford. The awkward position she was in must have made it difficult at first to see who had barged in. At least she had most of her clothes on. Wallingford was another story, however. There was no sign of his pants.

"Good evening, Inspector," I bellowed.

"What do you think you're doing?!" he bellowed.

"I might ask the same of you," I replied. "I'll bet Mrs. Wallingford is nowhere around, is she? You rascal."

So saying, I walked straight up to the man and hit him in the side of the head with the barrel of my pistol. He dropped to the floor like a sack of grain.

Mrs. Emma Ryder was hardly paying attention. She was standing beside her desk, pulling her skirt down, trying to brush off some dark smudges. She looked straight at me and said, "Did you like what you saw, Doctor? There's more. If the two of you—"

My own admonition echoed in my head: "Don't stop. Just don't stop." I thumbed back the hammer of my pistol, pushed her hard into the office wall and, before she could retaliate, pressed the cold barrel of the gun against her forehead, pinning her there.

"Where is the boy, Mrs. Ryder?"

The use of her real name seemed to give her some pause, but not much. Her eyes were alive with fury, and she tried to bat my arm with her left hand. I slapped it away and pressed the end of the barrel harder into her flesh. I shifted my weight, anticipating her next move, and it's a good thing I did, because in that instant she drove her knee into the top of my leg instead of my groin. I slapped her face, hard. The look she gave me was as pure in its hatred as any I had ever imagined, but there was something else in her eyes, too: She was enjoying this.

"The boy," I said, my face only inches from hers. "Where is he?"

She spat in my face. I jammed my forearm across her throat, and pushed hard upward so as to bring her up on her toes gasping for breath. It was then that I took a close look at the smudges on her uniform. Dried blood, at least one was, but most of the others were . . . what?

"Stove black," I said aloud. I spun the woman around

so that I was behind her. I knotted up the collar of her uniform in my fist, which had the effect of pulling the front of the collar tight against her throat. "Walk," I said. "As God is my witness, I will shoot you if I have to."

"Where do you think—"

"Shut up!" I said. "Brooks, we're going out back to the kitchen; it's off the day room."

At the mention of our destination, Emma Ryder twisted out of my grasp, turned and swiped at my face, trying to gouge me with her fingers. I jolted backward to avoid her, but slipped and fell, cursing my luck as I hit the floor, pistol in hand. She kicked viciously at my face a couple of times but missed, and as I got to my knees I whipped the barrel of my gun across her shin.

She started to scream, but Brooks threw the chain around her neck and pulled back on it hard with both hands. I scrambled to my feet. Emma Ryder straightened to the pressure on her neck, and her hands flew up to the chain, clutching at it, trying to relieve the pressure, but she could not. Brooks held her in front of him at arm's length.

"Walk," he told her. "Walk, or I'll strangle you."

Having to alternately push, pull or drag the matron made progress toward the kitchen slow, but in a few minutes we were there. I turned up the lights and looked around but saw nothing amiss. I opened the big pantry, walked inside, opened every door and drawer and found no trace of the boy. I lifted the lids on every barrel of flour and sugar. Nothing. I raced over to the ice room, pulled open the heavy door and poked about among the butter tubs and cuts of meat. I was quick but as thorough as need be. Still nothing. I went back out to the kitchen, then into an adjoining supply room, but Tommy was nowhere in evidence. I looked at my watch.

"Good God, it's a quarter-to," I said loudly.

I heard a thud. Then another. I turned, and the next thud was clearer. I was facing one of four big stoves. I raced to the first, threw open the oven door; nothing. Then the second; nothing. Then the third . . .

"Tommy!" I shouted. He had been gagged, trussed up like a holiday goose and stuffed into the cold oven. He had wriggled one foot free and used it to make the thumping noise I had heard. I pulled him out, slipped the gag below his chin and pulled a small ball of cloth out of his mouth. He coughed and choked and took several deep breaths.

"Easy, lad," I said. "You're lucky you didn't suffocate. Take some deep breaths. Are you all right?"

He nodded several times and snuffled. His face was scratched and swollen; his left eye was half closed from a bruise. I untied him and he threw his arms around me.

"There, there," I said. I patted his head, and touched some matted blood. I could feel him pull away. "You'll be fine," I said, but now my teeth were clenched in anger at the Ryder woman.

"Come on, now, Tommy," I managed. "There's no time. The night's not over. Brooks and I are going to need your help yet."

I heard a noise and turned to see Brooks was having trouble with the matron. She was kicking and clawing at him viciously.

I snatched a cast-iron skillet off the stove, took two steps toward the woman and whacked her in the head with it. She fell flat.

"Thanks, Doc," Brooks said.

"Quite the gentleman, aren't I, Brooks? Beating up on a woman. Blast! I hate this."

"I don't know how bad I'd feel about that," he said.

"Yes, well . . ." In exasperation I threw the skillet across the kitchen floor. We used a hank of rope from the supply room to tie up the matron, just as she had trussed Tommy: legs tucked up tight behind her, arms pinned to her sides. Brooks and I dragged her into the supply room, pushed her into a deep closet and slammed the door.

"Brooks, take the rest of that rope," I said. "We'll want to truss up our friend Wallingford, too."

"That inspector bloke?" Tommy piped up. "Ya got 'im, too?"

"We did at that," I said.

"Good goin', Doc. You, too, Mr. Brooks."

I sent Tommy to his room for warm clothes, told him to go quietly and meet us out front as quickly as he could.

Wallingford was still out cold, fortunately. We bound him hand and foot, gagged him securely and propped him up-

right in the matron's office closet with his hands tied over
his head to the clothes pole. Three bright white uniforms
hung next to him. "Quite a picture," I thought to myself.
"Still life with fool." I closed the door and was about to
leave when I noticed there was a key in the lock. I turned
it, put the key in my pocket, and we left.

We collected Tommy at the front door. There was no
sign of the attendant we had flattened on our way in. I
hoped he was all right, but there wasn't much time to think
about it. I checked my watch; it was ten minutes after nine.
We ran to the wagon. The night seemed even colder now;
the air crisp and sharp and so cold that when I inhaled, my
nostrils stuck together.

"C'mon, Tony," Brooks called to the horse. "Let's show
'em what you've got now." He snapped the reins and
shouted, "Heeyaah! Gittup! Heeyaah!"

The horse snorted and whinnied and sent a plume of fog-
like warm breath into the night air. He dug in hard, and in
an instant we were fairly flying down the street.

Over the clatter and clack of the horse's hooves, Brooks
shouted at me, "Where to, Doc?"

"Due west," I said. A specific destination was unrealistic;
there was too little time. "Just go due west as far as you
can until I tell you to stop."

Brooks nodded, shouted, "Heeyaah! Heeyaah!" and
snapped the reins. The horse lurched forward and picked
up more speed.

I looked at Tommy and saw that his teeth were chat-
tering. I pulled him close to me.

"Tuck in here, lad," I said. "Keep your head down. That
wind's sharp."

Brooks was a fair hand with a horse. The reporter kept
us moving at an optimum pace; never out of control, but
never far from the edge either. I kept my pocket watch
open, and at 9:25 told Brooks to pull over. We were on
High Holborn Street, across from the Staple Inn.

Tommy and I jumped off as soon as Brooks stopped. He
tied the horse's reins to a stanchion, and we unloaded our
cargo. We slipped the four sections of stovepipe into each
other. I took my bearings quickly, envisioning a map of the
West End, the rough position of Berkeley Square and our

approximate location, but I was no navigator and couldn't pretend otherwise. I shook my head in dismay, but we went ahead and stood the twelve feet of stovepipe straight up at the end of the wagon, hurriedly lashed it to the tailgate and then tilted the pipe westward at an arbitrarily selected angle of about seventy-five degrees. No time for science; just guesswork. I cursed loudly into the cold night, for I hated knowing that so much depended on so little. We lifted the end of the pipe off the ground just enough to allow receipt of the skyrocket. I pushed the missile into the bottom of the pipe, propped a stick under it to keep it off the ground, checked the fuse to see that it was intact and unbroken and looked at my watch.

"Here are some matches, Tommy. You get to do the honors."

The boy's eyes practically glowed with excitement.

"I'll tell you when," I said, "but as soon as that fuse catches, you run. Go as fast as you can over to that tree and watch from behind it."

We wrapped the chain around the pipe once, and quickly adjusted it so that equal lengths of chain extended from the front and back of the pipe. Brooks got up in the wagon and took one end of the chain; I stood fast on the ground and took the other. We pulled the chain tight so that the angle of the pipe could not change.

My watch read 9:28. "Okay, Tommy," I said. "Light it."

The boy struck a match and the wind blew it out.

"Cup your hand around it, Tommy," I said.

He did, got a flame, quickly touched it to the fuse, and as soon as he saw it catch and smoke curl up from it, he got up and ran.

"Good boy," I said.

I watched the flame chase up the fuse and into the stovepipe out of sight. At that instant everything stopped, including my breathing. There was no past. No future. Only this small gap in time and space. And then sparks erupted from the rocket and it rumbled and shook violently in the pipe as if it were a terrible powerful force fighting against all restraint, threatening to explode and carry Brooks and me to oblivion, but it did not. Instead, with a loud and startling, roaring *whoosh* that was so sharp and compressed that it almost sounded like an explosion, the skyrocket leaped through the tube and shot up into the cold black sky, dragging an impossibly long tail of golden sparks. I have no idea how high it went—certainly to the top of several buildings stacked one atop the other. And then, like magic, it erupted into an immense, broad and circular flower of the brightest, deepest red light imaginable. It hung there, suspended in the darkness, and for the merest fraction of a second it seemed to achieve solidity and substance. Then it dissolved, as if destroyed by its own daring. No sooner was the sky fully black again, then came the rocket's reverberating explosion, like a shot from a battlefield cannon.

As loud as the skyrocket was, I doubted that Holmes would hear it. We were too far away still, but he might, he just might, see it. That was possible. I took a deep breath and hoped to heaven that the rocket had flown high enough.

Chapter 35

In the sudden and inexplicable darkness that had enveloped the crowd of diners at Planetree, the woman's shriek was terrifying. First had come confusion, then silence, consternation and panicked flight. Men and women began pushing toward the exits, shoving, tripping, falling. A couple of stern male voices called for order, but no one listened. There were screams from women who were being stepped on or pushed or knocked to the floor. Men cursed at whatever stood in their way. The big double doors to the room rattled and shook; first one set, then the other.

"We're locked in," a voice cried. "The doors are locked."

There were some gasps and murmurs. Curses.

"Break the windows out," somebody hollered.

At that very instant, as quickly as it had disappeared, light filled the room again, not harsh bright electric light but the warmer, yellower gaslight to which everyone was more accustomed. The gaslights had been left intact as backup. Lady Armstrong had embraced modernity but not completely. She had reserved final judgment about this electric illumination, and in this instance her reservations had paid off.

The restoration of light had a generally calming effect on the panicked crowd, at least until the head table came into focus. Lady Armstrong sat slumped forward, her head flat on the table. Lord Armstrong was hunched over her, feeling for a pulse. Some of the diners shouted and pointed. Two more women screamed. One who was very near the table promptly fainted; her spouse tried quickly and dutifully to revive her.

Fully a minute passed before anyone noticed that Lady Armstrong's guard, Cuthbert Wilson, was sitting on the floor, slumped against the wall in a widening crimson pool. His head hung straight down. Both of his hands were clutched at his throat, fastened around the handle of a dagger that was protruding from it. The entire front of his tuxedo was bloody.

There were more screams. Then shouts. Two men ran to Wilson's side. "Get the police," one of them called out.

"Break out the windows," another voice shouted.

Some women began to cry.

Signore Famiglietti stood with his violin tucked under his left arm, his bow in his right hand, looking at the crowd. He seemed oddly forlorn, as though he did not understand what was happening, or what to do or where to go.

Two men from a table off to the side of the room stood almost as one, snugged their tuxedo jackets down over their bellies and walked toward the double doors the way prize-fighters walk into a ring, with fierce determination.

They gripped the handles on the doors and were about to test the locks when a gunshot interrupted the effort; small bits of plaster fell harmlessly from a pockmark in the ceiling. As did everyone else, the two big men turned toward the source of the gunfire, a tall gaunt man in a waiter's uniform. He was standing at the front of the room, opposite the high French windows, about twenty feet from the head table, a pistol in his hand.

"Take your seats, please, everyone. And do so now." His voice was as strong and clear as any trained actor's, and he assumed command on center stage as if he were born to it. "Enough blood has been shed here already, but I am an excellent shot, so please, do as I say. Until the police arrive, I will keep my pistol at the ready.

"You two large gentlemen by the door. Would you use some of the napery to cover up poor Mr. Wilson, and then carry him off to the serving area? And if someone would help Lord Armstrong by splashing a bit of water on our hostess, I think you will find she is quite alive."

He paused and the diners watched as two women seated nearby gently pulled Lady Armstrong by her shoulders off the table and set her back in the chair.

"The necklace is gone!" one of the women at a nearby table shouted.

A man near Lady Armstrong half rose from his chair and pointed at the hostess. "The Punjab stone. It's stolen!" he hollered. "Look! Look!" He pointed at Lady Armstrong's bare neck, which now wore only a red welt, a memento from her assailant.

"Quiet, please. Quiet," the man with the pistol shouted. "If the Blood of Punjab has left this room, then my name isn't Sherlock Holmes."

There were some gasps from the crowd. A few of the diners muttered.

"Stop it, all of you . . . please." It was Lady Armstrong. She was pale, her voice reedy and quavering. She was leaning on Lord Armstrong, who had helped her to her feet.

"Mr. Wilson was my body guard and loyal servant," she said. "I want his murderer found out. Tonight!" Her anger brought some color back into her face. "And where is my necklace?"

"If someone would be good enough to paw around near you under the table," Holmes said, "I expect you will find the answer."

"I've got the necklace," a diner to the left of Lady Armstrong shouted. He held it aloft for everyone to see. Some people clapped. "They didn't make off with it, after all."

The man handed it to his hostess and sat down. She nodded in thanks, looked at the gem and gestured to her son. He rose promptly, accepted the necklace, put it around her neck and shut the clasp. Lady Armstrong adjusted the beautiful jewel atop her décolletage. There was more clapping. Holmes cut it off.

"Necklace or no necklace," he said, "murder has been committed, and the killer is still among us. So is an accomplice. There needed to be darkness, you see, so while we all were enjoying Signore Famiglietti's concerto, someone threw the master electrical switch, which is downstairs.

"Lestrade?" Holmes called out in a loud voice. "Inspector Lestrade?" A key turned in the lock of one of the doors, and in walked Lestrade, with Jane Ryder in handcuffs. She looked embarrassed and angry enough to kill. She shook her arm free of the inspector and glared at him.

Lord Armstrong half rose from his table at the front of the room.

"Jane!"

His voice was a strangled, sorrowful exclamation. He looked at his nearly betrothed and then at Holmes. The detective shook his head once, as if to warn him against any further display. Armstrong seemed to sag and deflate like a punctured balloon. He fell back into his seat. Lady Armstrong looked at her son but said nothing.

"This is Inspector Lestrade, ladies and gentlemen, one of Scotland Yard's best," Holmes said. "He was not expressly in charge of this case, but he has been on top of it from the very beginning. And tonight he was waiting to see if someone would douse the lights, as we expected might happen, and a good thing, too, or that beautiful young lady he has in tow would be several miles distant by now. Some of you may know her as Jane Ryder from Chicago, in America. Her real name, according to a constable in Plymouth who was kind enough to respond to my telegram, is Butler, Jane Butler, a barmaid whose services were enlisted by Mr. Jack Ryder—and his wife, Emma.

"Those of you who have visited the Aurora Club undoubtedly know Mr. Ryder, who . . . Oh, well. He doesn't appear to be in the room at the moment. Regardless, I am quite sure that none of you has met his most attractive wife, Emma.

"You see, she has not been herself of late. Instead, she has been Mrs. Edna Phillips, the matron of Hope Settlement House. It was she who secreted the bomb that took the life of Mr. John Godey and very nearly a good many others. But don't be alarmed; I have reason to believe that as of this moment she no longer poses a danger to anyone.

"But why has all of this happened, ladies and gentlemen?"

"I don't give a hoot why it happened," a man shouted from the middle of the room. "This doesn't concern us. This is tawdry theater. I demand that you put an end to it right now." Voices rose in agreement from the crowd.

Holmes fired another shot into the ceiling.

"I'm sure that most of you do not care," he said, "but you will listen. My name has been bandied about in the press, and I intend to clarify a few things. If you think me mad, meanwhile, so be it, and—"

"And," Inspector Lestrade chimed in over Holmes' voice,

"if you all don't remain seated, I'll see to it that nobody leaves this room before daybreak tomorrow. Crimes have been committed here, and none of you is above the law. Is that clear? Now, you have my permission to continue, Mr. Holmes."

The detective nodded in thanks to Lestrade.

"A captive audience, indeed," Holmes said. "Less than two weeks ago I and my companion, Dr. John H. Watson, had become involved with the Armstrong household, and Jack Ryder was afraid that we intended to thwart his plans. Our involvement came about only because of a young boy who was invited to this affair tonight as a token of the city's unfortunates. That is Master Thomas Payton Rogers, ward and nephew of the late Mr. John Godey. You all have read about him, I am certain."

Some murmurs went up from the crowd as Holmes pulled some of the puzzle pieces into place.

"To be perfectly blunt, when John Godey got wind of the plan for this affair tonight, he smelled a rat. More to the point, he was afraid that the rat would somehow end up biting his beloved Tommy."

It was at that moment that Tommy and Brooks and I walked into the room. I spoke with the inspector very quickly, told him where to find Emma Ryder and gave him the key to the closet where Inspector Wallingford was stowed. Then I tipped my hat to Holmes, who smiled and nodded and resumed his rather theatrical postmortem of the evening's events.

"Yes, yes," Holmes said sharply, stifling the noise which had begun to arise from the crowd. "All of you here meant well, and none more than Lady Armstrong, I am sure. But what went wrong? The lights went out shortly after the beginning of what looked to be a magnificent performance." Holmes gestured to Signore Famiglietti. The man nodded and smiled, somewhat self-consciously for a renowned performer, I thought.

"Bèllo! Bèllo!" Holmes said, smiling first at the violinist, then the audience and then again at the violinist. The captive diners got the idea: Energetic applause rose and hung on the air.

Signore Famiglietti appeared reluctant, but then he took

a single, pronounced step forward. He raised his right arm
in thanks and slowly turned to all four corners of the room
while saying, *"Gràzie. Gràzie. Gràzie. Gràzie."* Then he
turned to Holmes, put the tips of the fingers and thumb of
his right hand together, touched them to his lips and, opening his fingers, tossed a final thank-you to the detective.

"Prègo," Holmes said, and turned back to his audience.

"Now . . . In the sudden darkness that cut short Signore
Famiglietti's concert tonight, someone quickly did for Lady
Armstrong's guard, Cuthbert Wilson, and in a way that
made it impossible for the poor devil to so much as whisper
an alarm. That was Jack Ryder, and in the very next instant
he violently snatched the Blood of Punjab from Lady Armstrong's neck, striking her a blow in the process.

"This was what I had feared, but I was powerless to
prevent it. I couldn't attack the person in the dark without
fear that another innocent person might be hurt or killed.
So I took counter measures, ensuring that the doors were
locked. Ryder figured out what was going on and dumped
the necklace just before I turned up the gaslights all over
the room. And here we are."

"All well and good, sir," said a ruddy-faced old fellow
seated near the center of the room, "but where is this
Jack Ryder?

"Lord . . . Basil Poundstone, I believe it is," Holmes
replied. The detective bent over and laid his pistol on the
floor as he spoke.

"Yes, yes. But you are talking in circles, sir."

"Not at all," Holmes said.

"Don't contradict me. You most certainly are. You noted
earlier that Ryder was not here, but just a moment ago,
you as much as told us that he killed Mr. Wilson, tried to
escape with the gem, but failed and is still here."

"I did not say that, Lord Poundstone," the detective
countered. "I said he did not *appear* to be present, and
that was precisely what I meant," Holmes said.

Then Holmes spun sharply toward the violinist.

"Perhaps you could tell us of Jack Ryder's whereabouts,
Signore Famiglietti."

It was Holmes' first and only mention of Ryder's name
in the same breath with Famiglietti's, and it sent the violin-

ist into motion. He was a picture of malevolent and deadly, fluid grace. The violin bow dropped from his right hand and clattered to the floor. He reached up behind the starched white collar of his tuxedo and took three or four short running steps. The handle of a dagger was visible only for an instant in his fingers. He used his momentum to increase the force of his throw, flinging his arm outward, fast and straight, his torso and hips twisting with the effort, his legs driving the entire balletic movement, which sent the dagger spinning and glinting in the gaslight directly at Holmes from no more than twenty-five feet. Famiglietti's knife made a brief whistling noise en route to its target of muscle and blood and bone.

But Sherlock Holmes moved quickly, too. In a single sweeping motion uninterrupted by so much as a blink, even as Famiglietti was uncoiling his throw, Holmes snapped his long arm straight out toward the moving violinist. A long dagger shot straight across his palm, handle first, directly at Famiglietti; it was the vicious knife that Holmes had collected after our fight with the toughs in St. Giles. He had thrown it underhand, very hard, and with a slight flip.

And in that cold uncertain instant between life and death, before either razor-sharp blade could find its mark, it was a gunshot that settled the fight. A bullet struck Famiglietti in the chest with brutal and absolute efficiency, stopping his athletic movement as abruptly as if he had run into a glass wall. The man was probably dead before his body hit the floor.

The blade of Holmes' knife was stuck deep in the man's left shoulder, just below his collar bone.

Famiglietti's blade thrummed in the wall directly behind where Holmes had just been, at a point clearly in line with his chest.

A few of the ladies screamed and then wasted their breath loudly decrying the ugliness of the scene; their spouses brought them up short, however. A couple of diners at a table near Holmes actually clapped. One had the temerity to offer, "Good show," and his wife kicked him. But they were hardly noticed. All eyes had turned to Lord David Armstrong, for it was he who had fired the shot that killed Jack Ryder. Wisps of smoke still twirled from the barrel of his pistol, which seemed frozen in his outstretched arm. Lord Armstrong's face was white. His eyes were glazed. His lips were pale and parted as if he would like to speak if only he knew what to say.

The little man was all alone. Holmes stood in silence looking straight at him. Lady Armstrong and her patrons had moved off, watching in horror. Only Inspector Lestrade and I stood near. When the action began, Lestrade had quickly cuffed Miss Butler to a door handle, and followed me to the front. Now he stood to Lord Armstrong's left, not three feet away. Lestrade's pistol was trained directly at the man's chest.

I stood to Lord Armstrong's right, and my revolver was aimed at the man's head. The barrel was only inches away, in fact.

Lady Armstrong's voice was a shriek. "David! David! You stop this instant. This very instant."

"Lower your arm very slowly, sir," Lestrade commanded. "Please. Don't make me shoot you. I will if I have to."

"He might hesitate," I said to Lord Armstrong under my breath, "but I will not."

"You put that gun down, David," his mother said in a dramatically softer voice. She must have realized that her son was nearly hysterical. "You did well, dear. The bad man is dead. Now it's over. Do what those men say. Please, dear."

I took a deep breath and kept my finger curled against the trigger of my pistol. Lord David Armstrong slowly lowered his gun toward the floor. I took my eyes off his face for an instant in order to watch the gun. That was when he turned the weapon upright toward his own head and fired.

But he was too slow.

I shouted, "Not bloody likely!" And even as my voice was rising, I drove my left fist into the side of his jaw and sent him reeling to the floor. I was tried of having to hit people, but at least Lord Armstrong's bullet went into the ceiling and not his own head.

His mother screamed; I was getting tired of that, too.

Lestrade nodded to me, put his pistol away, turned and hollered at the crowd:

"All right, ladies and gentlemen. It is time to leave now,

if you please. In an orderly fashion. Come now. Come. And Scotland Yard thanks you all for your cooperation."

The crowd was buzzing like a huge colony of overdressed bees. I couldn't see a mouth that wasn't moving, a set of eyebrows that wasn't arching in one instant, falling in the next. Some of the patrons dawdled, craning their necks in our direction. They'd be talking about this night for a good long time.

Holmes walked over to Ryder's body and, with his back to the milling crowd, quickly dug into the man's jacket; first one side, then the other. Then he picked up Ryder's violin and looked at it closely. By then I had reached him. Tommy and Brooks were with me. Out of the corner of my eye I could see Lady Armstrong approaching.

"What a fine instrument, Watson," Holmes said. "Not my Stradivarius, but a beautifully made piece all the same. Cremona, undoubtedly." He brushed the fingertips of his right hand softly, almost thoughtfully, across the instrument's amber surface and with the greatest care put it in its case, which lay on the floor nearby. He added the bow to the case and snapped it shut.

"Mr. Holmes," Lady Armstrong said. She looked pale and haggard and suddenly very old. "I suppose I should thank you for this."

"I regret that your banquet seems to have been ruined," Holmes said, "but I am sorrier about Mr. Wilson . . . and Lord David."

The woman stared at Holmes. "There are always Wilsons," she said. I don't think I had heard as callous a statement in a good many years; it turned my blood cold.

"As for the banquet, the charity pledges all have been most generous, and I am sure they will still make good on them."

She made no mention of her son.

Lestrade escorted Jane Ryder-née-Butler to a paddy wagon, dispatched various of his men to discreetly collect the bodies of Wilson and Jack Ryder and said good-bye.

"Maybe the new year will be better, eh, gentlemen?"

"Lord Armstrong," Lestrade said, "you must realize that this business is not over. We will be talking soon, you and me." Then he left.

Lord Armstrong was suddenly standing by his mother's side. He looked as pale as any cadaver I had ever seen. He was holding his jaw, which already was swelling. She discreetly took his hand in her own and squeezed it.

"You had better put ice on that," I told him without sympathy.

He nodded and stared at the floor.

The reporter turned to me. "Well, Doc," Brooks said, "you were as good as your word and then some. I've got a whopper of a story to write, so I'd better get busy with it. Thank you."

He shook hands with us and tousled Tommy's hair good-naturedly.

"I'll see you, chum," Brooks said. Tommy smiled and waved. Brooks nodded to the Armstrongs and left.

"I am afraid that young man is in for a grave disappointment," Lady Armstrong said as the big doors closed on the five of us.

"How do you mean?" the detective asked.

"I have a controlling interest in his newspaper and two others in the city, and I have close personal friends who have sway in equally prestigious ways at virtually every other newspaper in the city."

I was furious. "You will censor the coverage?"

"Not all of it. Of course not," she said. "We must take into account the public's need to be titillated, mustn't we? Some superficial version must be told. Two people died, after all. But there was that unseemly business Mr. Holmes made oblique reference to involving that dreadful Mr. Ryder's wife. And, that young Butler woman, whom I presume is, or rather was, some sort of mistress . . . I'm dreadfully sorry, David; really I am. And she did have a role in the attempted theft of my necklace. Then there's the matter of Mr. Holmes' name being cleared."

"Surely, you can't expect that given the number of people involved—"

"Oh, really, Doctor! Don't be naïve! All of the information will be dribbled out in little pieces over an appropriate period of time, and it will all be fed to the friendlier reporters in due course, but it will be very difficult for anyone to put all of the pieces together. And besides, the public's memory is only as long as the public is bright—which is to say, not very, as you well know. Other things will intervene, I am sure. Tomorrow's race results, for example."

"I find you repulsive, Lady Armstrong," I said.

She threw back her head and laughed a throaty, high-pitched laugh. Then she looked directly at me and narrowed her gaze.

"And you amuse me!"

"Stop this," Holmes said angrily, "both of you."

He stared at Lady Armstrong. "Why would you censor what has happened?"

"Because I can," the woman said. "Don't you understand anything? Because I can, and because someone really must. It simply would not do for the lower orders to have too clear a look inside the temple, so to speak. Surely, Mr. Holmes, a man of alleged breeding such as yourself can understand that."

"I understand," Holmes said, "but I strenuously disagree with it."

"That matters very little," she sniffed.

"I know," Holmes said, "but eventually the complete truth will be known. In fact, I can promise you that Watson and I will have a hand in seeing it happen."

"And by the time you do," Lady Armstrong said, "I will care even less about it—and the two of you—than I do right now."

Holmes shook his head in disgust.

Lady Armstrong scowled at him.

"You are insolent, Mr. Holmes. That's your problem. I think you may have great difficulty collecting your fee," she said. "Have you given that any thought?" She raised her head and stuck out her jaw and looked smug and contemptuous.

Holmes laughed. "Oh, I have given my fee what precious little thought it deserves, Lady Armstrong. And I expect that I will collect it from you with no difficulty whatsoever."

Before the woman could say anything, Holmes abruptly turned to her son. "And you, Lord David Armstrong, heir to her ladyship's kingdom, as it were, how do you feel knowing that history will record that you had neither decency nor honesty nor, much of the time, even sobriety?"

Lord Armstrong raised his head and glowered at Holmes.

"I beg your pardon!" Lady Armstrong said in her son's behalf.

"As well you might," Holmes shot back.

"Lady Armstrong, how do you suppose it came to pass that people such as Jack and Emma Ryder and the Butler woman ever got in 'the temple,' as you so grandiosely put it just a moment ago, hmm? Am I to interpret your silence as ignorance, or is it that you know all too well? Or do you merely suspect the truth?"

The woman stood staring angrily at Holmes, but there was a sense of uncertainty in her posture, which was not normal for her. It was as though she were poised to move in one direction or the other, but could not decide which.

"Lord Armstrong, the benefit dinner was your idea to begin with, was it not?" Holmes asked. "That's all right. You need not answer; you told us it was, early on. I believe you knew very well that if the occasion was grand enough, Mummy would drag out that monstrous gem of hers. Isn't that correct?" Holmes said.

The man's eyes were wide with anger now, and his ruddy face was decidedly redder than usual. I slowly slipped my right hand into my coat pocket and wrapped my fingers around the grip of my pistol.

"Why was it so important to have the stone here tonight? It's rather simple, really. You knew that an attempt would be made to steal it, and you had neither the courage nor the wherewithal to stop it. Jack Ryder had his talons sunk into you very deeply, didn't he? You owed him a great deal of money, and you could not pay it without your mother finding out, and we couldn't have that now, could we? And then tonight, when you saw Jane Butler in handcuffs, you realized just how much of a fool they had made of you.

"Was that why you killed him? Or was it to erase your debt? Or was it for both reasons? What about the story Miss Butler will tell? Hmmm And if not her, there's always Emma Ryder."

Holmes stepped closer to the man so that he fairly towered over him. He was pushing perilously hard, I thought.

Lady Armstrong shrieked at the detective. "Leave him alone!"

"I am sorry, Lady Armstrong," Holmes said.

Her son seemed to be dissolving in tears, quite literally. It was a pitiful sight. He just slowly slumped to the floor and sat down without so much as moving his feet. He put his head in his hands and wept.

Lady Armstrong looked down at him.

When Holmes spoke next, his voice was soft and solicitous.

"How much did you owe, Lord David? Ten thousand pounds? Twenty thousand? They cheated you, sir. They cheated you at every level and in the basest of ways, did they not?"

"I—I . . . saved your life," the man stammered. "You should be thanking me, you—"

Holmes ranged over the man and stretched his long sinewy arm toward the spot where Ryder's corpse had lain.

"Go down to Scotland Yard and look at the body," Holmes said. "See if you don't find a deep wound in his shoulder from my knife. I could argue convincingly before any court that the man already had lost the fight when you fired the shot that killed him. So I would advise you to not try my patience. Now, sir! Tell me: How much did you owe Jack Ryder?"

Lord Armstrong's voice was small and soft; I could barely make it out. He looked down at the floor as he spoke. "Forty thousand pounds."

I gasped.

Lady Armstrong's mouth fell open, and then she shut it so fast that her teeth made a noise.

Holmes nodded and turned to Lady Armstrong.

"My fee is precisely half of that amount then: twenty thousand pounds," Holmes said. "Within two days, and in a bank draft, if you please."

If the woman could have screamed and spoken at the same time, she would have, I'm sure.

"You can't be serious," she said to Holmes. "This is blackmail. I won't—"

"I am quite serious, Lady Armstrong," Holmes said. "And it isn't blackmail, not at all. It is my fee. And you are getting out of this fiasco rather inexpensively, if I do say so.

"You will not have to pay your wayward son's gambling debt, and let us not forget that if Dr. Watson and Lestrade and I—and that Brooks fellow, too—if we all had not ridden to the rescue tonight, then proper London tomorrow morning would be talking about the impending nuptials of Lord David and that young thing from the Plymouth docks.

"You do realize what the effect of that would have been, don't you? How long do you suppose it would have taken those leeches to bleed you dry? One year? Two or three perhaps? Certainly no more than that. And all because Lord David here let them in. Under the circumstances, Lady Armstrong, I don't think you could afford to have that known by your tight little circle of powerful friends, do you?"

The woman stepped toward Holmes, put both of her fists on her hips and shouted up into his face. "Who would believe you, detective? Ha! Inside of two weeks I will have turned your name into a curse in the finest households in London. Now get out."

I did not understand why at first, but Holmes no longer seemed angry with the woman. He smiled and sighed loudly and said in a calm and even voice, "My dear woman, you will pay me twenty thousand pounds within two days, in a bank draft, or . . ."

Lady Armstrong's lips quivered in fury. She opened her mouth and showed her little brown pointed teeth and started to speak, but Holmes held a finger up.

"Or," he said, "I'll not help you recover the Blood of Punjab."

The woman grabbed at her throat. She took her precious necklace in hand, then held the dark, blood-red heart of it away from her bosom. She looked down at the double-star ruby, just to be sure her senses had not deceived her. Then she looked abruptly back at Holmes, her face contorted.

"Yes," Holmes said, "it is a fake. A marvelously good one, to be sure, but a fake."

"No!" she screamed.

"Oh, yes," Holmes said. "Call in the experts; they'll all

tell you the same thing. The diamonds are good enough, but the ruby is art glass."

The color drained from Lady Armstrong's face. Her knees seemed to buckle, and she sat down hard in the nearest chair. Lord David knelt by her side.

"You bastard," she said to Holmes.

"On the contrary, Lady Armstrong. My pedigree is quite intact. You will have to excuse us now. I do believe this party is over."

Holmes opened the door and we filed out. He was last, and he stopped in the doorway, Famiglietti's violin tucked beneath his arm. His back was to the Armstrongs, and he spoke without turning around.

"Two days," Holmes called out, "and in a bank draft."

Chapter 36

We hailed a hansom cab, and I was surprised when Holmes told the driver to deliver us to Scotland Yard.

"Unfinished business," Holmes said. It was the only explanation he offered, and I was too tired to press the issue; I figured I would know soon enough. Tommy dozed off almost instantly.

"That was cruel, Holmes," I said.

"I know. I could see no alternative."

I did not argue. It was done. It was over. We rode in silence for several minutes.

"Why didn't you just shoot Jack Ryder? Was it really necessary to go up against him with a knife? That was his weapon of choice, after all."

"Professional courtesy," Holmes said.

"Rubbish! He didn't deserve any such thing," I said. "And he came close to killing you. Your shirt and jacket have quite a slash across the chest. You were not cut, I take it?"

"No," Holmes said with a quick smile, "but very observant on your part, Doctor. You do show promise."

"It can't be the company I keep," I said.

"Touché! You must tell me all about your adventure at the Hope Settlement House."

"You are trying to change the subject."

"Not successfully, I gather. Why are you so angry, Watson?"

"Damn it, Holmes!" I blurted. "Were you trying to get yourself killed?"

He looked at me in silence, without expression.

"I—I'm sorry, Holmes. I had no right. I . . ."

He turned and looked out the window. We rode in silence again, longer and more comfortably this time, because we had cleared the air.

"How did you know that Famiglietti really was Jack Ryder?" I asked.

"I had problems with Famiglietti's name from the start, Watson. You know that I diligently keep track of concerts in season and, more to the point, because of my research into medieval music I know something of the Continent's violinists and their history. I had never heard of this man, at least not as a part of this century. The only renowned Famigliettis I knew of from Cremona were contemporaries of the great violin makers there hundreds of years ago. That was the substance of the third telegram that I sent on Christmas Day; it went to the authorities in Cremona.

"They reported that, as I had believed, the entire Famiglietti line in that region had been extinct for more than five hundred years—victims of bubonic plague, every one. So this Signore Famiglietti had to be an imposter. The only reasonable candidate was either an accomplice or Jack Ryder himself.

"As Clough, the young Ryder had embraced the violin as if he were born to it. He had a gift. Pity that he chose not to hold it in higher regard."

"Indeed," I said. "Now where did you stay when you were hiding out?" I asked.

"In St. Giles," Holmes said. "Polly McGovern had an extra room."

"Inspired," I said.

"Thank you," Holmes asked.

"And how were you able to collect the telegrams? The police were on the hunt for you."

"Do you remember the policeman with the mutton chops?" Holmes asked.

"Ah, yes. From the Tisbury ruckus. Very good. Well, as an honorary member of the constabulary, you will be interested to know that when I charged into Emma Ryder's office, she was, uhm, being engaged by Inspector Miles Wallingford."

Holmes smiled. "You don't say? And where is he now?"

"We left the fellow trussed up to the clothes pole in his paramour's office closet," I said. "I gave Lestrade the key."

Holmes laughed. "Excellent, Watson! You may be developing a flare for this."

"Why, thank you, Holmes," I said. I told him we had left the matron in the kitchen supply closet, and he approved of that as well.

Tommy awoke the instant our hansom cab arrived at Scotland Yard. The three of us walked into the foyer. Holmes spoke quietly with an officer at the front desk and then turned to us.

"Tommy," Holmes said, "Dr. Watson and I have to see Inspector Lestrade for a few minutes, and while we do that, I want you to stay with this policeman. We'll be back for you shortly, I promise."

The boy was not pleased, but he did not argue.

We knew the way to Lestrade's office, and despite the lateness of the hour, or perhaps because of it, we were allowed to find him on our own.

Lestrade's office was much like him: unadorned, almost spartan. He had a simple oak desk and matching chair, a common desk lamp, two heavy straight-back chairs, positioned for visitors, five tall file cabinets, and a rather wide, heavy-looking safe that stood off in one corner.

He seemed surprised to see us, but pleased.

"Happy New Year, both of you," he said. "I was about to leave. It's been a pretty good night," he said, "at least from a simple policeman's point of view."

Holmes nodded but said nothing.

"You're not going to tell me anything that would change that, are you?" Lestrade asked.

Holmes smiled at him.

"Aaw!" Lestrade muttered. "You are, aren't you? Wait a minute. Doctor, lock the door."

He threw me the key. I did as he asked, and left the key in the lock.

"Now sit down, the two of you," Lestrade said.

He opened a desk drawer, withdrew an unopened bottle of good whisky, set it down on the desk and put a water glass next to it.

"It's the only glass I've got," he said, "so I guess we'll have to make do. I expected to be drinking this at home with the missus by now."

He filled the glass. We passed it around, and by the time Lestrade had it again, it was more than half empty.

"Now, Mr. Holmes," Lestrade said, pointing at the violin case on Holmes' lap, "unless you're going to play that fiddle you've brought with you, I think you should tell me what's going on."

"Oh, the violin is Scotland Yard's, Lestrade. Unless someone can rightfully lay claim to it. It's a fine old instrument, and I believe it is most valuable, so do put it in a secure place."

Holmes handed the case to the Inspector and said, "Thank you for your help in all of this, Lestrade. Without it, the outcome might have been dramatically different."

The inspector smiled and nodded.

"My pleasure," he said. "You've done me some good, too. I expect I'll be back in charge of this entire business before you know it. I've written out Wallingford's resignation for him. He just has to sign it."

"And he will?" Holmes asked with a slight smile.

"Yes, indeed," Lestrade said, "in return for some, uh, consideration."

"Mrs. Wallingford will not be told, then?" Holmes asked.

Lestrade shook his head.

"The inspector's paramour and Miss Butler are in stir?"

Lestrade looked at his pocket watch.

"They certainly should be, yes. Butler's still pretty feisty, but Mrs. Ryder seems to have lost her spunk now that she's a widow. She'll swing, and she knows it."

"And I suppose," Holmes said, "that Lord David Armstrong will not be held to blame for the shooting?"

I realized that Lestrade did not yet know of the pitiful Lord Armstrong's complicity, and that Holmes apparently was not going to tell him.

"There will be a coroner's inquest," Lestrade said. "Lord Armstrong probably will not have to attend in person. I suspect the results will be just inconclusive enough to be problematic from our perspective. To what extent? I don't know. It would be rather easy to argue that Lord Armstrong believed he was acting to save your life. Seems to me the poor sot's already in some hellish kind of prison, if you follow me," Lestrade said.

"Oh, I quite agree, Lestrade," Holmes said. He took another deep swallow of the whisky. I took two. Lestrade drained the glass and then poured another.

"What will become of Ryder's body?" Holmes asked.

"Well, his wife's out of the picture. I suppose the Ryder family can claim it if—"

Holmes shook his head.

"What do you mean, no?" Lestrade asked. "Any surviving Ryder can—"

"His name was not Ryder," Holmes said.

"Really? Well, who the blazes was he, then?"

"Clough was his name," Holmes said. "Jack Clough."

Lestrade's dark eyebrows knotted together in a frown. He was quiet. So was I, but for a different reason: The pieces suddenly started to fall into place like so many perfectly machined parts.

"Now, why's that name Clough seem so familiar?" Lestrade asked.

"The Mayfair robberies. Way back," Holmes said.

"All right. All right, I think I remember," Lestrade said. "Wait a minute."

He walked over to his file cabinet, shuffled through some folders and came up with the report he was seeking.

"Yes," Lestrade said. "His body was fished out of the Thames in late November, '69. Positive identification was impossible; too much damage and decomposition. We found the name 'J. Clough' scratched into the inside back of a leather belt that was still intact on his trousers. So we figured it was him."

"In fact," Holmes said, "the body was just some lost soul from the docks that Clough had killed and then disfigured. He secured his belt around him, weighted the body down and let Nature do the rest."

"You're sure of this, Mr. Holmes?"

"I am," the detective said.

Lestrade looked off into the corner, thinking, and then turned back to us.

"I don't see that it changes anything, really," he said.

"No, I suppose it doesn't," Holmes said, "but it does bring the overall picture into the light when you recall that one of Clough's partners was Charles Roberts, who—"

". . . was killed in one of the Mayfair burglaries," said Lestrade, who was reading through Clough's file.

"And?" Holmes asked.

"I'll be!" Lestrade exclaimed, shutting the file. "John Godey."

"The same," Holmes said. "Clough had made his way to America and established himself as Jack Ryder, and apparently had a rather fine time. Why not? As Jack Ryder, Clough got by on his wits, and always managed to stay one or two steps ahead of the authorities. Even that game had to play itself out eventually though. He returned home with his wife, Emma, and they determined to steal the Blood of Punjab.

"The key was to be his old partner, John Godey. Clough was outraged to find that Godey wanted nothing to do with him. Clough swore that if Godey didn't help him, Tommy would come to harm. Godey relented, but promised himself he would find a way to sabotage the burglary, and he did.

"The two of them watched the late-night habits of the household long enough to learn that the last room to be darkened was always the one near the top of the stairs on the north side of the house; they accurately deduced that this was the guard's bedroom. One moonless night in April, Clough and Godey cut a pane of glass out of the study window and broke into Planetree.

"Before they did anything else, Godey located a stand full of umbrellas and walking sticks, and he and Clough carried it to the first-floor hallway and left it outside of Wilson's room, where it stood to serve as an alarm should anything unforeseen bring the guard running. Clough, being the younger and more agile of the two men, went back down to the study ahead of Godey, not by much more than a few steps, but in the darkness Godey needed only a few seconds. He quickly wrapped a wire around the bottom of the posts atop the stairs at ankle height, pulled it taut and joined Clough as he was going into the study.

"On jobs such as this many years earlier, Godey had always carried a small canvas sack, and he brought one with him to Planetree. But in addition to tools, Godey had brought a vial of acid and a naphtha flare.

"The two men were back in the study for only a couple

of moments when Godey went into one of his terrible coughing fits. He scurried off to a far corner of the pitch-black room—trying to muffle the noise, or so it appeared to Clough—but what Godey really did was dump the acid onto the flare, drop it behind a couch and then, with the coughing gradually coming under control, move back to where his partner was. Unfortunately for Godey, the acid also had slopped onto one of the rugs and the back of his glove. There was nothing he could do but let it eat through to the top of his hand, take the pain and give nothing away.

"Apart from that little detail, Godey's bold, if unlikely, little plan was working almost to perfection. Everything happened all at once. His coughing fit had, in fact, awakened the guard. Wilson opened his bedroom door, pistol in hand and tried to steal down the hallway but instead set off the impromptu alarm. Meanwhile, the flare slowly ignited, and by the time Wilson struggled to his feet in a tangle of walking sticks and umbrellas, he could detect a strange glow coming from the ground floor near the study. Undoubtedly he thought 'Fire!' He raced to the stairs and hit the trip wire.

"The study was growing brighter by the second and filling with the sharp stench that Lady Armstrong described; it was from burning naphtha. As if that were not enough to startle and confuse Clough, then Wilson came thumping and tumbling down the stairs.

"Before Clough could figure out what was happening, and where, Godey hissed from behind him, 'Get out! Get out! They're on us! I'm right after yeh. Get out!' Clough dove out the window, trying to save his hide. Godey stomped out the flare, pulled off his gloves, wrapped them around the torch, stuffed it all in his canvas bag and then followed his partner. Clough never did quite figure out what happened."

Lestrade's thin, angular face seemed caught between disbelief and anger.

"How . . . ? Were you there, Mr. Holmes? I'll admit you've been able to figure out some things that might have taken us here at the Yard a bit longer to put together, but how could you possibly have figured all that out when—"

"Lestrade," Holmes said. "I am flattered, I assure you.

I had been able to deduce many of the points in the story I just told you, but . . ."

Holmes paused and from the inside of his coat pulled out a small battered notebook. He held it over the inspector's desk and dropped it.

"John Godey, bless his soul," Holmes said, "faithfully kept a journal. It's all in there. It was a habit he started in prison."

"And how did you come by it?" Lestrade asked, reaching for the book. "You can't withhold—"

"His lady friend thought we should have it," Holmes said.

"That McGovern woman?"

"The same," Holmes said. "Let me finish my little tale, Lestrade, hmm? I have reasons."

"Go ahead, then," Lestrade said.

"Clough was so shaken by the night's events at Planetree that he gave up on the notion of assaulting Lady Armstrong's safe, but he was more determined than ever to have the stone. That's when he and his wife recruited Miss Butler to snare Lord Armstrong. In a very little time they had maneuvered him into a big gambling debt and steered him toward the altar; he wasn't much of a challenge. The impending nuptials were to be announced tonight. That gambit alone would have earned them a fortune, quite literally."

Lestrade poured more whisky in the tall glass and took a sip.

"Well, at least he didn't get the Blood of Punjab," Lestrade said.

"Oh, that's right. You had left the party by the time I told Lady Armstrong the truth about the necklace."

"Which was?" Lestrade asked pointedly.

"Clough did steal it," Holmes said.

The inspector took another sip of whisky, deeper this time.

"The instant Lady Armstrong's dinner was plunged into darkness," Holmes said, "Clough stabbed Wilson, then walloped Lady Armstrong and snatched her necklace. But at the same time he dropped a wonderful fake beneath her chair. I suspect it was easy to have copied. So much publicity has always attended the Blood of Punjab that there were no shortage of photographs and detailed descriptions."

"Where's the bloody stone now, then?" Lestrade asked. "Lady Armstrong must be sick about it."

"I told her I would help her get it back," Holmes said, "assuming that she pays my fee promptly."

Lestrade straightened in his chair.

"Mr. Holmes, if you have that necklace, we might have a problem here."

The detective put both of his long arms straight up in the air and then stood.

"Inspector, you may search me," Holmes said.

"I don't really think . . ." Lestrade said.

"I insist. Please. My feelings will not be hurt."

Lestrade did, in fact, search the detective, and then he sat down. He seemed somewhat annoyed. I offered to let him search me, too, but he gave me a rather nasty look instead.

"I have a favor to ask of you, Lestrade."

The inspector raised his chin a bit, as if in question.

"I would like you to keep John Godey's diary confidential, if possible. I ask out of consideration for the boy, that's all. It is not an unreasonable request. If the Yard needs it as evidence, then I expect you will do whatever you have to do. But short of that, if . . ."

Lestrade rose from his chair, walked across the office and opened the big safe. Its massive door squeaked as it opened. Inside were sundry papers and handguns and ammunition. On the lower shelf Lestrade deposited Godey's journal. He was about to close the door but stopped. He returned to his desk, picked up the violin case, put it next to Godey's book and then locked the safe's door.

"There may well be enough evidence against the parties involved that we won't need the journal, Mr. Holmes, so unless I inform you otherwise, you may consider the favor done."

"Excellent, Inspector," Holmes said. "Excellent." The detective was busily scrawling a note on a pad of paper he had removed from Lestrade's desk.

"Now," Holmes said, "in return, if you send a couple of men around to the Diogenes Club tomorrow and present this note to old Phineas Cobb, he will gladly hand over two canvas sacks that Watson and I stored in one of the club's many closets several nights back. You will find exactly one hundred thousand pounds in there."

Lestrade's jaw fell open. He looked at Holmes incredulously.

"Yes, Inspector, it's a fortune, I know. I suggest that the Yard may want to quietly apportion the funds to the victims of those Mayfair robberies. Lord Cedric Atkinson suffered the biggest loss, I believe. There should be a rather considerable sum left over, Lestrade, so perhaps the Yard would see fit to help out the widows and children of its own officers."

"You seem to have this all planned out, Mr. Holmes."

"Actually, I cannot take the credit. The credit belongs to the late Mr. Godey."

"I don't understand," Lestrade said.

"His friend Polly McGovern told me it was what he always had wished he could do, make amends, properly settle all accounts before he had to meet his Maker. Well, now he has done that, you see."

"But one hundred thousand pounds," Lestrade said, "How on earth did . . ."

Holmes sighed heavily and then yawned. He got to his feet, took back the note he had written to Phineas Cobb and, catching my eye, nodded toward the door. I rose, unlocked the door, and Holmes and I stood in the portal, poised to leave.

"Now, wait a minute, both of you," Lestrade said. "All right. All right. As long as that money in the sacks isn't stolen—"

"Ryder's winnings," Holmes said.

"That much? Hard to believe."

"That's what he led me to believe, Inspector," Holmes said.

Lestrade was silent for a moment. Then he said, "Well, I guess it'd be a good deed for the Yard, I mean, to do as you suggest."

Holmes put the note to Cobb back on the inspector's desk and gave Lestrade a quick smile.

"We thank you," the detective said, "and so does Mr. Godey. Good night, Inspector."

I nodded to Lestrade, but as the door was closing, the policeman asked, "Now, what about the Blood of Punjab, Mr. Holmes? Holmes!"

The detective pretended not to hear. Lestrade didn't shout at us; nor did he follow as we walked to the front of the building to collect Tommy. Too proud, I suppose; maybe too tired.

"Holmes," I said, "may I assume that the real necklace is inside the violin case?"

"Of course," he said. "Where else? There's a compartment there for resin, strings and—"

". . . stones," I said. "How long do you suppose it will take Lestrade to figure it out?" I asked.

"Oh, not long . . . for a Yarder."

"Two days?" I offered.

"Approximately," he said.

"And by then Lady Armstrong will have paid your fee," I noted. "What a coincidence."

"I don't believe in coincidences, Watson," he said. "You know that."

Chapter 37

As we neared the entrance where we had left Tommy, the boy spotted us from quite a distance and came running all the way.

"I was afraid they'd locked you up," he said.

"Not this time," Holmes said with a soft smile. "Perhaps another."

He stepped between us, took Holmes' left hand and my right, and we walked out of Scotland Yard that way. We promptly boarded a hansom cab and settled in. Until the small carriage began to gently sway and I could once again hear the slow, rhythmic clacking of the horse's hooves on the cobblestones, I had not realized just how tired I was. Suddenly, I felt weary all the way through.

Tommy tried manfully to keep his eyes open but could not. We weren't en route for more than a minute when the boy nodded off, his head against Holmes' shoulder.

We sat in silence for some distance.

"Quite a night, eh, Watson?"

"Yes, Holmes. Quite a night, indeed."

"Yeah, Mr. 'Olmes," said Tommy. "Quite a bloody night, it was." The boy had awakened when the cab hit an upturned cobblestone.

Holmes reached into his pocket and handed him something.

"I believe this is yours, young man."

It was the engraved watch that Tommy's uncle had given him for Christmas.

"I didn't think Jack Ryder would need it where he was going," Holmes said.

"Thank you, sir," Tommy said. "It means a lot, it does." He sniffed a couple of times and wiped his eyes.

"You're entirely welcome," Holmes said.

The boy looked out of the cab window and then back to Holmes.

"This ain't the way to the Settlement 'ouse, Mr. 'Olmes."

"That's right," my friend said. "We're going to Baker Street. By now I am sure that Mrs. Hudson will have gotten one of her spare rooms on the ground floor all ready for you. If you would like, you may stay there."

"Just for tonight, y'mean?"

"Well, I think that is up to you," Holmes said. "Mrs. Hudson said the room is yours if you want it."

"Really?"

"Yes," Holmes said. "Really. You may stay at Baker Street for as long as you like. You may consider the house your home. That is what she said."

"Really?" Tommy asked.

"Yes," Holmes said. "Her exact words to me were, 'Tommy would be my little jewel, my little Covent Garden jewel.' Her exact words."

"Really?"

"Yes," Holmes said, "and do please find another word to express your sense of disbelief. I am tired of hearing you say, 'Really?' to everything."

Tommy turned to face me. "Is this for true?" he asked. I smiled and nodded. "Yes," I said. "Really."

Holmes gave me a withering look.

"Tommy," Holmes said, "I would not lie to you. Not even in jest. Don't ever forget that, hmm? But listen, if you choose to stay at Baker Street, you will have to abide by Mrs. Hudson's rules. Every one of them, mind you. And she will expect you to help her with the chores, and believe me, there are enough to go around."

"I'm a good worker, I am, Mr. 'Olmes," the boy said. "You'll see."

"I know you are," Holmes said, "but there's one final thing. A big thing. Your uncle John would have wanted you to have a proper education."

"Reg'lar schoolin', ya mean?"

"Yes," Holmes said.

"But I'm goin' to have to get back behind me cart tomorrow. Schoolin' and all that takes money, it does, and I got to earn what I need to live on. 'Ow am I supposed to go to school if—?"

Holmes interrupted him gently. "I guess you were not listening when I was having it out with Lady Armstrong. She is about to pay us a princely sum. I would say that twenty thousand pounds is much more than enough for an education, and there will be enough left over to pay for clothing and such. Then, several years from now, when you're old enough, you will have money that your uncle John has set aside for you."

"What?" the boy said.

Holmes smiled. "Maybe there is something wrong with your hearing, after all. I said, 'You will have money that your uncle John has set aside for you.' It is as simple as that . . . well, almost."

"But 'ow could he?" the boy insisted. "We ain't ever 'ad much."

"It's money from long ago," Holmes said, "back before he went to jail."

The boy seemed to grow smaller. He looked down toward the floor of the cab.

" 'At's money 'e stole, then?" Tommy asked in a small voice.

"Actually," Holmes said, "your uncle managed to get all of that money paid back, several times over."

" 'E did?"

"Yes," Holmes said. "He was a good man, Tommy, and he loved you very much."

"I know 'at, sir," Tommy said.

The yellowish gaslight from the city's street lamps seemed to flicker through the fog as our cab rolled toward Baker Street. There was enough light to make the tears shine on the boy's cheeks. He sniffled as discreetly and manfully as he could, but the tears were coming too fast. I handed him a handkerchief and patted his shoulder.

"It's all right," I told Tommy. "You're with us now."

The little boy used the handkerchief, sobbed a couple of times, and then sobbed some more, even harder. It was painful to watch. His small shoulders bobbed up and down, and his breathing came in gasps. He fell sideways into Holmes. The detective put his arm around the boy, gently pulled him close, and stroked his head until his breathing returned to normal.

The two of them stayed in that position for the rest of the ride, but Holmes kept his face turned toward the window. He seemed to blink quite a bit, and I recall that he had to clear his throat several times.

I suppose it was that damnable fog.